REGENCY

Mistletoe *and* MARRIAGES

ANNIE BURROWS
JOANNA MAITLAND

M&B™ and M&B™ with the Rose Device
are trademarks of the publisher.
Harlequin Mills & Boon Limited, Eton House,
18-24 Paradise Road, Richmond, Surrey TW9 1SR

REGENCY MISTLETOE & MARRIAGES
© Harlequin Enterprises II B.V./S.à.r.l. 2010

A Countess by Christmas © Annie Burrows 2010
The Earl's Mistletoe Bride © Joanna Maitland 2010

ISBN: 978 0 263 88830 0

26-1110

ROM Pbk

Harlequin Mills & Boon policy is to use papers that are natural, renewable and recyclable products and made from wood grown in sustainable forests. The logging and manufacturing processes conform to the legal environmental regulations of the country of origin.

Printed in the UK
by CPI Mackays, Chatham, ME5 8TD

A Countess by Christmas

ANNIE BURROWS

Annie Burrows has been making up stories for her own amusement since she first went to school. As soon as she got the hang of using a pencil she began to write them down. Her love of books meant she had to do a degree in English literature. And her love of writing meant she could never take on a job where she didn't have time to jot down notes when inspiration for a new plot struck her. She still wants the heroines of her stories to wear beautiful floaty dresses and triumph over all that life can throw at them. But when she got married she discovered that finding a hero is an essential ingredient to arriving at 'happy ever after'.

Look out for Annie Burrows's latest exciting novel, *Captain Corcoran's Hoyden Bride*, **available from Mills & Boon® Historical Romance in April 2011.**

Dear Reader,

When I was writing this story, set during a Regency Christmas house party, I spent a lot of time considering what is most important to me about the season. If I'm not careful, I have to confess, I can get totally stressed out by all the extra shopping, baking and general organising that the celebrations can entail. But sitting down to really think about the themes of this story reminded me that Christmas, for me, is essentially about family. I want to spend time with them, see them enjoying the day, finding them that special gift that will make them happy.

The hero of the story, Lord Bridgemere, has, like me, very strong views about the importance of family. Even though he finds many of his own relatives hard to get along with, he is determined to do the right thing by them, at least at this time of year. Even if he has to do so with gritted teeth.

And a man who is so determined to do the right thing deserves to find a woman who can see past the outer, prickly shell. And love him for who he really is.

And so I wish you and your own family all the joys and blessings of this season.

Merry Christmas!

Annie Burrows

In this, the fifieth anniversary of the Romantic Novelists'
Association, I would like to dedicate this book to all those
writers I meet up with regularly at local chapters.

Since I have joined the RNA I have found your support,
enthusiasm, friendship and advice invaluable.

And, if not for you,
I might never have found out about PLR!

Chapter One

An Invitation is extended to
Miss Isabella Forrest
To attend the celebration of the Season
at
Alvanley Hall

Helen was tired and cold. The private chaise she had hired for the last stage of the journey across Bodmin Moor was the most uncomfortable and least weatherproof of all the many and varied coaches in which she had been travelling for the past three days.

She shot her Aunt Bella an anxious glance. For the past half-hour she had kept her eyes fixed tightly shut, but she was not asleep. Helen knew this because every time they bounced over a pothole she emitted a faint moan.

She had never thought of her aunt as old until quite recently. Aunt Bella had always looked the same to her, right from the very first moment they had met. A determined-looking but kind lady, with light brown hair shot through with silver. There was perhaps just a little more silver now than there had been twelve years ago, when she had taken Helen home with her. But in the months since their local bank had gone out of business, and all their money had disappeared into some kind of financial abyss neither of them fully understood, she had definitely aged rapidly.

And now, thought Helen with a pang of disquiet, she looked like a lady of advancing years who had been evicted from her home, endured a journey fraught with innumerable difficulties in the depths of winter, and was facing the humiliation of having to beg a man she detested to provide her daily bread.

The transition from independent, respected woman to pauper had been hard enough for Helen to contend with. But it looked as though it was destroying her aunt.

At that very moment a flare of light outside the coach briefly attracted Helen's attention. They were slowing down to negotiate the turn from the main road onto a driveway, the wrought-iron gates of which stood open.

'Almost there, Aunt Bella,' said Helen. 'See?'

She indicated the two stone pillars through which their driver was negotiating the chaise.

Aunt Bella's eyes flicked open, and she attempted a tremulous smile which was so lacking in conviction it made Helen want to weep.

She averted her head. She did not want to upset her aunt any further by making her think she was going to break down. She had to be strong. Aunt Bella had taken her in when she had discovered nobody else wanted a virtually penniless orphan—product of a marriage neither her father's nor her mother's family had approved of. Aunt Bella had been there for her, looking after her, all these years. Now it was Helen's turn.

Through the carriage window she could see, one crouching on top of each pillar, a pair of stone lions, mouths open in silent snarls. Since the wind which howled across the moors was making the lanterns swing, the flickering shadows made it look just as though they were licking their lips and preparing to pounce.

She gave an involuntary shiver, then roused herself to push aside such a fanciful notion. She had only imagined the lions looked menacing because she was tired, and anxious about her aunt's health now, as well as already being convinced neither of them was truly welcome at Alvanley Hall. In spite of the Earl of Bridgemere sending that invitation.

He had sent one every year since Helen could remember. And every other year her aunt had tossed the gilt-edged piece of card straight into the fire with a contemptuous snort.

'Spend Christmas with a pack of relations I cannot abide, in that draughty great barracks of a place, when I can really enjoy myself here, in my snug little cottage, amongst my true friends?'

Yet here they were, whilst the cottage and the friends, along with Aunt Bella's independence, had all gone. Swept away in the aftermath of the collapse of the Middleton and Shropshire County Bank, to which all their capital had been entrusted.

Her feeling of being an unwelcome intruder into the Earl

of Bridgemere's domain only increased the further along the carriageway they drove. It had its foundation, Helen knew, in her aunt's statement that the Earl was as loath to open up his home to his extended family as she was to attend the annual gathering.

'It is about the only thing we have in common,' she had grumbled as she wrote her acceptance letter. 'A disinclination to go anywhere near any other member of this family. In fact, if it were not for his habit of going to Alvanley to preside over the Christmas festivities for the tenants at the family seat, nobody would know where to locate him from one year's end to the next, so assiduously does he avoid us all. Which is why he issues these invitations, I dare say. We would run him to earth there whether he did so or not. And at least this way he knows how many of us to cater for.'

Though torches had been lit and set at frequent intervals along the winding driveway, ostensibly to help strangers find their way more easily through the rapidly falling winter dusk, the only effect upon Helen was to make her wonder what lurked beyond the pools of light they cast. What was waiting in the depths of the menacing shadows, poised to pounce on anyone foolish enough to stray beyond the boundaries the Earl had set for those he so grudgingly permitted thus far?

It seemed to take an inordinately long time before the carriage drew to a halt in the shelter of a generously proportioned *porte-cochère*. A footman in black and silver livery came to open the coach door and let down the steps. Her aunt slumped back into her seat. The light streaming from the porch lamps revealed that her face was grey, her eyes dulled with despair.

'Aunt Bella, we have to get out now. We are here!' Helen whispered in an urgent undertone.

'No…' the old lady moaned. 'I cannot do this. I want to go home!' Her eyes filled with tears. She shut them, and shook her head in a gesture of impatience, as though reminding herself she no longer had anywhere to call home.

Their landlord had visited promptly, as soon as the rumours began to spread that Aunt Bella had lost her entire fortune. To remind her that their lease expired in the New Year, and that if she had not the cash to meet the rent she would have to leave.

Leaving her eventually with no alternative but to apply to the Earl of Bridgemere—the head of the family—for aid.

'That it has come to this,' Aunt Bella had said three days ago, when they had climbed into the mail coach at Bridgenorth. 'To be obliged to go cap in hand to that man of all men! But I have burned my bridges now. I can never go back. Never.'

She had sat ramrod-straight, refusing to look out of the window for miles lest she catch the eye of anyone who knew her. She had faced every challenge such a long journey had entailed with an air of dogged determination.

But it looked as though her redoubtable spirit had finally crumbled to dust.

Helen clambered over her, got out, and leaned back into the coach.

'Come!' she urged gently, putting her arms around her. 'Let me help you out.'

Helen had to practically lift her aunt from the coach. And had to keep her arm about her waist once she had reached solid ground to keep her standing. It was a shock to feel her trembling all over, though whether from exhaustion, fear, or the cold that had pervaded their hired carriage, she could not tell.

A second footman materialised. He was a little older than the first flunkey, and dressed more soberly. Helen assumed he was the head footman, or possibly even the under-butler.

'Welcome to Alvanley Hall, Miss Forrest—' he began, in the bland, bored tone of an upper servant who had spent all day parroting the same words.

'Never mind that now!' Helen interrupted. 'My aunt needs assistance, not meaningless platitudes!'

Both footmen goggled at her as though she had sprouted two heads.

She very nearly stamped her foot in irritation.

'Can't you see she can barely stand?' Helen continued. 'Oh, for heaven's sake!' she snapped, when they just continued to stare at her as though in shock. 'Make yourselves useful, can't you? Get her a chair. Or…no…' She immediately changed her mind as her aunt gave another convulsive shiver. 'We must get her inside first. Into the warm.'

Her aunt blinked owlishly about her. 'I do not think I shall ever feel warm again,' she observed.

And fainted.

To do him justice, the head footman had very quick reflexes. And very deft, sure hands. He managed to disentangle Helen from her aunt before she lost the fight to keep her from slithering to the ground, and scooped her up into his arms with an insouciance that suggested catching fainting guests was a task he performed every day.

Then he strode into the house without a backward glance, leaving Helen to her own devices.

After tamping down a fresh wave of annoyance she trotted behind him, arriving in the hall just in time to hear him addressing a young housemaid, who had been scurrying across the hall with a pile of linen in her arms.

'What room does Miss Forrest have?'

The maid's eyes grew round at the sight of the unconscious woman in his arms.

'Well, I just finished making up the drum room at the foot of the tower,' she began, 'but…'

'Very well. I shall take her up there myself.'

'B…but sir!' stammered the first footman.

The head footman shot him one look, which was so withering it was enough to reduce him to red-faced silence.

'Follow me, Miss…?' He raised one eyebrow, as though expecting her to enlighten him as to her name.

But Helen was in no mood to waste time on introductions.

'Hurry up, do! The sooner we make her comfortable the better!'

He nodded curtly, then demonstrated that he had caught on to the severity of her aunt's condition by striding deeper into the house. He bypassed the rather ostentatious staircase which swept upwards from the main hall, going instead along a corridor to a plainer, more narrow stone staircase, with wooden handrails darkened and glossy with age.

Helen had to trot to keep up with his long-legged stride,

and was quite out of breath by the time they came to a heavily studded oak door set into a small gothic arch that led into a perfectly circular room. With its unadorned ceiling, which contrasted starkly with the bright frieze running round the upper portion of the walls, it did indeed feel like being on the inside of a drum.

The footman laid Aunt Bella upon the bed, frowned down at her for a moment or two, then went across and tugged on a bell-pull beside the chimney breast.

'Someone will come and see to Miss Forrest,' he said curtly. 'I really should not be up here.' He stalked to the door, opened it, then turned to her. 'I am sure you know what is best to do for her when she has one of these turns.' He ran his eyes over her dismissively. 'I shall leave her in your... capable hands.'

Helen opened her mouth to protest that this was not a *turn* but the result of exhaustion, brought on by the sufferings her aunt had endured over the preceding weeks, but the footman had already gone.

How *dared* he look at her like that? As though she was a dead pigeon the cat had brought in! And as for saying he should not be up here! She tugged the strings of her muff over her head and flung it at the door through which he had just gone.

Pompous toad! For all his quick reflexes, and the strength it must have taken to carry her aunt's dead weight up all these stairs, he was clearly one of those men who thought that showing an ailing female any sort of compassion was beneath his dignity!

Unless he was just hiding a streak of venality beneath that

cool, efficient demeanour? She had heard another carriage approaching just as they had been going into the house. It probably contained one of the Earl's *titled* relatives. He had a score of them, her aunt had warned her as they had lain in bed the night before, neither of them quite able to do more than doze on and off because of the noise the other occupants of the coaching inn were making.

'Each one more pompous than the last,' she had said. 'Lord Bridgemere's two surviving sisters are the worst. Lady Thrapston and Lady Craddock are so starched up it is a wonder either of them can bend enough to sit down.'

Helen had giggled in the darkness, glad her aunt was still able to make a jest in light of all she was going through—and all she still had to face.

But she was beyond the stage of joking about anything now. With agitated fingers Helen untied the strings of her aunt's bonnet, loosened the top buttons of her coat, and pulled off her boots. Aunt Bella's eyes flickered open briefly as she tucked a quilt over her, but she did not really come properly awake.

Helen pulled a ladder-backed chair beside the bed, so that she could hold her hand while she waited for a maid to arrive.

Helen waited. And waited. But the promised help did not come.

She got up, crossed the room, and yanked on the bell-pull again. Then, in spite of the fact that the room was so cold she could see her breath steaming, she untied her own bonnet, shaking out her ebony curls and fluffing them over her ears, and peeled off her gloves before returning to her aunt's bedside to chafe at her hands. Even though a fire was burning in the hearth it was making little impact upon the chill that pervaded this room. Her aunt's hands remained cold, and her face still retained that horribly worrying grey tinge.

After waiting in mounting irritation for what must have been at least twenty minutes, she began to wonder if the bell-pull actually worked. They had not been quartered in the best part of the house. Even trotting behind the footman, with one eye kept firmly on her aunt, she had noticed that the corridors up here were uncarpeted, the wall hangings faded and worn with age.

This was clearly, she decided in mounting annoyance, all that an indigent, untitled lady who was the mere aunt of a cousin of the Earl warranted by way of comfort!

But then her aunt finally opened her eyes.

'Helen?' she croaked.

'Yes, dear, I am here.'

'What happened?'

'You…had a little faint, I think,' she said, smoothing a straggling greying lock from her aunt's forehead.

'How embarrassing.'

Her aunt might feel mortified, but the pink that now stole to her hollow cheeks came as a great relief to Helen.

'You will feel better once you have had some tea,' said Helen. 'I have rung for some, but so far nobody has come.'

Lord, they must have been up here for the better part of an hour now! This really was not good enough.

'Oh, yes,' her aunt sighed. 'A cup of tea is *just* what I need. Though even some water would be welcome,' she finished weakly.

Helen leapt to her feet. Though the room was small, somebody had at least provided a decanter and glasses upon a little table under a curtained window. Once her aunt had drunk a few sips of the water Helen poured for her and held to her lips, she did seem to revive a little more.

'Will you be all right if I leave you for a short while?' Helen asked. 'I think I had better go and see if I can find out what has happened to the maid who was supposed to be coming up here.'

'Oh, Helen, thank you. I do not want to be any trouble, but…'

'No trouble, Aunt Bella. No trouble at all!' said Helen over her shoulder as she left the room.

But once she was outside in the corridor the reassuring smile faded from her lips. Her dark eyes flashed and her brows drew down in a furious scowl.

Clenching her fists, she stalked back along the tortuous route to the main hall, and then, finding it deserted, looked around for the green baize door that would take her to the servants' quarters.

She did not know who was responsible, but somebody was going to be very sorry they had shoved her poor dear aunt up there, out of the way, and promptly forgotten all about her!

The scene that met her eyes in the servants' hall was one of utter chaos.

Trunks and boxes cluttered the stone-flagged passageway. Coachmen and postilions lounged against the walls, drinking tankards of ale. Maids and footmen in overcoats clustered round the various piles of luggage, stoically awaiting their turn to be allotted their rooms.

Helen could see that there must have been a sudden influx of visitors. She could just, she supposed, understand how the needs of one of the less important ones had been over-looked. But that did not mean she was going to meekly walk away and let the situation continue!

She strode past the loitering servants and into the kitchen.

'I need some tea for Miss Forrest,' she declared.

A perspiring, red-faced kitchen maid looked up from where she was sawing away at a loaf of bread.

'Have to wait your turn,' she said, without pausing in her task. 'I only got one pair of hands, see, and I got to do Lady Thrapston's tray first.'

The problem with having a Frenchman for a father, her aunt had often observed, was that it left Helen with a very un-English tendency to lose her temper.

'Is Lady Thrapston an elderly woman who absolutely *needs* that tea to help her recover from the rigours of her journey?' asked Helen militantly. Even though a very small part of her suspected that, since she was the Earl's oldest sur-viving sister, Lady Thrapston might well be quite elderly, she felt little sympathy for the unknown woman. She was almost certain that Lady Thrapston was getting preferential treat-ment because of her rank, not her need. 'I don't suppose *she* dropped down in a dead faint, did she?'

The maid opened her mouth to deny it, but Helen smiled grimly, and said, 'No, I thought not!' She seized the edge of the tray that already contained a pot, the necessary crockery, and what bread the kitchen maid had already buttered. 'Miss Forrest has been lying upstairs, untended, for the best part of an hour. You will just have to start another tray for Lady Thrapston!'

''Ere! You can't do that!' another maid protested.

'I have done it!' replied Helen, swirling round and elbowing her way through the shifting mass of visiting servants milling about in the doorway.

'I'll be telling Mrs Dent what you done!' came a shrill voice from behind her.

Mrs Dent must be the housekeeper. The one who by rights ought to have made sure Aunt Bella was properly looked after. It was past time the woman got involved.

'Good!' she tossed back airily over her shoulder. 'I have a few things I should like to say to her myself!'

It was a far longer trek back up to the little round room with a heavy tray in her hands than it had been going down, fuelled by indignation. She set the tray down on a table just inside the door, feeling the teapot to see if it was still at a drinkable temperature.

'My goodness,' said Aunt Bella, easing herself up against the pillows. 'You did well! Did you find out what was taking so long?'

'It appears that several other guests have arrived today, and the servants' hall is in uproar.'

Her aunt pursed her lips as Helen poured her a cup of tea which, she saw to her relief, was still emitting wisps of steam.

'I should not be a bit surprised to learn that *everybody* has arrived today,' she said, taking the cup from Helen's hand.

'Given the fact that we have only two weeks for all of us to make our petitions known, while Lord Bridgemere is observing Christmas with his tenants. And it is only to be expected,' she added wryly, 'that without a woman to see to the minutiae things are bound to descend into chaos.'

'What do you mean?'

'Only that he will not have either of his sisters acting as hostess,' Aunt Bella explained. 'Absolutely refuses to let them have so much as a toehold in any aspect of his life.'

'He is not married, then?'

Her aunt sipped at her tea and sighed with pleasure. Then cocked an eyebrow at Helen. 'Bridgemere? Marry? Perish the thought! Why would a man of his solitary disposition bother to saddle himself with a wife?'

'I should have thought that was obvious,' said Helen tartly.

Her aunt clicked her tongue disapprovingly.

'Helen, you really ought not to know about such things. Besides, a man does not need a wife for *that*.'

Helen sat down, raised her cup to her lips, took a delicate sip, and widened her eyes.

'I simply cannot imagine where I learned about…men's… um…proclivities,' she said. 'Or why you should suppose *that* was what I was alluding to.'

'Oh, yes, you can! And I do not know why you have suddenly decided to be so mealy-mouthed.'

'Well, now that I am about to be a governess I thought I had better learn to keep a rein on my tongue.' Once Helen had made sure the Earl would house her aunt, and provide some kind of pension for her, Helen was going to take up the post she had managed to secure as governess to the children of a family in Derbyshire.

Her aunt regarded her thoughtfully over the rim of her teacup. 'Don't know as how that will be doing your charges any favours. Girls need to know what kind of behaviour to expect from men. If they have not already learned it from their own menfolk.'

'Oh, I quite agree,' she said, leaning forward to relieve her aunt of her empty cup and depositing it on the tea tray. 'But perhaps my employers would prefer me not to be too outspoken,' she added, handing her a plate of bread and butter.

'Humph,' said her aunt, as she took a bite out of her bread.

'Besides, I might not have been going to say what you *thought* I meant to say at all. Perhaps,' she said mischievously, 'I was only going to remark that a man of his station generally requires…an heir.'

Quick as a flash, her aunt replied, 'He already has an heir. Lady Craddock's oldest boy will inherit when he dies.'

'So that only leaves his proclivities to discuss and disparage.'

'Helen! How could you?'

'What? Be so indelicate?'

'No, make me almost choke on my bread and butter, you wretched girl!'

But her aunt was laughing, her cheeks pink with amusement, her eyes twinkling with mirth. And Helen knew it had been worth ruffling a few feathers in the servants' hall to see her aunt smiling again. She would do anything for her dear Aunt Bella!

But Aunt Bella had still not got out of bed by the time they heard the faint echoes of the dinner gong sounding in the distance.

'I am in no fit state to face them,' she admitted wearily. 'Just one more evening before I have to humble myself—is that too much to ask?'

Aunt Bella had prided herself on maintaining her independence from her family, in particular her overbearing brothers, for as long as Helen had known her.

'All these years I have kept on telling everyone that I am quite capable of managing my own affairs,' she had moaned when the invitation to the Christmas house party had arrived, 'without the interference of any pompous, opinionated male, and now I am going to have to crawl to Lord Bridgemere himself and beg him for help!'

It was quite enough for today, Helen could see, that she was actually under Lord Bridgemere's roof. It would be much better to put off laying out her dire situation before the cold and distant Earl until she had recovered from the journey.

'Of course not!' said Helen, stacking the empty cups and plates back on the tray. 'I shall take these back down to the kitchen and arrange for something to be brought up.'

She had already asked the boy who had eventually dumped their luggage in the corridor outside their room if it was possible to have a supper tray brought up. He had shrugged, looking surly, from which she had deduced it would be highly unlikely.

So Helen once more descended to the kitchen, where she was informed by the same kitchen maid she had run up against before that they had enough to do getting a meal on the table without doing extra work for meddling so-and-sos who didn't know their place. This argument was vociferously seconded by a stout cook.

'Very well,' said Helen, her eyes narrowing. 'I can see you are all far too busy seeing to the guests who are well enough to go to the dining room.' Once again she grabbed a tray, and began loading it with what she could find lying about, already half-prepared. 'I shall save you the bother of having to go up all those stairs with a heavy tray,' she finished acidly.

There were a few murmurs and dirty looks, but nobody actually tried to prevent her.

In the light of this inhospitality, however, she was seriously doubting the wisdom of her aunt's scheme to apply to the Earl for help in her declining years. She had voiced these doubts previously, but her aunt had only sighed, and said, 'He is not so lost to a sense of what is due to his family that he would leave an indigent elderly female to starve, Helen.'

But the fact that his staff cared so little about the weak and helpless must reflect his own attitude, Helen worried. Any help he gave to Aunt Bella would be grudging, at best. And her aunt had implied that had it not been Christmas it would have been a waste of time even writing to him!

Thank heaven she had come here with her. She shook her head as she climbed back up the stairs to the tower room, her generous mouth for once turned down at the corners. If she had not been here to wait on her she could just picture her poor aunt lying there, all alone and growing weaker by the hour, as the staff saw to all the grander, wealthier house guests. Helen was supposed to have taken up her governess duties at the beginning of December, but when she had seen how much her aunt was dreading visiting Alvanley Hall, and humbling herself before the head of the family, she had been on the verge of turning down the job altogether. She had longed to find something else nearby, something that would enable her to care for her aunt in her old age as she had cared for Helen as a child, but Aunt Bella had refused to let her.

'No, Helen, do not be a fool,' Aunt Bella had said firmly. 'You must take this job as governess. Even if you do not stay there very long, your employers will be able to provide references which you can use to get something else. You must preserve your independence, Helen. I could not bear it if you had to resort to marrying some odious male!'

In the end Helen had agreed simply to postpone leaving her aunt until after Bridgemere's Christmas party. After all, she was hardly in a position to turn down the job. It had come as something of a shock to discover just how hard it was for a young lady of good birth to secure paid employment. After all the weeks of scouring the advertisements and writing mostly unanswered applications, the Harcourts had been the only family willing to risk their children to a young woman who had no experience whatsoever.

'I should think,' her aunt had then pointed out astutely, 'that if you were to tell them you mean to spend Christmas in the house of a belted Earl they will be only too glad to give you leave to do so. Think what it will mean to them to be able to boast that their new governess has such connections!'

'There is that,' Helen had mused. The Harcourts were newly wealthy, their fortune stemming from industry, and she had already gained the impression that in their eyes her background far outweighed her lack of experience. Mrs Harcourt's eyes had lit up when Helen had informed her that not only had her mother come from an old and very noble English family, but her father had been a French count.

A virtually penniless French count—which was why her mother's family, one of whom was married to the younger of Aunt Bella's horrible brothers, had shown no interest in raising her themselves. But Helen hadn't felt the need to explain that to Mrs Harcourt, who had indeed proved exceptionally amenable to her new governess attending such an illustrious Christmas party.

That night, though she was more tired than she could ever remember feeling in her whole life, Helen lay in the dark, gnawing on her fingernails, well after her aunt began to snore gently. She did not resent the fact they were having to share a bed yet again. It had been her decision to book only one bed between them on their journey south. It had saved so much money, and given both of them a much needed feeling of security in the strange rooms of the various coaching inns where they had broken their journey. And tonight the room was so cold that it was a blessing to have a body to help her keep warm. Besides, she would not have felt easy leaving Aunt Bella alone for one minute in such an inhospitable place!

If Lord Bridgemere could employ staff who would so casually ignore a guest who was far from well, it did not bode well for her aunt's future. Not at all. What if, in spite of her assurance that he would not permit a female relative to suffer penury, Lord Bridgemere decided he could not be bothered with her? What would she do? Helen wished with all her heart she was in a position to look after her aunt. But the reality was that there were precious few jobs available to young ladies educated at home—especially educated with the rather eccentric methods her aunt had employed.

Aunt Bella had decried all the received wisdom regarding which subjects were appropriate for a girl to learn. Instead, if Helen had shown an interest in any particular topic she had bought her the relevant books or equipment, and hired people who could help her pursue her interest. So she could not teach pupils watercolour painting, or the use of the globe. And the post she *had* been able to obtain was so poorly paid she would not be able to survive herself were her meals and board not included.

Not that she minded for herself. She was young and strong and fit. But her aunt's collapse today had shocked her. She had never thought of Aunt Bella as old and infirm, but the truth was that these last few months had taken their toll. And in a few more years she might well fall foul of some condition which would mean she needed constant care.

If her cousin's nephew proved as cold-hearted as Aunt Bella had led her to believe, and as the treatment she had received since arriving appeared to confirm…

She rolled over and wrapped her arms about her waist.

Her aunt's future did not bear thinking about.

Chapter Two

She woke with a jolt the next morning, feeling as though she had not slept for more than a few minutes.

But she must have done, because the fire had gone out and the insides of the lead paned windows were thick with frost feathers.

She got up, wrapped herself in her warmest shawl, raked out the grate and, discovering a few embers still glowing gently, coaxed them into life with some fresh kindling. Then she looked around for the means to wash the soot and ash from her fingers. There was no dressing room adjoining their tiny room, but there was a screen behind which stood a washstand containing a pitcher of ice-cold water and a basin.

Washing in that water certainly woke her up completely!

She did not want her aunt to suffer the same early-morning shock, though, so, having made sure the coals were beginning to burn nicely, she put the fire guard in place and nipped down to the kitchens to fetch a can of hot water.

By the time she returned she was pleased to find that the

little room had reached a temperature at which her aunt might get out of bed.

'You had better make the most of this while the water is still warm,' she told her sleepy aunt. 'And then I shall go and forage for some breakfast.'

'My word, Helen,' her aunt observed sleepily, 'nothing daunts you, does it?'

Helen smiled at her. 'Thank you, Aunt Bella. I try not to let it.'

She had discovered within herself a well of ingenuity over these past months, which she might never have known she possessed had they not been so dramatically plunged from affluence to poverty. Seeing her aunt so upset by their losses, she had vowed to do all she could to shield the older woman from the more beastly aspects of losing their wealth. She had been the one to visit the pawnbrokers, and to haggle with tradespeople for the bread to go on their table. Not that they had been in any immediate danger of starving. So many of the townspeople had banked with the Middleton and Shropshire that a brisk system of bartering had soon come into being, which had done away with the immediate need for cash amongst its former clients. The silver apostle spoons, for instance, had gone to settle an outstanding grocer's bill, and the best table linen had turned out to be worth a dozen eggs and half a pound of sausages.

Once her aunt had finished her toilet, Helen tipped the wastewater into the enamel jug provided for the purpose and set out for the kitchens once more.

At least this morning there was an orderly queue of maids

who had come down to fetch a breakfast tray. She took her place at the back of it, completely content to wait her turn. In fact she thoroughly approved of the way they all got attention on the basis of first come, first served. Regardless of whom they were fetching and carrying for. It was much more fair.

What a pity, she thought, her lips pursing, the same egalitarian system had not prevailed the evening before.

The kitchen maid scowled when it came to her turn.

'I don't suppose there are any eggs to be had?' Helen asked politely.

'You don't suppose correct!' her nemesis answered. 'You can have a pot of chocolate and hot rolls for your lady. Eggs is only served in the dining room.'

Really, the hospitality in this place was…*niggardly*, she fumed, bumping open the kitchen door with her hip. But then what had she expected? From the sound of it the Earl of Bridgemere thoroughly disliked having his home invaded by indigent relatives. And his attitude had trickled down to infect his staff, she reflected, setting out once more on the by now familiar route back up to the tower, because their master was a recluse. What kind of man would only open his doors—and that reluctantly—to his family over the Christmas season? An elusive recluse. She smiled to herself, enjoying the play on words and half wondering if there was a rhyme to be made about the crusty old bachelor upon whose whim her aunt's future depended.

Although what would rhyme with Bridgemere? Nothing.

Earl, though… There was curl, and churl, and…

She had just reached the second set of stairs when round

the corner came the broad-shouldered footman who had carried her aunt so effortlessly up to her room the night before.

Instead of stepping to one side, to allow her room to pass, he took up position in the very centre of the corridor, his fisted hands on his hips.

'I hear you have been setting the kitchen in a bustle,' he said. 'I hope you have permission to take that tray, and have not snatched it from its rightful recipient as you did last night?'

'What business is it of yours?' she snapped, thoroughly fed up with the attitude of the staff in Alvanley Hall. She knew they were not used to entertaining visitors, but really! 'And how dare you speak to me like that?'

His light coffee-coloured eyes briefly widened, as though her retort had shocked him. But then he said icily, 'Mrs Dent is most put out by your behaviour, miss. And I must say that I can quite see why. I do not appreciate servants from other houses coming here and thinking they know how to run things better…'

'Well, first of all, I am nobody's servant!' she snapped. At least not yet, she corrected herself guiltily. 'And if this place was run better, then I dare say visiting servants would abide by Mrs Dent's regime. As it is, I deplore the way rank was placed above my aunt's very real need last night.'

She had really got the bit between her teeth now. She advanced on the footman until she was almost prodding him in the stomach with her tray.

'If I had not gone down to the kitchens myself, I dare say she would still be lying there, waiting for somebody to notice her! And as for situating a lady of her age up so many stairs—

well, the least said about that the better! Whoever arranged to put her up in that room ought to be—' She could not think of a suitable punishment for anyone who treated her beloved aunt with such lack of consideration. So she had to content herself with taking her temper out on the unfortunate footman, since he was the only member of His Lordship's staff actually in range.

'She is supposed to be a family member, yet Lord Bridgemere has had her stashed away up there as though he is ashamed of her! No wonder she has stayed away all these years! Now, get out of my way—before I…before I…' She barely refrained from stamping her foot.

'Do you mean to tell me you are a *guest*?'

Helen could not tell what it was about him that irritated her the most. The fact that he had ignored all her very real complaints to hone in on the one point she considered least relevant, or the way he was running his eyes insolently over her rather shabby attire, his mouth flattened in derision. If she had been less angry she might have admitted that the gown she was wearing was one she had kept precisely because it *did* make her look more like a servant than a lady of leisure. Her wardrobe would now have to reflect the position she was about to take up. Nobody would take a governess seriously if she went about in fashionable, frivolous clothes. She had ruthlessly culled her wardrobe of such items, knowing, too, that the more fashionable they were, the more money she would get for them from the second-hand clothing dealers. For, although the bartering system had worked up to a point, cash had been absolutely necessary to purchase tickets from their hometown to Alvanley Hall, and to pay for their overnight stops *en route*.

This morning Helen had also wrapped her thickest shawl round her shoulders, to keep her warm as she scuttled along the chilly corridors. She'd knotted it round her waist just before she'd left the kitchen, to leave her hands free to deal with the tray, and now she noticed that it was blotched with ash from when she had made up the fire.

But it was not this man's place to judge or criticise her! Helen drew herself to her full height. Which was not easy to do when weighed down by a tray brimming with food, drink and crockery.

'I mean to tell you nothing! You are an impertinent fellow, and—'

He raised one eyebrow in a way that was so supercilious that if she'd had a hand free she might have been tempted to slap him.

'And my aunt is waiting for her breakfast! So stand aside!'

For a moment she thought he might refuse. But then something like amusement glinted in his eyes. His mouth tilted up at one corner in a smile full of mockery and he stepped to one side of the corridor, sweeping her an elaborate bow as she strode past with a toss of her head.

Well, really! What an abominable rogue he was! So full of himself!

And she could not believe he had goaded her into almost stamping her foot and actually tossing her head. Tossing her head! Like those village girls who loitered around the smithy in the hopes of glimpsing young Jeb Simpkins stripping off his shirt to duck his head under the pump. Who flounced off with a toss of their artfully arranged curls when he shot them a few pithy comments that left them in no doubt as to what he thought of their morals.

Not that she had been thinking about what the footman would look like with his shirt off!

Although he probably would have an impressive set of muscles, given the way he had so effortlessly carried her aunt up all these stairs last night…

She gave herself a mental shake. His physique had nothing to do with anything! He was a…a rogue! Yes, he was probably the type who snatched kisses from the kitchen maids and had stormy affairs with visiting ladies' maids, she reflected darkly. Oh, she could well understand why they would elbow each other aside for the privilege of kissing that hard, arrogant mouth, and ruffling that neat light brown hair with their fingers. For he had that air about him she noticed foolish women often fell for. That air of arrogant disdain which drew silly girls like moths to a candle flame. An air she had observed more than once in men who thought themselves irresistible to women, and who therefore mocked the entire female sex for their gullibility.

Well, she was not silly or gullible! And she had never been the type to find a man exciting merely because he had a rep-utation as a ladies' man. If she were ever to seriously consider marriage, she would want someone kind and dependable. Not a man who looked down his nose at women! And who was probably planning his next conquest before he had even buttoned up his breeches.

She drew herself up outside the door to her aunt's chamber, out of breath and more than a little shocked at herself. She could not believe the way her mind had been wandering since that encounter with the footman. Picturing him with his shirt off, for heaven's sake! Kissing kitchen maids and…and worse! Why, she could actually *see* the smug expression on his face as he buttoned up his breeches with those long, deft fingers…

It was just as well she was going to be a governess and not a ladies' maid. She did not know how any girl was expected to cope with encounters with handsome, arrogant footmen as they nipped up and down the backstairs.

A rueful smile tugged at her lips as she turned round and bumped open the door with her hip.

She rather thought that any girl who was the least bit susceptible would start to look forward to running into *that* particular footman. It had been quite exhilarating to give him a sharp set-down. To knock him off his arrogant perch and make him look at her twice. And if all she had to look forward to was the dreary grind of service, then…

She shook her head.

She was going to work as a governess, for heaven's sake! Flirting with the footmen on the backstairs was sure to result in instant dismissal.

Besides, the rogue worked *here*. It was unlikely there would be a man of such mettle working for a family like the Harcourts. Footmen of that calibre would not deign to work for anything less than a noble house. It would be very far beneath such a man's dignity to serve a family from *trade*.

Which was a jolly good thing.

★ ★ ★

She did not set foot outside the drum room for the rest of the day. Her aunt dozed on and off, declaring every time she woke that she felt much better, though to Helen's eye it did not look as though her spirits were reviving all that much.

Whenever Aunt Bella went back to sleep Helen sat by the window, making use of what pale winter sunlight filtered in through the tiny diamond-shaped panes to do some embroidery. There was little money to spare for Christmas gifts this year, and so she had decided to make her aunt a little keepsake, to remind her of their life together in Middleton whenever she used it. Fortunately needlework had been one of the subjects Helen had wanted to pursue. Largely because her mother had begun to teach her to sew, and her sampler had been one of the very few possessions she had managed to salvage from her childhood home.

She tucked her work hastily out of sight every time Aunt Bella began to stir, and occasionally broke off to watch the comings and goings of the other house guests. From up here in the tower she had an excellent view over the rear of the house, and the acres of grounds in which it was set. A party of gentlemen of varying ages went off in the direction of the woods with guns over their arms. A little later a bevy of females sauntered off towards the formal gardens which surrounded the house.

At one point she saw a group of children bundled up in hats and scarves, loaded up into a cart, and driven off in a different direction entirely from the way their parents had gone, their shouts and laughter inaudible from up here, but made visible by the little puffs of vapour that escaped from their mouths.

It looked as though the house party was now in full swing. She pursed her lips and bent her head over her embroidery. She had to admit that if, as her aunt surmised, all the guests *had* arrived on the same day, the servants might have some excuse for their attitude. They must have been rushed off their feet yesterday. Yet she could not quite rid herself of a simmering sense of injustice. She had only to look out of the window to see that His Lordship had organised entertainment for all the rest of his guests. Only she and Aunt Bella had been completely overlooked. Stuck up in a cold room in the tower and left to their own devices, she fumed, cutting off her thread with a vicious little snip.

Though later, as they prepared to go downstairs and mingle with the other guests for the first time, Helen knew that she must not let her poor opinion of him and his household show.

'Time to face the music,' Aunt Bella sighed, draping a silk shawl round her shoulders. 'I still do not feel at my best, you know, but I cannot hide up here for ever. Besides, I need to collar Lord Bridgemere's current secretary and arrange a private interview with him. The others will have already done so, I shouldn't wonder.'

Because this was the only time of the year he made himself accessible to his relatives, they had to make the most of this brief opportunity to lay their problems before him.

'I do hope it will not be too long before he can see me.'

Helen arranged her aunt's shawl into more becoming folds around her shoulders, and took one last look at herself in the mirror. She had only kept one of her evening gowns. In a deep bronze silk, with very few ribbons or ruffles, she felt that it looked elegant enough to pass muster should her new employers ever invite her to dine with them, without being too eye-catching. Though naturally, since she had bought it in better times, the colour of the silk flattered her creamy complexion. And she had spent hours finding exactly the right shade of chocolate brown for the sash which tied just beneath her bosom to match the deep brown of her eyes.

But it was not vanity alone that had made her keep this dress. Its colouring gave her an excuse to wear the amber beads that had belonged to her mother. She had been quite unable to part with them when disposing of other items of jewellery. They might have fetched quite a tidy sum, but they were worth far more to her as a memento of her mother than any amount of coin.

Both her parents had died when she was only ten years old, of a fever she had barely survived herself. She had recovered to find their chambers full of creditors, stripping the rooms of anything that would settle their outstanding accounts. She had grabbed the beads from her mother's dressing table and hidden them in her sewing case when she had seen what the adults all about her were doing. She ran her forefinger over them now, as she had been doing with increasing frequency over the past few months. They were a tangible reminder that she had been in dire straits before and come through them. Nothing could be worse than to find yourself an orphan, dependent on the whims of adults who saw you only as a problem they were reluctant to deal with. At least now she was able to provide for herself. And was not, like her aunt, reduced to turning to a wealthy relative for aid.

She whirled away from the mirror, reminding herself that the very least important aspect of tonight's dinner was the way she looked! She must forget about her appearance and concentrate on keeping her tongue between her teeth. Though she still seethed with resentment at the way her aunt had been treated so far, she must do nothing that might jeopardise her aunt's chances of getting into His Lordship's good graces.

They were halfway down the first set of stairs when the dinner gong sounded.

A footman with all the silver lace—the one who had opened the carriage door for them the night before—was waiting at the foot of the second set of stairs to direct them to the blue saloon where, he told them, everyone gathered before processing in to dine.

Her aunt tensed as they crossed the threshold. And Helen could hardly blame her. The amount of jewellery on display was dazzling to the eye, flashing from the throats and wrists of the silken-clad females lounging upon sumptuous velvet sofas. She could not imagine what people who looked so affluent could possibly want from the Earl! Although both she and her aunt had taken care with their appearance, too. They had their pride. To look at them, nobody would know that they had not two brass farthings to rub together. Perhaps she ought not to judge on outward show.

But the boom of male voices definitely struck a jarring note. Aunt Bella rarely had men in her house. And to be confronted by so many of them at once set Helen's senses reeling. She reached for her aunt's arm and linked her own through it.

A slender young man with an earnest expression hastened to their side.

'You must be Miss Forrest and…er…Miss Forrest,' he said, bowing. 'Permit me to introduce myself. I am His Lordship's personal secretary, Mr Cadwallader.'

'How do you do?' said Helen.

Her aunt drew in a deep breath.

'Young man,' she said, 'I would very much appreciate it if you could arrange for me to have a private word with His Lordship.'

'Of course,' he replied. 'Though that may not be for a day or so,' he added, with a smile Helen thought somewhat supercilious. 'His Lordship has many demands upon his time at present.'

Lord Bridgemere did not participate in many of the festivities laid on for his guests, Aunt Bella had told her, since he was either hearing petitions or deciding what to do about them.

It could not be much fun, Helen thought. But then it served him right for reducing his entire family to such desperation! Besides, he sounded like the kind of person who did not know how to enjoy himself. Even if he were not busy he would still probably not join in with the country pursuits she had seen the others enjoying throughout the course of the day from her window.

Aunt Bella nodded, her air outwardly gracious, but beneath her hand Helen could feel her trembling.

'I have seated you beside General Forrest this evening,' said Mr Cadwallader to her aunt, 'since I believe he is your brother.' He consulted the sheet of paper he held in his hand at that moment, thus missing the look of utter horror that flitted across Aunt Bella's face.

Helen gave her aunt's arm a comforting squeeze. As if this whole situation was not painful enough, now it appeared that the most odious of her brothers was here to witness her humiliation. And from what she remembered of him, coupled with her aunt's pithy observations over the years, he would be only too delighted to have the opportunity to crow over her downfall.

'And he will be escorting you in to dine.'

'He will?' Aunt Bella gasped. 'Does he know about this?'

For she had not spoken to either of her brothers for years. Twelve years, to be precise. And it was entirely because of this breach with her brothers that Aunt Bella had no recourse but to turn to the head of the extended family now she had lost all her money.

The secretary shot her a baffled look, before turning to Helen and saying hastily, 'And I have placed you opposite your aunt, between Sir Mortimer Hawkshaw and Lord Cleobury. Sir Mortimer will escort you into the dining room…' He trailed off, looking over their shoulders at the next person to arrive, and they felt obliged to move further into the room.

They had not advanced more than a couple of yards before Helen spotted the arrogant footman. One of the groups of gentlemen was breaking up, and he was moving from them towards the dining room doors, which the butler had just flung open. She supposed his duties would include circulating with drinks, and serving at the table.

Suddenly she became aware that the boat-shaped neckline of her gown was particularly flattering to her figure. And felt her cheeks heating at the realisation that he would have an exceptionally good view of her feminine attributes should he reach over her to pour wine.

What on earth had come over her? It had never occurred to her that a footman might *look* at her during the course of performing his duties. She did not think she was a complete snob, but never before had she thought of any servant as…well…as a man! What was more, she had never been the sort of girl who craved male attention. Her aunt was not of the opinion that it was every young lady's duty to marry as soon as possible, so had not encouraged her to mix with the so-called eligible young men of their district. And what she had observed of masculine behaviour, from a decorous distance, had given her no reason to kick against her aunt's prejudice against the entire sex.

Yet every time she saw this footman her thoughts began to wander into most improper territory!

Full of chagrin, she plucked up her shawl and settled it over her shoulders, making sure that it covered her bosom.

'Cold, love?' her aunt asked.

'Um…a little,' she said. Then, because she hated being untruthful, 'Though I think it is mainly nerves that are making me shiver.'

'I know what you mean,' her aunt murmured.

She glanced once more at the footman, warily. He was

standing in the doorway, tugging his wristbands into place as, wooden-faced, he watched the assembled ladies rise to their feet and begin to gravitate towards the dining room.

'So, Bella, you have decided to show your face in society again, have you?'

The booming voice of the ruddy-faced man who stood glaring down at her aunt jerked Helen's attention away from the fascinating footman. General Forrest was, naturally, older than Helen remembered him, though not a whit less intimidating.

He had not stopped shouting, so far as she could recall, from the moment she had arrived on his doorstep until the moment she'd left. 'The girl's mother has plenty of other sisters!' was the first thing she could remember him bellowing at his wife, who had shivered like an aspen leaf under the force of his fury. 'Pack her off to one of them!'

He had then slammed back into his study, where he'd carried on shouting at whoever was inside. When Isabella had eventually emerged, head high, lips pressed tightly together and a suspicious sheen in her eyes, the ten-year-old Helen had immediately felt a strong sense of kinship with her.

She had knelt down in the hall, looked the tearful Helen in the eye, and said, 'Would you like to come home with me? I should love to have a little girl to call my own. Without—' and she had glared darkly up at her glowering brother '—having to go through the horrid experience of having to marry some repulsive man to get one.'

Since the General had already made it perfectly clear he

did not want to be saddled with a half-French brat, she had slipped her hand into that of the older woman.

'If you insist on taking on my wife's niece, on top of all the other outrageous things you have done, then you will have only yourself to blame if I cut you out of my life!' he had bellowed.

They had not looked back. And, just before slamming the door shut on them, the last words he had uttered were, 'That's it! I wash my hands of you, Bella!'

As a child, General Forrest had seemed enormous to her. And, though Helen no longer had to crane her neck to look up at him, the years had added to his bulk, so that he still seemed like a very big man.

But he did not intimidate her aunt, who lifted her chin and glared straight back.

'Needs must when the devil drives.'

'Harrumph!' he replied, holding out his arm for her to take.

He completely ignored Helen. She battened down her sense of affront. Not only was she going to have to inure herself to a lifetime of snubs once she became a governess, but General Forrest had never thought much of her in the first place.

Helen looked beyond the General's bulk and saw, hovering in his shadow, the thin, anxious woman Helen dimly remembered as her real aunt.

A bored-looking man materialised at Helen's side, led her into the dining room, and showed her to a seat about halfway along the table. She assumed he must be Sir Mortimer Hawkshaw, though he did not deign to introduce himself or attempt to make conversation. It was galling to think that even *he* looked down his nose at her, she reflected bitterly. Though they both occupied the lowest social position, so he could only be another of the Earl's poor relations.

They all stood in silence behind their chairs, heads bowed, while an absurdly young clergyman said grace.

Helen could not help glancing down to the foot of the table, where an extremely haughty-looking woman who was dripping in diamonds and sapphires was taking her seat, and then turning to take her first look at her host, the head of her aunt's extended family. The man who held her aunt's entire future in his hands.

And felt her jaw drop.

Because, just being eased into the chair at the head of the table by the stately elderly butler who had earlier thrown open the doors to the dining room and declared dinner was served, was…

The man she had assumed from the first moment she had clapped eyes on him to be nothing more than a footman!

Chapter Three

How could he be so *young*?

When her aunt had spoken of her nephew, the head of her family, she had made him sound like a curmudgeonly old misanthrope of at least fifty years. Lord Bridgemere could not be a day over thirty.

And why did he not dress like an earl?

He was one of the wealthiest men in the country! She would have thought he'd be the most finely dressed man in the place. Whereas he was the most plainly, soberly attired of all the men at table. He did not so much as sport a signet ring.

Well, now she knew exactly what foreign visitors to England meant when they complained that it was hard to tell the difference between upper servants and their masters, because of the similarity of dress. Not that she was a foreigner. Just a stranger to the ways of grand houses like this.

And he did not act like an earl, either! What had he been about, carting her aunt upstairs, when there was a perfectly genuine footman on hand to perform that office? And as for loitering about on the backstairs…well, she simply could not account for it!

The Earl turned his head and looked directly at her. And she realised she was the only person still standing. And, what was more, staring at the Earl of Bridgemere with her mouth hanging open.

She sat down swiftly, her cheeks flushing hot. Oh, heavens, what must everyone think?

And what did *he* think? Did he find it amusing to masquerade as a servant and humiliate his guests? What an odious, unkind… If he was laughing at her, she did not care what anyone else thought of her, she would…she would…

She darted him an inimical glare. Only to find that he was talking to the lady on his left-hand side, a completely bland expression on his face, as though nothing untoward had occurred.

She felt deflated. And foolish.

But at least he had not exposed her to ridicule by any look, or word, or…

No, she groaned inwardly. She had managed to make herself look ridiculous all on her own!

Though it had been partly his fault. Why had he not introduced himself properly? Why had he let her rip up at him like that?

She tore her eyes from his and made an effort to calm herself while the real footmen bustled about with plates and tureens and chafing dishes.

Lord Bridgemere struggled to pretend that he was not painfully aware of Miss Forrest's discomfiture. What the devil had come over him this morning that he had bowed and grinned and left her thinking he was merely one of his own servants? She had been so shocked just now, upon realising her error, that she had made a complete spectacle of herself. And no gentleman would willingly expose any lady to such public humiliation.

Though how could he have guessed she would just stand there, gaping at him like that? Or that she would then glare at him, making it obvious to all that he had somehow, at some point, offered her some form of insult? None of the other ladies of his acquaintance would ever be so transparent.

No, they all hid behind their painstakingly constructed masks. The only expression they ever showed in public was mild boredom.

He fixed his gaze on his dinner companion, his sister Lady Craddock, although his mind was very far from her interminable complaining. Instead he was remembering the way thoughts of Miss Forrest imperiously ordering him about had kept on bringing a frisson of amusement to his mind, briefly dispelling the tedium of his day. When he had discovered he had made an error of a similar nature to hers, it had struck him as so funny that he had wanted to prolong the joke. He had even pencilled her name into his diary to remind himself, as if he needed any reminder, to make his way down to his study at precisely the same time he had run into her that morning in the hopes of encountering her again.

Extraordinary.

Most people would say he had no sense of humour whatever.

But they might, with some justification, accuse him of

wishing to revel in the novel experience of having a woman react to him as just a man, and not as the Earl of Bridgemere. The wealthy, eligible Earl of Bridgemere. And it *had* been a novel experience. Miss Forrest had not simpered and flattered. No, she had roundly berated him, her dark eyes flashing fire.

He had thought then what an expressive face she had. He had been able to see exactly what she was thinking. Not that he'd needed to guess. She had already been telling him!

Somewhere inside he felt the ghost of a smile trying to break free. Naturally he stifled it, swiftly. It would not do to smile whilst engaged in conversation with either of his sisters. The slightest outward sign that he might be interested in anything either of them had to say would rouse the other to a pitch of jealousy that would make the entire company so uncomfortable they would all be running for cover.

Even now, though, he could tell exactly what emotions Miss Forrest was grappling with. Chief amongst them was chagrin, now that her initial spurt of anger with him had simmered down.

She was quite unlike any of the other guests, all of whom wore the fashionable demeanour of boredom to cloak their dissatisfaction. And they were all of them dissatisfied with their lot, in one way or another. Which irked him beyond measure! They all had so much in comparison with the vast majority of the citizens of this country. Yet they still demanded more.

And Miss Forrest and her older namesake could not be so very different—not deep down, where it mattered. Or they would not be here. It would pay him to remember that.

Only once she felt more in control of herself did Helen raise her head and look about the table. There were at least forty people ranged along its length. For a while conversation was desultory, as the guests helped themselves to generous portions of the vast selection of delicacies on offer. Her aunt looked as uncomfortable as she felt, seated between her brother the General, who was applying himself to his plate with complete concentration, and a man who was conducting a very animated flirtation with the young lady seated on his other side.

It was during the second remove that the General remarked, 'I am surprised at you for bringing that person here, Bella,' motioning at Helen across the table with his fork.

Aunt Bella bristled, while Helen just froze. She had felt uncomfortable enough knowing that she had made such an error of judgement about the station of the man who had turned out to be her host. And in then betraying her consternation by standing there gaping at him like a nodcock. Now, since the General had one of those voices that carried, several other conversations at the table abruptly ceased, and she felt as though once again everyone was staring at her.

'Are you?' replied her aunt repressively. 'I cannot imagine why.'

'I suppose nothing you do ought to shock me any more, Bella,' said the General witheringly. 'You still enjoy courting scandal, do you not?'

'Even if that were true,' Aunt Bella replied with a tight smile, 'which it most emphatically is not, no true gentleman would even touch upon such a topic in company.'

Helen had the satisfaction of seeing the General flush darkly and shift uncomfortably in his seat.

But it was outweighed by the fact that she could also see her aunt's hands were trembling.

There was a moment of tense silence, punctuated only by the genteel clink of sterling silver cutlery on porcelain. Then the lady at the foot of the table drawled, 'The mutton is exceptionally well presented this evening, Bridgemere. You must compliment your cook.'

'I shall certainly do so, Lady Thrapston,' said the Earl dryly, 'since *you* request it.'

For some reason this comment, or perhaps the way it was delivered, made the haughty woman look quite put out.

Lady Thrapston, Helen noted with resentment as she recalled the way Aunt Bella had been neglected upon her arrival, could in no way be described as elderly. She was so stylish that if people did not look too closely, they might take her for a fairly young woman.

There was another uncomfortable pause in the conversation before a few of the younger men, led by a gaudily dressed youth who sat at Lady Thrapston's right hand, began to discuss the day's shooting.

Though the atmosphere had lightened to some extent, Helen was mightily relieved when the meal drew to an end and Lady Thrapston signalled to the other ladies that it was time to withdraw by the simple expedient of getting to her feet.

Helen hurried to the doorway, and waited for her aunt to catch up with her there.

'I am in no condition to go to the drawing room and face

any more of that,' said her aunt in an undertone. 'Not after the shock of discovering my odious brother is here!'

Thank heavens for that, thought Helen. But only said, 'I shall help you up to bed, then.'

They left the room arm in arm, and were ascending the first set of stairs when Helen said, 'Would you mind very much if I were to leave you for a little while?'

Aunt Bella's brows rose. 'You surely do not want to face that drawing room without me?'

'No!' She barely repressed a shudder. 'I most certainly do not!'

She chewed on her lower lip, wondering how much to confess to her aunt. She did not want to add to her worries by admitting she had mistaken Lord Bridgemere for one of his footmen and called him an impudent fellow. She cringed as the scene flooded back to her in all its inglorious detail.

'I have decided it would be a good idea if I had a word with that secretary fellow, that is all…' she began. She wanted to see if she could arrange an interview of her own, through his secretary, and get in an apology to Lord Bridgemere before he spoke to Aunt Bella. She would hate to think that her behaviour might prejudice him against her aunt in any way.

'Oh, Helen, what a good idea! I would be so relieved to learn exactly when I shall be able to speak with Lord Bridgemere. I do not think I shall rest easy until I have laid my case before him. And you are such a pretty girl. I am sure you could persuade the young man to arrange for me to see His Lordship before my brother has a chance to turn him against me. I could not believe he would be so unmannerly as to attack me like that over dinner! It shook me, I can tell you.'

Helen had never felt more uncomfortable than to hear the erroneous assumption her aunt had made.

Yet she did nothing to correct it. It would mean making too many explanations, which she was not sure would be helpful to anyone.

Fortunately it took quite some time to run Mr Cadwallader to ground, by which time Helen had managed to regain her composure.

Though he had dined with the guests, he had retreated almost immediately afterwards to a small book-lined room in the servants' hall.

'I am so sorry to bother you,' she said, knocking upon the door and putting her head round without waiting for him to reply, 'but I was wondering if it would be possible for me to have a private interview with His Lordship. As soon as possible. At least…before whatever time you have arranged for him to speak with my aunt.'

Mr Cadwallader looked up from the pile of papers he was working on and frowned.

'Miss Forrest, is it not?' He flipped open a leather-bound ledger and ran his finger down the page at which it opened. His brows shot up.

'Miss *Helen* Forrest?'

'Yes.' She nodded.

'It appears His Lordship has already anticipated your request. He has your name here for seven o clock tomorrow morning.'

'He has?' She swallowed nervously. What did that mean?

And was it a coincidence that he had her name down for seven? The approximate time at which she had run into him on the backstairs that very morning?

Forcing a smile, she said, 'Good. Wh…where shall I…?'

'Oh, you had better come in here, if he wishes to speak with you that early,' said the young man, snapping the book shut. 'His Lordship always comes down first thing to see to business before—' He pulled himself up, as though he had been on the point of committing an indiscretion, rose to his feet, and ushered her to the door.

Helen racked her brains as she returned to her room, but could not come up with any reason why he should have decided to arrange a meeting with her that boded anything but ill for her and her aunt. But at least she could see what he might have been doing on the backstairs. Those stairs were probably the most direct route from his secretary's office to his own room. He had probably been on his way down to that office, to see to whatever business he needed to get out of the way before…whatever else it was he did all day when he had a houseful of guests. None of whom, to judge by the set of his face at table, were any more welcome to him than she was. Her aunt had hit the nail on the head when she had described him as a man of solitary disposition. It was not only the plainness of his clothing that set him apart from the rest of the persons gathered about that table. An air of complete insularity cloaked him like a mantle.

And all she had accomplished during the two altercations she'd had with him had been to put herself at the head of the list of people who annoyed him. Oh, bother! Why was she always letting her temper get the better of her? And why did she have to have lost it with him, of all men? It was her French blood, her aunt would have said. She always blamed her French blood whenever she got into mischief.

She spent another rather restless night, and was pitched even deeper into gloom when she studied her reflection in the mirror the next morning. Somehow she felt that she would have a better chance to make her case without those awful dark smudges beneath her eyes.

But there was nothing she could do about them. She would simply have to appeal to the Earl's sense of fair play and hope that the General had not managed to turn him against her aunt at some time during the preceding evening.

If her own behaviour had not already done so.

She managed to find her way back down to Mr Cadwallader's office without a hitch. As she summoned up all her courage to knock on the door, she reflected that at least her experiences here were good preparation for her new role in life. She was having plenty of practice at taking backstairs, and haunting servants' quarters!

'Come in,' she heard the Earl say from behind the closed door.

She stepped into the room, turning and shutting the door behind her swiftly before anyone saw her. For some reason she did not want anyone to know she had arranged this interview. Not that there was any risk from the rest of the house guests, none of whom were early risers.

But one of the servants might have seen her, and… Oh, bother it all! She spun round, lifted her chin, and faced the

Earl, who was sitting behind his desk, idly twirling a pen between his long, supple fingers. What did it matter who saw her come here? She had every right to speak to the man…

Besides, he had been the one to send for her, had he not? Or would have if she had not spoken to his secretary first.

Lord Bridgemere made a motion with his pen towards the chair which was placed in front of his desk, which she interpreted as a signal to sit on it. On rather shaky legs she walked to it, and sank onto it gratefully, placing the candle she had used to light her way down on the floor by her feet.

He could see she was nervous. As well she might be, sneaking down here to meet him unchaperoned. She had taken care to make sure nobody had seen her, though, so at least she was not intending to attempt to compromise him. Still, he was going to take great care that she did not suspect he found her attractive, lest it occur to her to try her luck with him. She would not be the first young female to inveigle her way into one of his house parties with the intention of tempting him to abandon his single state. Though usually it was Lady Thrapston who brought them.

A horrible suspicion struck him then. Might Lady Thrapston have dragged the older Miss Forrest into her matchmaking schemes? Was this lovely young woman the bait by which he was to be hooked? He must observe the interaction between the two ladies closely over the next few days, to see whether they were engaged in some form of conspiracy. His sister might have finally realised that he would strenuously resist *any* female introduced to him by her, no matter how fetching he found her, and switched to a more subtle approach.

Helen was glad she had draped her thickest shawl round her shoulders before setting out from the little tower room, having checked this time that there was no soot on it. She had known the corridors would strike chill at this time of day, and the fire in this room had barely got going. Nobody had been in to light the candles, either. There was just her own nightstick upon the floor, and one very similar on the desk between them. It made the setting somehow very intimate. To think of them sitting alone down here, before anyone else was stirring, just barely able to make out anything in the rest of the room…

She shifted self-consciously in her chair, drawing the shawl more tightly round her shoulders.

Lord Bridgemere made no comment, merely lifted one eyebrow as he regarded her rather tatty shawl in that super-cilious way that had so incensed her when she had thought he was a footman.

Mutinously she lifted her chin, and ran her eyes over his own attire. He obviously intended going out riding. There was a whip and a pair of gloves lying on the table. But his jacket was of rough material, and the woollen scarf he had knotted loosely at his throat made him look more like a groom than the lord of the manor!

Their silent duel might have gone on indefinitely had not an odd, plaintive noise emanating from the direction of the fireplace drawn her attention. It appeared to be coming from a heap of mildewed sacking that somebody had care-lessly tossed onto the hearthrug.

'Oh,' she said, instantly forgetting her own grievances as

a wave of concern washed through her. 'Has somebody left an injured animal in here?'

Before the Earl could make any reply, something like a huge paw emerged and began energetically scratching at another portion of the tangled mass. A great shaggy head filled with immense teeth rose up, yawned, and then the whole settled back down into an amorphous muddy-coloured mass.

'It's a dog!' she said, then blushed at the absurdity of stating the obvious. Of course it was a dog. Not a heap of sacking. Why on earth would an earl have piles of mildewed sacks about the place?

'Yes,' he said icily. 'Do you wish me to have him removed? Does he offend you?'

'What?' She frowned. 'No, of course he does not offend me. He just took me by surprise, that is all.'

His mouth twisted into the same expression of distaste he had turned on the woman who had presided at the foot of his dinner table the night before.

'You think it beneath my dignity to own an animal of such uncertain pedigree? Is that it?'

It was a complaint he was always hearing from Lady Thrapston. Why could he not live up to his consequence? Why would he not go to town and ride around Hyde Park in a smart equipage? So that she could bask in his reflected glory, naturally. As though she did not occupy an elevated enough sphere in her own right!

And if he must have a dog, why could it not be an animal of prime pedigree, a gundog, the kind every other man would have.

As if he cared about appearances these days.

Helen was determined to hold her temper in check, in spite of his provoking manner. She managed to return a placating smile to his frown, and say, 'No, not at all.'

The smile and the soft answer did not placate him. Their only effect was to make his scowl deeper.

'I preferred you when you thought I was one of my servants,' he muttered.

At least when she'd thought he was a footman he'd had the truth from her. Now she knew he was the Earl of Bridgemere she was putting on a false face. Smiling when what she really wanted to do was take him down a peg or two.

His comment wiped the smile from her face. She barely managed to prevent herself from informing him that she did not like him in either persona! As a servant she had thought him impertinent, as well as resenting the improper thoughts his proximity had sent frolicking through her mind. As an earl… Well, she had already decided he was a cold, hard, unpleasant sort of man before she had even met him.

Now she *had* met him she could add eccentric and unprincipled to the list of faults she was tallying up against him. Stringing her along like that, when one word would have put her straight!

However, it would not do to tell him what she really thought. Forcing herself to adopt what she hoped was a suitably humble tone, she said instead, 'For which I do most sincerely apologise. It was just that you dress so…' She waved her hand at his attire, which was so ordinary that she defied anyone who did not know to guess that this man held the rank of Earl.

But her speech made no impact on the depth of his scowl.

'And then again, the way you just picked up my aunt and carried her upstairs, as though…'

'You expected me to stand back and watch as she fell to the ground? Is that it?'

He could not tolerate people who were too high in the instep to lend a hand to those less fortunate than themselves. It sickened him when he saw highly bred females hold scented handkerchiefs to their noses as they turned their faces away from beggars. And what kind of man would let a fainting lady drop to the stone flags rather than risk creasing the fabric of his coat?

'You were struggling with her dead weight,' he pointed out. 'And Peters was just standing there gaping. Somebody had to do something.' And from the way she had railed at him on the subject of rank and need he had thought she felt the same. 'As you so forcefully pointed out,' he reminded her.

His eyes had gone so cold and hard it made her want to shiver. She quailed at the reminder of exactly what she had said to him on that occasion. He was clearly still very annoyed with her for being so impertinent.

'Yes, I know I was terribly rude to you, but I thought…'

'That I was merely a servant, and so could be spoken to as though I were of no account. Yes.' He pursed his lips. 'It was a most edifying experience.'

Now she knew he was an earl she would modify her views, no doubt, as well as her manners!

'It was not like that!' Helen objected. 'If you do not wish to be taken for a servant you should tell people who you are! And not loiter around the backstairs the way you do!'

She could have kicked herself. She had sworn she would not antagonise him, and what was she doing? Answering him in a manner that was exceptionally impertinent.

And yet now his scowl had vanished. He leaned back in his chair, eyeing her with frank surprise.

'Do you have no control over your temper, Miss Forrest?'

It was intriguing. She knew who he was. He was certain she had some hidden agenda where he was concerned. And yet she could only play at being obsequious so long before something inside her rebelled.

'Very little,' she admitted guiltily. 'I always *mean* to say what is proper. But usually I just end up telling the truth instead.'

She clapped her hands over her mouth, appalled at having just given him such a clear demonstration of her lack of restraint.

But, far from looking offended, he began to smile. Until now she had only seen a hint of amusement putting a glint into those eyes which were normally so stony, so cold. It was a surprise to see how very different that smile made him look.

Oh, if he were just a footman, and he turned *that* smile on any of the maids, they would swoon at his feet!

'Let me assure you, Miss Forrest, that when the host of a gathering such as this appears on the doorstep to welcome his guests he generally assumes that they know exactly who he is.'

'Oh, well, y…yes,' she conceded. 'I suppose they would…'

'And as for *loitering*, as you put it, on the backstairs, I do no such thing. I never use the main staircase because—' He pulled himself up short, astounded by the fact that she had almost made him speak of a matter he never talked about with anyone. Not that most people needed to ask why he avoided setting foot on that staircase.

'I was simply taking the quickest route down to this room when I chanced upon you and ran foul of your temper,' he said irritably.

'Oh!' She sat up straight, feeling as though he had slapped her. All the melting feelings his smile had engendered vanished at once. 'Well, I think I had a right to be angry! My aunt had been treated abominably! And then, to add insult to injury, you accused me of setting the servants' hall in a bustle…'

He held up his hand. 'Unjust of me under the circumstances, I suppose.' Unjust to tease her, too. Had he not realised last night that this kind of behaviour was not that of a gentleman?

It was time to stop this—whatever it was that afflicted him whenever he came into Miss Forrest's orbit—and remember why he had wanted to speak with her privately.

'I had not all the facts at my disposal. I did not know that you were not a servant—'

'You see?' she could not refrain from pointing out triumphantly. 'It is an easy enough mistake to make…'

His lips twitched. Was it so surprising he could not remember who he was when she was around, when she clearly could not either? She was still talking to him as though she had the right to take him to task. As though they were equals.

'*Touché*. Let us cry quits over that issue. Agreed?'

'Oh, absolutely!' She beamed at him. Really, thought

Helen, he was being far less difficult to deal with than she had imagined he would be. He could be fair. She only hoped he would be as fair in his eventual treatment of her aunt.

Lord, but that smile packed quite a punch. Miss Forrest was not merely pretty, as he had first thought. She was dazzling.

And women who could dazzle a man, make him forget who he was, the very principles by which he lived his life, were dangerous. As he knew to his cost.

He pulled a sheet of paper across the desk and frowned down at it.

'As for the question of your aunt's accommodations,' he said coldly, 'it appears quite a string of errors have been made. About you both. I wondered at the time I took her up there exactly why my cousin's aunt had been put in a room that should more correctly have been allotted to a visiting upper servant. And upon making enquiries I discovered it had not.'

'Not?' Helen felt puzzled. One moment he had been smiling and approachable. The next it was as though he had pulled up the drawbridge and retreated into his fortress. Shutting her out.

'Ah, no. The room to which I took her is yours, Miss Forrest. And before you remind me yet again that you are not a servant, let me explain that until your arrival it was believed you were accompanying my aunt in the role of paid companion. I have checked the correspondence by means of which she informed Mrs Dent she was bringing along a young lady. She referred to you as her companion and, having read it myself, I am not the least surprised it created such confusion. We had no idea you are, in fact, a young relative of hers.'

Helen cast her mind back to the day her aunt had written that letter. Her nerves had been in shreds. When she had lost all her money certain people had begun to cut her in the street. And then their landlord, who had sometimes come in to take tea with them, had stood on the doorstep, coldly demanding cash and threatening her with eviction. She had known she could not apply to either of her brothers for aid. And then the annual invitation to Alvanley Hall had arrived, reminding her that there was still the head of the family, who might—just might—be able to solve her difficulties. Aunt Bella's hand had been shaking as she had penned her acceptance letter. It was hardly surprising that she had not made Helen's station clear.

When she nodded, he went on, 'I shall have her moved to the room she should have been occupying today. You will be relieved to hear,' he said dryly, 'that it is not up so many flights of stairs.'

She felt her cheeks colouring, but lifted her chin and said, 'Thank you.'

He regarded her wryly. 'I can see that hurt. And it may hurt you even more when you are obliged to retract your accusation that my staff ignored the needs of an ailing untitled lady to see to a woman of rank. The simple fact of the matter is that the bell-pull in that room does not work.'

Helen wanted to curl up somewhere and hide. She had briefly suspected something of the sort. But then she had lost her temper and gone storming down to the kitchens, flinging accusations in all directions. She could not have made more of a fool of herself if...if... No, that was it. She could *not* have made more of a fool of herself!

'I did wonder about that,' she admitted. 'But then I got so cross that I assumed the worst. I am sorry.'

The Earl cleared his throat, and for a moment he looked as uncomfortable as she felt. 'The only reason nobody came to see to her was that nobody knew she was there. For which oversight I hold myself entirely to blame. I assumed that my staff would take care of her. But immediately after your arrival my older sister Lady Thrapston moved in, and promptly commandeered the services of my housekeeper.' His voice dripped with disdain. 'She seems to think she has the right to order my servants about simply because she once used to live here herself. In retrospect I admit I should have taken a firmer stance over the matter, and personally ensured that at least one maid was not engaged in running round after Lady Thrapston. For which I apologise.'

'That is magnanimous of you,' she said, in some surprise. An apology from a man of his rank was almost unheard of!

She bit back the temptation to point out that during the course of his explanation he had proved that her accusation had, in fact, been correct. Or partially. For his staff *had* been so busy seeing to Lady Thrapston's demands that her aunt had been neglected. Only it had not been done deliberately. But after a brief struggle with herself she decided that it would not be wise to say so. She had more important things to consider than scoring points with this man. To start with she was going to have to go down to the kitchens and apologise in person to all the people she had offended down there. There was nothing worse than mistreating servants—simply because they could not answer back without risk of losing their employment.

And, for another thing, she had still not achieved her ultimate goal.

'I do hope,' she said, clasping her hands together tightly under cover of her shawl, 'that our misunderstanding will not cause you to think any less of my aunt.'

'Ah, yes,' he said, his face suddenly wiped of all expression. 'Cadwallader informs me that she has requested an interview with me to discuss a matter of some urgency.'

In the end, no matter how attractive he found her, it came down to this. Both she and her aunt were here because they felt that he, as head of the family, owed them something.

His face closed up further. Gone was the footman who had teased her and argued with her. In his place sat that cold, hard, remote man who had presided over the dining table the night before. 'Only slightly less urgent than your own request, I believe?' he added sarcastically.

Helen sat forward on her chair. His abrupt changes of mood were unsettling, but she could not waste this opportunity, since the conversation had swung in the direction she'd wished it to go.

'Yes, it was imperative I speak with you before she came to plead her case. I did not want you to be prejudiced against her on my account.'

'You think I am the kind of man who would take some

petty revenge on a third party in order to punish someone who has offended me? Is that it?'

Oh, Lord, how had she managed to make it sound so insulting?

'N…no—no, of course not…'

'And yet you insist it was imperative you see me first? What did you think this interview would achieve, Miss Forrest?'

Had she thought to seduce him into a more amenable frame of mind? Dear God, if that was her game…

'I have told you. I wished to apologise for the way I spoke to you and ask that you hear my aunt out on her own account…'

'Which brings us neatly to the matter about which I wanted to see *you*,' he said. 'A remark was made at table last night which gave me cause for concern. That you are not a person who ought to have been brought to Alvanley Hall at all. Would you care to explain what General Forrest meant?'

Chapter Four

'Oh…' She regarded him guiltily. 'Well, I am not strictly speaking a family member. Only Aunt Bella said that it would not matter so long as she notified you. Other people, she said, would be bringing maids and valets and grooms, and heaven knew who else, and you would be making provision for all of *them*…'

It struck her again, that if Aunt Bella had been thinking along those lines when she had written her acceptance note it was no wonder the housekeeper had assumed she actually *was* a servant.

His eyes narrowed. 'That is not the issue. What I wish to uncover is how your association with Isabella Forrest might affect any decision I make regarding the way I deal with her. General Forrest implied that there is some scandal regarding your connection with his sister.'

'That is exactly what Aunt Bella was afraid of! But she has done nothing of which she need be ashamed. The General just cannot stand the fact that she will not bow to his wishes—that is what I think!'

'From what I have so far heard, it is you, Miss Forrest, who has caused the most trouble between the two of them. I believe that her continued association with you—nay, her open acknowledgement of you—has in fact caused a complete breach between them.'

'That is simply not true! Aunt Bella was already at loggerheads with both her brothers before she even knew I existed. You see, much to everyone's surprise, she inherited a substantial fortune when she came of age.' Helen did not think she was betraying a confidence by telling him this much. It was public knowledge. 'She decided to use it to set up house on her own, even though both brothers fiercely opposed her bid for independence. If she no longer wished to live with either of them, they maintained, then she should regard it as a dowry and find herself a suitable husband. They insisted it was scandalous behaviour for an unmarried female to remove herself from their sphere of influence. Taking me in and declaring she would raise me as her own was just the last straw. I admit that neither of them have set foot in her house since the day she formally adopted me, but—'

'She adopted you? You are not, then, her natural daughter?'

'Good heavens, no! Who told you such a dreadful thing?'

He shook his head. 'It was implied…'

General Forrest had sidled up to him in the withdrawing room after dinner the night before and begun to drop a series of vague hints. Which, when added together, had left him with the distinct impression that Isabella Forrest had been a wild, ungovernable girl, who had been forcibly evicted from his life because of the advent of Helen into it.

What kind of man deliberately blackened his own sister's reputation? God knew, he had no great love for either of his, but even as General Forrest had been making those sly innuendoes he had felt revolted by the man's attitude, knowing he would never disparage anyone so closely related to him to a third party even if what he had implied was true. But Miss Forrest was now telling him a completely different version of events.

'If you maintain you are not Isabella Forrest's natural daughter, who exactly are you?'

'My father,' she said, tight-lipped with anger, 'was the Comte de Bois de St Pierre. A penniless French émigré when he met and married my mother, in spite of opposition from her family. They lived a simple but happy life together until their death. At which time I was ten years old. None of my father's family were left alive to take me in. And none of my mother's family wanted me. I was passed from one to another for several months before Aunt Bella came to my rescue. Though strictly speaking she is not really my aunt at all. We are only connected through General Forrest's marriage to one of my mother's sisters,' she explained.

'However, she declared she would be a better guardian to me than any of those more nearly related, since *she* would not resent my presence in her house. As I have already told you, she was already on poor terms with her brothers, on account of her lifestyle. Taking me in and legally adopting me was only the last straw. I admit they did break with her entirely after that…'

The Earl frowned. 'I fail to understand why that should be. What business was it of anyone else's if she chose to take in and raise a child nobody else wanted?'

'Exactly!'

The Earl was still frowning. 'What do you mean by "her lifestyle"? What was wrong with it?'

'Nothing at all!' Helen flashed. 'Except for the fact that she refused to marry.'

Helen's mouth twisted with wry amusement. When she had asked Aunt Bella, not long after first going to live with her, if she had really never wished to marry, she had given one of her contemptuous snorts and said, 'I had a Season without getting one single proposal. If they did not want me without money, then I certainly was not about to hand it, and myself, over to any of them once I'd got it! Besides,' she had pointed out astutely, 'men always think they know best. If I'd had a husband he would never have permitted me to adopt you. And then where would we both be?'

Helen had gone quite cold inside. If Isabella Forrest had been more conventional, and had meekly married to please her family, Helen shuddered to think where *she* would be. From that moment on she had never questioned the older woman's decision to remain single again. And as she had grown she had found that she too was rather strong-willed, and would likely find it just as difficult as Aunt Bella to have to defer to a man, whether he was right or wrong, simply because convention decreed it.

'Aunt Bella said she saw no reason to hand her fortune over into the hands of some man who would fritter it away.'

Instead she had managed to lose it all on her own. Helen blinked and hung her head. Her poor aunt's humiliation was complete. After a lifetime of striving for independence, she was reduced to begging a man—this man, the head of her extended family—for her daily bread.

'Did she formally adopt you?' Lord Bridgemere asked sharply.

Helen nodded.

'Which is why you go by the name of Forrest now. Although you were born Helen de Bois de St Pierre?'

'Helène, to be precise,' she informed him. 'But, since there is so much prejudice against the French on account of the war, my aunt thought it better to Anglicise me as much as possible.'

He nodded, as though accepting the wisdom of that, and then said casually, 'Did she by any chance make you her sole heir as well?'

She nodded again.

Well, that explained the General's antipathy to this young woman. He would still have had hope, whilst his sister remained unmarried, that some part of her fortune might revert to him upon her demise. Until she had adopted Helen and made *her* the sole beneficiary of her will.

It always came down to money in the end.

A cynical expression swept over his face as he clasped his hands together on the desktop, leaned forward and said, 'Speaking of which, perhaps now you would be good enough to get to the real reason why you requested this private interview with me?'

Helen frowned. 'I do not understand.'

He made a gesture of impatience. 'Do not take me for a fool, Miss Forrest. You all come here each Christmas for one reason and one reason only.' He got to his feet and strode to the window.

'I came with my aunt because I felt she needed my support. That is all.'

'You expect me to believe *you* want nothing from me?' he sneered, whirling round.

'Nothing at all. Except…'

'Yes, now we come down to it,' he said, his face a tight mask of fury. 'Think very carefully before you make your petition known to me. Because once you leave this room you will not get another chance to speak to me in private! I grant each of you one interview and only one.'

It was imperative he put her back with the rest of them. He should never have singled her out for special treatment simply because she had not known who he was when she first came here, and had made the mistake of letting him see her true self.

'My decision,' he warned her, 'whatever it may be, is irrevocable! Do not think you will be able to sway me from it!'

Helen got slowly to her feet. 'I do not know what suspicions you harbour where I am concerned, but I repeat: the only reason I came to you today was to clear the air between us and beg you to put any animosity you may feel for me to one side when you consider Aunt Bella's future. Neither of her brothers is likely to show her any mercy after the stand she took against them in her youth. She has nobody but you to depend on now. And if you will not take pity on her—'

'Do you not want me to take pity on you, too? Is your need not as desperate as hers?'

'No,' she replied calmly. 'My case is not at all desperate. I am young and strong and quite capable of looking after myself.'

'You expect me to believe you want *nothing* from me?'

His implication that she was not only dishonest but also incapable of looking after herself was really beginning to grate. 'Nor any man!' she flashed. No wonder Aunt Bella had taken the almost unheard of decision never to marry. 'I repeat: I am quite capable of looking after myself. And even if I were in need of help, why should I apply to *you*? I have no claim on you. We are not related.'

'That would not stop most women…'

'It would stop any woman with an ounce of pride!' she retorted.

'Of which I observe you have more than your fair share.'

Without her conscious decision, her hands curled into fists at her sides. At this very moment she wished she *were* a man, with the freedom to come to fisticuffs with him! Her only recourse as a female was to tell him exactly what she thought of his horrid opinions of women. But she could not do even that! She had come here to mend fences, to smooth the way for her aunt—not to start a completely new family feud.

He could see her battling with her temper. For one moment he had the impression she was about to fling herself at him bodily. He braced himself for the onslaught, imagining himself capturing her wrists as she tried to strike at him. Subduing her by twisting her arms behind her back. Showing her exactly who was in charge here by stopping that saucy mouth with a hard kiss.

Annie Burrows

He caught his breath. Took a step towards her.

'Miss Forrest...' His voice, he realised to his surprise, was hoarse.

She put up one hand, as though to ward him off.

'Enough!'

'But—'

'No,' she said through clenched teeth. 'I think I had better leave before one of us says something they will regret.'

It was not what he had been about to *say* she was saving herself from, he reflected grimly as she strode away to the door. But what he had been so sorely tempted to *do*.

'I think for once—' He flinched as she slammed the door shut behind her, sank into his chair, and finished softly, 'I completely agree with you.'

He felt stunned. Yet strangely energised. He wondered if this was what it felt like to be struck by lightning. There had definitely been something elemental about that encounter.

Miss Forrest, he acknowledged with a hollow laugh, could truly be described as a force of nature.

After breakfast Mrs Dent herself came to the drum room, gushing apologies, and a veritable army of staff moved all their possessions to a new suite of rooms, down on the main floor where the other guests were staying.

'Since we have discovered you are a guest, and not a servant, your things will be moved down here, too,' the housekeeper said to Helen.

Adjoining her aunt's bedchamber was a small but beautifully

decorated room, which would afford Helen privacy whilst keeping her close enough to her aunt for peace of mind.

It took most of the rest of the day to organise things to their satisfaction, but as dusk began to fall her aunt remarked, 'I think we had better go down for dinner a little earlier this evening. I do not want anyone to think I am hiding away, as though you or I have anything to be ashamed of.'

An image of the Earl circulating amongst his guests flashed into her mind. The prospect of perhaps speaking to him filled her with mixed feelings. So far their exchanges had been pithy, and strangely stimulating. But tonight, with other people present, they would both be obliged to limit themselves to polite commonplaces. Which would be most unsatisfactory.

Though in all honesty it was unlikely he would deign to speak to her in public. Why should he? He was the head of a large and wealthy family, with immense responsibilities. Whereas she, in another week or so, was to become a governess. What was more, their encounter this morning had hardly ended on…friendly terms.

'Do not look so downcast,' her aunt remarked. 'You will be more than a match for any of them. You are far more clever, as well as having more spirit than any other woman present.'

Helen was loth to admit that it was the prospect of having to interact with one person in particular that had resulted in her looking a little wistful, so she answered, 'Thank you for saying that. But I think I shall have to make an attempt to quench that spirit tonight. I would not wish to say something I ought not, and perhaps give His Lordship cause to think you have not brought me up to know how to behave.'

He had already indicated that his decision regarding Aunt Bella's future hung in the balance. He was half inclined to believe she was Aunt Bella's illegitimate daughter, and that they had both come here to wheedle something from him to which they were not entitled. Unless she could convince him that the General had lied... She shook her head. It was out of her hands now. She had told him the truth, and thank goodness she had, but it was up to him to make up his own mind.

As had become their custom since letting their maid go, they helped each other to get changed. On their way downstairs Helen decided that she would have to make some alterations to her gowns so that she would be able to dress and undress herself unaided in future. Fortunately she was clever with a needle.

The liveried footman was once again on duty at the foot of the stairs, to remind them of the way to the blue saloon. There were already several of the other house guests present, ranged in groups of twos and threes.

Her aunt took a seat on one of the sofas dotted about the room, and Helen sat beside her.

'You have already met Lord Cleobury,' she said in a low voice, cocking her head towards the gentleman who had sat next to Helen at dinner the night before. 'And if I am not mistaken that clerical gentleman, the one who gave thanks for our meal last night, is none other than Barnaby Mullen. Another very distant connection of His Lordship's. I should not be a bit surprised...' she lowered her voice still further

'…if he is not angling for a living. His Lordship has several in his gift.'

Helen took ruthless advantage of the fact that Lord Bridgemere happened to be engaged in an earnest-looking conversation with the young cleric to turn her head and look at him. It almost surprised her to see that he looked the way he always did. What had she expected? That their confrontation this morning, which had left her so shaken, would have made some kind of physical impression on him? He did not even turn his head and look back at her. It was as though he was completely unaware she had entered the room.

He probably was.

At that moment Lady Thrapston walked across her field of vision, severing her tenuous connection to Lord Bridgemere.

There was no need for her aunt to inform her who *this* woman was. She and her aunt watched in silence as Lord Bridgemere's oldest sister sashayed across the room. Tonight she was wearing emeralds to complement the sumptuous outfit of green satin she was wearing.

Helen frowned. Lord Bridgemere had said they all came to Alvanley Hall at Christmas because they wanted something from him. What could a woman as obviously wealthy as this possibly need?

Then Aunt Bella gripped her hand, and said in a voice quivering with suppressed excitement, 'And this boy just coming in now is the one I was telling you about. Bridgemere's heir. The Honourable Nicholas Swaledale.'

Unlike His Lordship, the heir—who was not really a boy at all, although he was certainly not very much past twenty—

was dressed in an extravagantly fashionable style. There were
fobs and seals hanging from his cherry-striped satin waistcoat, jewels peeping from his cravat, and he wore his hair
teased into a fantastic style with liberal use of pomade. Helen
tried very hard not to dislike him just because of the way he
looked. For he, she recollected, was the youth who had
steered the dinner conversation away from her the night
before, after General Forrest had been so rude.

'And, *oh*,' Aunt Bella continued wickedly, 'how annoyed
Lady Thrapston is that her younger sister produced him,
when all *she* managed to have were girls!'

'He does not look to me,' Helen observed, 'like a very
happy young man.'

'Money troubles,' Aunt Bella explained darkly. 'His father
is not a wealthy man. But because of the title he expects to
inherit once Bridgemere dies, he tends to live well beyond
his means.'

An idiot, then, as well as a fop, thought Helen as she
watched the youth saunter across the room and take a seat
in between two damsels who blushed and simpered at
him. One of them Helen recognised as the young lady
who had been flirting with Aunt Bella's dinner partner the
night before.

'I wonder if he is sitting with them on purpose, to annoy
his aunt?' mused Aunt Bella aloud. 'Oh—I should perhaps
explain that those are the two of Lady Thrapston's daughters not still in the nursery. Octavia and Augustine.'

Even as he acknowledged the adulation of his female
cousins, she could still detect a faint sneer hovering about

the heir's mouth, which unhappily put her very much in mind of his Aunt Thrapston.

'Which are his parents?' Helen whispered. 'Are they here?'

Aunt Bella made a motion with her fan, to indicate a very ordinary-looking middle-aged couple perched on the edge of a pair of spindly-legged chairs. The lady had been sitting beside Lord Bridgemere at dinner the night before. Talking non-stop and irritating him, she saw on a flash of insight. As much as his other sister had managed to irritate him from the foot of the table, with her condescending remarks about the quality of the food.

What a family!

'You know my brother the General, of course, and his *charming* wife,' her aunt said sarcastically as the couple strolled into the room arm in arm.

When the General saw them, his brows lowered into a scowl.

'I wonder why they have come this year?' her aunt mused. 'He usually goes to spend Christmas with Ambrose.'

It was a great pity he had not gone to spend *this* Christmas with Ambrose, Aunt Bella's oldest brother, sighed Helen. His estate was just outside Chester. Which would have put him at the very other end of the country.

'I can only assume his pockets are to let.'

'Whatever do you mean?'

'Oh, come! You know full well that none of us comes here without a very compelling reason. Had I no need, even *I* would have given my cousin's nephew a wide berth. Indeed, I do not think I have seen him for over fifteen years.'

Helen shifted in her seat. 'It sounds a very odd way of conducting family relations…'

But it helped to explain Lord Bridgemere's conviction that she had come cap in hand, like everyone else. And when she had been so insistent upon speaking to him in private, to put her case, it could only have reinforced that impression.

She wished she had not been so quick to take offence. For suddenly she could see exactly why it had been so hard to convince him that she, personally, wanted nothing from him for herself.

'Perhaps I am being a little harsh in regards to his sisters,' Aunt Bella murmured. 'Not that it is fondness for their brother that brings *them* here, either. It is just that neither of them can bear the thought that the other might somehow steal a march if they are not here to keep an eye on their dealings with Bridgemere.'

How awful! Did nobody ever come to see him merely because they liked him?

Although her aunt had said he actively discouraged visitors by being purposefully elusive. She could not help allowing her eyes to stray in his direction, her heart going out to a man she now saw as an island in the midst of a sea of greedy, grasping relatives. She wondered which had come first. His reclusive habits, or his family's attitude towards him as nothing more than an ever-open purse?

She was startled out of her reverie by the General who, after standing stock still, glaring at them for a few seconds, marched right up to them and demanded, 'I want to know why you have come here, Bella.'

'I do not think that is any of your business,' Aunt Bella retorted.

'Still as argumentative as ever,' he growled. 'And just as prone to stirring up a hornets' nest with your effrontery!'

'I have no idea what you mean,' she replied coldly.

'Don't you? Don't you indeed?' he said. 'You have shunned your entire family for years, and then you march in here, bold as brass, with some devious scheme in your head involving this baggage, I don't doubt…'

'The reason I came here has absolutely nothing to do with Helen—' Aunt Bella began.

'Then why is she here? You have no business bringing that charity case to a family gathering.'

'She is not a charity case. She is family,' Aunt Bella protested. '*My* family.'

Oh, no! Saying such a thing was playing right into the General's hands. Anyone who overheard Aunt Bella's remark would be only too ready to believe she was her natural daughter!

'Well, at least we have that out in the open. You think more of that chit than you do your own family, and that's the truth! Years and years you've frittered your money away on her, and now, when I—'

His wife was tugging urgently on his sleeve.

'Please…not here, not now…' she begged him.

He shook her off as though she were a bothersome fly. 'Well, let me tell you something, madam. *I* know my duty to family. And I have made it my business to keep in His Lordship's good graces over the years. I have let him know what kind of person you are, and if you think you can persuade him otherwise you are very much mistaken.' A nasty smile spread across his face before he turned and stalked across the room, his little wife trailing behind him.

Helen could hardly believe that he bore so much animosity towards both her and his own sister that he would stoop to such tactics. He was a blustering bully! No wonder Aunt Bella had been so determined to make a bid for independence as soon as she'd had the means to do so.

She could not help herself. She just had to see what impression this little scene had made upon Lord Bridgemere. Her eyes flew to his face. To her relief, he was watching the General stalk across the room, his anxious little wife in tow, with barely concealed distaste. As yet she had no way of knowing whether it was dislike for the creation of a scene or a complete rejection of his version of Aunt Bella's past that was bringing that look of cold contempt to Lord Bridgemere's eyes.

But at least he was wise to the kind of man the General was now.

'Do not worry, Aunt Bella,' she murmured, patting her aunt's hand. 'Lord Bridgemere is no fool. I do not think he will accept anything the General says or implies without checking the facts for himself.'

'You seem to have formed a very high opinion of His Lordship, Helen. How on earth did you come by it?'

'I can see it in his face,' she hedged, unwilling to admit she had been to see him in private. Because then she might have to admit to her other encounters with him. 'He did not like the way the General attempted to browbeat you like that in public.'

'You may be right,' Aunt Bella said, though she did not sound all that convinced.

Fortunately for Helen, at that moment another guest caught her aunt's eye.

'My goodness, can that be Sally Stellman? Lady Norton, I should say. I have not seen her since my own come-out. After she married we lost touch, but…'

The lady in question, who was just entering the room, clearly recognised Aunt Bella, too. She tugged upon her husband's arm, steering him straight towards their sofa.

'Bella!' she cried, detaching herself from her husband and plumping herself down beside them. 'It *is* you! I thought it was last night, but you retired so early I never had the chance to renew our acquaintance. How lovely to see you again after all these years!'

The chance for the two ladies to say any more than that was abruptly curtailed when the butler announced in sonorous tones that dinner was served.

Sir Mortimer came to escort Helen in to dine, as he had the night before. This time he did not look bored. No, he looked downright reluctant to associate with her. She had no idea whether it was because he might have heard the rumour the General had started about her being somebody's love-child, or if it was because of the way she had made a fool of herself the night before, or…

Oh, she had never known a Christmas like it. Peace on earth? There was precious little peace here. Let alone goodwill towards men. Why, the whole place was a seething maelstrom of repressed resentments.

She was sorely tempted to remove herself from the field of combat by taking her meals up in her room from now on, if the atmosphere was always going to be as fraught as this in the public rooms. Since she had spent part of the afternoon apologising to the kitchen maid and the cook for her outburst on that first night, she was no longer in *their* black books. In fact, after they had all matched her apology with an explanation of their own errors, which had echoed what Lord Bridgemere had already told her, they had said she was a rare lady to come and make peace with them, when most of the gentry did not give two hoots for the feelings of those below stairs.

Only it did seem a little cowardly to hide away upstairs. And to desert her aunt in her hour of need. She lifted her chin as her reluctant dinner partner escorted her to table. She was as well born as any of them! Better than some. And if Lord Bridgemere did not object to her presence, then nobody else had a right to make her feel like an interloper.

She darted a glance in his direction.

His gaze swept round the assembled guests, his face closed entirely. Until it came to her. She thought for just an instant that he hesitated. That his features softened very slightly.

Her spirits rose. He believed her! Just that slight thaw in her direction, coupled with the utter contempt with which he had regarded the General, was enough to remove the burden of worry that had so weighed her down.

She smiled at him.

His face closed up. He bowed his head.

For the young clergyman was clearing his throat before saying grace.

A stillness gradually descended over them all as they followed the Earl's lead in giving thanks for the food they were about to receive.

Helen clasped her hands at her waist and bowed her own head, truly thankful that it looked as though Lord Bridgemere was not going to believe the General's lies.

She did not notice Lady Thrapston's beady eyes going from her radiant face to her brother's bowed head.

And, since she swiftly bowed her own head, in respect to the convention, absolutely nobody saw the speculative expression that came over Lady Thrapston's face.

Chapter Five

The meal turned out to be every bit as delicious, and the atmosphere quite as poisonous, as it had been the previous night. Only this time when Lady Thrapston got to her feet and the ladies withdrew, Aunt Bella whispered, 'I'm blowed if I'm going to let my brother make me feel as though we have no right to be here. Especially since I have not seen Lady Norton for such a long time. I am looking forward to catching up with her news. Will you come with me?'

'Of course,' Helen replied. She had already decided that nobody was going to make her creep away and hang her head as though she had no right to be here herself. Lifting her chin, she took her aunt's arm and joined the procession of ladies making their way to the winter drawing room. It was the room, her aunt explained, that guests always used in the evenings when they came for Christmas, since it boasted two fireplaces—one at either end of the room.

Lady Thrapston's daughters made straight for the pianoforte as soon as they entered the drawing room. They played and sang competently, but the way they commandeered the instrument put Helen's back up. Acting as if they owned the place! It reminded her very forcibly of the way their mother had swanned in on the day of their arrival, and been so full of her own importance that poor Aunt Bella had been completely overlooked.

'Be very careful where you choose to sit,' whispered Lady Norton, who had come in just behind them. 'If you are too close to Lady Craddock's camp then Lady Thrapston will take you for her mortal enemy.'

Helen realised that the layout of the room was most unfortunate. People naturally wished to sit as close to one of the fires as they could, but since Lady Craddock had appropriated the sofa nearest the hearth at one end, and Lady Thrapston a matching one at the other, several ladies, apart from her and her aunt, were hanging about in the doorway as though plotting a course between Scylla and Charybdis.

'Is there no neutral ground?' Aunt Bella whispered to her more knowledgeable friend.

'The gaming room. It is just through that door,' she replied with a laugh. 'Only I am not permitted in there until Norton comes.'

Aunt Bella's eyebrow shot up.

'I will explain later,' she said, with a meaningful nod in Helen's direction.

Helen smiled politely, though she took exception to the way the woman was trying to monopolise her aunt and exclude her.

'Look,' she said, indicating a quartet of chairs grouped

around a table towards the centre of the room. 'That looks a safe enough place to sit.'

'We shall have our backs to the piano, though,' said Lady Norton. 'Lady Thrapston might take it as an insult to her daughters…'

'Especially since I intend to sit and gossip with you, rather than listen to their uninspired performance,' agreed Aunt Bella cheerfully. 'But, since I do not care what that woman may think of me, I think we may as well risk it.'

The three of them made their way to the table and sat down, laying their reticules on its highly polished surface before anyone else could steal a march on them.

'You know why they are all here this year, don't you?' Lady Norton said, when the music came to a particularly noisy section that ensured nobody could overhear what she was about to say.

'Augustine is of an age to make her come-out, and I have heard that Lady Thrapston is angling to get her brother to open up Bridgemere House for at least part of the season in her honour.'

'Do you think he might?'

Lady Norton snorted. 'He did not do so for Octavia. Why should he make an exception for Augustine? Besides, their father is still alive. And I am sure Bridgemere will point out that *he* can well afford to launch his girls creditably.'

'Then why on earth is Lady Thrapston making the attempt?' Aunt Bella was leaning forward, her eyes shining with curiosity. Helen had not seen her this animated since well before the collapse of the Middleton and Shropshire Bank.

'Bridgemere House is so much larger than their own London house. And Lady Thrapston, apparently, thinks it is about time Bridgemere spent some time in town again. What better time than to launch his supposedly favourite niece into society?'

'You mean he has not always been such a reclusive person?' Helen asked.

But before Lady Norton could elaborate, they all became aware that the General's wife was approaching their table. With a conciliatory smile, she indicated the one remaining chair and said, 'I do apologise for my husband's outburst earlier. I hope you will not hold it against *me*.'

Before anyone could say anything she sat down and added, 'It is such a pity we have got off on the wrong foot. Especially since the few days we are all going to spend here gives me such a wonderful opportunity to get to know *you* better, Helen.' She turned an anxious smile upon her. 'The breach between my husband and his sister has kept us apart for too long, don't you think?'

'Well, I…' It was such an about-face that Helen did not know what to think.

Mrs Forrest smiled sadly. 'It must have been a terrible blow for you to lose both your parents at such an impressionable age. I would have loved to have raised you myself, but as you know the General is not a man one can cross…'

Helen frowned, trying to recall if her impressions of that time might be faulty. She had not thought her aunt had seemed terribly keen on taking her in, and could certainly not remember her attempting even the smallest argument with the General on her behalf. But then, she had already been through several households where neither adult had wanted the expense of her upkeep, and had begun to feel like a leper.

'Your mother and I were…well, sisters, you know,' she said airily. Then she glanced over her shoulder, as though checking to make sure the gentlemen were not yet joining them, and said, 'I may not stay and chat with you now, but perhaps we could take a walk about the grounds tomorrow? While the men are out shooting?'

Helen hardly had to think about her response. Here was a woman who had known her mother. Though she had no complaints about the way Aunt Bella had raised her, she had never met either of Helen's parents. It would be wonderful to have somebody to talk to who had known them both.

'I should like that very much,' she said.

As soon as they had made arrangements about where to meet, and at what time, Mrs Forrest got to her feet and went to join a group of ladies who were seeking a fourth for a hand of whist.

'She did not invite *me*, I hope you notice, Helen,' said her aunt darkly.

Immediately Helen felt contrite for arranging to meet Mrs Forrest without considering how this might affect Aunt Bella.

'Did you *want* to go out walking tomorrow?' said Lady Norton. 'If you do, then you and I could take a stroll together. Though myself I dislike going out when it is so cold. I would much rather stay within doors and amuse myself with a hand or two of piquet.'

Aunt Bella turned to her with a smile. 'Then that is what we shall do while Helen renews ties with her mother's family. If that is *really* why Mrs Forrest has attempted to detach her from my side.'

'What do you mean?' asked Helen with a frown.

'Well, has it never occurred to you that if she really thought so much of her sister's child she would at the least have written, or sent small gifts for birthdays and Christmas?'

Helen's heart sank. 'Perhaps the General would not permit it.'

'Yes, that *might* be it. But I would not be a bit surprised to learn that she has some other motive than reconciliation on her mind. Take care, Helen. She may smile and say all the right things here, where there are plenty of eyes on her. But I have a strong suspicion she is up to something.'

And so Helen was on her guard when she went to meet her aunt the next morning. And it was just as well, because they had scarcely left the shelter of the house before Mrs Forrest unsheathed her claws.

'We wish to know *exactly* what you are doing here, young woman,' she began coldly. 'And to warn you that whatever your intentions may be we intend to see to it that your days of being a drain upon Isabella's resources come to an end. If my husband had been the head of the family, instead of that ineffectual brother of his, he would never have permitted things to go this far. Indeed, Isabella should never have been permitted to make a home for herself, unprotected, to fall prey to unscrupulous people who only have an eye to her fortune!'

It was so obvious that Mrs Forrest considered Helen to be one of those unscrupulous persons with an eye on Aunt Bella's fortune that for a brief second she almost blurted out the truth. That there was no longer any fortune for the General to be getting into such a pother about. She found it incredibly sad that this woman had brought her out here simply to squabble over money—non-existent money at that—when they could truly have been spending the season putting aside past misunderstandings and learning to deal better with each other.

Not that she could say as much. For it would feel like a betrayal to talk about Aunt Bella's financial losses behind her back—especially to this woman.

And Aunt Bella had been upset enough about the way the loss of her fortune had affected Helen as it was.

She had gripped Helen's arm so hard it had almost been painful. 'Helen,' she had said, with tears in her eyes, 'I cannot believe I have let you down so badly. I thought I had provided for you. Everything I had would have been yours when I died and now it is all gone. You have nothing. Now or in the future.'

'Aunt, please, do not talk this way,' she had remonstrated. 'You *have* provided for me. You gave me a home. You took me in and raised me as though I was your own child when nobody else wanted me. And do not forget how very poor my parents were. Had they lived, I would *never* have had any expectations for my future.'

Her aunt had seemed much struck by that point. Then Helen had said, 'Besides, you gave me such a broad education that I will surely be able to find work eventually.'

'There is that,' Aunt Bella had said. 'It will be some comfort to know that I have at least ensured you may keep your independence. I have not raised you to think you have to rely on some man, have I?'

No, she had not. To begin with she had loved Aunt Bella so much it had never entered her head to form any opinion that ran counter to her own strongly held beliefs. But as she had grown, and observed the fate of other women of her class, she had begun to regard women who relied entirely on their menfolk with a tinge of contempt. They were like the ivy that had to cling parasitically to some sturdy tree for its support, having no strength in themselves.

Helen eyed her real aunt with a heavy heart. If this woman had kept her, what would she be like now? Cowed and insecure? Afraid to lift her head, never mind her voice, should the General or any other man express his disapproval of something she had done?

Thank heaven she had met Bella Forrest, who had always encouraged her to think for herself. To trust in her own instincts and follow her own heart.

She forced her lips into the semblance of a polite smile.

'I am quite sure you do not include *me* amongst the ranks of people attempting to part Aunt Bella from her fortune? Because you *know* that I was merely a child when she first showed an interest in me....'

'But you are not a child now, are you?' Mrs Forrest put in swiftly. They came to the end of the gravelled path along which they were walking, and passed through an arch in a closely clipped yew hedge into an enclosed garden. 'Though you have got your claws into her now, I am warning you that we intend to take steps to protect her. Steps that should have been taken years ago!'

'This is ridiculous! I—'

But before she could finish her observation she noticed that another party was already strolling across the lawn within the sheltered enclosure. The Countess of Thrapston and her two daughters came to an abrupt halt, and turned round to stare at the sound of raised voices. Helen suspected— although they were all wearing different bonnets and coats— that these were the same females she had observed from the drum room, walking through the formal gardens on her first day here. Oh, how she wished she had observed them more closely. If she had realised this was a favourite walk of theirs she would not have allowed her aunt to strike out in this direction! It was upsetting enough to be having this altercation. It was made ten times worse to have this haughty woman and her proud daughters witness it!

Mrs Forrest recovered first. 'Oh, Lady Thrapston,' she gushed, dropping into a deferential curtsey. 'I am so sorry if we have intruded upon your walk. But really, this girl is such an aggravating creature that she quite made me lose my temper.' She shot Helen a malicious glance. 'I dare say you overheard how she has latched onto my husband's poor sister, and for years has taken shameless advantage of her generous nature?'

'Poppycock!' snapped Helen, finally losing her battle to keep a civil tongue in her head.

'You deny that you have wheedled your way into a defenceless woman's affections? To the extent that she has made a will in your favour? And that you now stand to inherit a fortune that should by rights return to her real family upon her death?'

So *that* was what this was all about. General Forrest cared nothing for his sister's welfare. He was just desperate to claw back some of the money he believed she had.

At least there was one slur upon her character she could refute without betraying her aunt's confidence, though.

'I do not expect,' said Helen through gritted teeth, 'to receive anything more from Aunt Isabella in future.'

'No?' said Mrs Forrest, with a sarcastic little laugh. 'You do not, surely, expect me to believe that?'

'I do not care what you believe—though what I have just told you is the truth. I intend to work for my living.'

'Oh, really!' scoffed Mrs Forrest. 'As if *any* woman would choose to work for her living if she had an alternative!'

Helen was not about to tell this woman she *had* no alternative. Particularly since the Thrapston ladies were all listening avidly.

Instead, drawing herself up to her full height, she said, 'On the contrary. I am pleased to tell anyone who may be interested that a few days hence I shall be a completely independent woman. I have already secured a post as governess to the children of a family in Derbyshire.'

The girls looked horrified.

'I do not scruple to tell you, young lady,' said Lady Thrapston, shaking her head, 'that it is not at all the thing to boast about taking employment. No true lady would stoop to such measures. I have heard that Isabella Forrest is something of an eccentric, and if this is an example of the kind of thing she has taught you—'

'Though, if it *is* true,' Mrs Forrest interrupted, 'my husband will be most relieved. Perhaps he need no longer be at outs with Bella, and then she might—'

Helen was by now beside herself with anger. She clenched her fists. What right had Lady Thrapston to make any sort of observation about her conduct? None whatever! And how dared Mrs Forrest assume Aunt Bella would meekly make a will in her brother's favour after the way he had treated her?

Her eyes narrowing, she took a pace towards the three Thrapstons.

She had just taken a breath to make a pithy rejoinder when the hedge to the south of where they were standing suddenly erupted. A dog that was very nearly the size of a pony got its shoulders through and then, barking joyously, bounded straight towards them. From the long, matted hair Helen recognised the hound which had been sprawled on the hearthrug in His Lordship's study the morning before.

Helen had never been so glad to see such a disreputable-looking animal, or so impressed by the effect it had on her erstwhile tormentors. Emitting shrill shrieks, Lady Thrapston and her daughters darted round behind Helen before the dog managed to reach them. Mrs Forrest, even less stalwart in the face of danger, simply took to her heels and fled. Helen could hardly wait to inform Aunt Bella just how athletic her sister-in-law was. How it would make her laugh to hear of that sudden turn of speed!

The hearthrug dog, meanwhile, had reached its target and leapt up, setting its paws on Helen's chest and licking her face. Only the press of females cowering behind her stopped her from falling flat on her back.

'Eeurgh!' Helen could not help exclaiming, screwing her eyes tight shut, wishing that she could somehow stop her nostrils, too. She was not used to dogs, and found the exuberance of his slobbery greeting somewhat too pungent for her liking. Though she did not feel the least bit frightened. She had no doubt it was a doggy sort of friendship the great beast was demonstrating, and felt rather scornful of the two girls who were now squealing with fright, cowering behind her and Lady Thrapston.

'Esau!' the Earl's voice boomed across the lawn. 'Devil take it, what *do* you think you are doing?'

The dog looked in the direction of his master's voice, drool dripping slowly from his lolling tongue.

The Earl forced his way through the hedge just where the dog had broken through. He took the situation in and snapped his fingers. 'Heel, I say! *Heel!*'

To Helen, it looked as though the dog sighed and shrugged its shoulders before obediently dropping to the ground and loping across to his master's side, where he flopped to the ground and rolled on his back, paws waving in the air.

'I am *not* going to rub your stomach, you hell hound!' the Earl snapped.

The dog merely looked up at him adoringly and wriggled encouragingly.

Helen, already struck by the humour of the situation, could barely stifle her giggles. She reached into her pocket for a handkerchief, covering her grin under the pretext of vigorously wiping away the slobber that coated her cheeks.

'Really, Bridgemere,' said Lady Thrapston, emerging from behind Helen. 'Have you no control over that animal?'

'Better than *you* have over your own manners,' he replied coldly. 'You have a very carrying sort of voice, My Lady, and I beg leave to inform you that you have no business berating Miss Forrest upon her future plans. Plans which, in any case, *I* regard as admirable!'

'Excuse me…' Helen put in, suddenly cross all over again. Though it was quite pleasant to hear the Earl say that he found her admirable, she was not in the least bit pleased that he was saying what she would have said herself, had the dog not put a halt to proceedings.

The Earl made an impatient gesture with his hand.

'Not now, Miss Forrest!' he snapped, his eyes fixed upon his sister. 'I find it remarkably refreshing to hear that there is at least one woman in England who does not have marriage to a wealthy man as her goal after having been launched expensively into society!'

At that point Helen's temper came to the boil. It was beyond rude for these two aristocrats to stand there arguing about her as though she was not present. Besides, it was perfectly clear they were not arguing about *her* at all, but about what Lady Thrapston expected Bridgemere to do for her daughters.

Who were both close to tears.

'Don't you assume you know anything about me or my

goals, My Lord!' she said. 'It is only women with a dowry and a family behind them who have the luxury of taking the route of which you speak! And, since I have not a penny to my name, I should have thought it would be obvious even to you that route is not open to me!'

'You see?' said the Countess. 'Even this creature would rather marry than work for a living! You have heard it from her own lips!'

The Earl swung to her, his eyes blazing, as though he felt she had betrayed him.

Not a penny to her name? What nonsense was this? From the preliminary enquiries he had made, it was generally known that she stood to inherit a substantial fortune from Isabella Forrest. Who was already keeping her in some style.

'N…no, I did not mean that, exactly…' Helen stammered, her eyes flicking from brother to sister and back again.

'Come, girls,' said Lady Thrapston imperiously. 'We shall return to the house, since His Lordship chooses to exercise that beast where his guests *should* feel safe to walk!'

Her nose in the air, she swished across the lawns, her two subdued daughters scurrying along behind her.

The dog rolled itself upright and woofed once after them, as though in triumph.

Helen stood frozen to the spot by Lord Bridgemere's glacial stare. He waited until the other ladies were out of earshot before speaking again, while Helen braced herself for yet another battle royal.

'I trust you are unharmed?' he said, completely taking the wind out of her sails. 'For some reason,' he drawled, as though there was no accounting for the working of a dog's mind, 'Esau regards you as a friend. The moment he heard your voice he made straight for you to make his presence known.'

'Straight, yes,' she agreed. 'Straight through the hedge,' she amended, a bubble of mirth welling up inside her as she recalled the consternation he had caused. Then with a perfectly straight face she reached up and plucked a yew twig from the front of Lord Bridgemere's waistcoat. 'And you came *straight* after him,' she observed, tossing the twig to the ground.

'He frightens some females,' he countered. 'He is so large and…'

'So sadly out of control.' She shook her head in mock reproof.

His brows drew down into a scowl. 'No, that is not the case at all. He is very well trained…'

Abruptly she averted her face, as though glancing towards the dog, who was now sniffing away at the foot of the hedge. But not quite quickly enough to hide the laughter brimming.

He caught at her chin and turned her face towards him, studying it in perplexity. Then suddenly comprehension dawned.

'You…you are teasing me!'

For a moment she felt as though her fate hung in the balance. It was the height of impertinence for one of her station to treat a man of his rank with such lack of respect.

But then he smiled.

Really smiled—as though she had just handed him some immensely rare and unexpected gift.

Her stomach swooped and soared—just as it had done when, as a little girl, she had taken a turn on her garden swing.

She had thought him attractive, in a dangerous sort of way, when she had believed he was merely a footman. Had imagined maidservants queuing up to kiss that mouth when it had been hard and cynical. But the intensity of that smile was downright lethal. As she gazed, transfixed, at those happily curved lips, with his hand still cupping her chin gently, she wished that he would pull her closer, slant that mouth across her own…

With a gasp, she pulled away from him.

His smile faded. He looked down at the hand that had been cupping her chin as though its behaviour confused him.

'E…Esau?' she stammered, determined to break the intensity of the mood. 'You called him that because he is so hairy, I take it?'

'And he has a somewhat reddish tinge to his coat,' he agreed mechanically. Then, as though searching for something to say to prolong their odd little conversation, 'Under the mud which unfortunately he chose to roll in this morning.' He looked down at her attire ruefully. 'And which is now liberally smeared all over your coat.'

For the first time Helen took stock of the damage the encounter with his dog had wrought upon her clothing. Helen had wrapped a shawl over her bonnet before setting out. It had slithered to the ground when Esau had jumped up, and the other ladies had trodden it into the ground. Her gloves and cuffs were shiny with the aftermath of Esau's affectionate greeting, and her shoulders bore the imprints of his enormous muddy paws. And, worst of all, when he had dropped to the ground his claws had torn a rent in her skirt.

'You must allow me to replace it.'

'Must?' Taking exception to his high-handed attitude towards her, she took a step back. 'I *must* do no such thing!'

'Do not be ridiculous,' he snapped, his own brief foray into good humour coming to an abrupt end. 'I saw the way my sister used you as a human shield to protect her own clothing from Esau's unfortunate tendency to jump up on people he likes. And she can easily afford to replace any gowns his paws might ruin. I suspect that you cannot. I have just heard you declare you have not a penny to your name! And I doubt if you have more than two changes of clothing in that meagre amount of luggage my staff carried up to your room.'

Helen stiffened further. 'Mud brushes off when it dries. And I am quite capable of darning this little tear,' she said, indicating her skirts. 'Any competent needlewoman could do it! And, contrary to your opinion, I *do* have a clean gown into which I may change. I am not a *complete* pauper.'

'Nevertheless, you are not the heiress that General Forrest has assumed, are you? What has happened between you and your aunt? Why do you have to go out and work for your living? Will you not tell me?'

'It is not your affair—at least not my part of it.'

She was not going to confide in him. It shook him. Most people were only too ready to pour out a litany of woes in the hope that they might persuade him to bail them out.

He had already told Lady Thrapston that he admired her,

but if he were to say it again now it would be with far more conviction. For he realised that he really did.

'That damned pride of yours,' he said, shaking his head. 'Nevertheless, Miss Forrest, you have to admit that it is entirely my fault that your clothing has been ruined. As Lady Thrapston pointed out, I should not have returned to the house by this route when I knew that visiting ladies like to take their exercise in the shelter of the shrubbery. Please,' he said, stepping forward and grasping her by the elbows, 'allow me to make amends.'

For once he would like to be able to do a small thing for someone he suspected had suffered some kind of financial reversal. And what was the cost of a coat to him?

Esau, as though sensing the tension between them, bounded over and sat at Helen's feet, gazing up at her with his head on one side.

'It would be quite inappropriate for you to do so,' she pointed out.

It felt as though the sun went behind a cloud when he let go of her arms and stepped back.

'But thank you for your kind offer,' she said, in a desperate attempt to undo the offence she could see he had taken at her refusal.

It was no use. His face had closed up.

Which was ironic, considering the last time they had spoken he had complained that people only came to him because they wanted something!

'No very great harm has been done by your dog. In fact,' she said, reaching out one hand and tentatively patting the great shaggy head, 'I am rather grateful to him for putting such an abrupt end to my walk.'

'You do not like the gardens?'

'The *gardens* seem very pleasant, My Lord, from what little I have seen so far.'

'Perhaps you would enjoy seeing more of them,' he said, as though he had just been struck by a brilliant idea, 'if you had a more congenial escort? I confess, though I generally only permit Esau to accompany me on my morning ride, I—'

He pulled himself up short, frowned, and made her a stiff bow. 'Miss Forrest, since you will not permit me to replace the clothing Esau has ruined, perhaps you will allow me to make amends in another way. Let me show you these gardens tomorrow, early. Before anyone else has risen. Before the sun has burned the frost away.'

'Oh.' Helen blinked up at him. 'I thought you said you preferred to be alone...'

'To *ride* alone,' he corrected her, with some signs of irritation. 'But I have not asked you to ride with me. Just to walk. Will you?' He clutched his riding crop between his hands, his whole body tensing as he added, 'Please?'

For one wild, glorious moment Helen had the feeling that her assent would really mean something to him. She wondered, given all that she had learned about him, how long it had been since he had asked anyone for anything.

Her heart went out to him. How sad to think that he might be so lonely that he was more or less begging her for an hour or so of her time. She suddenly saw that it was a rare thing for him to come across a person with whom he might spend time safe in the knowledge she would not be pestering him for some kind of favour. Lord, he must be one of the loneliest men on earth.

Especially if he had to resort to asking *her* to go for a walk with him. She was a virtual stranger to him. And whenever they had met they had ended up arguing.

She chewed on her lower lip. Going for a walk with him, unchaperoned, would be a rather shocking thing for her to do. Especially considering the vast difference between their stations. And yet…and yet…

She was quite certain she would never meet a man like him again.

In the dreary years of servitude that lay ahead of her, would it not be a comfort to look back to this time and recall that once, at least, a handsome, eligible man—a man who made her heart flutter—had urged her to cast convention aside and spend time alone with him? Oh, not that anything would come of it. He could not possibly have any romantic feelings towards her. It was just a walk.

Sometimes, she decided, the conventions were ridiculous. As if he would stoop to attempting to seduce *her*, of all people. A guest under his roof!

She brightened up, knowing that she would be quite safe.

'If the weather is fine, I think I should like that very much,' she said.

While Bridgemere had been awaiting her answer he had felt as though he was teetering on the brink of a precipice. And now he wondered if he had tumbled headlong into it.

For the sense of relief and gratitude he felt when she said yes was out of all proportion.

He was more than a little irritated with himself for letting her affect him so much.

'I will wait for you in the mud room at first light, then,' he said brusquely. 'Cadwallader will give you the direction.' He glanced down at her feet. 'Wear sturdy footwear.'

And then he whistled for his dog and strode away, leaving Helen to trail back to the house in a state that was becoming all too familiar after an encounter with Lord Bridgemere. A turbulent mix of exhilaration, irritation, yearning and trepidation—and now, as if that were not quite enough to contend with, more than a dash of compassion for the man who was expected to bear everyone else's burdens but had nobody to help him bear his.

Chapter Six

The next morning Helen woke early. She had escaped up to bed as soon as she could, uncomfortable about lingering in the winter drawing room amongst so many antagonists, leaving Aunt Bella to enjoy some hands of cards with Lady Norton. Helen was not sure what the time had been when her aunt had tiptoed back into their room. She looked down at her now, where she lay sprawled on her back, snoring gently, with a fond smile. It must have been well past midnight. Not even the sounds of Helen rising and having her wash had managed to rouse her this morning!

She rubbed a small patch of frost from the inside of the windowpane with the corner of her towel to see a still star-spangled sky. Not a cloud was in sight. It would be bitterly cold outside. Not that even a blizzard would have doused the excitement that was welling up inside her. Lord Bridgemere had asked her to go for a walk with him. Her! When he so famously shunned others. She simply added several flannel petticoats beneath her gown, as well as a knitted jacket under her coat, and a woollen shawl over her bonnet.

And left the room with a smile on her face and a spring in her step.

Lord Bridgemere was waiting for her in the mud room, similarly bundled up against the cold.

'I would prefer not to take a lantern,' he informed her. 'The sun is only just rising, but I believe we can make our way where we are going quite safely without one.'

'Oh. Very well.' She smiled at him, quite content to go along with whatever he suggested.

He opened the door for her, and with a slight dip of the head extended his arm to indicate she should precede him.

She wanted to laugh out loud. She had expected nothing but slights and insults in her new life as a humble, hard–working governess, but here was a belted earl opening a door for her! Sharing his morning walk with her simply for the pleasure of her company. Well, wouldn't this be something to look back upon when she eventually moved to the Harcourts' home?

She smiled happily up at him as she passed him in the doorway. And breathed in the sharply fresh air with a sense of relish. She had always loved this time of day. It was like having a blank sheet of paper upon which she could write anything.

She darted a surreptitious glance at him as he closed the door behind them. Then averted her gaze demurely when he took her arm to steady her as they set off across the slippery cobbles of the kitchen court. He did not look at her. He kept his eyes fixed ahead, on where they were going. Once they left the cluster of buildings at the back of the main house he led her away from the formal gardens, where she had walked before, and up a sloping lawn towards a belt of trees.

After a while she took the risk of studying his face through a series of glances as they walked along. Most particularly her eyes were drawn to the mouth that had been haunting her imagination from the very first moment she had seen him. When she had thought he was a footman. Now she knew he was an earl, he was no longer beneath her socially, and so…

Guiltily, she tore her eyes from his mouth and cast them to the ground. He was as far from her socially as ever! She ought not to be thinking about kisses—especially not where he was concerned. For it could only end badly for her. Aunt Bella had already told her the man was not the marrying kind. And she had too much pride to become *any* man's plaything.

No matter how tempting he was, she thought, darting another longing glance at his handsome profile.

No, far better to have some innocent, pleasurable memories from this outing to keep her warm in the bleak years ahead.

And she did feel warm, just being with him arm in arm like this. Her heart was racing, and her blood was zinging through her veins in a most remarkable way. She heaved a sigh of contentment, making her breath puff out in a great cloud on the still winter air.

'Am I setting too fast a pace for you, Miss Forrest?' Lord Bridgemere enquired politely.

'Oh, no,' she replied. 'Not at all.'

'But you are becoming breathless,' he said with a frown. 'Forgive me. I am not used to measuring my pace to suit that of another.'

'I suppose Esau has no problem keeping up with you, though?' she observed.

He frowned, as though turning her remark over in his mind, before replying rather seriously, 'No, he does not. He is an ideal companion when I ride, since he eats up the miles with those great long legs of his. It is, in fact, when he has not had sufficient exercise that he becomes…exuberant.'

Some of her pleasure dimmed. He was having to deliberately slow the pace he would have preferred to set because she was with him. And the way he was smiling now, after talking about his dog, made her feel as if he would be enjoying himself far more if it was the dog out here with him!

It was some minutes before either of them spoke again. Lord Bridgemere seemed preoccupied, and Helen, even though he had slowed down considerably, had little breath left to spare for speech.

It had been getting steadily lighter, and just as they reached the trees the sun's rays struck at an angle that made the entire copse glisten diamond-bright. Since the frosted branches almost met overhead, they looked like the arches of some great outdoor cathedral.

'Oh!' she gasped, stopping completely just to gaze in awe at the magical sight. 'I feel as if, I am in some…church,' she whispered. 'Or a temple. Not made by human hands, but by…'

'Yes,' he said in a low, almost reverent tone. 'That is exactly how I feel sometimes out here, at sunrise.'

She twirled round, her head arched back, to admire the spectacle from every angle. It made it all the more wonderful that through various gaps in the branches she could make out the moon against the pearly dawn sky, and just one or two of the last and brightest of the stars.

'Oh, thank you,' she breathed. 'Thank you for bringing me here to see this.'

'I *knew* you would appreciate it,' he said, his eyes gleaming with what she thought looked like approval. 'You are the one person I know who would not grumble about the necessity of rising early to witness this,' he said. 'Most of my other visitors prefer staying up all night drinking and gaming, then sleeping half the day away. It does not last long, this rare moment of utter perfection. But just now, as the sun strikes the frosted branches, it makes everything so…' He frowned, shaking his head as though the right words eluded him. 'One can almost embrace winter. For only in this season can one experience this.' He turned around, just as she had done, only far more slowly, as though drinking in the frozen splendour of their surroundings.

Then, without warning, his face turned hard and cynical. 'Nature has a remarkable way of compensating for absence of life. None of this would be possible without bitter cold. And long, dark nights. You can only see this when the branches are stark and dead.'

He turned to her with a twisted sort of smile on his lips. 'Of course before long the very sunshine that creates this glorious spectacle will melt it all away. You can already see the mist beginning to rise. In another hour all that will be left of your mystical temple to nature will be dripping wet branches, blackened with mould, and pools of mire underfoot..Come,' he said brusquely, 'there is something else I wish you to see.'

Puzzled by his abrupt change of mood, Helen plunged through the copse after him. He did not seem to care if she could keep up or not now, and she was soon quite out of breath.

'There,' he said, as he emerged from the trees into a small clearing.

She saw an ancient ruin with a tower at one end, half overgrown with ivy, and at its foot, a sheet of ice almost the size of the front garden of their cottage in Middleton.

'We nearly always get some ice forming up here over winter,' he said. 'The position of the trees keeps the sun from melting it away each morning. This year I have had the staff deliberately extend it. The lake here is too deep to freeze, except a little around the edges, so proper skating is out of the question, but I thought the children would enjoy sliding about on this. What do you think?'

'Me?'

'Yes. You are going to be a governess. You know children. They always seem to love to skate. Don't they? I know I did as a boy.'

Helen's heart plummeted. She had been having fantasies of stolen kisses. He had been thinking of asking her professional opinion, as a woman experienced with children, about his plans for amusing the children of his guests.

Oh, well. She shrugged. It had been only a wild flight of fancy on her part. What would a wealthy, handsome man like him see in an ordinary, penniless woman like her? At least now she did not have to be quite so concerned about what he thought of her.

The notion was quite liberating.

'Only as a boy?' she repeated, grinning up at him. 'Don't you still enjoy skating?'

And, before he had the chance to say a word, she gathered her skirts and made a run at the ice. When her boots hit the slippery surface she began to glide. It had been a while since she had last been skating, and then she had worn proper skating boots. Staying upright whilst sliding rapidly forward in ordinary footwear was a completely different sensation. To keep her balance she had to let go of her skirts and windmill her arms, and lean forward…no, back…no…

'Aaahh!' she squealed as she shot across the ice like a missile fired from a gun. She had totally misjudged how far her run-up would propel her.

She screamed again as she reached the perimeter of the ice, and realised she had no means of slowing down without the blades she was used to wearing for skating. She hit the slightly sloping bank running. Momentum kept her going, forcing her to stumble rapidly forward a few paces, before she managed to stop, with her gloved hands braced against an enormous bramble patch.

'That was amazing!' she panted, straightening up with a huge sense of achievement. She had not fallen flat on her face! Only her skirts had snagged amongst the thorns. Head bowed, she carefully began to disentangle the fabric, to minimise the damage.

'You might want to do something about these, though,' she remarked. 'Somebody might hurt themselves.'

'Only,' he bit out, striding round the ice patch with a face like thunder, 'if they have no adult to supervise them, and to prevent them from going wild. What the devil were you thinking?' He grabbed her by the shoulders and gave her a shake. 'You little idiot! You could have gone headlong into those brambles and cut yourself to ribbons!'

He had scarce been able to believe it when she had flung herself out onto the ice like that. And when he had heard her scream... For one sickening moment he had pictured her lying injured, her face distorted with pain, frozen for all eternity in agonised death throes...

And then, when he had realised that scream was border-ing on a cry of exhilaration, that she was relishing the danger, totally oblivious to the effect her reckless escapade might have upon him...

She gazed up at him in shock, all her pleasure from the little adventure dashed to pieces.

'If you think me an idiot,' she retorted, stung by his harsh words, 'you should not have asked for my opinion!' She swatted his hands away from her shoulders, taking such a hasty step backwards that her skirt ripped. 'And *now* look what you have made me do! Whenever I come anywhere near you it ends in disaster!'

Disaster? he echoed in his mind. This girl had no notion of what disaster truly was. She had come nowhere near disaster.

He tamped down on his surge of fury, acknowledging that

it was not her with whom he was angry. Not really. God, Lucinda! Would her ghost never leave him be?

Nobody deserved to die so young. No matter what she'd done. For a moment he was right back in the day he had heard of Lucinda's death, ruing the decision he had taken to wash his hands of her. He should have stayed with her, curbed her. She had been so wild he ought to have known she could be a danger to herself. He had lived with the guilt of her death, and that of the innocent baby she'd been carrying, ever since. Guilt that was exacerbated by the knowledge that a part of him had been relieved he was no longer married to her. Yes, she had set him free. But death was too great a price for any woman to pay.

It was with some difficulty that he wrenched himself back to the present, and the woman who was examining the damage to her gown with clear irritation. It was only a gown. Just a piece of cloth that had been torn. Had she no sense of perspective?

'I have already told you I am willing to replace your gown…'

'That was another gown!' she snapped, made even angrier because he had not noticed she was wearing an entirely different colour today. 'And I have already told you that giving me such things is out of the question!'

That was correct. He had forgotten for a moment that she was merely a guest in his house. That he had no right to buy her clothing. To question her conduct. To be angry with her.

To care what happened to her.

Helen saw his face change. He no longer looked angry. It was as though he had wiped all expression from it.

'I asked for your opinion,' he said in a flat, expressionless tone, 'because you are never afraid to give it. You tell me the truth. Because you care nothing for what I may think of you.'

'Oh, well,' she huffed, feeling somewhat mollified. It was true that, from what she had observed, most of the people who had come here for Christmas had some kind of hidden agenda. 'Then I apologise for my angry words.' She had lashed out in a fit of pique because he very clearly had no problem keeping his mind off *her* lips. No, he could not possibly have entertained one single romantic thought towards her, or he could not have chastised her in that over-bearing manner. Speaking of having some responsible adult to watch over the children, implying he thought *she* was most definitely not!

'Though,' she said ruefully, 'I do not know as much about children as you seem to imagine. The post I am about to take is my first. However, I do think this will be a lovely surprise for them.' Her eyes narrowed as she looked back at the glassy smooth surface he had created. Then she looked straight at him. 'Or for any adult who does not have too inflated an opinion of their own dignity.'

'So you think I have an over-inflated view of my importance?' he replied coldly. 'You think me a very dull fellow, in fact? As well as being hard and unfeeling when it comes to the plight of elderly relatives? I see.'

He gave her a curt bow. 'Perhaps it is time we returned to the house.' He eyed her nose, which had a fatal tendency to go bright red in cold weather. His lips twisted with contempt. 'I can see that you are getting cold.'

She knew it looked most unattractive, but did he really have to be so ungentlemanly as to draw attention to it? Anyone would think he was *trying* to hurt her.

As if he wanted to get back at her for hurting him.

Oh. No…surely not?

But if that were the case…

'I never said I thought you hard and unfeeling. Well, not exactly! Don't go pokering up at me like that!' she protested.

To his back.

He was already striding out in the direction of the house. She would have to trot to keep up with him, never mind catch up with him. She stopped, hands on her hips, and gave a huff of exasperation.

If only it had snowed recently. There was nothing she wanted so much as to fling a large wet snowball at him and knock his hat off!

Except, perhaps, put her arms round him in a consoling hug and tell him she had never meant to insult him. Though she would have to catch up with him to accomplish that. And he had no intention of being caught.

'Ooh…' she breathed, shaking her head in exasperation with herself. What on earth had made her fancy there had been a glimmer of attraction burning in his eyes when he had invited her to come walking with him? Well, if it had ever been there it was gone now. He had just looked at her as though she were something slimy that had crawled out from underneath a rock.

It was not the kind of look she was used to getting from men. Aunt Bella had reminded her only recently that she was a pretty girl. Had urged her to win Mr Cadwallader over with one of her smiles. Had she become vain in recent years? She lowered her head in chagrin as she began to trudge back to the house in Lord Bridgemere's wake. Though she had never actively sought it, she *had* come to regard flattering male attention as her due.

There were some who would say she was getting a taste of her own medicine, no doubt. Because whenever one of the men of Middleton had sidled up to her in the market, or some such place, under some spurious pretext, to tell her how pretty she was, she had felt nothing for them but contempt. And now the first man she had met who had actually awoken some interest was completely impervious to her charms. He had not paid her a single compliment, nor tried to hold her hand, or snatch a kiss. And yet whenever she was in Lord Bridgemere's vicinity kissing seemed to be all she could think about.

Whereas he, to judge by the stiff set of his shoulders as he drew steadily further and further away, found her annoying.

She flinched, wondering why that knowledge should hurt so much. These days he was out of her reach socially, anyway. Perhaps, she decided glumly, it was just that he represented *everything* that was now out of her reach. The social standing and the affluence that she had taken for granted when she and Aunt Bella had been so comfortably off.

There was nothing so appealing as something that you knew you could never have.

That afternoon Helen took the opportunity to slip away to the library, since the light in there was so much better than it was in their room, with her sewing basket tucked under her arm. She had told her aunt that she intended to make a start on the alterations she had already decided her gowns needed, and the minor repairs her encounters with Lord Bridgemere had made necessary. But really she wanted to get on with the little gift she had been sewing for Aunt Bella. Besides which, the floor-to-ceiling windows contained some heraldic designs which she wanted to sketch. She had decided to use them as a basis for another project which, it had occurred to her, she must complete very swiftly, since it lacked only three days until Christmas.

She made herself comfortable upon one of the window seats with which the room was blessed, and bent her mind to the task in hand. She was not sure how long she had been sitting there when she became aware she was no longer alone.

She looked up from the tangle of silks on her lap to find Lord Bridgemere standing in the doorway. His face was, as usual, hard to read.

Helen felt her cheeks grow hot, and knew she was blushing. It was the first time she had seen him since that early-morning walk of which she'd had such high expectations. And which had resulted in her making such a fool of herself and caused her a morning of quite painful soul-searching as she'd faced up to several unpleasant truths about her character. She had come to the conclusion that whenever Lord Bridgemere looked at her what he saw was a very vain and silly woman.

'I was just passing,' he said, moving his arm towards the corridor outside. 'And I saw you sitting here alone.'

And had been transfixed by the way the sunlight gilded her hair, the pout of her lips as she concentrated on whatever it was that she was doing.

He cleared his throat. 'Why are you on your own, Miss Forrest? Is your aunt unwell?'

Even as he said it he knew that she would not be down here if that were the case. She would be upstairs, nursing her adopted relative. Or down in the kitchens, making some remedy for her. She would not have bothered to ring the bell. A smile kicked up one corner of his mouth as he pictured her marching into the kitchens and elbowing his servants aside to concoct some remedy which only she knew how to make to her own satisfaction.

'Far from it,' replied Helen, wondering what could have put that strange smile on his face. Did she have a smut on her nose? Or was he just recalling one of the many ways she had made a fool of herself since she had come here?

'Aunt Bella is in the card room with Lady Norton. They plan to spend the afternoon drinking tea and gossiping about the fate of mutual acquaintances.'

Her face was so expressive he could not miss a little trace of pique at the way the older woman was treating her. There was something going on between these two ladies that he needed to uncover. The general belief was that Helen was the older Miss Forrest's sole heir. But she had told him she needed to go out to work because she was penniless.

Yet she was still fiercely loyal to her adopted aunt. Whatever had happened between them, it had not soured her.

He found himself walking towards her.

'And what is it you are doing?'

'Oh, nothing much!' Helen quickly stuffed her rough sketches of the Bridgemere coat of arms into her workbasket, and held up the bodice of one of the gowns she was altering. 'Tedious stuff. Making buttonholes and such,' she said.

His brows lowered slightly. 'Is there nothing more amusing you could be doing?'

Helen grappled with a sense of exasperation. She had accused him of neglecting her and her aunt, had felt resentful of the amusements he had provided for the other guests. Yet now he was here, playing the gracious host, she felt uncomfortable. She was not an invited guest. She had done nothing but cause trouble since she had entered his house. And he must have a thousand and one more important things to do with his time. He ought not to be wasting it on her.

'Please do not trouble yourself with me. I am quite content. I…I would actually prefer to be doing something useful than frittering the time away with cards or gossip.'

'Is that so?'

Sometimes Miss Forrest said things that were so exactly what he felt about life himself that it was as though…

He sat down on the window seat beside her and took hold of the piece of material draped across her lap.

'Oh, be careful of the pins!'

He let it go. He had only focussed on it because he had not wanted to look into her face. Lest she see…what? A quickening of interest that she very obviously did not return? She thought him hard and unfeeling, full of his own importance. And worst of all dull. There was no worse character flaw a man could have in the eyes of a girl as lively as this. Had not Lucinda told him so often enough?

It took Helen a great effort to sit completely still. The material which he had dropped back onto her lap was warm from his hand. The fleeting sense that it might have been the touch of his hand on her leg had created an echoing warmth in the pit of her stomach. Which was even now sinking lower, to bloom between her thighs.

Oh, Lord, she hoped he had no idea how his proximity was affecting her! Why did it have to be *this* man, the one man she knew she could never have, who was making her respond in such a shocking way?

'If you really would enjoy being useful, it occurs to me that there is a way in which we could help each other,' he said, laying his arm casually along the edge of the windowsill.

Did he know that extending his arm like that made her feel enclosed by his arms? Was he doing it on purpose, to make her even more conscious of him?

And in what way could she possibly be of any help to him?

Unless she had betrayed her interest in him?

He had no need to marry, but if a woman was silly enough to let him know how physically attractive she found him, might he think he could cajole her into a brief affair?

'I don't think there can possibly be any way I could be of help to you,' she said primly, averting her head. If he was going to insult her by suggesting what she thought he was, then she had no intention of letting him see how much it would hurt!

'You said this morning that you do not have much experience with children, Miss Forrest. And it just so happens that there is a whole batch of them here. They have come with their parents, who have consigned them away upstairs with their nurses. If you wanted to gain some experience with working with children before you take up your first post, then here is an ideal opportunity.'

Experience with children. Of course. She let out the breath she had been holding, chiding herself for once again rating her charms far more highly than Lord Bridgemere obviously did. Here was she, thinking he was about to make her an improper suggestion, while nothing could have been further from his mind. Would she never learn?

'The children of your guests?' she echoed faintly. 'You wish me to go and help…?'

'I have already enlisted the services of Reverend Mullen. He has written the script, which he tells me he has based mostly on the gospel of Luke…'

'Wait a minute. Script?' She raised her head to look at him, quite puzzled. 'What script? What are you talking about?'

'I forgot. This is your first visit to Alvanley Hall, and you are not aware of the traditions that prevail.' He leaned back, his eyes fixed intently on her face. 'Each year I throw a ball for my tenants on Boxing Day, as part of my gift to them to reward them for all their hard work and loyalty to me throughout the year. Out at one of the barns on the home farm. The children who are brought by their parents to stay at the Hall always put on a little entertainment for them to start the evening's festivities. The villagers always perform their mummer's plays for me on Christmas Day, and so I return the favour by getting up this party for them. And, of course, it helps to keep the children occupied during their stay here.'

'Of course,' she echoed faintly, still feeling somewhat resentful that it had not occurred to him to make her a proposition. Which she would naturally have refused! But still…

'So would you, then? Like to become involved in putting on the production for my tenants?' Or did she consider it was beneath her to spend her time coaching the children to perform for rustics?

She was not quite sure how she could be of *any* help, since he had already told her that Reverend Mullen was writing the script and coaching the children through their parts. She had no experience whatever of amateur theatricals. And the children had their own nurses to see to whatever else it was they needed.

Yet it would be a good opportunity to see how the children of the very upper echelons of society were organised, even if she could contribute very little.

The experience would be of more benefit to her, she suspected, than to Lord Bridgemere.

'Thank you, My Lord,' she said through gritted teeth, wondering why his eyes had turned so cold. 'I should find the experience most beneficial.'

It was ridiculous to let the Earl's treatment of her hurt so much. It was not as if she had seriously believed there could ever be anything between them. And as for those brief flashes of feeling as though she was totally in tune with him…well, they had clearly existed only in her own mind.

Lord Bridgemere might have paid her a little attention, but she could see now that it had only been to assess how he could make the best use of her.

'Thank you,' he said, getting to his feet. 'I must leave you now. Cadwallader has arranged a full afternoon for me, and would be most put out if I ruined his timetable. Can you find your own way up to the nursery?'

'If not, I can always ask for directions,' she replied acidly.

She got to her feet and began tidying her work away as soon as he'd left the room. Though she disliked being on the receiving end of Lord Bridgemere's demonstration of his organisational skills, she *would* appreciate the experience of working with some children before she took up her new post. Even though she had decided, when all the money had disappeared, that she would find consolation in moulding young minds in the way Aunt Bella had moulded hers, she was a little nervous about how exactly she would go about the task. Lord Bridgemere could not have hit upon a better way of helping her become accustomed to her new station in life.

Drat him.

Helen enjoyed the rest of the afternoon much more than she had expected. To begin with, the Reverend Mullen welcomed her with an enthusiasm that was a balm to her wounded pride.

'Ah, good, good— His Lordship has managed to persuade you to lend your talents to our little endeavours,' he beamed, when she entered the huge attic space which had been converted into a rehearsal area. 'I have cast the children as best as I can,' he said, 'and rehearsed them once or twice, but they are in dire need of costumes. His Lordship told me you consider yourself a most competent needlewoman, and would be able to help on that front.'

Helen's lips compressed as she recalled flinging those very words at Lord Bridgemere on the day she had rejected his offer of a new gown to replace the one Esau had spoiled.

But it was hard to stay cross for very long in the atmosphere of jollity over which the Reverend Mullen presided. He was scarcely any older than Nicholas Swaledale, she reflected, yet two youths could not have been more different. The Reverend was earnest, diligent and…well, *worthy* was the word that kept on springing to mind in his regard.

And the children, unlike their parents, all seemed to regard their visit to Alvanley Hall as the highlight of their year.

'Christmas last year was horrid,' said the tubby lad who was to play the part of Joseph, while she was measuring him for his costume. 'Mama and Papa wanted us to keep out of the way while they had their parties. And they forgot all about us. We never got a big feast, like we had the year before at Alvanley. Will we be having a children's feast, this year, Miss Forrest?' he asked excitedly. 'We had cake and jelly and ices last time, I remember.'

'I do not know. This is the very first time I have been here.'

Immediately 'Joseph's' expression turned pitying. 'Never mind, you're here now. Perhaps you will be able to come to our feast with us, and then you'll see!'

'I think I should like that.' She laughed. Far more than

the deadly formal banquet she guessed would be provided for the adults.

It would be wonderful to stay up here with the children and servants…

She sucked in a sharp breath. Why had she not seen it before? He had not invited her. She was here as the companion of Aunt Bella, nothing more. He had placed her in a room he'd told her was allotted to upper servants, and when he'd seen her making use of his library, as though she was a guest with the right to make free with the public rooms, he had sent her up here, where the Reverend Mullen could find fitting work for her to do!

She flushed angrily. He thought of her as a servant! It was not his wish to help her gain some experience with children that had prompted him to send her up here. No, he was just putting her in her place! Keeping her out of sight of his relatives, several of whom clearly objected to her presence.

'Did you prick your finger?' asked the pretty little girl who was to play the part of Mary.

When Helen had first come up here the child had run her eyes over her rather plain gown and looked as though she had immediately relegated her to the status of servant. But in spite of that she stopped sifting through the pile of materials that had been provided to make up the costumes the moment Helen gasped.

'I am always pricking my finger when I sew my sampler. You should use a thimble,' she said, nodding sagely.

'Thank you,' said Helen amending her impression of her as a haughty little madam. 'I shall remember that.'

'We get nice presents here, too,' she said absently, resuming her search for something she deemed fit to appear on stage in. 'All of us. *Nobody* is forgotten,' she said, with such a wistful air that Helen suspected she must have suffered such a fate herself. 'And we get to stay up really late to put on our play. And all the grown-ups watch us and clap their hands. Even Mama and Papa.'

Helen could barely refrain from putting her arms round the child and giving her a hug. Her words spoke volumes about the way she was usually treated in her own home.

'I would rather they didn't,' said the slender boy cast in the role of the angel Gabriel, who was sitting on a nearby stool, glumly studying his copy of the play. He was clearly nervous about performing in front of an audience. 'I would rather just stay up here with a book.' He coughed in a most theatrical manner. 'I don't think I will be able to say my lines. I think I'm catching cold.'

'You had better not, Swaledale,' observed 'Joseph'. 'Or you will miss the skating.'

Helen looked sharply at 'Gabriel'. If his name was Swaledale then he must be the younger brother of Lord Bridgemere's heir. Now that she knew he was related, she thought she could see a resemblance. He did have a rather sulky mouth.

'Miss Forrest,' said 'Joseph', turning to her, 'His Lordship has made a skating pond, especially for us children. We are all going to go down tomorrow if the rain holds off. Will you be coming with us?'

'I am not sure,' she replied, tight-lipped. The Earl had

specified that he wanted *responsible* adults to watch over his precious young relations, implying that she did not qualify.

'Mary' pouted. 'I expect it is only for boys. The girls will have to stay indoors and…learn lines, or something equally tedious!'

'No, no, Junia, dear,' said Reverend Mullen, who had been passing with a sheaf of scripts in his hands. '*All* the children are to gather in the stableyard, first thing in the morning, where a cart is to be ready to carry them to the pond. Those who do not wish to skate do not have to. They may watch. There will be a warm shelter where hot chocolate and cakes will be served.'

'Joseph's' eyes lit up.

'And did I not tell you, Miss Forrest? His Lordship particularly wants you to accompany the nursery party, since you are such an enthusiastic skater.'

'Are you?' said Junia, dropping a length of purple velvet and looking up at her wide-eyed. 'Would you teach me to skate?'

'Of course I will,' replied Helen, suddenly understanding why her parents sometimes overlooked her. Junia, she recalled hearing, was the name of another of Lady Thrapston's daughters. Her mother must have been furious she had produced yet another girl, when there, in the form of 'Gabriel', was the proof that her sister, Lady Craddock, had produced not only an heir for Lord Bridgemere, but also a potential spare.

As Reverend Mullen hurried away, bent on his next task, Helen's mouth formed into a determined line. No child over whom *she* ever had any influence would be made to feel

inferior because of their sex! She would make sure their accomplishments were applauded, their talents encouraged,
and—she glanced at the slender, pale young 'Gabriel'—their
fears soothed.

Junia sat back and beamed at her. And Helen's opinion of
her mellowed still further. She probably could not help being
a little haughty, considering who her mother was. The poor
girl had clearly been taught that certain behaviour was
expected of a young lady. But Helen was going to see to it
that tomorrow, at least, she had the chance to break out in
the direction her natural inclination carried her!

Then she turned to 'Gabriel'.

'You know, you do not have to say very much,' she said,
eyeing his script. 'From what I have seen of the way
Reverend Mullen has written it, you mostly have to stand
there, looking imposing, while Junia recites the Magnificat.'

'And keep the little angels in order,' said Junia.

Many of the younger children, who could not be
expected to learn lines, would be dressed as angels and simply
moved about to represent the heavenly host watching over
the events taking place in Bethlehem.

He sighed despondently. 'They won't mind *me*,' he proph-
esied gloomily. 'Nobody ever takes any notice of me.'

'They might,' said Helen on a burst of inspiration, 'if you
arm yourself with some treats as a reward for good behaviour.'

'I say, Miss Forrest,' he said, brightening up immediately,
'that's a capital notion. I might ask Cook for some jam tarts,
or something!'

Helen had visions of half a dozen little angels, their faces smeared with jam. 'Something like ginger snaps?' she suggested. 'Easier to stow in your pockets for distribution at the proper time. I shall go and have a word with Cook about it later on.'

How fortunate she had already mended fences below stairs, she reflected as Gabriel grinned at her.

Goodness! Helen was beginning to think she might have some natural talent when it came to dealing with children after all.

Chapter Seven

Alas, she had not so much success with adults!

The very moment she walked into the blue saloon that evening she felt out of place. And self-conscious because she had so badly misinterpreted Lord Bridgemere's motives in singling her out for attention. Right now he was moving from one group of guests to another, playing the part of dutiful host. Something inside her squeezed painfully as she saw afresh that it was the duty of a good host to pay a little attention to each of his guests. And she had mistaken his willingness to spend a little of his time ensuring she enjoyed some of the beauty of his estate at dawn's first light as personal interest in *her*. His subsequent attitude had shown her how he really viewed her.

And yet, even knowing this, she was still painfully aware of exactly where he was at any given moment. It was as though she was attuned to the low, melodious timbre of his voice. And, her attention having been caught, she could not prevent her eyes from seeking him out. And then she would feel deflated whenever she caught sight of the back of his head, his light brown hair gleaming in the candlelight. For he would always be intent upon somebody else. So far as he was concerned she might as well not exist.

It was even worse once they sat down to dine and she had an unimpeded view of him at the head of the table. For he talked quietly to those seated on his right hand, or his left.

And ignored her completely.

By the time the ladies withdrew, all Helen wished to do was escape to her bedchamber, where she might have some chance to wrestle her tumultuous feelings into submission.

But Lady Thrapston beckoned to her the moment she crossed the threshold, and she did not see how she could refuse her imperious summons to take a place on the sofa beside her.

Under cover of the noise her two daughters were making at the piano, Lady Thrapston fired her opening salvo.

'I have been observing you,' she said, with a grim smile. 'And I feel obliged to warn you that your tactics will not work with Bridgemere.'

'Tactics?' Helen was so surprised that she hardly knew how to answer Lady Thrapston. They had a knack, she reflected wryly, Lord Bridgemere and his sister, of reducing her to parroting one or two words of their speech.

'Do not play the innocent with me. You fool nobody with all that nonsensical talk about not wishing to marry! It is quite obvious that you have set your cap at Lord Bridgemere.'

Helen's first instinct was to deny the allegation indignantly. She had just opened her mouth to make a pithy rejoinder when she heard her aunt laughing at something

Lady Norton had said. And she closed her mouth abruptly. She must not let her temper get the better of her. Aunt Bella was still awaiting Lord Bridgemere's verdict, and until then it would not do to create an even worse impression upon him than she had already done.

She contented herself by lifting her chin and glaring at Lady Thrapston.

'Nothing to say for yourself?' the haughty matron said. 'But then what *can* you say in your defence?'

Helen wondered if she had just made a tactical error. For it looked as though Lady Thrapston thought her dart had gone home. Her next words confirmed it.

'With my own eyes I have watched you making a spectacle of yourself. And let me tell you this. Fluttering your eyelashes at him over the soup plates is one thing, but it has come to my attention that you have now gone to the lengths of luring him to some out-of-the way spot in an attempt to compromise him.'

'That is not true!' Helen gasped. She had not done any luring! Lord Bridgemere had *invited* her to go out walking with him.

How dreadful that somebody had seen them and run to Lady Thrapston with such a tale. She felt quite sick that somebody disliked her enough to do such a thing, without a shred of evidence.

Especially since she would never dream of setting her cap at any man, or luring him into a compromising position.

But she *had* felt acutely disappointed that his attitude towards her had been so completely impersonal, she admitted to herself. And, her conscience whispered, she'd also had to chastise herself several times for entertaining inappropriate thoughts regarding Lord Bridgemere. Lady Thrapston had obviously noticed that she could not help finding him most attractive. Even when he had made it perfectly clear he was immune to her, she reflected with chagrin.

Her cheeks flushing guiltily, she said, 'I am aware that His Lordship would never consider marrying someone like me.'

Lady Thrapston nodded grimly. 'I trust you will remember that, my girl. If you know what is good for you, you will take care to keep well away from him for the remainder of your visit. It would not do for rumours of indecorous behaviour to accompany you to your new post, would it?'

Was this a threat? Helen reeled at the thought of the damage Lady Thrapston could do to her future if it was. A judicious word in her employer's ear, from a woman of her rank, and her job could well disappear. Nor, if gossip spread about her supposed conduct, would it be easy for her to find another.

Helen wished she might make some clever, cutting rejoinder, but for once she knew it was imperative she keep her tongue between her teeth.

'No,' she whispered. She dared not risk antagonising Lady Thrapston, and have her spread unfounded gossip about her. What General Forrest had begun was bad enough.

'You may return to your aunt,' said Lady Thrapston, a small, but self-satisfied smile playing about her mouth.

She had the look of a woman who had just successfully put a designing trollop in her place, fumed Helen as she walked, stiff-legged and straight-backed, to her aunt, and sat down, her fists clenched in her lap.

It was so unfair!

She caught her lower lip between her teeth, unable to deny that, had she behaved with greater propriety, the woman would not have had cause to think what she had. Her eyes did keep straying towards Lord Bridgemere whenever he was present. Something about him drew her like a magnet. And, from what Lady Thrapston had just said, her attraction towards him must be written all over her face.

She sighed. A proper young lady should never reveal what she was thinking. Her aunt had informed her of that fact many times, without ever managing to teach her how such a feat might become possible. With the result that everyone must be able to tell exactly what she was thinking just by looking at her. She glanced round the room, wondering what everyone had just made of her encounter with Lady Thrapston. And noted several ladies staring at her in a disapproving manner. Lord, did *everyone* think she was fast?

She supposed she could hardly blame them. For she *had* snatched at the chance to spend a few moments with him alone. Even though she had known full well it was most improper behaviour. Oh, she might not have actually set her cap at Lord Bridgemere, but her conduct towards him had definitely been questionable. And had laid her wide open to Lady Thrapston's charges.

Not that his sister need worry. Lord Bridgemere had already taken steps to ensure she kept her distance. He had made sure that she would be busy all day long. Well away from him!

She went cold inside as it occurred to her that *he* might have thought, as Lady Thrapston had, that she was deliberately attempting to entrap him.

How humiliating.

And she had nobody but herself to blame.

'I think I should like to retire early tonight,' said Aunt Bella. 'I have been tired all day after last night's dissipation.'

'I shall come up with you,' said Helen with heartfelt relief. 'Do you wish to go now?' She desperately wanted to get out of the room before the gentlemen joined them. She did not think she could bear to have Lord Bridgemere look at her with the kind of censure Lady Thrapston had just turned on her.

'If you would not mind,' said Aunt Bella gratefully. 'Lady Norton makes me feel old. I simply cannot keep up with her.'

'We are used to living much more quietly,' said Helen, taking her aunt's arm as she rose to her feet. 'That is the problem. Though I, for one,' she muttered under her breath, 'have no wish to fit in with these kind of people.'

Going to bed early solved nothing. Helen lay wide awake, going over and over Lady Thrapston's acid comments, castigating herself for the way she had behaved since coming to Alvanley Hall, and bitterly regretting that second helping of pickled cabbage. She had the worst case of indigestion she could ever remember. Eventually her discomfort became so acute that she knew she would have to find some remedy. In the past she had found that taking a hot drink and walking about provided some relief.

She had no intention of ringing for a servant in the middle of the night. Besides, she knew the way to the kitchens. She could quite easily make herself a cup of tea without disturbing anyone. She got out of bed, thrust her feet into slippers, pulled on her wrapper, and tiptoed across the room so as not to wake her aunt. Then, remembering how cold the corridors could be at any time of the day, she darted back to get her thickest shawl for good measure.

She was halfway down the backstairs when the door at the foot of the staircase opened and somebody with a candle and booted feet began to mount. Assuming it must be a footman, she kept descending until she got to the bend in the stairs, where she gathered the skirts of her nightgown tightly and pressed herself against the wall of the half-landing, to give the man room to get past her.

'Well, well, what have we here?'

Helen grimaced as she recognised in the flickering candlelight not a footman, but the flushed features of Nicholas Swaledale. His neckcloth was awry, his waistcoat buttons undone, and he was swaying ever so slightly with each breath he took.

In other words, he was thoroughly foxed.

And he was standing right in the centre of the narrow staircase, blocking her path. Running his bloodshot eyes insolently over her.

Her nightgown was not in the least bit revealing. On the contrary, it covered her in voluminous folds of flannel from neck to toe. And yet it was a garment designed for wearing in bed. And the smirk on his face told her he was well aware of the fact.

Helen had never felt so vulnerable.

She had never come across a drunken young man on her own in her entire life, and was not quite sure how to deal with him. If he had been sober she would have curtsied, greeted him formally, and then gone on her way. Perhaps that would be the best thing to do. Remind him of his manners.

'Good evening sir,' she said, dipping her knees in a curtsey as though they were in a drawing room.

Swaledale sniggered as she straightened from her curtsey.

'You don't need to p'tend to be all prim and proper with me, Helen,' he said, climbing up another step so that his face was level with hers. 'Or sh'll I call you Nell?'

He stepped onto the landing and swayed towards her.

Now was not the time to argue about the over familiarity of using her given name. It was the fact that he was standing far too close that was bothering her the most.

She already had her back to the wall. All she could do was turn her head aside as stale brandy fumes assailed her nostrils.

'Please stand back and let me pass,' she said.

'Why? Where you goin'? Or c'n I guess?' His expression turned nasty. 'Off for a little midnight trysht with Bridgemere, are you? Shneaking down backstairs so nobody will see wass goin' on…'

'There's nothing going on!'

He made a derisive snorting sound. 'The way he goes on about you fair makes me sick. "Paragon!"' He lurched and hiccupped, dripping candle wax onto her shawl. 'Never askin' nobody for nothin', but just goin' out and findin' work. Praising your frugalishity to make the rest of us feel guilty…'

'Fru…frugalishity?' She couldn't help herself. She giggled.

It was just so wonderful to learn that, however he treated her to her face, and whatever suspicions he might harbour in regard to her obvious attraction to him, Lord Bridgemere was still holding certain aspects of her behaviour up to others as an example. And the sudden lift this knowledge brought to her spirits burst forth in a wild surge of hilarity at this drunken youth's muddling of the English language.

With a newfound boldness she reached up and pushed him in the chest, intending to step round him and carry on her way.

But his reflexes were amazingly quick, considering he was slurring his words so badly. He grabbed her wrist and, after a brief struggle, managed to twist her arm behind her back and pin her to the wall.

'Don' laugh at me!' Swaledale's expression had turned ugly. He was leaning against her heavily, his eyes glazed. She could feel the heat of his candle scorching her cheek. She jerked her head away from the naked flame, afraid now that he was so drunk he could easily burn her, entirely by accident.

'Thass wiped that smirk off your face,' he said with a satisfied grin. 'Slut.'

She went still. This kind of behaviour from a man was totally outside her experience. She knew she had no hope of breaking free. And she feared that if she antagonised him further he might really hurt her.

'I am not laughing at you,' she said, in as calm a tone as she could muster, considering her heart was lurching about in her chest. 'Please, won't you let me go now?'

He chuckled.

'No. Don't think I will. Not yet.'

To her utter disgust, he pushed his mouth against hers and licked all the way round her lips.

With the candle held so close to her cheek, she dared not move. All she could do was keep her mouth pressed tightly closed as the revolting assault went on and on. It was just like being slobbered on by Esau! Though at least she had known the dog was trying to be friendly. There was nothing friendly about what Swaledale was doing. It was a deliberate insult!

She whimpered in distress.

He growled. And ran a line of wet kisses down her jaw to her neck.

'What the *devil* do you think you're doing?'

From the staircase below Lord Bridgemere's voice boomed, echoing from the bare woodwork.

'Oh, thank heavens!' Helen cried as Swaledale spun round, letting her go. She wiped her face and neck with the sleeve of her nightgown. Her arm was shaking, she noted. As were her legs.

And she felt sick.

'Having a little bit of sport,' said Swaledale defiantly, 'with a game pullet. Where's the harm in that?'

'The harm,' said Lord Bridgemere coldly, continuing to mount the stairs, 'is that the lady does not appear to me to be willing.'

'She's no lady,' Swaledale sneered. 'Just some jumped-up servant…'

'All the more reason for you to keep your hands off her!'

Helen could not believe how much that hurt. He had not denied Swaledale's assumption that she was a menial. No, his retort only went to confirm that he really did think of her as a sort of servant.

'I will not have my house made unsafe for females whatever their station in life!' Bridgemere continued. 'And if this is an example of what my staff may expect if you take over the reins…'

'Whadya mean, *if*? I'm your heir! When you're gone it will all be mine…'

'*When* I'm gone, and not before!'

He had reached the landing, which now seemed very crowded. Helen was already flat against the wall, and the two men were standing toe to toe.

'I thought I made that quite clear this afternoon,' said Lord Bridgemere in anger. 'You cannot keep running through your allowance, assuming I will mop up all your debts! If this is the way you repay my generosity, then I shall have to think very carefully about doing so again.'

'This is all *your* doing,' Swaledale muttered, giving Helen a dirty look.

'It is nothing to do with Miss Forrest! Oh, for heaven's sake, go to your room and sleep it off!' he said, running the flat of his hand over the crown of his head. 'We will talk again when you've sobered up.'

To Helen's relief, Swaledale turned and lurched off up the stairs.

But then Lord Bridgemere rounded on her.

'As for you, Miss Forrest, what the devil do you think you

are doing, loitering about the backstairs in your nightgown? Have you no sense at all?'

'Loitering?' she retorted, unbelievably hurt by his accusation of deliberate immodesty.

Tears sprang to her eyes as she recalled the way Lady Thrapston had made her feel earlier, when she had accused her of setting her cap at Lord Bridgemere. It was so unfair. She might have been a little reckless, but she had never deliberately set out to lure anyone.

'I assumed that as a guest in your house I would be perfectly safe. I never dreamt I would be accosted and mauled about like that!'

'Well, now you know better.' He laughed bitterly. 'That was just a sample of what you can expect in a devil of a lot of households.' He grabbed her by the shoulders. 'You stay in your room at night, with the door locked,' he grated, shaking her.

He was furious to discover *any* female being subjected to this kind of treatment under his roof. But to think of her going off to some household where there was nobody about to check her natural exuberance, to watch over her, to keep her safe, was ten times worse. He had to make her see that she must modify her behaviour.

'You can never assume anything about men when they have been drinking,' he warned her, 'except that you need to steer clear of them. If you will go prowling around in a state of undress you will have only yourself to blame when some drunken buck helps himself to what is on offer.'

'On offer?' She batted his hands away, her candle guttering as wax splashed down the front of her nightgown. 'How dare you? You make it sound as though what happened was my fault!'

He stepped back and sighed. 'Just get back to your room,' he said wearily. 'And take this as a salutary lesson.'

He was doing it again. Talking down to her as though she was an imbecile...or a child.

'I will not go back to my room,' she said defiantly. 'I have not got what I came down for.'

'If you do not stop acting like this, even I might be tempted to give it to you.'

It was an insult too far. Oh, he might well have commended her frugality to his heir. But only, as the obnoxious toad had said, as a rebuke to a spendthrift youth who seemed to think the world owed him a living.

He really did think she was a...a designing hussy. That she was here on the backstairs in her nightgown for some nefarious reason. And if he could believe that, then he did not know her at all! With a wild sob, she slapped him as hard as she could across the face.

He went very still. Though the breath hissed through his teeth, he said nothing. Merely stared coldly down at her as the marks of her fingers began to bloom across his cheek.

That glacial self-control told her all she needed to know. Her slap had not hurt him anywhere near as badly as his words had wounded her.

Her breath hitched in her throat as tears streamed down her face.

She felt her self-esteem shrivel to nothing. It was pointless to argue that she had done nothing wrong. In the eyes of the world, a woman who wandered around a house at night in a state of undress, as he had put it, was inviting the wrong sort of attention.

'I d…didn't mean to…'

'I know,' he said, and suddenly he pulled her into his arms and held her. Just held her close while she wept all over his dinner jacket.

It was just what she needed. Someone to hold her and comfort her after the horrible way Swaledale had treated her. Even after the horrible way Lord Bridgemere had spoken to her.

But after only a short while she became aware of the danger of drawing such comfort from Bridgemere, of all men. She knew he would bring Swaledale to book for this night's work. But he would not always be around to fight her battles for her. She was going to have to stand alone. This feeling of security that being in his arms produced was deceptive.

Besides, clinging to him like this when he already thought so poorly of her could only be confirming all his worst assumptions.

Shakily, she pulled herself away, and wiped her face with the back of her hand.

'*Now* will you go back to your room, Miss Forrest?'

He looked completely exasperated. To him, she must seem like a tiresome child, always blundering into scrapes that he was tired of rescuing her from. Or a servant who did not quite know her place and constantly needed reminding of it.

Not as an equal.

And not, by the way his face had shuttered, as a woman—
a desirable woman who might stand a chance of success if
ever she *were* brazen enough to attempt a spot of luring!

It felt as though a door had just slammed shut in her face,
locking her out, leaving her forever in the cold. Alone.

With a sob, she whirled round and pounded back up
the stairs.

The next morning, gritty-eyed from lack of sleep, Helen
stumbled outside to the stableyard. She had promised Junia
she would help her learn to skate or, to be more accurate,
slide about on the ice, and nothing was going to make her
break her word to a child.

'Good morning, good morning!' chirped Reverend
Mullen, rubbing his hands together for warmth. 'A fine,
frosty morning. Perfect for the children's outing,' he
beamed.

Helen managed to muster a polite smile as she clambered
up into the back of the cart that was already half filled with
excited children, all bundled up warmly, with hats and
scarves concealing most of their faces.

She had seen them going off in this cart on her first
morning here, she remembered, with a pang of nostalgia.

Back then she had felt like an unwelcome intruder. Now,
although she was caught up in Lord Bridgemere's plans for
his guests, she still felt painfully aware that she did not belong.
He would be glad, no doubt, when she left, considering all
the trouble she had caused.

She sighed as a groom slammed the tail of the cart closed.

Reverend Mullen leapt up in front, next to the driver, and they lurched off, out of the cobbled yard and round a winding drive towards the copse.

The ride through the estate was like rubbing salt into a raw wound. Alvanley Park was just so beautiful this time in the morning. Every bush, tree and lacy spider's web was gilded with frost, which sparkled as the sun caught it. As they swept round the lake she saw tendrils of mist rising from its surface, as well as from the grassy slopes upon which the sun's rays beat down. And she could not help recalling the walk through the woods they were approaching now by the lane. The fleeting feeling of intimacy she had known with the owner of all this magnificence.

Which had melted away like the frost in the sunlight. Leaving behind, as he had predicted, a black mire of misery.

The cart could not get right into the grove in which Lord Bridgemere had created the ice slide. They all had to clamber down from the cart and walk the last few yards.

When they emerged from the last stand of trees Helen was astounded by the transformation that had been wrought on the place overnight. There were coloured lanterns hanging from the overhanging branches, so that what had been a dank, dark place now looked festive and inviting. The door to the tower stood open today, and inside she could see a fire burning in a massive great hearth, so that anyone who got too cold could go and take shelter there.

And, she noted with tears in her eyes, what looked like horse blankets had been draped over the offending brambles, so that if anyone else was careless enough to overshoot the slide they would not get scratched.

Lord Bridgemere had thought of everything, she sniffed. He had taken as much care over this treat for the children as would be given to an entertainment arranged for adults on such estates. He cared equally for all his guests, be they high-born or low, be they young or old.

Why did more people not see this? Why had her aunt described him in such terms that she had thought he was a total misanthrope? He was nothing of the kind!

'Miss? Miss?'

Junia was frowning up at her. 'You said you would teach me…'

Blinking away her tears, Helen saw that some of the boys had dashed straight out onto the ice and were already sliding around, whooping and hollering at the tops of their voices.

Reverend Mullen strode out after them, waving his arms like a shepherd with an unruly flock of sheep, shooing them all to one end so that the smaller ones, and those who were more timid, would have a space where they need not fear getting knocked down.

'I did,' she said, taking Junia's hand. 'Let's show these boys how it's done!'

It was impossible to stay feeling sorry for herself for very long. Soon she was having as much fun as the children. Even Junia forgot her starchy manners and laughed happily as she mastered the art of staying upright whilst sliding about.

Some while later Helen heard the unmistakable sound of

Esau's deep throaty bark, carrying to her from the pathway where they had abandoned the cart.

Her heart began to pound heavily. If Esau was there, Lord Bridgemere would not be far behind. Indeed, the moment she lifted her head to gaze in the dog's direction she spotted him, astride a glossy bay stallion, his brows knit in a ferocious scowl as he called his hound to heel.

Esau stood for a second or two, his tail waving in the air, his nose well up, as he watched all the activity on the ice. He would have loved to join the children. But he was so boisterous, and so big, he would be bound to frighten the little ones. Lord Bridgemere called him again, and the dog bounded back to his master's side.

He looked up then and saw her, standing stock still, staring at him.

Her cheeks flushed, remembering the last time she had seen him. How little she had been wearing. And how wonderful it had felt when he had put his arms round her.

And how exasperated he had looked at her clinging to him and weeping all over him.

He had not repulsed her, though. He was too kind for that.

She began to raise her hand, to wave a greeting, but quickly perceived how such a gesture would be interpreted. People already thought she was setting her cap at him. Even such an innocent gesture as waving to him would give them more fodder for gossip. Besides, he had not come down here today to see her. He would want to check for himself, considering all the trouble he had gone to, whether the children were enjoying themselves.

Sucking in a sharp, painful breath, she deliberately turned her back on him, gripped Junia's hand a little more tightly, and pushed herself and her charge in the opposite direction.

Lord Bridgemere felt as though she had slapped him all over again. Last night he had assumed it had been Swaledale she had wanted to strike, that *he* had been the one who had made her so angry.

But now he was not so sure.

The reproachful look on her face before she had deliberately turned her back on him had made him wonder if she could possibly have discerned the effect she'd had on him last night. But, hell, what man could hold a woman like her in his arms and *not* become aroused? She was so warm, so soft, and so very much alive! And as he had held her it had been as though her life force had flowed into him, making him feel, making him want…

If she had not run upstairs like a frightened little girl she would have discovered he could behave every bit as badly as Swaledale. And there would have been nobody to stop him.

Who would dare? They courted him, fawned over him, said *yes, My Lord*, and *no, My Lord* until he could barely stomach the sight of them. All except this proud, vibrant girl, who had barely stopped challenging him from the moment she had set foot in his house. Effortlessly breaching the walls he had built up so painstakingly. Dull but safe bulwarks comprised of duty, cemented together by plentiful application of steady routine. She made him act upon impulse. Brought him back to life…

But with life came pain. He felt it now, in the wake of her reproachful rejection. Almost as badly as he had felt it last night when she had slapped him.

His face twisting in self-disdain, he turned his horse away from the clearing and cantered away into the woods.

Chapter Eight

Upon her return to the house, Helen went straight upstairs to change out of her outdoor clothes.

She was still feeling somewhat disturbed after that fleeting glimpse of Lord Bridgemere. As soon as he had ridden away her pleasure in the morning's activity had dimmed. She had so wished he might have come and joined them. If not for her sake, then for his own. He ought to have been able to take part in the fun everyone else was having. Instead, he had kept his distance.

Dispensing largesse to others whilst staying aloof from them was what he did best. She sighed sadly. Each night, for instance, he provided wonderful food and plenty of drink. Yet he ate but sparingly, and remained sober when the other gentlemen drank to excess. She shuddered as she remembered Swaledale's beastly behaviour. And perceived that Lord Bridgemere would detest being as out of control as that youth.

She wished he were not always quite so serious, though. For a man so young, he carried a great weight of responsibility on his shoulders. She wondered how often he was truly free from care. She wished she might see him smiling more often. Laughing at life's simple pleasures.

But his life was not simple. A great many people depended upon him. And, particularly at this time of year, he had to make a great many decisions about their welfare.

She found herself yawning as she went along the corridor that led to the rooms she shared with Aunt Bella. Heavens, but she was tired! She had barely slept since coming here. And each day had been filled with such emotional turmoil she was quite wrung out with it all. She would be glad when it was time to leave and take up her new post. Being around the insular Lord Bridgemere was too emotionally exhausting.

Yet another shock awaited her when she opened her door. For Aunt Bella was sitting on the chair before the fire, sobbing helplessly into her handkerchief.

A shaft of cold dread struck her in the midriff. For it had been her aunt's turn, this morning, to visit Lord Bridgemere in his study and plead her case.

'Oh, Aunt Bella, whatever is the matter?' she cried, darting across the room and falling to her knees at her aunt's feet. 'What did he say to you to make you weep like this? What is to become of you? Oh, I cannot believe he could be so cruel!'

She could not help thinking of how coldly he had looked at her after she had slapped his face last night. But, surely...? He had vowed he was not the kind of man to take a petty revenge on a third party! Yet her aunt was weeping as though her heart had broken, when she never cried. She had not even cried when their landlord had threatened to evict them from the home that was so dear to her. No, she had just metaphorically rolled up her sleeves and sought a solution for them both.

'C…cruel?' her aunt sniffed, dabbing at her eyes. 'Oh, he has not been cruel at all. So kind. So very kind…' She attempted a wavering smile, but then burst into tears again.

'But you are crying…'

Aunt Bella balled her soggy handkerchief and took a deep breath.

'I have maligned that boy,' she sobbed. 'He was not a b…bit censorious of the way I chose to live all those years, nor did he make me feel inc…competent when I told him what had happened to the b…bank. No snide comments about females not being fit to manage m…money matters and how it would have been better to have been guided by my b…brothers even if I did choose not to marry.'

She drew in a shuddering breath. 'He…he said that this k…kind of thing happens all the time, which is why more experienced men of business n…never put all their eggs in one basket. He laid the blame squarely on my man of business, Ritson, for not spreading my capital amongst a diverse range of enterprises. I told him about the time I wanted to invest in the canal company,' she said, her tears ceasing to flow as the light of indignation came to her eyes, 'and that little manufactory that wanted capital to make modernisations, and how Ritson talked me out of it as being too risky. Risky!' She squeezed her handkerchief so hard Helen knew she was imagining fastening those fingers round

Mr Ritson's neck. 'Lord Bridgemere told me that had I had my way on just those two ventures I would now be as well off as I had ever been!'

Helen settled back on her heels, drawing off her gloves with profound relief. Her aunt was drying her eyes, though she had known that she was much more her old self when she had mimed wringing Mr Ritson's neck. Helen could not help admitting to herself that a great deal of her relief stemmed from knowing her faith in Lord Bridgemere had not been misplaced. For a moment, when she had feared he might have refused to help her aunt in her hour of need, it had felt as though her whole world had turned upside down.

'I had been so afraid, Helen, that he would insist my brother resume his responsibilities towards me, even though we have been at daggers drawn all these years. After all, he must be in some kind of trouble himself, or he would not be here, would he? And I thought the price Lord Bridgemere would make him pay for bailing him out would be taking me under his wing again.' She shuddered eloquently.

'Thank heaven it was no such thing. To begin with, His Lordship has offered to look into my finances for me, and see if anything may be salvaged,' she said, dabbing at her nose. 'And if I am really as poor as I fear, he will make arrangements for me to find a new home in which I may be happy. What do you think of that?'

'That,' said Helen, untying the strings of her bonnet, 'it is most thoughtful of him…'

A wave of tenderness towards him swept over her. How tactfully he had dealt with what could have been a most

painful interview for her aunt. Aunt Bella was a proud, independent woman. It had not been the poverty so much
as the prospect of having to beg for help that had been
making her ill.

'He *is* thoughtful, Helen.' Aunt Bella frowned. 'You
know, I had gained the impression that he had grown
hard and unapproachable in recent years. But perhaps it
was just my reluctance to have to approach anyone for help
after I had fought so hard to maintain my independence
from my overbearing brothers which coloured the way I
regarded him.'

In short, she had resented having to humble herself. And
therefore resented *him*.

And she, Helen, had absorbed those same views. Her
aunt's bitterness had made her suspicious when she need not
have been, and angry with him without cause. He had never
been intentionally unkind. It had not been his fault that her
aunt had worked herself up into a state about casting herself
on his mercy. It had not been his fault that she had ended
up in that little tower room untended, either. She recalled
his chagrin upon discovering the mistake which had resulted
in his elderly relative lying up there unattended for hours.

She really had behaved dreadfully, Helen reflected, yet
another wave of self-disgust churning through her. She remembered the coldness of his eyes after she had slapped him,
now piercing her deeply in such rebuke that it was all she
could do to keep her chin up.

The only fault she could find with him now was that he
tended to be rather aloof.

She groaned inwardly. But if she had a family like his would not she, too, take care to steer clear of them from one year's end to the next?

'Oh,' said Aunt Bella, leaning back and shutting her eyes. 'It feels as though an enormous weight has rolled off my shoulders.'

'I am so pleased for you, Aunt Bella,' she said. But a wave of sorrow swept through her. Everyone was here because they wanted something from him. But where did he turn when *he* needed help? She shook her head at the ridiculous notion. A man like him would never need help from anyone. Least of all her.

'Before I forget,' said Aunt Bella, sitting up and opening her eyes, 'I should tell you that a letter has arrived for you.' She pointed to the console table just inside the door. 'I put it over there.'

Getting to her feet, Helen went and picked up the single sheet of paper, and broke open the wafer.

'It is from the Harcourts,' she said, quickly checking the signature. 'They want me to go to them straight away. Some domestic crisis.' She frowned at the few lines scrawled upon the page, which explained very little.

'Oh, Helen, I shall be so sorry to see you go.'

'I shall be sorry to have to leave,' Helen admitted. It was ironic that only a few minutes since she had been wishing she could leave Alvanley Hall, and the agonising pain of becoming increasingly infatuated with a man so very far out of her league. Yet now the Harcourts had summoned her the prospect that this was it, she must bid him farewell and never see him again, felt perfectly dreadful. As though a huge dark cloud was hovering above her.

Helen smiled bravely. 'At least I shall not be worrying about your future, now that Lord Bridgemere has turned out to be so very kind.'

She crumpled the letter in her hand.

'I am just going to take off my coat, Aunt Bella,' she said, darting into her own room to conceal the fact that there were tears in her eyes. 'And then I will see about getting you some luncheon.' She removed her bonnet, hastily dabbing at her eyes with the ribbons. 'This afternoon,' she called, 'I have promised to help Reverend Mullen again, with the theatricals for the children.'

'That is fine by me, dear,' she heard her aunt reply from the other room. 'I shall have forty winks and then go down and join Lady Norton in a hand or two of piquet.'

Helen scrabbled in her coat pocket for a handkerchief and blew her nose. There. She was fine again. Fixing a smile on her face, she returned to the main room.

'I should not be a bit surprised,' her aunt said, 'if His Lordship does not try to see if he can somehow kill two birds with one stone by housing me with her.'

'Do you really think so?'

'Lady Norton,' her aunt said, lowering her voice and leaning towards her niece, 'has such a passion for gambling that even here her husband watches her like a hawk. We play for ivory counters, from some old gaming boxes we found, because he has forbidden her ever to play for money again. And she seems quite scared of disobeying him. His Lordship may well agree to pay off her debts, if that is what they are asking for, in return for taking me in. Though of course that is only conjecture.'

'Would you like to go and live in such a household?'

'Do *you* really want to go and work as a governess for strangers?' Aunt Bella fired straight back at her. 'What we both want,' she said, her lower lip quivering, 'is to be able to go back to the way things were in Middleton. Living simply and quietly, dependent upon nobody, and able to please ourselves. But if you can go out to work for a living,' she said, lifting her chin, 'without uttering one word of reproach to me or anyone else, I can certainly go and act as companion to a woman who is in need of a steadying influence in her life. Not only against her addiction to gambling, but also as a shield against that overbearing husband of hers. And if that *is* the solution His Lordship finds for me, I shall certainly consider it quite seriously. I always liked Sally. After all these years, it is amazing to find that I still do.

'But in any case, I have no need to rush into a decision. Although His Lordship will not be remaining here long after Twelfth Night he has said I may as well stay on, since there are umpteen empty rooms and a small kernel of servants who keep the place up.' A determined look came over her. 'Though you may be sure that if I do stay on here I shall find some way to make myself useful. I dislike the thought of being a charity case.'

Helen was quite sure that Lord Bridgemere would make sure Aunt Bella never felt that way. She sighed. There was really no need for her to stay at Alvanley Hall any longer now that her aunt's future was assured. There was no excuse she could give to put off answering her employer's summons.

'I had better write to the Harcourts straight away and tell them I shall make my way there as soon as is practicable.'

'I wish you need not go,' said Aunt Bella, twisting her handkerchief between her fingers. 'I am quite sure that His Lordship would make some provision for you, too, if you were not too proud to ask him.' She held up her hand as Helen opened her mouth to make her objections known. 'No, you do not need to say it. You have no claim upon him. I know how hard it would be for you to accept his help, since I have found it so difficult to come here myself, and it is his *duty* to look after me. But this one thing I will say. It would be foolish of you not to ask his help with the travel arrangements. You have already partaken of his hospitality, and this would only be an extension of that.'

Helen thought he would probably be so relieved to know she was leaving he would be tempted to load her into the coach himself. He would think it well worth a little inconvenience if it meant ridding himself of a woman he regarded as a conniving hussy who prowled round the house in her nightwear, hoping to lure him into her clutches.

'Do you know?' Aunt Bella continued. 'He said that if we had written to confide the difficulties we were experiencing he would have sent his own coach to fetch us here. He said he was mortified to think of the struggles we had endured, the deleterious effect the rigours of our journey had on my health. Imagine that.'

Helen sighed. She could imagine it all too well. Lord Bridgemere was, beneath that forbidding exterior, a good man. A decent man.

'Then I will ask him if he would be so kind as to make the travel arrangements for me.'

It would probably be best if she went to Mr Cadwallader and asked him to arrange an appointment. She did not want to have to suffer the indignity of approaching Lord Bridgemere in the blue saloon before dinner tonight, with all those beady eyes on her. All those ears straining to overhear what was her business alone. Besides, she knew only too well that it was completely beyond her capabilities to conceal the effect he had on her. And there was nothing more pathetic than females who made fools of themselves over men who were just not interested.

He would probably not have time to schedule such an appointment before tomorrow. Christmas Eve. She frowned. The day would be packed with so many activities, he might well be too busy to fit her in at all. And had he not said that he only granted each of his guests just one appointment, anyway? And then it would be Christmas Day, and of course he would not make his coachman set out on such a long journey—not on a day which ought to be a holiday for all.

It would be Boxing Day at the earliest before she could leave. And she would probably have to ask Cadwallader to arrange everything without speaking to Lord Bridgemere himself.

But she rather thought that seeing their new governess draw up outside their house in a coach with a crest on the door might compensate the Harcourts for her not arriving sooner.

Two more days. That was all she had left.

And then the rest of her life to recover from the impact the handsome, self-contained Earl had had upon her heart.

It was a relief to return to the noisy chaos of the schoolroom. Since the children's costumes had all been agreed upon, and suitable materials found, her task that afternoon was to make them up. Lord Bridgemere, she discovered when she went to sit at the large table by the window, had also hired a couple of girls from the village to help out with the sewing.

They were inclined to be on their best behaviour, until Helen explained, 'I have only come here as companion to my aunt. She is the one who really has the right to be here. Once Christmas is over I will be going off to work as a governess.'

After that they began to chat more freely with her as they sat tacking together swathes of velvet, calico and silk for angels, shepherds and kings.

From them, she learned that all the villagers were really looking forward to the ball Lord Bridgemere always arranged for them on Boxing Day.

'Puts on a right good do,' said the plumper of the two, whose name was Maisie. 'And not just for the gentry staying at the house. But for all of us ordinary folk, too.'

'Speak of the devil,' said her thinner companion, jabbing her in the side with her elbow.

Helen looked up to see that the door to the attic room was open and Lord Bridgemere was leaning against the frame, his arms folded, watching over the activity with what looked to her like satisfaction.

Reverend Mullen suddenly noticed him, too. He clapped his hands and said, 'Children, children! Make your bows to His Lordship, who has most generously spared us a few minutes out of his busy day to come and visit us!'

Was it her imagination, or did some of Lord Bridgemere's satisfaction dim?

If it did, it was only for a second, because as the children all stopped what they were doing and turned towards him he produced a smile and said, 'Well, I happen to know that Cook is sending up a tray of her ginger snaps, so how could I stay away?'

At that very moment two maids came into the room, bearing trays of drinks and biscuits which they carried to a table at one end of the room. The children, to Helen's amusement, promptly forgot their company manners to swarm round the refreshments table.

Far from looking offended, Lord Bridgemere was smiling again.

His smile dimmed as he turned towards the table where Helen was working. By the time he reached them his face showed no emotion whatsoever.

'I did not intend the refreshments for the children alone,' he said. 'I do hope you ladies will take a break from your work to sample some of Cook's baking.'

'Why thank you, Your Lordship,' said Maisie, getting up and dropping a clumsy curtsey, her face pink with pleasure. Her friend, too, looked similarly flustered at having Lord Bridgemere address them directly.

It seemed Helen was not the only female upon whom he

had such a disturbing effect. Her heart sank as she saw that he had been as impervious to her blushes and sighs as he was to those of these village girls. In his mind he probably consigned her along with them as foolish females who were well beneath his notice! Head lowered, she followed her two companions to the refreshments table.

'Did you enjoy the ice this morning, children?' he asked, when they were all seated with their beakers of milk.

There was a rousing chorus of yeses and thank-yous through milk-moustached smiles.

'Do not forget,' he said solemnly, 'that tomorrow, Christmas Eve, I am relying on you to gather enough greenery to decorate the Great Hall. I need holly and ivy, and mistletoe if you can find it. I think there may be one or two boughs in the apple orchard…'

He frowned, as though uncertain, when Helen was sure he knew exactly where it was to be found. He was deliberately turning the ritual of bringing greenery in for Christmas Eve into a kind of treasure hunt for the children.

The boy who was playing the part of Gabriel, the younger Swaledale, was wriggling where he sat. 'We'll find some for you, sir!' he said earnestly.

'Why, thank you, Charles,' Lord Bridgemere replied, bringing a flush of pleasure to the lad's thin cheeks.

'I know that some of your older brothers and sisters may stir themselves, and there will be a few servants free, but without your help…' He shook his head in mock solemnity.

'We'll do it!' several of them shouted.

Helen couldn't help smiling. It would be servants and

perhaps some of the ladies who fashioned the gathered greenery into garlands and wreaths. But after the way he had just spoken the children would feel a real sense of achievement. When Christmas morning came, and they saw the house festooned with the greenery they had helped gather, they would really feel a part of the Christmas celebrations.

No wonder those who had visited before had such fond memories of Christmas at Alvanley Hall.

'Thank you,' he said solemnly. Then, 'Now, make sure you wear suitable clothing. Holly is very prickly. I do not want anyone to forget their gloves. Reverend Mullen, could you perhaps find a few spare pairs of gloves, in case anyone forgets to bring their own?'

Helen could have kissed him. None of the children would want to be left out of the adventure from lack of proper clothing. Yet a few of them, as she had discovered during that morning's outing, simply did not have any. Peter, the little boy who was to play the part of Joseph, for instance, had come back from the skating party with the joints of his fingers horribly distended by angry looking chilblains. If she was being charitable, she would hazard a guess that his parents, Lord and Lady Norton, had so many worries of their own that outfitting their only son for winter had slipped their minds. Except that every time she saw Lady Norton she acted as though she had not a care in the world. It was her husband who went about looking burdened with woes.

She shook her head, her lips pursed. Peter's mother, she feared, did not care about her son, and even if his father did he was such a bellicose kind of man that in all likelihood nobody would dare approach him and remind him of any oversight he might have committed.

Still, once his son left Alvanley Hall Helen had no doubt that he would have been discreetly supplied with enough warm clothes to see him through the rest of the winter. She was convinced that nobody would demand any child return their 'borrowed' gloves.

Lord Bridgemere had such a tactful way of providing for those in need without making them feel like paupers.

She sighed.

It was at that moment, while she was sighing adoringly at his back, that he turned round abruptly and looked straight at her.

Her cheeks flamed guiltily. She swiftly lowered her head and stared fixedly into her half-empty beaker, but she was all too aware of him stalking towards her.

Oh, heavens. After all the lectures she had already given herself about the inappropriate nature of the way she looked at him, he had caught her doing it again!

'Miss Forrest? May I have a private word with you?'

He motioned with his arm to indicate his wish that they step outside.

Her heart sank. She could feel another stinging rebuke coming her way. Yet she placed her beaker on the tray and followed Lord Bridgemere across the room to the doorway. He held the door open as she passed him, then stepped out into the passage, leaving it open behind them. Nobody would be able to hear what they were saying, but since they were in full view of Reverend Mullen, the children, their nurses and various household staff, there would be no possibility of anyone accusing either of them of the least hint of impropriety.

'I spoke with your aunt this morning,' he began, surprising her into raising her head and looking at him properly for the first time since he had caught her making sheep's eyes at him.

He did not look annoyed. More…troubled.

'Her case was far more desperate than I had been led to believe.' He frowned. 'She ought to have written to me straight away,' he said, running the flat of one hand over the crown of his head.

'Oh. Well, perhaps… Only we did not know where you might be found…'

'Nonsense!' He turned and paced away from her, and then back, as though he was seriously agitated. 'A letter addressed to me and sent here would have made its way to me easily enough. I always keep my steward apprised of my movements in case he needs to contact me urgently.'

He was pacing back and forth now, a frown pleating his brow.

'He always forwards any mail. It is unthinkable that she has lost her home because she left approaching me this late. Had she applied to me at once I might have been able to do something to prevent her losing her independence. That she thought me so lacking in proper feeling that she regarded me as a last resort…'

Helen laid a hand upon his sleeve as he passed, arresting his movement. 'Please, do not upset yourself. It is not your fault that she resisted applying for charity.'

'I cannot help blaming myself, though,' he said irritably.

'I have gained something of a reputation over the past few years for being unapproachable. Particularly to my own family. I have sent several of them away with a flea in their ear when I thought they were trying to sponge off me. More than once. But you must believe me, Miss Forrest,' he said earnestly, laying his hand over her own, 'I would never permit anyone for whom I am responsible to suffer unnecessary hardship. Not real hardship.'

'I know that.' She turned her hand over and squeezed his, reassuringly. 'I know.'

She was not sure why he was so determined to convince her that he was not an ogre. When, from what he had just told her, he appeared to have deliberately fostered that image. But it made her feel so happy to think he did not want *her* to think badly of him that she smiled.

'And I want to thank you for the very tactful way you handled the situation. My aunt has been so proud of maintaining her independence from her brothers that the act of asking you for aid now might well have broken her. But she is easy in her mind now, for the first time in months. Because of you.'

'Rubbish!' He stepped back smartly, releasing her hand as though it had stung him. 'I only did what any decent man would do.'

Helen let her own hand fall to her side, humiliatingly aware that she had overstepped the bounds of propriety with him yet again.

'Oh, no,' she insisted, with a shake of her head. 'Some men would have casually crushed her with their condescension. You listened to her. Really listened to what she needed and made it available.'

But he did not look any less troubled.

'It occurred to me, as your aunt was telling me about her plight, that when she lost her fortune you lost your inheritance too. That is why you told me you are now penniless, even though everyone else believes you are an heiress.'

'Well, yes,' she admitted hesitantly. 'Though I do not see that it is any concern of yours.'

'Do you not? Do you not think any man would be concerned to see a young woman, brought up in affluence, suddenly obliged to go out to work for a living?'

It warmed her heart to see him so concerned on her behalf. Though there was nothing he could do for her—not really.

'Miss Forrest,' he said, 'you have no family to speak of. Nobody to whom you can apply for aid. Would it make a difference to your future plans if I were to make it known that I am willing to provide you with a dowry?'

'Wh…what?' Helen could not believe her ears.

'You ought to marry,' he said. 'I know you say you do not want to, but I cannot believe you are completely sincere. It is the main ambition of all my female relatives. And of all the ladies of my acquaintance you are the one I could actually see making some man a comfortable sort of wife. You are unselfish. You unfailingly put the welfare of others before your own.'

She went up to bed early with her aunt, missing out on the entertainments the other ladies enjoyed. He had found her sitting, uncomplaining, mending her meagre supply of clothes whilst her aunt was playing cards with another of the matrons. And as for the effect she was having on the children! He had seen little Junia blossom under her kind ministrations, and even the younger Swaledale boy casting off his habitually sulky attitude.

'I have never seen a woman bear misfortune with such fortitude,' he continued. 'You do not pout, or whine that life is unfair. You just take it all on the chin, with that rueful little smile of yours.'

He reached out with one forefinger, running it over her chin, before abruptly snatching it back and saying gruffly, 'You deserve to find happiness. Not to be shut away in some schoolroom for the rest of your life.'

He blinked then, as though he could not believe what he had just done.

And, as for Helen, she could not believe what he had just *said*! He admired her so much that he would insult her by offering her money so that she could go out and marry someone else! She could feel her heart pounding hard in her chest. He thought she would make *some man a comfortable sort of wife*, did he? She clenched her fists.

'How can you still keep on trying to ram your charity down my throat when I have made it quite plain I shall never accept anything from you? Besides, a dowry is the very last thing I need! I shall *never* marry,' she said furiously, as much to herself as to him.

She had learned a lot about herself during the days she had been at Alvanley Hall, and honesty compelled her to admit that the only reason she had never thought much about marriage was because she had never met a man like Lord Bridgemere before! No other man had ever had a strong enough pull to tempt her to break faith with Aunt Bella, who was so very opposed to the institution.

'I could not possibly marry *some man* just so that I might have somebody to keep me in suffocating indolence,' she spat. 'I could have been married by now, you know, without a dowry. There were men in Middleton who were quite keen,' she declared defiantly. *He* might not find her attractive, but others had.

'Even after we lost all our money, if I had given certain gentlemen a little encouragement, they would have been only too happy to take me into their homes and smother me with their generosity.' She laughed bitterly. 'But I was too proud, I suppose *you* would say, to sell myself to some tradesman with greasy skin and hairy knuckles.' She shuddered.

And then, of their own volition, her eyes strayed to his hands. His nails were neatly manicured, his fingers long and lean. She knew there was strength in those hands. He had held her by the shoulders, shaken her in anger.

Held her to his heart and briefly made her feel as though there was nowhere on earth she would rather be…

She tore her eyes from their greedy perusal of his hands, forcing herself to look him in the face even though she feared he would be able to see exactly what was in her heart. What did it matter now? He clearly felt nothing for her beyond a mild sort of admiration of her character. Else he would not have just offered her a dowry so she could go out and find some other man to marry.

'In short, sir, the only reason I would ever marry would be for love. I have absorbed my aunt's belief in independence too much to even consider marrying some man so that he might support me. I would rather provide for myself.'

She flushed and hung her head. She could not maintain eye contact with Lord Bridgemere whilst speaking of love. She was more than halfway to that state with him, she thought, and it felt unbearably humiliating to know he did not return her feelings.

'I see.' His voice sounded particularly hard. 'Then there is no more to be said.'

Why did she always have to fling his offers of help back in his face with such vehemence? It made no difference that she was correct—that it would be improper of her to accept money or indeed any substantial gift from a man who was not related to her. He wanted to help her, dammit! He could tear his hair out with frustration at knowing there was nothing he could do for the most deserving case he had encountered this year. What was the point of having so much wealth if he could not use it to benefit someone he actually *wanted* to help? Not because he felt it was his duty, but because…well, because he just wanted to!

And all she could do was stand there, her eyes flashing angrily, telling him she did not need him at all. She could manage quite well on her own, thank you very much!

He had turned and walked halfway down the corridor before Helen remembered she still had to ask him about transport to her new home.

'Wait!' she cried.

He turned, reluctantly, and looked back at her with barely concealed impatience.

'I *do* need to speak with you,' she said. 'I have something to ask of you.'

'What? You?' He laughed mockingly. 'The proud, independent woman who wants nothing from any man. Least of all me!'

Her eyes widened in shock and he realised he had been unnecessarily curt with her. He held up his hand and continued on his way.

'Not now, Miss Forrest,' he said, shaking his head. He was not completely in control of his emotions. What he ought to have said was, *yes, Miss Forrest, ask me anything and I shall give it to you.* But she had got him so riled up that he no longer knew what he was saying.

'Oh, but it will not take a minute—'

'I said not now!' he snapped. 'Speak to Cadwallader.' He sighed, running his hand over his head wearily. 'He arranges all my appointments. I will hear your petition,' he said coldly, 'when it is more convenient to me.' When he had regained some vestige of self-control.

Helen frowned at his retreating back, wondering how it was possible to feel so much admiration for a man who was so difficult to understand. Whose moods could change so abruptly.

She sighed and turned back towards the schoolroom.

It hardly mattered anyway. She would be gone from here in just a few more days. And their paths would never cross again. Gradually, without the stimulus of his presence, these turbulent feelings he stirred up would wither away. Until he became nothing more than a distant memory.

The prospect of becoming a governess had never seemed more dreadful.

Chapter Nine

Lord Bridgemere had organised Christmas Eve so that it would be one continuous round of pleasure for his guests.

Helen started her day by clambering into the cart that conveyed the nursery party into a section of the woods where evergreens were predominant. The children were still rushing about excitedly when Lord Bridgemere himself appeared on horseback, followed by a small party comprised of the younger, unmarried ladies and gentlemen, resplendent in highly fashionable riding habits.

Lady Thrapston's daughter Augustine, who looked as though she was not long out of the schoolroom herself, looked rather wistfully at the children playing tag amongst the trees. Then she darted a furtive look at her companions, as though checking to see if anyone had caught her out, and adopted the same air of languid boredom worn by the other members of the riding party.

Making Helen feel sorry for her.

She was just thinking what a shame it was that Lady

Augustine no longer felt free to be herself now that she wasn't a child, when she caught Lord Bridgemere smiling sadly at his niece. And she knew he was thinking exactly the same thing. When he turned slightly, and their eyes met, it was as though they were of completely one mind. Though they were yards apart, she felt as though they were connected intimately by sharing one and the same thought.

She felt quite a wrench when he looked away.

'I need some of you older boys for a special task,' he said, leaning his forearm across the pommel of his saddle. 'Any volunteers?'

Charles and Peter's hands shot up.

He looked them over critically for a few seconds, before nodding solemnly and saying, 'You will follow me to a copse where I have discovered a holly tree with the biggest, reddest berries you have ever seen.'

'I have found something even better,' Swaledale informed the girls in his party, with a suggestive waggle of his eyebrows. 'Mistletoe.'

Helen could not help casting them a withering look as they rode off after him, giggling and blushing. They would not be so keen on gathering mistletoe with him if they knew how disgusting he could be!

Once more she found Lord Bridgemere watching her when she glanced in his direction, only this time, since her mind was on that encounter on the backstairs, she felt her cheeks heat, and it was she who looked away first.

She heard his horse champ at the bit as he tugged on the reins, wheeling the creature round, and once the boys had darted off after him she permitted herself the luxury of watching him riding away into the forest. Charles and Peter were puffed up with pride at being handpicked for a task which was too difficult for the very little ones. They looked adorable as they trotted off behind him. It was such a pity their parents were not here to see this.

But then there was no reason, really, why their parents should not see this if they wanted to. She sighed and went back to the main group of children, who were pointing out likely-looking branches of fir to the bevy of gardeners who were in charge of the pruning hooks. She knew that there were other entertainments designed for those who preferred to remain within doors, but she could not understand why some of them at least had not come to witness this. What could be more enjoyable than watching their children's happy little faces and sharing in their delight at the magic of Christmas time?

The trouble with this house party was that children were either woefully neglected by parents who regarded them as just one more problem they wished they did not have, or, worse, as in the case of Lord Bridgemere's family, moved about like pawns in the complex power struggle that was raging between the various sets of adult siblings.

Every time the adults came together at mealtimes, or in the withdrawing room afterwards, it turned into yet another skirmish. Lady Thrapston, Helen suddenly realised, was fighting a desperate rearguard action in wearing all that jewellery and flaunting her status by lording it over the foot of the dining table. And whenever Nicholas Swaledale walked into a room, or contributed to the conversation, his mother Lady Craddock was able to shoot her sister a look of spiteful triumph. Though she had only married a baron, and not a very wealthy one at that, she *had* managed to produce two sons, whereas Lady Thrapston had only girls. Poor little Junia was the ultimate disappointment to her mother.

It made Helen's blood boil.

Even more determined that these children should have at least some happy memories of their childhood to look back upon, she flung herself into the task of making the gathering of the greenery as much fun for them as she possibly could.

A brace of footmen, who had travelled to the site in a second cart, loaded the fragrant boughs and the long swathes of ivy they'd pointed out, into a farm wagon. Occasionally members of Lord Bridgemere's riding party returned, with the much prized holly and mistletoe, and soon the cart was piled high with a wonderful assortment of glossy green leaves, bright waxy berries and bristling bluey-green fronds.

In what felt like no time at all they were climbing back into the cart for their homeward journey, the children bubbling over with satisfaction at a job well done.

The riding party followed behind the convoy of open carts, but to her surprise Lord Bridgemere drew up alongside the one that contained the children, just as Reverend Mullen produced a tin whistle from his pocket and began to play Christmas carols. Lord Bridgemere sang out in a fine baritone, the servants in the cart that followed joined in, and then so did the children, with as many of the words as they could remember.

It was an episode Helen knew she would remember for the rest of her life, coming home from gathering in the greenery, with Lord Bridgemere riding alongside. His powerful voice rose effortlessly above that of the servants following behind, soaring up through the branches even as it reached into the very depths of her being. It put her in mind of the way she had felt that morning when he had taken her to the frost-spangled clearing. There was something about singing hymns outdoors, in nature's own temple, that was particularly moving, she thought. She had certainly never had tears in her eyes when she had sung any of these carols before.

Surreptitiously, because she felt a little foolish, she dabbed away at her tears with the end of her scarf, lifted her chin, and forced a smile to her lips. She kept it fixed there, resolutely, when they returned to the stableyard. Lord Bridgemere dismounted, while she accepted Reverend Mullen's hand to help her out of the cart.

Lord Bridgemere hustled his own party towards the house, while she kept the children together and herded them towards the back door that led through the servants' hall and thence to the stairs up to the nursery wing. He paused in the doorway, watching the children swarming into the house, before giving her an impenetrable look and following his own party indoors.

When they reached the nursery Helen saw that Lord Bridgemere had arranged yet another treat for the youngsters. Not only were a couple of maids waiting, with jugs of steaming hot chocolate and plates of those delectable ginger snaps, but there were several bowls of chestnuts for them to roast over the schoolroom's open fire.

She put Junia, Peter and Charles in charge of roasting the nuts and handing them out to the younger ones. When she knelt on the hearthrug, a little distance away, to make sure there were no burnt fingers or, heaven forbid, singed clothing, a couple of those still in leading strings escaped from their nurses and came to sit on her lap.

It was not long before the warmth of the fire after their outing, coupled with all that hot chocolate and all those biscuits, made them drowsy. Their nurses returned to take them from her and put them down for a nap, and gradually a contented hush settled over the room, punctuated only by the crackle of the fire or a murmured comment from one of the older children, who were now sprawled on their tummies, imagining, Helen surmised from their rapt expressions, dragons, volcanoes, or firework displays amongst the glowing coals.

She had a feeling that Lord Bridgemere would have enjoyed being up here, witnessing this moment of utter peace and harmony, far more than being in the rather contentious atmosphere that would surely be prevailing downstairs.

As her thoughts inevitably turned to him, the remembrance of their last encounter up here, just outside the nursery door, shattered her whimsical mood. Even though she felt as though she was beginning to understand something of his views, he most certainly did not feel the same burning, physical ache for her that she felt for him. Or he would not have offered her a dowry to marry some other man. The fact that he had immediately thought of a financial solution to her problems showed that he did not really separate her in his mind from any of his other guests. Who were his family, after all.

And she was not even that.

She was up here practising being a governess. Thanks to Lord Bridgemere, she had grown more confident that she would be able to cope within the sphere of her new life. She had grown fond of these children, and fiercely protective of them, in the short time she had become part of their world.

But it was not her world. And Lord Bridgemere's offer to pay her off showed her that she did not have so much as a toehold in it.

There was to be dancing after an early dinner that evening, in honour of the day. She was sure most of the other ladies would spend the entire afternoon beautifying themselves. But—she smiled wryly to herself—*she* would much rather be doing something useful than wasting hours in front of a mirror. She would have quite enjoyed joining the team who would be making the greenery up into garlands and wreaths, and helping Mrs Dent decorate the ballroom. But on the whole she thought she would get most pleasure from just staying up here with the children. They would be rehearsing their play again later, and she wanted to be on hand to put finishing touches to their costumes. And just be there, to support them as they got to grips with their parts. Junia was word-perfect already, but Charles, who was playing Gabriel, was still nervous enough to need all the encouragement he could get.

It took her, just as she had suspected, less than an hour

to wash and change into her best gown, brush her hair and pin it up in the simple style she had perfected when they'd had to dismiss their maid. All she had to do then was fasten her mother's amber beads around her neck, drape her evening shawl over her elbows, and she was as ready as she would ever be.

Which was not all *that* ready, she reflected upon entering the blue saloon. Everywhere she looked there were crisp ringlets, sumptuous satins and glittering jewels, casting her own plain bronze gown and simple string of beads into the shade. Making her even more aware that she did not belong here.

But it struck her, once they had all sat down to dine, that the amount of personal wealth on display had not brought any one of these people happiness. All round the table she could see one discontented face after another. Most of them never seemed to stop grumbling. It was as though whatever they had was never quite enough to satisfy them.

And the battle which raged between Lady Thrapston and her sister Lady Craddock created a maelstrom of tensions. Maintaining neutrality was hard, but since both ladies were influential in their own ways, risking making either of them an enemy by openly befriending the other made it by far the safest course to steer.

And that was quite apart from the rift that existed between Aunt Bella and her brother General Forrest, which had created still more eddies.

After dinner everyone went to the ballroom, which had been opened up and decorated for the occasion. It really looked magnificent, Helen mused. The floor had been polished to a high sheen, and every chandelier and wall sconce was festooned with ivy, while garlands of pine and fir had been draped over picture frames and mantelpieces. The staff must have worked really hard to achieve so much in such a short space of time. Particularly since there was to be a sumptuous supper later, to round off the evening.

The orchestra which had been hired for the event was still tuning up when Helen walked in. After swiftly examining the seating arrangements, she and her aunt went and took seats in a quiet corner, rather than on the front row of chairs which ringed the dance floor. She did not expect anyone would ask her to dance. The other guests either regarded her as one of the serving classes or somebody's love child. Lady Thrapston, she suspected, given the way she studiously looked straight through her as she glided past, thought she ought not to be there at all.

Well, she was not going to stay for very long. Her aunt would probably move into the card room with Lady Norton as soon as they had watched the opening few sets, and when they made their move she would get to her feet too, say she was tired after the exertions of the day, and claim she needed an early night. There was no way she was going to sit here like a wallflower, watching other, more socially acceptable ladies dance!

The first set was drawing to a close, and her aunt and Lady Norton were shifting in their seats, plucking at their shawls and generally getting ready to leave the dancing for the younger ones, when to Helen's surprise Lord Bridgemere threaded his way through the chairs until he came to a halt right in front of her.

'The next dance,' he said without preamble, 'is to be a waltz. Do you know the steps?'

'I...I do,' she stuttered, her heart bouncing around inside her chest at the possibility he might be going to invite her to dance.

For a moment she wondered if he regretted whatever impulse had brought him over, as he just stood there, gazing down at her with a slight frown on his brow. But then he seemed to make up his mind. He held out his hand, and said, somewhat impatiently, 'Come on, then!'

Both her aunt and Lady Norton dropped straight back down into their seats when she rose and followed him onto the dance floor. Though they could hardly be more surprised than she was!

Or anyone else.

She was very conscious of the hush that fell over the assembled guests as they stood in the very centre of the dance floor, waiting for the music to begin. She was convinced that everyone must be watching her with disapproval, though how they thought she had managed to get Lord Bridgemere to invite her to waltz with him was beyond her!

But she was blowed if she was going to let anyone, or anything, spoil this moment. Resolutely lifting her chin, she looked up into his face, willing the rest of the room to the edges of her notice.

A smile pulled at the corner of his mouth as he saw what she was doing.

'That's it, Miss Forrest,' he said, very softly. 'Look at me, not at them.'

And, as if holding her to the challenge, he kept his own

eyes fixed upon hers as the music began and he guided her into a set of basic steps.

She had never danced the waltz whilst looking deep into her partner's eyes before. It was unlike anything she had ever experienced. He filled her consciousness to the exclusion of almost everything else. The music seemed to come from very far away. It was the subtle direction of his hands, the angle of his body, that guided her through the figures of the dance. Once he had ascertained the level of her skill he began to introduce ever more complicated figures, smiling at her every time she rose to the occasion. It was exhilarating to find they were so perfectly matched. Before long she could anticipate his next move, so that she felt as though he was not leading her and she following, but that they were moving as one.

By the time the dance ended there were several other couples on the floor, though she had not noticed them joining in. She had been aware of nothing but the feel of his hand at her waist, the scent of his cologne filling her nostrils, and the steady regard of his eyes, holding her to him with a power that felt stronger than bands of steel.

Lord, she would remember this night, this magical waltz, for the rest of her life! This whole day, in fact, would have a special place in her memory. For he had been at the centre of everything. Even when he had not been in the room with her she had felt his influence holding sway over all her pleasures.

She moved away from him with reluctance when he stood still, removed his hand from her waist, and bowed to her. The music had ended, she realised, and with it the magic.

He turned to lead her back to her seat, breaking the eye contact which had held her in thrall throughout the waltz.

And then he brought her right back down to earth with a bump by saying, 'I have made it a tradition to answer the petitions of my family by means of a note which they receive at the breakfast table on Christmas morning. But in your case, since I do not yet know what you want of me, I have requested that Cadwallader free up a quarter of an hour *after* breakfast tomorrow. I hope that will be convenient?'

Her heart abruptly plunged. The interview would truly mark the end of her time here. While she was helping with the children, or dancing in his arms, she could make herself forget for just a few moments that she did not truly belong here. That their time together was only temporary.

'Of course,' she replied, dropping like a stone onto her chair.

'Until tomorrow, then,' he said, and strolled away without a backward look.

Her aunt laid a hand on her sleeve and whispered, 'Well, that was a surprise. You should have seen the look on Lady Thrapston's face! The only person who looked more affronted was Lady Craddock!'

'You have set the cat among the pigeons, Miss Forrest,' said Lady Norton with glee from behind her fluttering fan.

Her suggestive smile made Helen feel horribly exposed. Did everyone here know she was completely infatuated with a man beyond her reach? What a fool she must look!

'Oh, no, I am sure it was just a duty dance,' Helen replied hastily. 'He is the sort of man who would take pity on any unattached female who is not likely to have many partners. Even one who is destined to become a governess.'

'Oh,' said her aunt, her puzzled expression clearing. 'Yes, I expect that must be it. In which case, since you will not be needing me to act as chaperon—' she cast a quelling look at Lady Norton '—I shall be off to the card room. Will you come too?'

'No, thank you,' Helen said, drawing on the ready-made excuse she had prepared. 'I was up very early this morning...'

It was more important than ever that she escape to her room. Waltzing with Lord Bridgemere had been delightful, but it must only have confirmed to the onlookers what they had already suspected.

She could not face anyone now! She wanted to slip away and go over every second of that dance—commit it all to memory, so that she could take it out and re-examine it at her leisure in years to come.

She gave her aunt a swift peck on the cheek, and quietly slipped away to the exit.

But Lady Thrapston had somehow managed to guess what she meant to do. When Helen left the ballroom, she was waiting for her in the corridor.

Laying her fan on Helen's forearm, she said, 'I warned you about making up to my brother. But I can see you have not paid any heed. Every person watching that dance must have seen that you have so far forgotten your station you have fallen headlong in love with him!'

'Unfortunately, my lady,' Helen said sadly, 'my heart does not seem to have heeded the warning either you or I have tried to give it.' She knew her case was hopeless. He could not feel much for her if he was prepared to pay some other man to marry her—which was what his offer of a dowry amounted to.

'Then I pity you,' said Lady Thrapston coldly. 'For he will break it.'

'Oh,' said Helen with a wry smile, 'you do not need to tell me that he is impervious to me as a woman…'

'Far from it,' said Lady Thrapston, with a shake of her head. 'If I thought that, I would not have taken the trouble to try and warn you. It is my belief that he is, in his own way, quite taken with you. He has singled you out for the sort of attention he has not granted another woman for years.'

Had he? Helen's heart, which had been so heavy ever since he had told her she ought to marry *some other man* promptly soared. And with it her self-esteem. She had *not* misinterpreted the heat she had sometimes thought she saw in his eyes. Especially just now, on the dance floor.

'And if you continue to encourage him, you might even persuade him into indulging in an affair. I dare say,' Lady Thrapston said with a contemptuous sniff, 'he is ripe for one!'

Helen's hopes plunged back down to earth. An affair. That was all a girl like her was good for. She had suspected the same thing herself at one point, before she had begun to think he did not reciprocate the physical attraction she felt for him at all.

'But I do not think you are the kind of girl who would survive such an encounter. So I urge you to beware. For you will not succeed in dragging a proposal from him, no matter what you do!'

No, a man who had any honourable intentions towards a woman could not possibly offer to sell her on to another man.

Lady Thrapston went on. 'Believe me, there is nothing I would like more than to see him married again and setting up his nursery. And to that end I have introduced a succession of gels to him who are far prettier and much more suitable than you—without success. Of late I have come to the sorry conclusion that his heart is buried in the grave with Lucinda.'

'L…Lucinda? Who is…was she?'

'His wife.'

The words sank into her brain like a stone dropped into a pond, sending ripples of shock vibrating through her. He had been married? And widowed? Why had her aunt never mentioned this?

'When she died,' Lady Thrapston continued mercilessly, 'he was so heartbroken that he shut himself away from the world, and even now, all these years later, he can hardly bear to live without her. I have watched him year upon year, and I have to tell you that even when he forces himself to come out of his self-imposed seclusion in honour of this season he can hardly bear the celebrations without her.'

Now his behaviour made so much sense! She had wondered how he had got the reputation of being a surly recluse, but she could see it all now. He was a broken-hearted widower, who had only slowly and painfully pieced his life back together after the love of his life had died.

And as for Lady Thrapston's attempts to get him to remarry! Well! She had probably been thrusting marital prospects under his nose with total insensitivity to his pain well before he was ready to take such a step. And not out of concern for him, either! No, it would all have been part of her ongoing battle with Lady Craddock. All Lady Thrapston was keen for him to do was—how had she put it?—set up his own nursery. So that Lady Craddock's son would be cut out of the succession.

But if he really was attracted to her, as Lady Thrapston seemed to think... A sharp pain seared through her. She could understand now why at times he seemed to enjoy her company and then abruptly withdrew into stony hostility. Any tender feelings he might have would seem like a betrayal of his first love! He would resent them. He would resent *her* for making him feel them.

'Thank you for telling me this, My Lady,' said Helen jerkily, dropping an abrupt curtsey. 'Unfortunately for me,' she said with a grimace, 'it comes a little late. Oh, do not worry—I have no intention of becoming his mistress. I have too much pride to allow *any* man to use me in such a fashion! I have honest work to go to. In fact I shall be leaving to take up my job in just a few days. I am sure,' she said bitterly, 'that once I have gone he will forget all about me.'

'But you will not forget him, will you?' Lady Thrapston's face softened into an expression of pity.

'No,' replied Helen. 'Never.'

That night she cried herself to sleep. The more she learned about Lord Bridgemere, the more he tugged at her heart. And the further out of her reach he receded. She might have tempted him out of his customary isolation into a solitary walk, and a waltz which had shocked his family, but only the day before he had offered to buy her a husband. He evidently found her attractive, but would rather see her married to some other man than risk furthering their relationship in any way whatever. What more evidence did she need to prove that his heart was buried in the grave with his late wife? Oh, Lord, but there was nothing more painful than unrequited love. She sobbed. She hurt. She physically hurt inside at the knowledge that he did not, could not, return her feelings. That she had no hope.

She woke with a heavy heart on Christmas Day. She was dreading her interview with Lord Bridgemere, when she would ask for his assistance with her travels. When she would bid him farewell for ever. He might feel a little sorry she was leaving, if he *had* begun to feel some slight attraction towards her, but on the whole he would be relieved that the temptation she represented would be permanently removed from his life.

On Christmas morning it was the custom, she had been told, for everyone to gather for breakfast together. In years past she and her aunt had always exchanged gifts at the breakfast table too, so the day before she had given her gifts to Mrs Dent to place at the correct table setting.

When she reached the dining room she saw that there was a small packet beside each place setting. She felt a little perplexed as she sat down. Lord Bridgemere had told her that he gave everyone a note informing them of his decision regarding whatever petition they had made. But not that he enclosed with it a small gift.

Beside her, Aunt Bella suddenly burst out laughing. She

had opened the present Helen had given her, which was a quarter of peppermint drops twisted into the set of handkerchiefs Helen had embroidered for her.

Helen was a little put out. They had agreed that they would only give each other small token gifts this year, considering the state of their finances. She had known peppermint drops were a particular favourite of her aunt's and had thought the gift would please her. Not make her laugh out loud!

Aunt Bella prodded her in the side between whoops of laughter.

'Open yours, open yours!' she chortled.

The moment Helen complied she saw the joke. Aunt Bella had made her a reticule and stuffed it to the brim with those self-same sweets.

They were both giggling like a pair of giddy schoolgirls when Lord Bridgemere came to the table.

He gazed coldly round at the occupants of the table, instantly sobering Helen and her aunt, then took his seat and flicked open his napkin. The butler hastened to his side and poured coffee, whilst everyone else, as though at some hidden signal, began to open the present that lay beside their plate.

Everyone had received something from Lord Bridgemere. Even her. And, while it had been impossible to accept any gift from him on any other day, it was not as though he was singling her out today. She reached for her parcel with trembling fingers.

Inside was a beautiful silk damask shawl. One side had a rose ground and the other gold, so that it could be worn either way to go with different outfits. She felt quite touched by the thoughtfulness of the gift, since one of the shawls she had brought with her had been ruined by a combination of her encounter with Esau in the garden, when it had been trampled into the mud, and Swaledale on the staircase, when his candle had singed it. But her pleasure in Lord Bridgemere's gift dimmed somewhat when she looked up and saw that every other female at table was also in receipt of such a shawl. Just as the men had all received cufflinks along with their promissory note.

At that moment Lady Augustine gave a cry of delight as she unfolded the note which had fallen out of her shawl. Her mother, Lady Thrapston, swiftly quelled her outburst with a withering look, which reduced her to stammering her thanks to Lord Bridgemere with red cheeks. But it was too late. The damage was done. Several of the other guests were looking at her with envy, and when they also thanked Lord Bridgemere for whatever it was he had given them it was stiffly, as though they felt disgruntled.

Apart from Lord Norton, who looked downright relieved.

Then Aunt Bella, as if impervious to the atmosphere of jealousy and resentment that was brewing, beamed at Lord Bridgemere and said, 'Are you not going to open *your* present now?'

Though conversation up to that point had been stilted, Aunt Bella's comment had the effect of stifling it completely.

Lord Bridgemere looked down at his plate, registering surprise to see the small neatly wrapped packet that Helen had asked Mrs Dent to place there for him. Tentatively he pulled on one of the trailing ends to release the bow that held it all together, and frowned down at the pair of embroidered handkerchiefs within.

'Is this from you?' he asked her aunt.

'Oh, no. From Helen,' she informed him.

Lady Thrapston shot her a scandalised look. 'It is not the done thing, Miss Forrest,' she said. 'Everyone knows that it is not the thing at all.'

'Nevertheless,' he said, as Helen's face flamed with mortification, 'I am touched by Miss Forrest's gesture. She is the only one who thought to give me anything.'

Helen caught General Forrest glaring at her, his cheeks growing ruddy with suppressed fury. She guessed he was among those who had not received all he had hoped for, and by the look on his face, after the way Lord Bridgemere had publicly defended her for committing what was clearly a social *faux pas*, he was inclined to lay the blame on her.

'You always say you have need of nothing!' snapped Lady Thrapston.

'You are correct, as always,' he replied coldly, getting to his feet. 'Miss Forrest? A word in private?'

Oh, yes. The interview. Head lowered, so that she did not have to see the way everyone must be staring at her, she left the table and made for the exit.

'Please—come in and take a seat,' he said, opening the door for her and ushering her into his study.

She walked carefully to the chair he had indicated beside his desk, since her knees were somewhat shaky, and sank onto it as gracefully as her emotional state permitted.

In the few moments it took for him to shut the door, walk round the desk and take his own seat, she drank him in.

She already had a treasure trove of precious memories she could examine in the years ahead. On long, dull evenings she would be able to look back upon their walk through the wintry woodland. Smile at the time his dog had almost knocked her down, scattering his female relatives with his exuberant greeting. Picture him sitting astride his horse, his hound at his side, watching the children sliding around the ice lake he had created just for them. And, best of all, that waltz. Those magical few moments when he had held her in his arms and the rest of the world had ceased to exist.

But this would be the last time she would have a few moments of privacy with him. And she wanted to be able to remember every single second of this, their last encounter, bittersweet though it must inevitably be.

His clothing was understated, as usual. Over the days she had been at Alvanley Hall she had come to see that it was his quiet, self-assured presence that made people take notice of him. He had no need to wear elaborate waistcoats or deck himself with jewels to draw attention to himself. He was confident in who he was and what he was. She had mistaken that very confidence at first for arrogance. Other people, she knew, saw that same demeanour and whispered that he was cold and insular.

But how could he be anything else when he was fulfilling all his duties, caring for the needs of all his dependants, whilst nursing a broken heart?

'I wonder, Miss Forrest,' he said, tossing the offending

handkerchiefs onto his desk, 'how you managed to find the time to embroider these for me. You always *seemed* so busy. If you were not running errands for your aunt, you were helping entertain other people's children. And yet I know you must have stitched these since you came here. You copied the emblems from the heraldic glass in the library windows, did you not?'

'Yes. But it did not take me as long as you might suppose.' She'd had no idea that giving him such a trifling gift would cause such a stir. If she could downplay the time it had taken her to do the embroidery, perhaps he would not make so much of it! 'Though the design looks complicated, it was actually quite simple to prick out the outline and fill it in with satin stitch. As for your initials—why, they are only done in chain stitch, after all, which is mere child's play.'

'I fail to see why you thought it was necessary to give me anything at all,' he said angrily. 'What was your motive? Were you trying to impress me? Is that it? I can assure you there was no need.'

He could not believe how angry it had made him to think that she felt free to give him a gift she had laboured over with her own hands but was always so reluctant to accept anything from *him*!

He was angry, too, at the knowledge that every time he touched these small squares of cloth he would see her, sitting in the library with the sun gilding her hair. Or trying out the skating pond he had fabricated for the children, shriek-ing with laughter as she careened across the ice. Then taking Junia kindly by the hand and reassuring her that there was nothing to fear when he knew she would have had more fun racing with the older boys.

Angry, most of all, at how easily she could touch him. Move him. Make him feel…things he had not felt, not wanted to feel, for years!

And, worse, though he had accused her of trying to impress him—which was what he knew such a gift would signify from any other woman—Miss Forrest saw no need to make the attempt.

He had grown cynical, he realised, over the years. To even think that Miss Forrest would act as so many others had done… Why, he only had to look at her open, honest face, see the affront flashing from her eyes… No, Miss Forrest had not been trying to ingratiate herself with him.

She never would.

By the looks of her, she was about to give him what for even for suggesting it!

Helen took a deep breath. 'I was doing no such thing,' she retorted, sick of everyone attributing the worst interpretation to her behaviour. 'It is common courtesy to give one's host a small gift! And it has always been the custom for my aunt and I to exchange presents upon Christmas Day. I gave *her* handkerchiefs I had embroidered, too. Just as you gave identical gifts to each of your female guests. Honestly,' she huffed, 'I had no notion that extending that custom to you would cause anyone offence!'

He leaned back in his chair, half closing his eyes and taking a deep breath. Being on the receiving end of one of Miss Forrest's tirades was refreshing. Almost like coming upon a hidden spring whilst taking a ride on a hot summer day, and feeling all the dust being washed away by even the briefest of dips into it.

Helen shifted uncomfortably in her chair. He had been regarding her steadily for such a long time that she felt like some kind of exhibit in a museum. She had never been able to understand his abrupt changes of mood. But at least now that Lady Thrapston's revelation had made her face the fact that she had fallen in love with him she knew why it did not make her like him any less. On the contrary, seeing he was in a bad mood just made her wish she could do something to cheer him up. To wipe away that disgruntled expression and see him smile again.

Which was, of course, quite impossible. He did not need her. He did not need anyone. Had he not just said so?

'Are you having some difficulty,' he asked eventually, with a wry smile, 'in making your request known to me now that it comes to the point?'

Oh, yes! Of course! She had almost forgotten the whole point of coming in here. Seeing his mouth hitch at one side into that little smile had put everything right out of her head.

So now she felt like an idiot on top of everything else.

What had he said? Was she finding this difficult? 'Oh, yes.' Because this was it. The beginning of the end.

The end? She mocked herself. Nothing had really started except in her own fevered imagination!

'What I wish to ask for might sound a bit presumptuous,' she began nervously. 'After all, I know I have no claim on your generosity…'

'It never stops anyone else,' he said bitterly.

She got to her feet. The last thing she wanted was for him to regard her in the same light as he did the rest of his troublesome guests, who only came to Alvanley because they wanted something. The only thing she wanted from him was his heart. Though, since it was impossible for him to give her that, she could at least command his respect.

'It does not matter, then. If you are so averse to helping me I shall see to it myself.'

'Sit down!' he barked. 'If you have something you want, just *ask* me, dammit!' Whatever she wanted, if it made her less hostile towards him, he would give it, he realised. Could you buy someone's regard?

Not Miss Forrest's. No, she would toss her hair and, eyes flashing, inform him that she was not to be bought...

But at least she was subsiding onto her chair, twisting her fingers together nervously on her lap. Nervously? Then whatever she wanted to ask him must not be the trivial thing he had assumed was all she would ever bring herself to request of him. He sat forward, every sense on the alert.

Helen had never imagined it would be this hard to ask for his help. She was, she discovered, every bit as proud and prickly as her aunt. Though at least half the trouble was that she simply did not really want to leave.

This experience would be good for her, she decided, lips firming with determination. She would be always having to ask employers for time off, or permission to do one thing or another. Asking him for the loan of one of his carriages would humble her in a way that would make later slights and slurs seem like nothing.

'It was my aunt's idea,' she began. 'She said you would not begrudge me the use of one of your carriages. She seemed to think you would have me taken the entire way, but if you could just arrange for me to reach the nearest staging post I have enough money for my ticket. Or if not it really does not matter. I can quite easily walk. Only there are my trunks...' she mused with a frown.

'What the blazes are you talking about? Take the stage? When?'

'Tomorrow. I—'

'Out of the question!' He slapped his hand palm down on the tabletop. She could not leave! He had known, of course, that once this house party broke up she would be going to work for a family somewhere—but that was at least a week away!

'You have promised to help the children prepare for their nativity play,' he said, a sense of desperation making him grasp at the first excuse he could come up with that was sure to touch her. 'You cannot break your word to a child!'

'I have no choice. My employers have sent a letter demanding I go to them at once.'

'Nonsense! You are staying here as my guest. Nobody leaves until Twelfth Night!' His heart was pounding. He felt slightly sick. Unless he could stop her somehow, tomorrow she would walk out of his life and...

He would never see her again. It was one thing spending time with a guest under his roof. Quite impossible for an earl to go seeking out a lowly employee of some family he did not even know and begging for an hour or two in her company!

If he let her leave tomorrow she would be lost to him.

'Do you dislike it here that much?'

He knew his relatives were insufferable, but she had always seemed so cheerful in spite of it all. Nothing seemed to get her down for long. Yet now she was talking about leaving. As soon as she possibly could.

'Have you not enjoyed your stay here?'

He felt as though someone had punched him. Perhaps it was him, specifically, she wished to get away from? She had slapped him once. And last night he had brought down upon her the censure of the entire assembly by singling her out as the only female he'd danced with all evening. Had he pushed her too far? It had been selfish of him, he knew. But she had looked so enchanting, sitting there tapping her foot in time to the music. He had been sure she wanted to dance. And none of the others would have asked her! Besides, he had wanted the excuse to hold her in his arms without having to wait until she was in floods of tears again.

'It is not that,' she sighed. 'I was supposed to start working for the Harcourts on the fifteenth of December. They let me have a few days' grace when I explained about my aunt and how I needed to see her settled. They said I could have until the New Year, but now that I know you will be looking after my aunt there is no reason for me to delay even that long. Especially not now they have written to say they cannot do without me any longer.'

'Well, nor can I, dammit!'

'What?'

Helen gazed at him in shock, doubting she could have heard him aright. By the look on his face, *he* could hardly believe what he had said, either.

He clenched his hands into fists on the desktop.

'You heard me. I said I don't want you to leave. Miss Forrest, the only thing that is making this house party bearable this year is the thought of running into you as I go about my daily business. Playing with the children. Busily sewing away in my library. Or putting my blasted sister to the rightabout!'

He dragged in a deep breath and got to his feet, pacing away from her to the hearth, then whirling round. 'I know we do not always speak. But that is just it. We do not have to. Everything you think is written on your face.'

He loved watching her. Not just because she was pretty—although she was, exceptionally so. It was because more often than not she was like a visual echo of what he was already thinking. And it soothed him.

'I know exactly what you think of General Forrest's boorish manners,' he continued, 'and his incredible insensitivity to his sister. I know what an overbearing snob you think my sister. I see you wondering how on earth I can stand to have such a complete and utter tick as Nicholas Swaledale as my heir, and for the first time in my life I feel…' He turned and took a few paces, before saying, 'I feel as though I have an ally in the midst of an enemy camp.'

And if she left he would be utterly alone.

'And now you say you intend to desert me! Well, I won't

have it—do you hear?' He marched up to her and stood, hands on hips, glaring down at her. 'I forbid you to leave!'

'You have no right,' she said, tears springing to her eyes.

For one moment he had seemed so agitated at the thought of her leaving that she had almost started to hope he might be going to tell her that he had feelings for her. And then he'd ruined it all by saying he forbade her to go! Giving her a direct order as though she was a member of his staff!

Which was how, she reflected bitterly, he had always thought of her. A useful person to have about, but nowhere near his equal!

She got to her feet, quivering with indignation. 'No right to forbid me from doing anything I want, sir! Just as I have no right to refuse my employer's summons. They have already been more than lenient with me…'

'I will write to them for you, then.' He grabbed her upper arms. 'Tell them I cannot spare you. That they must do without you until the celebrations here are at an end.'

She felt a clutch of panic. 'Oh, please do not do that! I will lose my job, and then what would become of me?'

'Does your job mean so much to you?'

'Of course it does! If I lose this post I must seek another, and it was difficult enough to secure this one…'

Of course. She had no money. And it was unfair of him to ask her to jeopardise her whole future without some concomitant sacrifice from him.

He slid his hands down her arms until they were loosely clasping hers. He looked down at them, head bowed. The only person who would have the right to help Helen whether she wanted him to or not would be her husband. He had never thought he would put his head in that particular noose again…but had he not already told her that he thought she would make some man a comfortable sort of wife?

He looked into her eyes, which were troubled, almost afraid, and felt a rush of resolution surge up within him.

At least he would not spend any more sleepless nights wondering what sort of people she was going to work for. Imagining her being accosted by some drunken buck on some other set of backstairs because she was too damned innocent to know girls could not go wandering about a house at night half dressed! Fearing that next time there might not be anybody around to rescue her.

The sacrifice would be worth it if it meant knowing she was being properly looked after.

'Do you really want to leave?' he asked her gently. 'Do you dislike Alvanley Hall so much that you would rather go elsewhere?'

'No.'

He took a deep breath. 'Is it me, then? Have you taken me in dislike? Do you wish to put some distance between us?' If that was the case he was not going to make himself look ridiculous by offering her his name!

'No! Oh, *no*,' she said with feeling.

'Then I will offer you a position here,' he said, gripping her hands a little tighter. 'How about that?'

'What sort of a position?' she asked, bewildered. 'You do not have any children…'

'More's the pity! My sister's boy is proving to be more and

more of a disappointment to me the older he grows. After that incident on the stairs I am beginning to feel quite perturbed at the thought of leaving the estate and the people for whom I am responsible in such careless hands. If I had my own son,' he said, 'I could train him up from the day of his birth. I am only in my thirties—the age at which most men consider marriage for the first time. With luck I might live long enough to bring him safely through the troubling years of growing to maturity, and go to my grave with a clear conscience.'

'What are you saying? You want me to kick my heels here, with my aunt, while you find a wife and then breed a son so that I can educate him?'

'No, you little idiot!' he shouted angrily. 'I am not saying that at all! I am asking you to marry me!'

Chapter Ten

'M...marry you?' She tugged her hands free and felt behind her for the chair. She had to sit down. She could not believe he was really asking her. She had cried herself to sleep the night before because she'd been so sure he would never, ever propose to her. Apart from the fact he was still mourning for his late wife, she was a nobody. Nothing. If this time at Alvanley Hall had taught her anything it was that she did not know how to move in the upper echelons of society. She had no idea how to be a wife to a man like him.

He could not possibly mean it!

A strange spasm passed across his face as he eyed the way she clasped her trembling hands together in her lap.

'May I point out that I have neither hairy knuckles nor greasy skin?' He held his hands out to her, palm down.

For a moment she could not understand why he was holding out his hands to her like that. Was he making some kind of jest? But when he turned them over, so that she could inspect them thoroughly, it came to her that he was referring to the conversation they'd had about marriage before. When he'd offered her a dowry and she had thought he wanted to be rid of her.

'I own I am much older than you, but you did not specify at what age a suitor would become unpalatable.'

She looked up into his face and frowned.

'Are you being serious?'

'Yes. Will you have me, Helen? You…you have already given me one gift this Christmas. Agreeing to become my wife would be the greatest gift of all.'

He looked so sincere her heart skipped a beat. But she did wish he had not spoken of *having* her. It made her think of bedrooms. Her entire body blushed. Would she have him? Oh, yes—in that respect in a heartbeat!

She wanted to go to bed with him and know what it felt like to become completely one flesh with him. That dance last night, she realised, had sensitised her whole body to his. As they had moved about the room, scarce an inch separating them from chest to thigh, she had resented even that inch.

Her face flooded with heat. She had told Lady Thrapston in no uncertain terms that she would not become any man's mistress. So why had she not leapt up and shouted, *Yes, yes, I will marry you!* and flung her arms round him and kissed him? What kind of woman was she?

'I d…don't know,' she said, hanging her head. 'I never thought…'

'For God's sake don't say, *Oh, dear, this is so unexpected*!' He laughed bitterly.

His proposal could not have surprised her any more than

it had surprised him! But that was always how it was around Helen. She got under his skin to the extent that he never knew what he was going to do or say next. And he really disliked the feeling of uncertainty she was engendering. He had known who he was before she came along.

'Well, it *is* unexpected!' she retorted, lifting her head to glare at him. Especially since his proposal had come without a single word of affection, let alone a hint that he might perhaps, in some way, love her. Even just a little.

'Look,' he said, running the palm of his hand over his head, 'perhaps you had better go away and think it over.' A cold, sick feeling gripped him at the prospect she might refuse. She was not like other women, who regarded him as a prize. There was no telling what she would decide. Certainly, by the looks of her, his proposal was not filling her with rapturous joy.

'You have nothing to fear from me if you refuse. I shall not make things difficult for you. I would appreciate it, though, if you would let me have your answer by this evening,' he said, going to his desk and sitting down on the other side of it.

That was better. Putting a barrier between them helped him to revert to his sane, rational self. Because for a moment there he had experienced an almost overwhelming urge to get down on his knees and beg her not to leave. It shook him. He hardly knew her, and already she had reduced him to that!

'There will be arrangements to make for your departure. I shall, of course, put my carriage and a driver at your disposal should you decide against the match,' he said, forcing himself to focus on practicalities. 'But travelling tomorrow is out of the question. Apart from your promise to the children, I make Boxing Day a holiday for all my staff. I will not have them put out.'

That was better. He was calm, cool, and in control of himself. There was no more risk of an inappropriate descent into some kind of emotional outburst.

And if she left that was what he would go back to. No swift surges of joy, but no risk of pain either. Just the safe, orderly, contained life he had made himself live since Lucinda's death.

The coldness of his eyes, the clinical way in which he addressed her, struck a chill through Helen. It was not just that he did not behave like a lovestruck suitor. It was far worse. He looked to her very much like a man who had just said something that on reflection he wished he had not said at all.

'Of course not,' she said, wounded. 'I would not wish to put anyone out.'

With that, Helen stumbled from the room, staggered a few feet along the corridor, and collapsed onto the nearest chair. For she was shaking. She did not think she had ever felt so confused.

Oh, not about her own feelings. She loved him. From the moment they had met he had affected her as no other man had ever done. And, in spite of that moment of self-doubt just then, it was *not* just a physical attraction. The more she learned about him, the more he drew her to him.

But what did *he* think of *her*? Apart from mentioning that they thought alike on a number of issues, that proposal had given her no clue. No, wait—he had said he thought of her as an ally against his family. Well, that was not saying very much, was it? Nobody with a shred of decency could fail to take his part against them!

Though how could she possibly refuse the one thing he had asked of her? At breakfast she had heard him agree that he needed nothing. That he never asked anybody for anything.

But he had asked *her* to mother his children, so that he could raise up a son he could be proud of.

Dared she reach out and take the little that he seemed to be offering her? Since that talk with Lady Thrapston she knew that loving *any* woman was completely beyond him. For one wild moment she was filled with the desire to pour out her own heart on his wounded soul. To love him and love him! She might not be able to heal his broken heart, but he had asked her to provide some measure of comfort by giving him children of his own, so that he would at least not have to dread leaving his tenants to Swaledale's tender mercies. Could she really do that? Dedicate the rest of her life to bringing some sunshine back into his dark, lonely existence?

It was the only Christmas present he wanted. And did he not deserve it? He was the best of men. The very best. Surrounded by a pack of greedy, grasping relatives who had been, and still were, totally insensitive to his pain.

It would take some getting used to, this inequality in their feelings for each other, but in time he was bound to grow fond of her at least.

Wasn't he?

She rubbed at a tension spot on her forehead. He might

not feel any great affection for her, but he had certainly demonstrated that he had a great deal of respect for her. A man did not ask a woman to marry him unless he felt…

Oh, what was the use? She had no idea what was going on in the aggravating man's head! And even when she thought she might be getting a glimpse of what he was thinking, his mood could change in the blink of an eye.

She got to her feet and strode along the corridors and up to her room to dress for church. If she dithered about down here any longer she would be late.

From her pew, she kept sneaking peeks at Lord Bridgemere. He did not look a bit like a man who was waiting for an answer to a marriage proposal. He seemed so calm and collected as he stood and knelt and sat through the service. While she was still a mass of quivering nerves. Had that proposal really meant anything? By the look of him he would just shrug and go on with his life as though nothing untoward had occurred if she turned him down.

That was why, it suddenly struck her, she had not leapt at his proposal. Because he had not spoken of love. He had only given her a *practical* list of reasons why they should marry.

Very well—she would look at it from a practical point of view herself. She had never really thought seriously about marriage as an option. She cared too much for Aunt Bella to question her strongly held views upon the subject and, because no man had tempted her to abandoning her comfortable single state, she had never given the matter any deeper thought.

But Aunt Bella and she were going to have to go their separate ways now anyway. She would, in fact, be likely to have less contact with Aunt Bella if she went to live the proscribed life of a governess than she would if she married Lord Bridgemere. And she did not think that her aunt would disapprove of the match all that much, considering how highly she had spoken of him after that interview.

If she had met him and fallen for him when they had been living in Middleton things might have been very different, but as they were…

Very well. There was no risk of offending Aunt Bella.

But what else would marriage mean? Well, she would become a countess, for one thing, with unassailable status and untold wealth. She would never have to worry about finding the money to settle outstanding bills, or sell off her gowns to put food on the table.

Most girls would jump at the chance to marry an earl. Any earl. Let alone one who was so handsome. And with whom she had grown so infatuated. She ought to regard getting a proposal from a man who was renowned for being a recluse as a triumph. Especially since his own sister had despaired of ever getting him to take such a radical step.

She glanced round the packed pews at the other members of his family. They would all say she was not good enough for him. And yet he had seen something about her he liked enough to tempt him from his single state. Yes, there was no doubt about it: he was quite a catch.

So why did she not feel triumphant?

In the pew beside her, Aunt Bella stifled a yawn as the local vicar mounted the pulpit to deliver his Christmas sermon.

Here was another factor to consider. If she were to become Lady Bridgemere, she could make sure that her aunt would never have to worry about money again. By golly, how she would enjoy ensuring Aunt Bella had every luxury her heart could crave! Never mind finding some small nook amongst Lord Bridgemere's vast holdings in which she could eke out her declining years. Or palming her off on one of his other relatives in return for bailing them out of their financial embarrassments! It would be wonderful to pamper the darling who had taken her in and comforted and cared for her when she had been just a forlorn little girl.

Yes, there were plenty of solid, practical reasons for accepting his proposal.

So why hadn't she? What was holding her back?

If all these very practical reasons were not making her thrill to the idea, what would convince her to marry a man she knew didn't love her?

When they returned from church, everyone went to the great hall for mulled wine and spiced cake.

The hall, like the ballroom, was festooned with greenery brought in from the woods. One of the suits of armour, Helen noted with amusement, now sported a crown of holly, bright with berries, his upraised gauntleted hand clutching a bunch of mistletoe.

Chairs had been set out in a semi-circle, and gradually

everyone took their places. Except the children and Lord Bridgemere, who were all gathered up in the minstrels' gallery. He must have gone straight up to the nursery wing on returning from church, to make sure they would have the best view of the mummers who had come over from the village.

One of the villagers banged on the drum he was carrying, and everyone stopped talking. The man with the drum stepped forward, tilted his face up towards the minstrels' gallery, and said, 'We come to perform for you, Your Lordship, to thank you for the way you always look after us, whether you're here or busy elsewhere. We know there's unrest in some parts, but as for us we give thanks daily that God has seen fit to grant us such a fair and charitable master as you.'

Lord Bridgemere's face took on that wooden cast Helen had seen him adopt on several occasions. For the first time she realised he was struggling with strong emotion. For a moment her mind went back to the way he had looked immediately after proposing to her. She had thought he looked completely cold then, but that was not it at all. He'd looked just as he did now! Her heart sped up. Did that mean his feelings *were* engaged? Perhaps so strongly that he felt the need to conceal them?

Perhaps there was hope. Perhaps he might come to care for her in time…

He made a slashing motion through the air with one hand, as though he did not want to hear any more, which made him look harsh. Yet it did not stop the villagers from beaming up at him.

They knew him. Had known him and his moods for years.

They could see straight through that cold, forbidding exterior to the man he was beneath. And they loved him for what he was. That flicker of hope grew bright enough to drive away some of her fears and doubts. Lord Bridgemere was a good man. It was why they loved him. Why *she* loved him.

Though *her* love for *him* was not the issue.

To the accompaniment of a fiddle and drum, the villagers in their garish costumes then performed a rollicking version of *Saint George and the Dragon*, which ended with a rousing song about shepherds increasing their flocks.

When they'd finished, the assembled house guests clapped politely. Then Lord Bridgemere cleared his throat and said, 'Singing so loud is thirsty work. The traditional wassail cup is over there.' He indicated the table round which they had been clustering earlier. 'I would advise the Methodists amongst you to partake only from the jugs at either end of the table. Not the punchbowl.'

They gave him three rousing cheers. Though, judging from the enthusiasm with which most of the men made straight for the punchbowl, not many of them belonged to the abstemious new religious sect.

'We'll drink to your good health, then, My Lord,' piped up the drummer, who had been among the first to get to the punchbowl.

'Drink rather to the season,' he replied.

'To Christmas!' they roared.

He stood there for a few moments, watching the villagers enjoying themselves with a satisfied smile hovering about his mouth. She had heard that he only came here at Christmas to preside over the festivities for his tenants, but somehow she had always assumed it was a matter of duty. Of keeping faith with the generations of tradition he had to uphold as lord of the manor here. But now she was of the opinion that it was far more than that. He really cared about these people.

Could she settle for that much? As his wife, the mother of his children, of course he would care for her—at least as much as he cared for these people.

Wouldn't he?

She did not feel up to following the rest of the guests to the dining room and taking luncheon when they began to file out of the great hall. It was too much to expect her to make appropriate responses to the barbed insults and snide comments that passed for conversation around that table. Not while her own mind was in such turmoil.

So she informed her aunt she would spend the rest of the day with the nursery party, and set off up the stairs.

She dawdled on the landings, since she was not quite ready even to deal with children in her given state. She gazed out of the windows that lit the deserted stairwell, basking in the absence of other people. She needed space to think. She had only until tonight to make her decision.

She sighed, rubbing at a dirty spot on the window with her cuff so that she could see out more clearly. She only wished it were that easy to clarify her thoughts.

She'd had her life mapped out before coming to Alvanley Hall. That was why his proposal had thrown her into such turmoil. If she married him, her whole life would undergo a radical change.

Most women would think the changes all for the better, but they would be women who thought of marriage as the height of their ambition. Whatever her circumstances, marriage had *never* been part of her plans. This was the first time in her life she had ever really had to examine what she thought about the institution.

When she had thought herself financially secure she'd believed she would be content to live exactly as her aunt had done. Alone, or with a companion, finding fulfilment in the simple life of a country town. Even when all their money had vanished overnight it had never occurred to her to look to a man to take care of her.

Or that she would fall in love.

That fact alone ought to have made her accept him like a shot.

Instead, it was that very fact which made marrying him such a scary prospect. When she had told him she would only marry for love, it was the first thing that had come into her head, she realised. And even then she had been vaguely thinking about an *equal* love. A man and a woman falling in love with each other, as her parents had done, and then finding they could not bear to be apart. Marriage naturally flowed from such strong feelings. She could see exactly why marrying, in their case, had been so right.

But in this case it was all lopsided. She had fallen headlong in love with him. But he appeared to have looked her over, noted down her admirable qualities as though he had some kind of a mental list, and decided that, yes, she would do very well in the role.

Many women would regard that kind of proposal as a triumph. The kind of women who regarded marriage as the *only* respectable state for a female of good birth. Unfortunately she was just not of their number!

Her breath was steaming up the window, obscuring the view she had dirtied her gown to obtain, just as her infatuation with Lord Bridgemere had clouded her judgement. Before coming here she would never have dreamt of marrying a man who saw her as nothing more than a means to prolong his bloodline. Where had her pride gone? She deserved more than that! More than the kind of marriage she'd had such a clear vision of immediately after his proposal, with her pouring out her heart and him taking it as his due.

Her lips tight with strain, she trudged off up the stairs again. She wanted him—oh, yes, how she wanted him! But could she pay the price? That was the question.

When she reached the schoolroom, she was amazed to see the air thick with glistening soap bubbles. Several of the children were sitting at a table, industriously dipping little clay pipes into dishes of soapy water, while the smaller ones were dancing about madly trying to burst them before they popped of their own accord.

Her mouth relaxed into a smile. It was impossible to remain out of sorts in such an atmosphere.

'Merry Christmas, miss!' said one of the nurserymaids as she scurried past with an empty coal scuttle.

'Merry Christmas to you, Jenny,' Helen replied.

'Miss Forrest!' cried Charles, scampering up to her. 'Look

what I got for Christmas!' It was a clasp knife and *exactly*, he stressed, what he had been wanting.

Every child, it appeared, had mysteriously received exactly what they had wanted most. She smiled to think of Lord Bridgemere skilfully yet subtly extracting the information from them over the few days they had been here, and then sending somebody—Cadwallader, probably—to make the purchases in the nearest town.

'There were bunches of grapes hanging from the rocking horse when I woke up this morning,' said Peter, pausing for a moment in his endeavours with his clay pipe. 'And twists of barley sugar and peppermints…'

'I got a doll,' said Junia, holding it up.

Her heart squeezed inside her chest. He was such a darling to do all this for the children. To make sure Christmas reached to the very furthest corners of his domain—be it to the neglected children, thrust out of sight of their selfish parents, or to the meanest cottager inhabiting his estates.

He was a man who ought to have his own children. He wanted a son and heir. She had already noticed that he seemed to approve of the way she was with other people's children, and now something had made him decide he wanted that for his own.

And if they were hers, too…

Already she had grown fond of this group. It would be quite a wrench to leave them. If she really did become a governess her life would become a continual round of growing fond of children who were not hers and then having to bid them farewell when they outgrew her and she had to move to a new post. If she married Lord Bridgemere it would save her from all that heartache. She could have her own children. Raise them exactly as she pleased. Love them unreservedly.

Whatever problems she might have with their father.

But was it enough?

It was not long after a joyful and rather chaotic Christmas lunch, which had started with ham and sausage and finished with jellies and creams, that the door opened and to her utter astonishment Nicholas Swaledale and Lady Augustine came in.

The maids glanced at them and dropped curtsies, but did not greet either of them warmly, as they had done Helen. Because they were gentry, she realised, whilst over the week she had been there she had almost become one of them.

She had to lower her head to conceal a smile when Swaledale waved his hand regally, as though granting them permission to carry on.

Then Junia squirmed down from her chair and ran over to them.

'Gussy, look!' she cried, her eyes alight with happiness as she held up the doll to show her sister. 'Look what I got for Christmas!'

Swaledale took a hasty step back. 'For the Lord's sake, make sure that child keeps her sticky hands off my clothing, if you please.'

Lady Augustine cast him a look of irritation, then hunkered down and put her arm round Junia's shoulders.

'Oh, what a lovely doll,' she said. 'I *do* like her dress!'

'Would still rather be playing with them, wouldn't you,' Swaledale drawled, 'than partaking of more adult pursuits?'

'I just wanted to see what they'd all got for Christmas,' snapped Augustine. 'And you needn't have come with me if you dislike children so much. In fact,' she said, getting to her feet, 'I wish you had not if you are just going to be nasty.'

'But how else was I to manage to get a few words with Miss Forrest?' he replied glibly. 'Now that she has taken to hiding herself away up here?'

'We have nothing to say to each other, sir,' said Helen.

'Oh, but I disagree,' he replied. 'Run along, Gussy, do. What I am about to say to this person is not for your ears.'

Helen was the one who tried to move away but, like a snake striking, his hand shot out and grabbed her arm. His grip was so tight that she knew if she resisted the way he was tugging her to a quiet corner his fingers would leave a bruise.

'Think you are very clever, don't you?' he breathed, once they were out of earshot of anyone else. 'I saw you dancing with him last night. You think you have him eating out of your hand. Though I can't say I blame him for making the most of what you're offering. One taste of you was enough to make me want more. And you looked very beddable in that nightgown, with your hair all down your back, from what I can recall. Was pretty castaway, was I not?' He sniggered, as though they were sharing some dirty secret.

Helen felt the bile rise in her throat as his proximity brought the whole episode rushing back to her so vividly that she could almost feel his tongue sliding across her face. Instinctively she tugged her hand free and put it to her cheek, as though erasing the very memory of his intrusive kisses.

'You know, flinging yourself at him won't get you anywhere.

Even if you've gone so far as sacrificing your virginity you won't get a marriage proposal from him. He will cast you off without a backward glance when he's done with you!'

'How dare you?' she gasped. Lord Bridgemere had already offered her marriage—and how could this toad imply that his uncle would seduce a female living under his roof? It would be completely out of character! Naturally she was not going to tell Swaledale about the proposal. That was strictly between her and His Lordship! But one thing she *could* refute.

'Lord Bridgemere is an honourable man. He would never take advantage of an innocent woman then discard her!'

'My, my, you *are* hot in his defence. He must have really turned on the charm. He can be charming, so I believe. But you would change your tune if you knew what he is really like.'

'I *do* know what he's really like.'

'Oh, do you?' He smiled nastily, leaned closer and murmured, 'Do you, perchance, happen to know exactly what became of his first wife?'

'What do you mean?'

'It is strange, but nobody who was around at the time is at all willing to talk about it. Suspicious, wouldn't you say— the way they all clam up and look shifty, saying the accident was nobody's fault? It is almost as if nobody dares to lay the blame at his door. But then the people round here need to keep on his good side. You have seen the power he wields over them.' He smirked. 'But my mother has told me there is quite a scandal there. If you know him as well as you say you do,' he said suggestively, leaning closer still and lowering his voice, 'then you will already have discovered he has the devil's own temper when roused. And Lucinda roused him all right…from what I hear.'

Helen could not help flinching to hear yet another person speak of the very great love Lord Bridgemere had had for his first wife. When he saw *her* as little more than a potential mother for his children.

Swaledale must have seen the hurt flicker across her face and decided he had achieved what he had set out to do, because with one more smirk he turned and stalked over to where Lady Augustine was dipping a clay pipe into a dish of bubbles.

'Playtime over, Gussy,' he said. 'Time to return to the world of adults.'

Her face red, Lady Augustine handed the pipe back to his younger brother, whom he had completely ignored, and they left.

Junia stuck her tongue out as the door closed behind him, and Helen couldn't blame her. What a toad he was! What a liar!

Lord Bridgemere would never hurt a lady! And as for implying he could fly into some sort of rage. Hah! Were they talking about the same man? Lord Bridgemere was always fully in control of himself.

She felt a small hand tugging her fingers out of the fist she had unconsciously clenched them into. She looked down as Junia looked up. 'He always makes me want to hit him as well,' she said.

Helen knelt down and gave her a swift hug. He would make a *saint* want to hit him. In fact, even though she could not imagine Lord Bridgemere ever raising his hand to a lady, she could see him becoming so angry with Swaledale that he would do whatever it took to prevent him inheriting his title.

She went cold inside. He would even enter a loveless marriage, provided the woman in question could make him *comfortable*. That was what he thought of her, was it not? That she would make some man a comfortable sort of wife?

And perhaps, if loving his first wife so much had made him grieve for so many years, he would only risk marrying again if he could be sure he would never experience the same sort of hurt.

He obviously thought *she* would not give him a moment's worry or heartache because he felt certain that his heart would never be deeply touched by her. How could it be? It was buried in the grave with his first wife!

Her hands went to her beads, which she had put on in honour of Christmas Day, even though she did not usually wear jewellery during the daytime, and she thought again of her parents, who had married for love. Their love for one another had carried them through the opposition of both their families, various financial hardships—oh, all their difficulties. She had not seen it as a child, but now she perceived that it had been the best for them, that they had died together. Neither would have wanted to outlive the other.

They'd been as essential to each other as the air they'd breathed.

And was she, their daughter, seriously contemplating marrying a man who, though he had shut himself away in mourning for years after the death of his first wife, would regard her as *comfortable*?

Comfortable for him, perhaps. But what would such a match be like for her? She had already imagined herself pouring her love into his wounded soul. But if his heart remained closed, as was clearly his intent, then how long would it be before loving him without hope proved too much for her? She was not a saint! Far from it. She had only a very limited supply of patience. And a great deal of pride. And a temper that she often had a struggle to contain.

It would not be very long before she became disgruntled. She would shout at him. He would coldly withdraw.

Eventually, from being merely cool towards her, he would grow increasingly irritated by her outbursts. Which would hurt her terribly.

Before much longer they would become one of those couples who lived in a state of cordial dislike. Given his propensity to remove himself from unwelcome society, he would probably disappear to the estate furthest flung from wherever she was, and she did not want to be reduced to the kind of woman who followed around after a man, begging for scraps of attention like some…spaniel! She would not do it. She had too much pride to beg anyone for anything!

No, she would stay exactly where she was, proudly refusing to show how much he hurt her.

It would be hell on earth!

She hugged Junia swiftly, got to her feet and, after waving goodbye to the children and wishing them a happy Christmas, left the nursery to go and find Lord Bridgemere.

She was going to tell him she could not marry him. The prospect of living like that was too dreadful.

Chapter Eleven

For a man who wanted an answer to his proposal before nighttime he was being extremely elusive. But at length, just before dinner, she ran him to ground in his study.

'Please take a seat,' he said, when she hesitated just inside the doorway, her heart in her mouth. He was dressed for dinner, as was she by now. His face was shuttered. He had never looked more unapproachable.

She took a seat. She bowed her head. She was on the verge of tears. Was she doing the right thing? Was she walking away from what could be her heart's desire?

No. She swallowed down an incipient sob. The vision she'd had of marriage to Lord Bridgemere had convinced her he would utterly destroy her. This brief interview would be painful, but at least all her memories of him would be good ones. She would not grow bitter with resentment. Turn into a shrew that no man could like, never mind love.

She took a deep breath, raised her head and looked at him.

'I am conscious you have paid me a great compliment by

asking me to marry you,' she began, using the phrases she had rehearsed so many times in her head. 'I am flattered by your proposal. But on reflection I am afraid that I m…must…' *Oh, no! She could not burst into tears. How undignified that would be.* She took another deep breath, clenching her hands into fists on her lap. 'I am sorry, but I c…cannot m…marry you.'

There! She had done it.

Oh, God. It felt as though her heart was going to break. It hurt to breathe.

'I see.' For a moment he looked completely blank. Then he frowned slightly at her, as though she were something of a puzzle, got to his feet and walked past her to the door. 'There is no more to be said,' he said tonelessly, opening the door. 'I trust you enjoy the rest of your stay. I will make the necessary arrangements for your departure on the twenty-seventh.'

He made a gesture with his arm to indicate she should leave.

And she no longer felt as though she might burst into tears.

She had suspected that he would simply shrug and get on with his life if she refused him. And just look at him! That was exactly what he was doing. Calmly ordering her from his study—from his life.

Oh, how right she had been to refuse him.

She leapt from the chair and stalked past him, her head held high. Since he was holding the door open for her he did not even afford her the satisfaction of slamming it in his face.

She was halfway along the corridor before the breath got stuck behind the hard lump of misery in her chest and she had to sit down swiftly on one of the chairs that were ranged along the walls. Oh, what a fool she was! She knew she had made the right choice, to avoid exposing herself to a lifetime of pain, and yet it still hurt.

She suspected it would hurt for quite some time.

But in the distance she heard the dinner gong sound, and knew she must somehow put on a brave face and go and find her Aunt Bella. If she did not turn up for dinner, her aunt would worry about her and demand to know what was wrong with her. And she did not feel up to speaking about it. Not even with her.

This cut too deep. And somehow she did not think Aunt Bella would understand. She had never had any time for men. She might applaud Helen's decision to reject a proposal of marriage, but it was highly unlikely she would understand the pain it had caused her to do it.

She paused just inside the doorway of the blue saloon, wondering how on earth she would survive another evening closed in with Lord Bridgemere's extended family.

One or two glanced her way, before turning away abruptly in dismissal. Aunt Bella smiled vaguely in her direction, but she was deeply engrossed in conversation with her friend Lady Norton.

Helen had never felt so alone. So utterly, hopelessly lost.

And then Reverend Mullen approached her. 'Good evening,' he said with a friendly smile. 'I have the honour to escort you in to dine tonight,' he said, taking her by the arm and drawing her into the room. 'And may I say what a pleasure it will be to have a like-minded person with whom to converse…'

In a daze, she watched his mouth moving as he no doubt said a lot of very kind things to her. But Lord Bridgemere had just at that moment entered by the far door, and he was walking across the room. Nobody else existed.

He looked, she thought on a fresh wave of misery, just as he always did. Calm, controlled. Perhaps just slightly irritated. Just very slightly.

As he might have been by any minor setback that had occurred during the course of his busy day.

Nobody, but nobody, would be able to tell from his demeanour that he was a spurned suitor.

But then he was not. He had not courted her as a suitor would a woman he cared for deeply. He must have proposed to her on some kind of a whim!

'I say, Miss Forrest, are you quite well?' The Reverend Mullen's voice swam to the forefront of her consciousness briefly. She saw his concerned face, peering intently at her.

'No…no. Actually, I do feel a little unwell,' she said. 'I think that perhaps I shall go to my room…'

There was certainly no way she could sit through dinner, watching him carry on as though nothing had happened between them, when she felt as though… Oh, the only way to describe it was as though she was dying inside.

It was not long before her aunt came to join her. Helen had undressed and got into bed, though she was not sleepy. She saw no point in sitting up, brooding. She wanted to pull the blankets over her head and will the day to end. It was sure to hurt less in the morning.

Wasn't it?

'What is the matter, dear?' her aunt enquired, laying her hand upon her forehead. 'You do not seem to have a fever.'

'No, it is not a fever,' she sighed.

'Then what is it? What can I do to make you feel better?'

There was nothing anyone could do to make her feel better. She suspected she was not going to feel any better for some considerable time. She had thought earlier on that she could not possibly open her heart to Aunt Bella, but there *was* nobody else. And her aunt deserved some sort of explanation for why she was missing her dinner.

'Aunt Bella, have you ever been in love?'

Her aunt looked at her sharply. 'Ah, so that is it after all. Sally said you had fallen for Lord Bridgemere. The fellow has played fast and loose with your feelings, has he?'

'No,' sighed Helen. 'He asked me to marry him. And I refused.'

Aunt Bella looked completely confused. As well she might.

'Have I done the right thing?'

Aunt Bella pulled up a chair and sat down beside the bed. 'I do not know, Helen. I am not the best person to talk about romantic love between a man and woman, if that is what ails you. I have no experience of it myself. And from what I have observed in others it brings nothing but pain and disillusion.'

'So you would say it is better not to marry if you are not sure…?'

'Oh, unquestionably. A woman is better alone.'

Alone. The word tolled like a death knell in Helen's heart.

She would always be alone. She would never meet another man who would match up to Lord Bridgemere.

'That is what I thought. Only it does hurt so…'

And finally Helen burst into tears. Tears she had been holding back since the moment she had reached her decision.

'H…he does not l…love me, you s…see,' she sobbed. 'So of course I c…could not marry him, c…could I?'

'Not if you have any sense of self-worth, no,' said Aunt Bella prosaically.

For a while Helen just wept, while her aunt patted her on the back.

'In time I expect the pain will ease,' said Aunt Bella, offering her a handkerchief when Helen began to weep a little less bitterly. 'People do not really die of broken hearts. Not sensible people, at any rate. I could tell, really, I suppose,' she admitted, 'that you fell hard for him the moment you clapped eyes on him. You have never been able to hide what you are feeling,' she said, gently brushing a strand of hair from Helen's tearstained cheek. 'Did he try to take advantage of you? Is that what upsets you so?'

Helen shook her head furiously. 'No! It is because he said I should be a comfortable wife!'

Aunt Bella's brows shot up. 'You? Comfortable? Are you sure?'

When Helen nodded, Bella clicked her tongue. 'The man's an idiot. Only a grand passion would induce *you* to marry. And there is nothing comfortable about that sort of relationship, I should not think.' She frowned. 'You would not have wanted to upset me by marrying for anything less.

I have always been so scathing about the institution, have I not? Have I been utterly selfish? I have worried recently that I did you a great wrong by not taking you to London and introducing you to some eligible men. Just because I never wished to marry, there was no reason to assume that you would not.'

'Oh, Aunt Bella, no! Please do not think that. I never wanted a Season. Besides, I am certain that had I said I wanted one you would have gone along with my wishes. You always let me have whatever I wanted.'

Aunt Bella looked a little mollified.

'And,' Helen continued, 'this week, mixing with the kind of people we would have run into in London, has shown me that I should not have enjoyed it all that much. I do not regret anything about the way you brought me up, Aunt Bella. Please do not think so!'

Aunt Bella produced another handkerchief and blew her own nose on it. 'And yet if you had married someone you would not now be obliged to go and work as a governess. Be reliant upon strangers. We know nothing of these Harcourts. I worry that—' She broke off and dabbed at her eyes. 'You have been so brave about it, but this week I confess I have often felt so uncomfortable about the way things have turned out that I have actually been avoiding you. Sticking my head in the sand, I suppose you would say. Because every time I am with you I—' She broke off again, on a little sob.

Helen knelt up in bed and put her arms about her aunt. 'Please do not worry about me. You have taught me to be strong and resourceful. I have appreciated the way you have brought me up even more this week, after renewing my acquaintance with General Forrest and his wife. I shudder to think what I would have ended up like had I stayed with them!'

'And yet you refused Lord Bridgemere. When most women would think marrying him would be far preferable to going out to work for a living. Helen, what have I done to you?'

'Taught me to have pride,' she said. 'The man is still in love with his first wife, Lucinda. If I married him he would expect me to simply accept what is left over—like a beggar taking crumbs from his table!'

Aunt Bella frowned. 'Lucinda? In love with her, was he? I should not have thought it myself.'

'Wh…what do you mean? Lady Thrapston said—'

'That woman! Twists the facts to suit herself, she does. Lord Bridgemere could not have been much more than seventeen when he married Lucinda Ellingham. She was of much the same age. The match was arranged by their families.'

'Oh?' Helen had a peculiar cold sensation in her insides. Had she just made the most colossal error? 'B…but why did he shut himself away from everyone after she died? Lady Thrapston said his heart was buried with her in her grave.'

Aunt Bella flung up her hands in annoyance. 'What a piece of melodramatic nonsense! Honestly! Does he strike you as the sort of man who would care that much about any woman?'

That remark did not help Helen as much as her aunt had probably intended. Though it might be some consolation to hear he had not been so enamoured of his first wife as she

had been led to believe, it still did not bode well for any relationship they might have had.

'S…Swaledale said—'

'Helen, if you have been listening to the tales those two
have been telling, then I despair of you. Surely they contra-
dicted each other on every conceivable point?'

Now she came to think of it, they had. Lady Thrapston
had said Lord Bridgemere was a man with a broken heart.
Whilst Swaledale had implied he had a guilty conscience.

'So…are you saying he did not love her?'

Aunt Bella shrugged. 'That I cannot tell you. It was a long
time ago, and I have never been that close to him. Does it
make so much difference?'

Helen's shoulders slumped. 'Probably not. He does not
love *me*, and that is the main reason I could not accept. I sat
down and really thought about marriage for the first time
today. And I saw that the kind of match I want would be
the kind my parents had. The grand passion, as you so rightly
said. They were so very much in love, my mother and father.'
She shook her head sadly. 'Bridgemere I think admires me
a little. But he does not love me the way I need to be loved.
He would have made me miserable.'

'I expect so,' said Aunt Bella tartly. 'That is what men are
best at. Making women miserable.'

Helen could not help smiling weakly at that remark.

'That is what Swaledale said. That Lord Bridgemere
would make me miserable. According to him, Lord
Bridgemere has a dreadful temper. And, what is more, he
implied his first wife's death might not have been an

accident. He said that nobody ever dared question Lord Bridgemere too closely about the incident, as though there was something sinister about her death that he wished to keep quiet.'

Aunt Bella snorted contemptuously. 'Well, from what I recall of that time it would have been no surprise if Bridgemere *had* lost his temper with Lucinda. She acted like a spoiled child instead of a wife with a position in society to live up to. But as for implying he had anything to do with her death—why, that is absolute nonsense! He may have blamed himself for not being here to curb her excesses perhaps…'

'It happened here?'

'Yes. She fell down the grand staircase and broke her neck. During one of the riotous parties she liked to throw. The rumours that came my way were to the effect that she was intoxicated. *Not* that Bridgemere had anything to do with it. And if Swaledale implied otherwise I should say that it stems from spite, because he feared what he could see was going on between you and His Lordship. That young man must be terrified of being cut from the succession.'

'I…I never thought of that…' Helen whispered. Oh, Lord, what had she done? She shut her eyes and wrapped her arms round her waist.

But it did not take her long to realise that it made no difference what had gone on in that first long-ago marriage, even though it had cast such long shadows over his life. The reason she had not accepted Lord Bridgemere's proposal was that he did not love her now, today. Not because of anything that might or might not have happened in his youth.

'Shall I send for a supper tray?' said Aunt Bella, dabbing at her eyes and sitting up straight. 'It is bad enough that the wretched man has upset you so much. I see no reason why we both need to go hungry on his account as well.'

They were not going to discuss the matter any further, Helen could see that. Aunt Bella disliked emotional scenes of this sort. They had made their peace with each other, dealt with Lord Bridgemere's proposal, and that was the end of that.

Helen blew her nose one last time, knowing the subject was closed. When Aunt Bella drew a line under any topic there was no point in trying to revisit it.

Helen woke next morning with a throat that felt raw from weeping quietly into her pillow and eyes that were heavy from lack of sleep.

It was her last day at Alvanley Hall. And she did not know how she was going to get through it. He would be somewhere near all the time. She might see him unexpectedly at any moment. And every time she saw him it would be a like a fresh blow. To know she might have married him if she'd had less pride. To know that because of it she would likely never see him again.

Oh, how she longed for the day to be over, so that she could leave tomorrow and start to get on with the rest of her life without him. To begin to allow her wounded heart to heal.

This must be what purgatory was like. Neither one thing nor the other. Just enduring the present punishment for a decision she was bitterly regretting even though she knew it had been the right one.

For once she had no wish to go up to the nursery. Children were perceptive. They would be bound to ask her what was the matter. Or Reverend Mullen would enquire after her health. She was afraid that she might start to cry again, and upset them. As well as drawing the kind of attention to herself she desperately wished to avoid.

But she had no wish to sit in her room moping all day, either.

Fortunately she knew exactly where another pair of willing hands would be welcome, and that was at the barn on the home farm, where the tenants' ball was to be held tonight.

As she had suspected, Mrs Dent welcomed her with open arms, and promptly handed her a broom. Once Helen had finished helping sweep the floor she went and stood with the village girls who had also come up to help, and had a drink while they all watched the men setting up trestle tables along one wall. From then on her feet hardly touched the ground. There were cloths to spread, garlands to make, wreaths to hang and, to the accompaniment of much giggling, kissing balls to fashion from mistletoe and hang in as many strategic locations as possible.

Much later she went to the nursery, to take an early tea with the children since she was feeling a little shaky. She could not say she wanted to eat anything, but she knew there was a lot of the day left to get through, and the last thing she wanted to do was faint away and ruin the children's big moment on stage.

She helped them into their costumes and handed Charles, swathed in silk as the angel Gabriel, the supply of ginger snaps which she had fetched on her way up through the kitchens, so that he could bribe the little angels to behave themselves. Then she helped Reverend Mullen and the nurserymaids to get them all downstairs and into their cart for the short drive over to the barn.

Their party was the last to arrive. The house guests were sitting on benches directly in front of the raised platform on which the band would later play music for the dance, and the villagers, dressed up in their Sunday best, were standing behind them.

There was an empty seat next to Lord Bridgemere, on the front row. He got to his feet the moment he saw her and indicated that she should come and sit beside him.

Helen's heart sank. It was further proof, as if she needed any, that he had not a grain of sensitivity. How could he think she would want to sit so close to him when her whole being was grazed red raw from rejecting his proposal?

Yet how could she refuse his invitation with everyone watching? It would look as though… She grappled with the possible interpretations the others would put on her actions, then gave up, too weary to take any thought to its logical conclusion, and sank onto the seat beside him.

'Are you feeling any better?' he murmured as she took her seat. 'You did not take dinner last night.'

How could he think she could have sat through another interminable meal with his family when her heart had felt as though it was breaking?

'I feel…'

She felt dreadful. And sitting so close to him was not

helping. If she should reach out, just a little, she would be able to touch him. When she knew that really he was forever out of her reach. For two pins she could throw back her head and howl with misery. She had to bite down hard on her lower lip, to stop it quivering.

'Hush,' she said, keeping her face fixed straight ahead, for she dared not look at him lest he see exactly how much she was hurting. 'The children are about to start.'

Something inside Lord Bridgemere had settled when she took her place beside him. He had been worried about her all day. He had upset her somehow by proposing marriage. Though he could not tell why. He had thought she liked him. But last night in his study she had looked as though she could not wait to get as far from him as possible. She had not been able to look him in the face from the moment she'd entered. Had run from the room positively bristling with indignation when he had decided he might as well put a period to that embarrassing little scene.

But at least she did not have such a disgust of him that she could not even bear to sit beside him now.

Strange how badly he had misinterpreted her. He had thought he could always tell exactly what she was feeling. He had caught her looking at him sometimes with what he had thought was her heart in her eyes. He would have sworn she would leap at the chance to marry him.

Instead she had turned him down. Had run from the dining room the second he'd entered it as though she could not bear to so much as look at him and gone without dinner rather than endure another second in his presence. And she had clearly been avoiding him all day. He'd respected her wishes, leaving her to her own devices though he would much rather have made the most of this last day they would ever have together. But he was too much the gentleman to trample all over her feelings.

Whatever they were. He glanced at her out of the corner of his eye. She looked as though she had slept as poorly as he had done. The feeling of numbness that had descended over him when she had turned down his proposal had stayed with him through the night. He just could not believe she would walk away from him when she could be his wife. *Why?* he had wanted to shout when she had stammered through that painful little rejection speech. Why could she not stay with him? Did he mean nothing to her at all? He had lain in bed all night feeling…empty. Completely empty.

But she was sitting next to him now.

He barely restrained the urge to reach out and take hold of her hand.

Reverend Mullen had done a masterful job of coaching the children, who acted out the story of the nativity quite beautifully, even if several of the tiniest angels could clearly be seen munching biscuits throughout. To end the performance the whole audience joined in with a heartfelt rendition of 'Hark the Herald Angels Sing', then the seated guests applauded the children's effort politely, while the villagers whooped and cheered.

When the applause had died down, all the seated specta-

tors got up and made their way to the exit, intent on returning to the chilly grandeur of the big house. Instinctively
Helen made a move towards the children, intending to help
their nurses wrap warm coats over the tops of their costumes
for the ride home.

'Miss Forrest,' said Lord Bridgemere, putting his hand on
her arm to stay her.

'Please, don't go.' His heart was hammering so hard it was
a wonder she could not hear it. There was so little time left.
Mere hours before the coach would come round and carry
her away. How could they waste them sleeping? Or in his
case pacing his room, wondering what he could have done
to make her accept rather than reject him.

Her heart leapt within her breast. Was he asking her to
reconsider? Had he, on reflection, decided he could not bear
the thought that she was leaving tomorrow?

'It is your last night here,' he said. 'Your last night of
freedom before you have to try to behave with propriety all
the time, as befits a governess.' He tried to make a joke of
it, so that she would not hear how close he was to begging
her to spend the evening with him.

Her heart plunged. It was not a renewal of his proposal,
then. How foolish of her! Why would it be? She'd only ever
been supposed to be his 'comfortable' wife.

'There is to be dancing. And I should like you to be my
partner for the opening set even if you do not care to stay
longer. Will you stay for just one dance? Please?'

He held out his hand to her. The rest of the room was in
a bustle as the children were shepherded out of the door.

The villagers cleared away the chairs, and musicians mounted the stage and began tuning up.

But where she was standing there was nothing but Lord Bridgemere, holding out his hand to her with an intensity in his expression that produced an echoing yearning deep within her. As he had said, this was her last night. The last time she would ever see him. And he wanted her to spend it with him.

What else could she do? Go up to her room and finish her packing? Sit on her bed and spend the whole night weeping?

Or make the most of this chance—this one last chance to be with him?

She put her hand in his and he smiled.

'Thank you,' he said quietly, and led her to the head of the first set that was now forming to the cheers of the locals.

Helen had never seen Lord Bridgemere looking so carefree as he did that night.

He was dressed fairly casually, so that he did not look so very different from the other young village men in their Sunday best. When the first dance was finished he proceeded to dance with his tenants' wives and daughters, whilst the farmers and their sons swept her up into the merriment. Though even when she was not his partner, she still felt as though she was dancing with him. The nature of the country dances was such that they all continually moved up and down the set, so that she never knew when he might take hold of her hand or swing her round by the waist in performance of one of the figures. So long as she was dancing and he was dancing it was as though they were dancing together, no matter who their nominal partners happened to be.

Which was why she stayed. And kept on dancing. Until she was so tired that she was forced to go to the refreshments table for a glass of the local cider.

It was only moments before Lord Bridgemere joined her.

'You have enjoyed your last night here, I think,' he said, accepting a drink from the girl who was serving. 'Rather more than you have enjoyed most of the rest of your stay at Alvanley Hall.'

She nodded as they both sipped their cool, refreshing drinks. In spite of everything she was glad she would have the memory of this night to look back on. When she had glimpsed yet another facet of Lord Bridgemere's character.

'I have, too,' he said. He moved a little closer and lowered his head, so that she could hear him above the music that was striking up again. 'We only danced the once, but somehow, because you were here, too, and happy, it made it…very special.' He smiled at her, ruefully.

Helen closed her eyes. Hearing him say that was unbearably poignant. She wanted to savour his words without giving away her state of mind. She was not wearing her best bronze gown tonight, but a simpler dress that she'd thought more appropriate for the activities in which she had envisaged taking part. And he was standing so close that she could feel his body heat through the thin muslin.

Her heart began to pound. Her eyes flew open. And she saw him looking down at her with sadness in his eyes.

'It is almost midnight,' he said. 'I really think we should leave. Some of these men have been partaking of the ale I have provided somewhat too freely and the atmosphere is about to become rather boisterous. I should like to take you back now.'

Take her back. She had not given a thought as to how she would get back to the house. But the prospect of leaving did not sound quite so terrible now she knew he meant to escort her. The dancing might be over, but there was still the walk home.

'Thank you,' she said. 'I shall fetch my coat and bonnet.'

Lord Bridgemere waited for her by the door, leaning against the frame with his arms crossed over his chest. She had not liked it when he'd spoken to her of his feelings. From being relaxed and seemingly happy in his company she had completely withdrawn. And when he had suggested they leave her relief had been palpable.

She really did not want to marry him.

Helen thought Lord Bridgemere had never looked more isolated as he lounged against the doorpost, watching his tenants enjoying the festivities. It was as though a great gulf separated him from other, lesser beings.

As if to confirm her opinion of his exalted status, the moment she joined him the band stopped playing, the villagers stopped dancing, and everyone turned to look at him.

'I usually make a sort of farewell speech when I leave the ball,' he explained to her. 'It will not take a moment...'

But before he had the chance to say anything to his tenants the fiddler, who had been imbibing steadily all night, suddenly yelled, 'Don't leave without giving her a kiss, Your Lordship! Don't let that mistletoe go to waste!'

Everyone was either roaring with laughter or pointing at

the kissing ball under which, he now perceived, he and Helen were standing.

She was looking up at it, too, but then she glanced at him, her cheeks turning fiery red.

That reckless spirit that she so often managed to provoke in him surged to life. She might rather become a governess than his wife, but, dammit, this was Christmas. He had every right to kiss the woman he wanted to marry under the mistletoe. Whether she wanted him to or not!

In a spirit of defiance, he reached up and plucked a berry from the already much used bough.

'It would disappoint them if I did not oblige,' he said, tucking it into his waistcoat pocket. Then he took her firmly by the upper arms, and drew her close. 'You do not mind, do you?'

She was staring at him wide-eyed, lips already slightly parted. 'N…no,' she stammered. 'W…we would not want to disappoint anyone, would we?'

'Not at Christmas,' he said, his heart pounding in his chest as he drew her closer still. 'I make a point of giving everyone exactly what they want at Christmas.'

Then he bent down, just slightly, and brushed his mouth against hers. She shut her eyes. He felt a quiver run through her body.

He stepped back. She opened her eyes and looked at him. As though what he had done had stunned her.

And then a sheen of tears began to form in her eyes.

He flung his arm about her shoulders and turned her to shield her from view. Waving his arm at the revellers, he pulled her out of the barn and into the yard, to the accompaniment of cheers and applause.

How little his tenants knew! They thought he was going to have a romantic walk home with his sweetheart by starlight. Not escort a reluctant and probably highly offended female back to the Hall.

'Miss Forrest—' He pulled himself up short. He was not going to apologise for kissing her. He had asked her if she minded, and she had not refused. If she had disliked it so much it had made her cry…

Dammit, he had never meant to ride roughshod over her feelings. Just because he wanted her it was quite wrong of him to conveniently forget the fact she did not want to marry him!

Beside him in the dark he heard her give a little sniff, as though she was trying hard not to weep.

'Hell,' he growled, coming to a complete halt and pulling her into his arms. 'I never meant to make you cry. I would not have kissed you if I had known you would dislike it so much. You should not have said you did not mind if you did!' he finished, confusion and frustration making him spit the words at her angrily.

She raised her head and looked up at him. 'I d…did not mind at all!' she said, confusing him even more.

'Then why the devil are you crying?'

'I am not crying,' she said, averting her face.

He took hold of her chin and turned her face up to his, so that he could see quite clearly the silvery tracks glinting on her cheeks that exposed her lie.

'Then what are these?' he said, brushing his thumbs across the tearstains. 'Miss Forrest, what is the matter with you? If you do not explain, then how am I to make it right for you?'

She took a breath, as though she was going to speak, but then shook her head, looking so woebegone it tore him up inside.

'You cannot make it right for me, Lord Bridgemere. The reason I am crying is something you can never mend for me.' She reached up and placed her palm against his cheek. 'Though I wish with all my heart that you could.'

Chapter Twelve

It was no use wishing, though, was it? He did not love her. And that was that.

Reluctantly she removed her hand from his cheek and let it hang at her side.

'Tell me what I can do to make you happy,' he said.

Her mind went back to the way she had felt when he had kissed her under the mistletoe. She had known he was only kissing her to amuse his tenants. She had known she had to keep that thought very clear in her head and not permit herself to indulge in any kind of romantic fantasy. And, as if to reinforce her strict warning, he had barely brushed his lips across hers.

So briefly, and yet it had felt so sweet. Like a benediction which she had felt all the way down to her toes.

And so powerful that it had completely erased the shame she had felt after Swaledale assaulted her.

What would make her happy would be another kiss just like that one. Only given because he wanted to give it, not because she or anyone else had asked for it. She smiled sadly.

'There is nothing you can do, truly.' She had finally, she reflected ruefully, had her curiosity satisfied in regards to Lord Bridgemere's mouth. And the memory of that kiss would be something she would treasure for the remainder of her life.

She shivered, suddenly picturing all those cold, lonely years without him.

'We should not be standing here like this,' said Lord Bridgemere. They had paused beside the gate after he had closed it behind them. They were still only a few yards from the barn. Helen could hear the sounds of merriment spilling through the gaps in the barn door, along with the light from the lanterns.

'You are getting cold,' he said with concern.

Helen had been driven over in the cart, with a thick rug tucked over her lap and the bodies of all the children squeezed up against her to keep her warm. It was much colder now than it had been earlier. The clouds that had made the day so dull had cleared and frost coated every surface, so that every branch and twig and blade of grass, even the old farmyard gate, glittered brightly in the light of the almost full moon.

Lord Bridgemere began to unbutton his coat.

'No,' cried Helen, thinking he meant to take it off and lend it to her. 'If you remove your coat then *you* will be cold. As soon as we start walking again I am sure I shall get warm.'

He paused, but then resolutely went on unfastening his coat. 'I have a better idea,' he said. 'Stand still.' He opened the front of his coat, stepped forward and wrapped his arms about her, enveloping her in the thick folds of material and his own body heat. 'If you turn a little and put your arm about my waist we can share the warmth of my coat as we walk home,' he said. 'So neither of us need feel the cold.'

For a few seconds Helen stood quite still, revelling in the feel of his arms about her. But eventually, when she felt she had absolutely no excuse for stretching the moment out any longer, she said, weakly, 'Y…yes, that is a most practical solution.'

'I thought so,' he said softly. 'Though I don't suppose we will be able to walk very fast like this.'

As she turned he kept both his arms about her, so that his coat completely enfolded her.

'N…not very fast, no,' she agreed, as he attempted to match his stride to accommodate her stumbling steps.

It was highly improper to cling onto Lord Bridgemere as he held his coat about her for warmth, but who was ever going to know? They were the only two people out here tonight. And even if somebody did spot them, what could they do? For once Helen was just going to do exactly as she wished and hang the consequences!

Slowly, entwined like lovers, they picked their way along the frozen rutted lane. As soon as they drew away from the farm buildings the deep silence of a winter's night descended. She was more than ever aware of how utterly alone they were under the vast canopy of stars. And also of how very intimate it felt. Why, even their breath mingled visibly, as it rose above their heads before dissipating into the clear cold air.

Neither of them said a word. Helen was afraid to break the

spell that seemed to be holding them suspended in this moment out of ordinary time, and every time she peeped up at him Lord Bridgemere looked as though he was concentrating on where he was putting his feet. Though he did not seem to be in any hurry. And that was good enough for her—for now. She shut her eyes briefly, revelling in the feel of his body flexing beneath her hands with every step he took.

But all too soon they were entering the kitchen court and crossing the slick cobbles. And then he was removing one arm to reach out and open the door. His coat was still round her. He still had one arm about her shoulders as they stepped inside, into the unlit lobby of the servants' hall.

The door creaked shut behind them, blotting out even the moonlight, and as they both stood quite still in complete darkness Lord Bridgemere remarked, 'Nobody seems to have thought of leaving a lantern lit.'

'I expect,' replied Helen, 'the servants know exactly where it is, and can put their hand upon it and get it lit in an instant.'

'No, I do not think that is it. I think it is more likely that there are usually plenty of people about down here and lights all over the place.'

But tonight the servants were all still at the barn, dancing. The gentry were all above stairs, for once fending for themselves. They were utterly alone.

And somehow, even though they were no more alone than they had been on the walk back here, being within doors, with her arm about his waist and his arm about her shoulder, felt a whole lot more intimate. And risqué. Especially since there was now absolutely no excuse for them to be touching each other.

With great reluctance Helen began to slide her arm out from round his waist.

Lord Bridgemere sucked in a sharp breath. She felt his body jerk.

'No,' he said, turning as she moved her arm so that it stayed imprisoned under the fabric of his coat.

They were standing face to face now, although it was still too dark to see. But she could feel the warmth of his breath fanning her cheek, so she knew he was angling his head down towards hers. And then he slid his arm from her shoulder, lower down her back, and exerted a slight pressure. Only a little, but it was all the encouragement she needed to move closer to him and lay her head against his chest. The buttons of his waistcoat stung cold against her cheek, but she did not care. For Lord Bridgemere had given a great sigh and put his other arm around her.

Helen slid her other arm about his waist and held him, too. For a moment or two it seemed to be enough. They stood, clinging together in the dark, as though neither could bear the thought of letting the other go. But then the tenor of his breathing changed.

'Is there mistletoe hanging above this doorway, do you suppose?' he said.

It was far too dark to see. So there was no point in raising her head to look.

'There might be,' she said wistfully.

'If there was, would there be any chance you would let me kiss you again?'

Beneath her cheek Helen could feel his heart beating

very fast. And he was breathing hard, as though he had been running, not walking slowly with her cradled in his arms like some precious, fragile piece of porcelain.

And in the dark, with nobody to see them, and the minutes before she had to leave ticking away urgently in her mind, she gave him the only answer possible.

'Yes, I am sure there is mistletoe here. And yes to the other question, too.'

It would be too brazen to actually say *Yes, I want you to kiss me*. But he knew what she meant, because the moment she lifted her head from his chest and raised her face he swooped down and took her mouth.

This time his kiss was not the polite brush of the lips he had given her in the barn, with all his tenants watching. It was too dark here for anyone to see anything—even each other—and it was as if the very darkness freed him from all restraint. His lips moved urgently across her own, nipping and tasting her. He stroked his tongue across the seam and when she gasped he plunged it into her mouth with a groan. It was as if he wanted to devour her.

Helen was in such bliss that she yielded to every prompt he gave her, opening her mouth wider to allow him deeper access, tentatively tasting him as he was tasting her. He tasted sweet, like the cider they had both been drinking. His lips were soft, but the skin of his cheek felt rough, even though he had looked cleanshaven in the moonlight earlier. But she did not dislike the sensation of his jaw abrading her chin. It made her thrillingly conscious of his masculinity.

All her senses seemed particularly acute. She expected it

was because she could not see him with her eyes. She was aware, for example, that he smelled slightly different. Or perhaps because he had been dancing the scent of his skin was slightly stronger than usual. For whatever reason, she felt as though she was breathing in the heat of his body, along with the more familiar smell of cologne and clean linen she usually associated with him.

And the darkness freed her from some of the restraint she would have felt in bright light. She felt bold enough to reach up and loop one arm about his neck and press her body closer to his. He encouraged her by holding her harder, as if he wanted to meld their bodies into each other.

Excitement flared through her when his hands slid down to her waist, tracing the shape of her body through her clothing. She did not feel cold any more. In fact she felt warm in the most unlikely places. Not just where his hands were touching her, but in the pit of her stomach, the tips of her breasts and, most shockingly, in the secret folds of skin between her legs.

Under his coat she ran the hand that had been round his waist up his back, then down his side, tracing the tapering shape of his torso. He growled low in his throat and his hands went round her back and down, to cup her bottom, pulling her hard against his body.

She could feel something hard pressing into her stomach. She only wondered what it was for a split second before re-alising it was his arousal.

She revelled in the knowledge that he wanted her in this most primal, basic way. And the heat that had begun to bloom between her legs became an ache of need.

He flexed against her, his fingers kneading at her bottom in time with the undulation of his hips. And her legs almost gave way.

She staggered backwards and he came with her, their mouths still fused together, their feet shuffling and dragging as they stumbled across the corridor, locked together in a dance of urgency. As soon as her back hit the wall he let go of her, but only so that he could fumble open the buttons of her coat and delve inside. His hands felt hot as they shaped her breasts.

She felt lost. Confused. But whatever the question that was niggling at the back of her mind she was too caught up in sensation to want to know the answer. Lord Bridgemere was trailing hot kisses down her neck, along her collarbone, and then the upper slopes of her breasts. Her gown had a square-cut neck, and he deftly scooped one breast free so that he could suckle it.

Helen gasped. The pleasure was so intense she hardly knew what she was doing any more. Her fingers kneaded his shoulders as he laved her nipple, while his hand caressed the fullness of her breast. She found that she was writhing against him, her hips gyrating in time with his own undulations.

He kept his mouth at her breast, but his hands slid down her sides, then grasped handfuls of her skirt, hitching up her dress until he could reach beneath. She gasped again when his hands found the bare skin above the tops of her stockings.

He was going to touch her there!

Oh, yes!

But then somewhere in the depths of the house a door slammed.

Lord Bridgemere jerked upright. And swore.

Her skirts fell decorously to her ankles, but one breast was still hanging out of the bodice of her gown.

Her eyes had grown used to the dark by now. She could see him looking down at her breast, which she knew must be glistening with moisture from his tongue. He looked appalled.

'Miss Forrest, forgive me,' he said, stepping back and disappearing into the shadows.

She felt cold and alone—and humiliated. With trembling fingers she straightened her gown, then pulled the edges of her coat together to cover herself up.

'I should not have—' he began.

Oh, this was terrible! Bad enough that she had let him put his hands and mouth all over her. But now his moment of madness was over he was going to make some feeble excuse about having drunk too much, or give some other reason that would negate everything she had felt and reduce it to an impulse he now regretted.

She did not want to hear it!

It had been glorious. Wonderful! And she would not let him destroy it with his words.

Clapping her hands over her ears, she stumbled away from him.

'No, wait—please. I…'

'Don't say it!' she cried, breaking into a run. She knew her way about down here sufficiently to know that so long as she kept to the centre of the corridor there was nothing she could trip over. 'I don't want to know!'

Lord Bridgemere stood stock still, listening to the sounds of her footsteps fading into the distance.

Then he reached out and touched the wall against which she had been standing. Whilst he had… God! He had practically ravished her! He could not believe he had lost control like that. He had never known such passion. Such driving need. If not for hearing that door slam, which had brought him back to his senses, who knew what might have happened? No wonder she had fled from him! Had refused to listen to his apologies! What he had almost done was beyond forgiveness.

He was no better than Swaledale, preying on an innocent, unprotected female in a deserted corridor.

He closed his eyes and pressed his forehead against the cold, smooth surface, gritting his teeth as he struggled to bring his body back to something resembling normality. But in the dark he could still feel her little hands, clinging to his shoulders. Could still smell her sweet, womanly fragrance hanging in the air. Could taste her in his mouth. Feel her nipple beading under his questing tongue.

He had to move away from this spot. She haunted it!

Muttering a curse, he pushed away from the wall and set out for his bedroom. His valet, like the other servants, would be kicking up his heels over at the barn, so he had no need to maintain any kind of pretence when he got there. He shut the door behind him and leaned against it, bowing his head as a wave of self-loathing swept over him. He was *worse* than Swaledale. At least the youth had the excuse of being so drunk he'd hardly known what he was doing. But he was without excuse. It was desire alone that had made him act like a ravening beast.

The two scenes swam into his mind, overlapping as he saw himself as the predator and Miss Forrest as his victim. He saw Swaledale slobbering down her neck while she stood rigid, her face averted, sick with terror and not knowing what to do. And then himself, scooping her breast out of her gown to suckle at it while she…

He straightened up abruptly. She had been writhing against him. Clinging to him.

She had been with him every step of the way!

He recalled now her little gasps and moans of pleasure. The way her hands had tentatively begun to explore his body. It had been her eager yet innocent response that had ramped up his own arousal to almost overwhelming proportions.

He walked to the bed and sat down heavily, remembering suddenly that he had not just pounced on her but had asked permission to kiss her.

And she had said yes.

They had *both* imagined mistletoe to give themselves the liberty to do exactly what they wanted, even though they both knew it was wrong.

So…why had she fled from him? Could it possibly be that she did not blame him for the whole episode, but that she, too, had abruptly come back down to earth and been ashamed to have let things go so far? Ashamed, most of all, that it had been he who had called a halt to proceedings. If he had not stopped, he did not think she could have done so!

He gave a great sigh of relief, running the palm of his hand over his hair. That was more like it. That was Miss Forrest all over. She acted on impulse and thought about what she had done afterwards. She had not been able to resist his advances, and the moment they had been interrupted she had been as full of remorse as he had been.

How her pride must have stung to know that any man had the power to make her sigh and moan with desire. Particularly one she had refused to marry.

His sense of relief ebbed away as bitter regret swamped him. Shakily he covered his hands with his face and hunched over.

How could she have let him put his hands all over her when she knew she would be walking away from him in the morning? He had thought she had a deep vein of integrity running through her. She was so proud she would not marry him, even though he was one of the wealthiest men in the country.

What was it about him that made her still want to leave when she had just acted as though she wanted him with every fibre of her being?

He leapt up from the bed and paced across the floor. God in heaven, but he wished he understood her! What was the key that would unlock her mystery? He thumped the windowframe, turned, and paced back towards his bed.

There was no logical reason why she should not marry him if she could respond to him as she had just done downstairs!

No logical reason, no. But when had logic ever played a

part in anything Miss Forrest did? She was not a cold, cal-culating woman. From the first he had thought she was a force of nature. As well try to capture lightning in a bucket as to think Miss Forrest would tamely settle with him when she wanted—

What the hell *did* she want? He turned and stalked back to the window. She had made it clear she had no ambition to net herself a wealthy, titled husband. What was it she had said about those tradesmen who might have offered for her had she given them any encouragement? He had thought it sounded proud at the time. Had thought she did not want to be demeaned by taking a step that would see her descend the social scale.

But then she had spurned him, too.

Just what did she want from a husband, then, if it was not money, or a title, or even physical gratification?

And then her voice came to him—proud and clear and defiant. *The only reason I would ever marry would be for love.*

He sat down hard on the bed, winded.

He should not have given her a practical list of reasons for marrying him. He should have romanced her!

He thought back to that stilted little speech he had made. To the reluctance he had felt to enter the married state again, which must surely have transmitted itself to her. His cursed pride had made him disguise how much her answer mattered to him. He had let her think he did not care much either way. When the reality was that the thought of living without her was almost unbearable. He groaned out loud. What a fool he had been! He suddenly perceived he had not offered her the one thing that she might have valued.

His heart.

He laid his hand upon his chest, feeling it beating. Pounding. Because he was afraid there was nothing he could do to stop her leaving.

Two days ago he would have said it did not matter. He would have expected to feel some regret, but would have thought it would fade in time, and that as he went back to his orderly existence the routine of carrying out his duty would soothe the passions she had roused.

But that was before he had kissed her.

If he let her slip through his fingers now, without making one last effort to persuade her…

He got to his feet and went to the door. Opened it. Then remembered that she was sharing a suite of rooms with her aunt by adoption. He could not go in there and try to make love to Helen with her aunt watching his every move. If a man invaded her rooms she would probably set up such a squawk that she would set the whole house in an uproar.

He shut the door and stood there, his mind whirling.

He could not let Helen go. Not without putting up a fight.

Then his face set. It was *his* coach she was relying on to take her away in the morning. Driven by *his* coachman. Without his say-so the man would not carry her off his lands.

He flung open his door and strode purposefully along the corridor. To judge by their reaction when he had kissed Miss Forrest in the barn, his tenants would be only too pleased to help him carry out the plan that was forming in his mind. They could all see the impact she'd had on him. And, to a

man, they would welcome her as their new countess. She
had impressed them all as much as she had impressed him.

He just hoped a sufficient number of them were still
sober enough to be able to carry out the work needed to
bring his plan to fruition.

Chapter Thirteen

Helen and her aunt ate a very subdued breakfast in their room the next morning. They were both too upset by the prospect of parting to try and speak to each other, lest one of them break down. They just hugged each other fiercely when a couple of under-footmen came to collect her trunks. And both walked down to the coach with their lips firmly pressed together.

Although Helen felt further from tears than her aunt looked. It was as though there were some hurts that just went too deep. She had lain in bed the night before feeling strangely numb. It reminded her a bit of the way she had felt when her parents had died and her future had seemed so vast and terrifyingly empty. She had known then that she would have to be brave to survive. And somehow, last night, she had felt that shedding any more tears over Lord Bridgemere would only weaken her resolve to survive life without him.

She paused before getting into the coach that was to take her away from Alvanley Hall for ever, swiftly glancing along the rows of windows and wondering if *he* stood behind one of them, watching her go. Naturally he could not come and bid her farewell in public. An earl did not condescend to notice the departure of a woman who was destined to become a governess.

A man who had been disappointed in love would not be able to bear the parting, either, she reflected wistfully.

But a man whose emotions were not engaged at all would probably have gone out riding, as was his habit, with his enormous hound loping at his side.

Suddenly Helen's breath hitched in her throat, and she had to duck her head to hide the way her eyes were smarting as she took the footman's extended arm and he helped her climb into the coach.

She understood the difference between passion and love. There were places men could go to in just about every town to slake the kind of need Lord Bridgemere had been exhibiting last night. Which she, to her shame, had not even attempted to deny. To think she had once joked with her aunt about a man's *proclivities*!

Aunt Bella fumbled a handkerchief out of her pocket and, pressing it to her eyes, abruptly turned away and marched swiftly back to the house.

The door slammed shut, the coach lurched, and she was off. And, perhaps because she was finally alone, and nobody would be able to either hear or see her weep, she found she could no longer stem the flood of feelings that pride had kept so firmly held back. She delved into her reticule and held a handkerchief over her face while she released all the misery that had formed into a cold, hard lump in her chest.

Lord Bridgemere desired her. Enough to make marrying her and getting her with child no hardship for him. But he had never—not once—spoken of having any feelings for her that would make sacrificing her independence worth the risk. And so now she was leaving behind the only other person in this world that she loved, Aunt Bella, to start a new life alone.

All too soon, it seemed to her, the coach came to a halt. She looked up, stunned, when the driver came and opened the door himself.

'Is there a p...problem?' she asked, hastily wiping her nose. Beyond him she could see trees. They had not even left Alvanley land yet, so far as she could tell.

The driver's face softened at the sight of her red swollen eyes, and the way she was blowing her nose.

'I do not think so,' he said, confusing her still further. 'But it's just that I can't take you no further than this. Coach won't get up the track.'

'Track?' Helen peered past him as he stood back, opening the door wider and gesturing that she should get out.

'You will have to walk the last little bit,' he said, holding out his hand in readiness to steady her. 'That is if you want to speak to His Lordship. He is waiting for you up yonder.' He jerked his head to the right, and quite suddenly Helen recognised where they had stopped. They were at the end of the lane that led to the woods that sheltered the children's skating pond.

'His Lordship wants to speak to me?'

The driver grinned at her. 'Says I wasn't to take no for an answer.'

'There really is nothing more to say to him,' she said aloud. But her heart was pounding. Could she really leave without finding out what he wanted to say to her? It could not, of course, be what she most wanted to hear. 'I should just go on my way,' she said. But if she left, and did not hear him out, she would always wonder what he had wanted to tell her. It would drive her mad with curiosity!

And so, against her better judgement, she found herself taking the driver's hand and getting out of the coach. And standing looking at the narrow path that wound through the thick belt of trees with her heart in her mouth.

And wonder in her eyes.

For strung amidst the dark, oppressive branches were dozens of coloured lanterns, lighting the way. She followed the route they lit for her stumbling feet, emerging in a matter of moments into the clearing where the children had skated. There had been another heavy frost overnight, adding a coating of what looked like swansdown to the pond where the children would no doubt be skating later on. And beyond it the old tumbledown ruins of the watchtower. The door was closed today, but through the arrow slits she could see a golden glow, and she knew Lord Bridgemere was inside, waiting for her, a fire already prepared so that they should not grow cold while they discussed…whatever it was he had summoned her to discuss.

Her heart pounding, she began to pick her way round the edges of the shallow dish of ice. She had still not reached the door before it flew open, and Lord Bridgemere was standing there, a dark silhouette against the golden glow of the fire.

'Miss Forrest, you came!'

She paused, astonished by the eagerness of his greeting and the slight tinge of surprise she could hear in his voice—as though he had not been certain she would come. Had he really thought she could have insisted the driver turn the coach round and take her away?

He was standing to one side now, holding out his hand to her, 'Come into the warm, please,' he said. And she realised she was standing stock still, just gazing at him in surprise. 'I promise you have nothing to fear from me.'

She knew that! It was just surprising to hear uncertainty in the voice of a man who had always seemed to her so very certain about everything.

She stepped over the threshold, and paused again in utter amazement. When he had opened it up for the children's use she had thought it pretty rustic. It had a flagged stone floor and whitewashed walls, against which the fire-blackened beams stood out in stark contrast. There had been a table positioned a safe distance from the generously proportioned hearth from which the maids had dispensed hot drinks, and several mismatched dining chairs had been ranged about the walls, so that the smaller children or the nurserymaids would have somewhere to sit while they warmed themselves.

But today the place looked completely different. There was a sumptuous deep red carpet spread over the flags. The table had gone. And a pair of sofas had been draped with yards of heavy red velvet, heaped with cushions, and situated on either side of the fireplace. From every exposed beam hung garlands of fir and ivy, so that the air within was redolent of the greenwood.

But what struck her most of all was the mistletoe. There were bunches of it everywhere. There were two over the doorframe, and another hanging from the central rustic candleholder. There were bunches hanging in the arrow slit windows, and dangling from the mantelpiece, and even a small sprig of it, she noted, her cheeks flaming, tucked into Lord Bridgemere's buttonhole.

He saw her looking at it.

'There will be no need for either of us to hope there might be mistletoe around today, Miss Forrest,' he said, shutting the door. 'I have made sure that wherever in this room you stand I will have the right to ask you for a kiss.'

'B…but I am leaving…' she said faintly.

He shook his head. 'I do not think I can permit that.' He turned his back on her to lock the door, then dropped the enormous iron key into the capacious pocket of a coat that was hanging on a peg nearby. He turned back to her, and with his hands on his hips shook his head. 'No, I cannot permit it. If I have to keep you locked up in here for days until you see sense, then so be it!'

He stalked up to her, grim purpose writ all over his face.

Helen did not know what to make of what sounded like a declaration of intent to imprison her. She supposed, fleetingly, that she ought to be afraid. But, perversely, her heart was beating wildly with excitement. All that mistletoe, coupled with the look on his face, made her think he fully intended to kiss her senseless, as he had done last night. And she wanted him to! Wanted him to kiss her until *he* was wild and out of control, too.

But she could not let him do any such thing. It would be madness. She had a job to go to. Her own way to make in the world. Yielding to him just because he felt like kissing her was absolutely out of the question!

As he had been advancing on her she had been steadily retreating, until the backs of her knees hit the sofa, and she dropped far from gracefully onto the soft, velvety surface, her eyes never leaving his intent face.

But, to her surprise, the moment he caught up with her, instead of joining her on the sofa and perhaps flinging her down and behaving like a proper kidnapper, he dropped to his knees before her. Seized her hands and looked up into her face, his eyes pleading.

'Miss Forrest, you were right to refuse me when I asked you to marry me.'

Now Helen was really confused. If he thought she was right not to have accepted his proposal, then why had he bothered abducting her?

Her heart sank. Was he going to ask her to become his mistress? Because she had responded to him with such passion last night, did he think she was more fitted to that kind of position in his life?

She stiffened with anger.

'I know, I know,' he was saying, sensitive to her reaction. 'That proposal was…an insult to a woman like you! It was just that hearing you were going to leave took me by surprise. I could not bear to think of you leaving. But I did not think about *why* I was so upset by the notion of never seeing you again. All I could think of was that I had to prevent you going. Had to do whatever it would take to make you stay and give me the right to care for you. I proposed to you out of panic. And then reeled with shock at having said the words I swore I would never say to any woman again after what happened with Lucinda.'

He paused, an expression of anguish flickering across his face. And Helen's anger cooled in the face of his misery. It appeared Lady Thrapston had been in the right. He *had* loved his first wife. So much that it was causing him agony to so much as mention her name!

'And then last night I behaved like a brute beast. I knew you were leaving, that I had no right to kiss you like that, never mind the other liberties I took with you!'

At the mere mention of those liberties Helen could feel his tongue sweeping over the breast that his hands had freed from its confinement. She remembered the delicious shivers that had racked her whole body when he had bunched up her skirts and slid his hands between her thighs.

'I do not want your apology—' she began.

But he let go of her hands, got to his feet, and said fiercely, 'I have no intention of apologising! I am merely trying to explain things!'

He paced away from her, as though grappling with some internal demons before being able to speak again.

'I suppose I could blame the moonlit walk home with you in my arms. Or claim I drank rather more than I should have at the tenants' ball. But the truth was,' he said, his eyes bleak, 'that you were utterly irresistible. At one point I was almost completely overwhelmed by my desire for you. I think I was on the point of ravishing you up against that wall,' he said bitterly. 'Which is not at all like me. You see, I have not looked at any woman in that way since Lucinda died. I had thought I would never feel desire again. And then you came into my life, and I began to feel again. It has been like coming back to life. Or…or like spring bringing everything into flower after a long, cold winter.'

'Did…did you love her that much?' she blurted. It hurt so much to think he seemed angry with her for making him feel again. As if she had done it to him on purpose!

'Love her? I did not love her! What the devil made you think I loved her?'

'Y…you said it was like winter. That you had not been happy for years or thought of another woman… What am I supposed to think?'

He came back to the sofa, sat down heavily, and reached for her hand. 'I did think I loved Lucinda at first,' he grated. 'When my guardians told me they had chosen her to be my wife I was thrilled. She was so beautiful. So captivating. She dazzled me. But whatever it was I felt for her it was turned completely on its head within a month of marrying her. When I discovered what she was really like. And when it ended I swore I would never let another woman take me for a fool again. Because my first marriage, you see, was an un-mitigated disaster.

'Lucinda was a consummate actress,' he continued. 'She pretended to be all sweetness and light, fooling my guardians, fooling me, into thinking she would make the ideal Countess of Bridgemere.'

Helen's mind flew back to what Aunt Bella had said about Lucinda acting like a spoiled child instead of a wife with a position in society to live up to. And how she would not have been surprised if His Lordship *had* lost his temper with her. And wondered whatever she could have done to make him speak of her with such bitterness even after all these years.

'She *was* a virgin when we wed. I'll grant her that,' he said, giving Helen a pretty good idea of what the answer to her unspoken question was going to be. 'I can only suppose she must have thought she ought to bow to the conventions until her position became unassailable. But once I had relieved her of that impediment she saw no more need for discretion. She took her first lover within a month of marrying me…'

Helen gasped. Even in a marriage arranged by families, where no love existed between the parties, convention demanded that a wife stay faithful at least until she had presented her husband with an heir.

'At first I refused to believe the evidence of my own eyes. Until she grew so indiscreet that even I, besotted as I was, could no longer pretend. I went through two years of utter hell, trying to make her change her ways. In the end I realised I was just too dull for her… You see, I had become Earl at only nine years of age. My mother bore my father several daughters, only two of whom survived infancy, but I was the only son. My guardians cosseted and sheltered me. They did not want to risk sending me to school, where I might come into contact with some disease or other, and so they brought in tutors. I had very little contact with any life beyond the environs of Alvanley Hall. *They* selected Lucinda, for her pedigree and wealth, and brought her here. She burst into my life like… I don't know how to describe her. A whirlwind, perhaps. With hindsight, I can see that she needed more than just to live quietly in the countryside. But back then I had no idea how to handle her. She did not respond to threats or begging.'

He ran his hand over the crown of his head. 'I blamed myself, my own lack of experience, for her inability to remain faithful. And so did she,' he said, his mouth twisting with bitterness. 'She told me to my face that I was dull, provincial, not as exciting as her other lovers…'

'Oh, no…' Helen reached out and grasped his hand. How cruel of that Lucinda, to destroy his youthful optimism, his hopes of a happy marriage, his very self-confidence! 'You are not…'

But he placed one finger to her lips, to silence her. 'Please hear me out. I need to tell you all.'

She nodded and he removed his hand, though her lips tingled where his finger had rested, albeit briefly.

'Had I been older, more worldly-wise, I might have handled the situation better. I dare say there are any number of men who have unfaithful wives and manage not to go to pieces.'

'You were just a boy!' she protested.

'And a coward,' he condemned himself bitterly. 'I left her here at Alvanley Hall and began an existence entirely separate from hers. Nursed what I thought was my broken heart…'

His face twisted with contempt. 'But you are right. I was just a boy. A green boy. I did not know what love was! I did not know anything!' He gripped her hand so hard it was almost painful.

'When she died, and I came back here to deal with things, even I who thought I knew what she was like was shocked by the things my tenants told me had gone on in my absence. Perhaps the worst thing, though, was to learn that she was pregnant when she died. With a child that could not possibly have been mine. Had she lived, I would have been forced to acknowledge it. That was the worst betrayal of all. And when I learned about that I was glad she was dead. I felt as though I had been released from prison. I watched them shovelling earth onto her coffin and felt nothing but relief. And I swore on her grave that I would never let my family arrange a marriage for me again. I did not care about my so-called duty to produce an heir. I already had a nephew who could step into my shoes should anything happen to me. And so I told them when we got back to the house that I would not be browbeaten into another arranged match. And when they kept on badgering me about doing my duty to the family name I told them that so far as I was concerned the whole family could go to hell!

'Even now I can barely tolerate having any of that generation near me. Only once a year do I permit them into my house, and that is largely because I do, in truth, have a duty to my family as much as to my tenants. And for one season of the year—just one—I do the right thing. Not the thing I want. In honour of the season.'

Helen could have wept. After shunning people for so long, hiding away and recovering from what his first wife had done to him, he had at long last reached out to someone. To her. He had asked her to marry him only a week after they had met. He might not have declared his love for her in the conventional way, but now he had explained why he was the way he was that proposal told her how very much he needed her. And she had refused him. Turned her back on him in his hour of need! Oh, he had not deserved that! If only she had understood!

'I am so sorry I refused you—' she began, but once again he silenced her.

'You did the right thing. I am glad you refused me.'

'What?' Now Helen hurt on her own behalf. For he was telling her that she had destroyed any chance for them to be together!

'Your refusal made me really think. You brought me down to a level I have never visited before. You see, all my life I have been taught that I am my rank. I am Lord Bridgemere. But the rank means nothing to you, does it? I began to see that if I really wanted you to marry me I would have to offer you something more than rank or wealth. Something that would be of value to you. And then last night, after having you in my arms, I knew I would never forgive myself if I let you walk away without offering it to you. Miss Forrest, last time I proposed to you I told you that if you agreed to marry me it would be the best Christmas present anyone could give me. But last night showed me that is simply not true.'

'No?' A pang of dismay shot through her.

He shook his head. 'The greatest gift you could give me would be your heart. As I…' He swallowed, took a deep breath, and then said, 'As I give you mine. I am sorry I was so often cold and distant with you. I kept telling myself I was being a fool to expose myself to the risk of so much hurt again. But when you said you were leaving, and I pictured my entire future without you, that was far worse!'

He dropped to his knees, seized her hand and kissed it.

'Besides, what I feel for you is nothing like what I felt for Lucinda. She dazzled me. But from the moment you walked in I felt as though you knew me.'

'I thought you were a footman,' she protested weakly.

'You brought me down to earth. You would not let me behave in that pompous, arrogant manner which keeps everyone else so very far from me. And you spoke as I would have spoken, you thought as I think. You made me laugh. Miss Forrest, you once told me you would only marry for love. And love is the reason I have had you brought here and am proposing to you again. I do not fear loving you, Miss Forrest, for I know you will not despise the love I bear you as…as *she* did. Quite simply, I need you. To work alongside me. To make me laugh. Make me weep. To rebuke me when I grow too pompous. To…to complete me. I have been so empty and lonely for so long…'

'Please do not say any more,' she begged him, tears streaming down her cheeks.

A look of utter hopelessness came over his face. 'I know you do not love me yet, but in time do you not think you could learn to? I swear, I will be the most devoted husband any woman has ever had. If you cannot agree to marry me now, then at least stay on at Alvanley longer and grant me the chance to court you, to woo you as you deserve. You have not known me long enough to decide whether or not you can love me…'

'I do not need time to know whether I love you or not. I already do!'

He shook his head. 'You cannot mean that.'

'Why not?'

'Because I have always been a dull fellow. And marrying Lucinda left me twisted inside. I have become suspicious and insular and moody. Not at all the kind of man to attract a vibrant, passionately warm woman like you…'

She shook her head, her eyes shining with love. 'You are upright and noble and good.'

He was still frowning, as though the notion any woman could love him was preposterous.

'And handsome,' she declared, as though that was the clincher. 'I can see now,' she said, 'that for years you have thought yourself unable to inspire a woman's love. You have been so used to thinking people only come near you when they are desperate for your aid. You don't mix in society enough to see that there are many, many people who would value you for yourself. As I do.'

He shook his head. 'There *is* nothing in me to inspire a woman's love. I did everything I could for Lucinda, and she still could not love me.'

'Let's leave Lucinda out of this, shall we?' said Helen tartly. 'She is not typical of womankind, let me tell you! You had a particularly unfortunate experience with her, but it was not your fault. Not your fault at all! *You* were not the one who failed in that marriage.'

'Miss Forrest,' he said, 'if you love me…if you truly love me…'

'I do!' she said, stroking his cheek very gently.

'Then do you think you might change your mind about marrying me?'

'Yes,' she said simply. 'So long as I know you love me, too.'

He wrapped his arms round her waist, burying his face in her lap. She felt his great shoulders heave as though with relief. Then he looked up into her face, searching her features intently.

'You say you love me? You really believe you love me?'

'Yes. Yes, I do!'

'And I, in spite of swearing I would never let another woman touch my heart, have fallen in love with you, too. I did not want to, mind,' he said ruefully. 'I did my utmost to evade the silken coils you were winding round my heart.'

'You make it sound as if I did it on purpose…' she objected.

He shook his head vehemently.

'No. I have had experience of a woman who truly tried to entrap me. What happened between us was something very different. We neither of us sought it. It was…a gift. Love came unbidden, unsought. And we are both richer for it.'

'Yes,' she said, her face lighting up. 'That is exactly how it happened! That is exactly what I feel!'

For a moment or two they just gazed at each other, as though neither of them could quite believe in their sudden reversal of fortune. And then Helen reached out and plucked the bunch of mistletoe from his buttonhole.

'I know this is not quite the done thing,' she said, plucking a berry and holding the sprig above their heads with a hopeful expression.

'You never do what anyone would expect, do you?' he said, his eyes lit with adoration.

Sometimes her impulsiveness had put him very much in mind of the way Lucinda had been. And it had made him wary of her. But it had not taken him long to see that the similarities were only on the surface. Lucinda had never thought of anyone but herself—never considered anything but her own pleasure.

Helen was all heart.

'Which is why I love you.'

And then he pushed himself up off the floor so that he could reach her lips and kissed her. With tears now streaming unchecked down her face, Helen flung her arms round his neck and kissed him back. And, just like the night before, the moment their lips met she felt as though she was entering a different world. A world of sensation, of need. She clung to him. He traced her shape, running his hands all over her body as though he could not quite believe she was real and he had to make sure.

And before long Helen felt restricted by the barrier of clothing that separated them. She was glad when he tore open the buttons of her coat, undid the hooks at the front of her gown, and freed her breasts from their confinement. For a while she was content to lie back and let him feast on her. But soon that was not enough. She had to get rid of some of his clothing, too. Pushing him half off her, so that she could reach his own buttons, she pushed aside his jacket, undid his waistcoat, yanked his shirt from his breeches, and sighed in satisfaction when her fingers finally met with skin.

He shuddered as she ran her hands up the satiny smooth muscles of his back, then tore away his neckcloth and cast it to the floor, before lowering his mouth to her bared bosom once more.

Helen moaned as he began bunching up her skirts. At last she could move her legs apart, so that he could lie between them. This time when his hand slid over the tops of her stockings she arched up to meet his questing fingers.

'Miss Forrest, are you sure?'

She looked up at him in astonishment when he reared up and slowly began to remove his hand. He could not stop now! Not when he was finally touching her where she had been aching for his touch since they had been interrupted the night before.

'Helen—my name is Helen,' she managed to gasp, grabbing his hand and holding it still. 'You cannot address me in such a formal manner while you are doing that!'

'Sebastian,' he said, and, as though sealing a pact, he slid one finger inside her.

'Sebastian!' she breathed. 'Oh, Sebastian!'

He began to probe and withdraw. She reached for him then. He sucked in a sharp breath as she fumbled open the flap of his breeches.

'Helen, are you sure?' he asked again. And then groaned

as she delved inside and tentatively caressed him. 'Oh, God,' he breathed. 'If you don't stop doing that I shall not be able to hold back...'

'Good,' she purred with female satisfaction. 'I don't want you to hold back.' She wanted to shatter his self-control. Make him break through his rigid self-restraint and just once behave completely outrageously!

So she stroked him again, exploring the length of him with inquisitive fingers, revelling in the way he jerked in her hand, his whole body quivering with the force of what he was feeling.

And then he snatched her hand away. Not to stop her, but so that he could take charge. He grabbed her by the hips and tugged her down so that she lay flat on the sofa beneath him. Then pushed one of her legs down to the floor and hooked her other knee up so that she was fully opened to him.

For a moment as Helen glanced down at him she feared it was going to be impossible. She knew, of course, that people had been doing this for centuries. That it brought men and women great pleasure. But when he entered her, just as she had feared, there was such a fierce stab of pain that she thought the pleasure might be gone for good.

And then Sebastian stilled. He kissed her cheek softly, and stroked her hair back from her brow, and told her how much he loved her. The pain ebbed a little. And then he gave a groan and began to move again.

And just like that she forgot the pain as a fresh wave of sensation swamped her. Sensation which built and flooded her as he loved her with his hands and his mouth, his whole body.

But, most importantly, with his heart and soul.

And then she grew quite frantic with need, writhing and bucking under him, until it rose into a crescendo of ecstasy and every part of her throbbed with untold pleasure.

And Sebastian came with her, shuddering and throbbing deep within her.

Leaving her feeling complete. At peace.

And boneless.

He seemed to be feeling much the same as her, since he collapsed on top of her, his head buried in her neck.

'You are so generous,' he said at length, when he had got his breath back. 'I noticed that about you from the start,' he murmured into her ear, 'that you have a kind heart.'

'The start?' she said, lazily running her hands across the width of his shoulder.

'Was that while I was shouting at you to make yourself useful?'

He reared up and looked down into her face, a grin tugging at the corner of his mouth.

'That incident certainly served to make me take notice of you,' he said. 'After that I could not help watching out for you, to see what you might do next. Most girls of your age would do nothing but complain about their lot. But you never did. Not once. All you seemed to care about was your aunt's health.'

'Well, I love her.'

'You have a loving disposition,' he agreed, his eyes growing dark. 'I want that love for myself,' he said. 'I am greedy for it.'

'You have it.'

He kissed her then—not wildly, as he had done earlier, but with a tenderness that made her heart melt.

'So,' he said, after a short interval, 'now we have a wedding to plan.' His face abruptly fell. 'You know what this means?' he said.

'No,' said Helen, a shiver of foreboding slithering down her spine. Surely he had not had second thoughts?

'It means giving a grand ball. Half the county will have an excuse to come traipsing through Alvanley! And more than half of those currently staying up at the Hall will use it as an excuse to stay on for at least another month!'

He sat up and began to restore order to his clothing.

'You…you do not need to give a ball on my account,' said Helen. 'We can get married quietly. I only want a simple ceremony, with my aunt as witness. I do not care about anyone else…'

'Oh, no,' he said grimly. 'You deserve better than that. If I do not throw a ball and celebrate our union publicly people will think I am not proud of you. And I am,' he said gruffly. 'I want to show you off. You are going to be such an asset to me, and I mean to show everyone right from the start that this is no convenient marriage I am entering for dynastic reasons, but a love match that I enter into with my whole heart.'

'And so you will throw a ball…?'

He nodded, his face set.

'And invite your family to stay on while the banns are read?'

He squared his shoulders. 'I will.'

Helen giggled. 'Oh, Sebastian, you must love me very much to go through all that for my sake.'

He looked down at her where she lay, her white limbs still spread against the red velvet, her hair tumbled across the cushions, and his heart turned over.

'I do,' he said. And then, with a wry twist to his lips, 'Just think if that bank had not collapsed, and your aunt had not lost all her money, you would never have come here for Christmas and I would never have met you. I would still be cold and lonely and utterly without hope.'

She sat up, put her arms round his neck, and laid her head on his shoulder.

'And if you were not so determined to honour the season each year, in spite of wanting to have nothing more to do with the family that caused you so much unhappiness, I would never have found you.'

He turned and hugged her tight. 'When I was a very small child I had a nurse who told me that Christmas is a time for miracles. And somehow, deep down, I don't think I ever quite let go of the notion that it was the one time of year when hopes and dreams might come true. Every year when I came back here I wondered if this would be the year when things would change for me. And this year—thank God—at last it has. For this year you came. And brought love with you.'

'Thank God, then,' she agreed soberly. 'Thank God for Christmas.'

★ ★ ★ ★ ★

The Earl's
Mistletoe Bride

JOANNA MAITLAND

Joanna Maitland was born and educated in Scotland, though she has spent most of her adult life in England or abroad. She has been a systems analyst, an accountant, a civil servant and director of a charity. Now that her two children have left home, she and her husband have moved from Hampshire to the Welsh Marches, where she is revelling in the more rugged country and the wealth of medieval locations. When she is not writing or climbing through ruined castles, she devotes her time to trying to tame her house and garden, both of which are determined to resist any suggestion of order. Readers are invited to visit Joanna's website at www.joannamaitland.com

Dear Reader,

After ranging widely across Europe with my spying brothers in *The Aikenhead Honours* trilogy, it was delightful to return to English Regency Society for Jon and Beth's story. As you will see, it begins with one strange Christmas encounter and ends with another, bang in the middle of a grand Christmas house party.

In the Regency period, before Queen Victoria and Prince Albert imported the tradition of Christmas trees from Germany, Christmas was symbolised by the burning of the great Yule Log and by rooms decorated with holly, ivy and, of course, mistletoe. I confess I couldn't resist including the old tradition of removing a berry for every kiss. Once all the mistletoe berries were gone, there could be no more kissing, so it paid to be forward enough to grab your girl early. But would the forward man's advances be welcome to his chosen lady? In at least one case here, they definitely are not.

Mistletoe is important to several of my characters in rather unexpected ways, but you'll also meet a hidden folly being put to highly unconventional uses and an extraordinary and scandalous challenge from Beth that Jon, for all his experiences as a battle-hardened soldier, finds it very difficult to deal with.

I hope you enjoy the twists and turns of my Christmas tale and also your own Christmas kisses under the mistletoe, if you are lucky enough to have some to hang in your house. Happy reading and happy holidays!

Joanna

Dedicated to
the Romantic Novelists' Association
in its 50th Anniversary year
with grateful thanks for
all the inspiration, support and friendship
I have found there

Prologue

It was cold. So very cold.

Sharp icy fingers were probing into the hidden crevices of her clothing and scratching at every inch of exposed skin. The sleet-laden wind was whipping across her cheeks like scouring sand, rubbing them raw. Every breath was a torment to her aching lungs.

But she had no choice. She must go on. Away from all those pointing fingers. To somewhere safe, somewhere she could breathe again.

She had no idea where she was or where this lonely rutted path might lead. She raised her chin to peer ahead, brushing aside the wet strings of her hair and screwing up her eyes against the sleet in an attempt to see her way. Overhanging trees, mostly naked against the onset of winter; an under-layer of shrubs, some evergreen, but most of them bare and soggy black in the storm; a sodden path strewn with drifts of dead leaves that would soon be swallowed up by the deep, oozing mud. And beyond the trees, the path led into darkness.

She shivered, drew her thin shawl tighter around her shoulders and bent her head against the keening wind. If she stopped now, here, alone, the weather would win their unequal battle. She was not ready to yield. Not yet.

She plodded on, forcing herself to lift her weary feet, one step, then another, trying to ignore the freezing water in her boots and the squelching of the mud as it tried to hold her fast and suck her down. She was so very tired. If only—

For a second, the wind changed and whipped at her skirts from behind. She saw— No, she fancied she saw a simple fence, of posts and rails, of the kind that might border a country road, but it was gone in the blink of an eye. No matter how much she strained, she could not find it again. She had probably seen only what she longed to see: some sign of human habitation, of human warmth, of hope.

There was no hope.

The last light of the short December day was almost gone. Soon she would be alone, in the dark, in this strange wooded place, on a path that led to nowhere. Why on earth had she followed it?

At the time, it had seemed the most sensible course. What else could a woman do, abandoned at a lonely crossroads by the coach driver who had taken her up?

She had travelled many miles with him, naively believing that he was helping her out of the goodness of his heart. In truth, he was merely waiting to bring her to a suitably lonely place, where he could present his ultimatum: her money, or her person. Once he discovered that she had neither money in her pocket nor any willingness to pay him in kind, his bluff good nature had vanished. He had brought her even further from any chance of rescue, and pushed her out on to the deserted road, without even allowing her to take down her battered travelling bag. He would sell the contents, he said, to make up for the fare she owed him. He had whipped up his horses then, disappearing without so much as a.glance at the woman he was leaving to the mercy of the storm.

She struggled to put the evil man from her mind. She must find the strength to go on. She must not give in to exhaustion. She *must* go on.

Beyond a huge oak tree, she found herself in an odd sort of dark clearing. It was edged with dense evergreen shrubs surrounding a broad area of churned mud and tussocks of grass. For a second, the wind dropped. In the sudden lull, she tried to tuck her hair back under her dripping bonnet. But the strings parted under the strain just as the wind returned, howling around her. Her bonnet was torn off and disappeared into the darkness, leaving her unbound hair whipping her face like slapping fingers.

She was too tired to wonder for more than a second why she should be suffering so. She knew only that she needed to find shelter soon, or the storm would surely best her.

There was that plain fence again! Or was it?

She took a few steps away from the path, trying to avoid the mud. The grass felt spongy beneath her feet, and treacherous, as though it might give way at any moment and plunge her down into some sucking void.

But those shrubs over there were thick and still densely green. Beneath them, she thought she could make out a kind of haven where they overhung a patch of more sheltered ground, full of dead leaves blown into heaps. It even looked fairly dry. She could take refuge there, just for a while, until the worst of the storm was over and she had regained a little of her strength.

She moved more quickly now. Being out of the wet was a prize worth the effort. She focused all her remaining strength on gaining it. But, in her haste, she forgot to watch where she was putting her feet. Her ankle turned. The laces of her boot snapped with a loud crack. Before she realised what was happening, the boot was gone, sucked away, and her stockinged foot had taken one more unwary step, sinking deep into the mud.

She cried out in shock and fear. Slimy hands seemed to be trying to drag her down. She tried to tell herself that it was nonsense, wild imaginings, but her senses were bewildered. She could not make them obey her.

She tugged hard, desperate to release her foot, but she did not have the strength. Her flailing arms found one of the branches of the evergreen. Something to give her purchase. She hung on to it with both hands and pulled again. No use. Still she could not—

Suddenly, she was free! She stumbled forward a single step, then pitched head first into the base of the shrub and the pile of leaves. Her head and her right arm crunched against unyielding wood. Her nose and mouth filled with debris and dirt. She tasted decay and mould. She was clawing at her face, desperate to breathe. It took her several moments to regain enough control to force the terrors from her mind.

Eventually, she spat out the last of the leaf fragments and forced herself up. Pain lanced through her injured arm. Was it broken? She could not tell.

The wind was howling even louder. The evergreens around the clearing bent before it with an angry but defeated hiss. Yet the branches above her did not swish away. They seemed to bend over her, caressingly, like a loving mother soothing her child to sleep. Soothing, soothing.

She let her body relax again into the leaf litter, pillowing her pounding head on her good arm, resting her cheek against her wet, ungloved palm. It would do no harm to close her eyes, just for a space, just until the storm abated. Then she would go on. She had to go on.

Closing her eyes changed everything. Soon she could no longer feel the pain or the cold seeping into her bones. The storm seemed less hostile. She could barely hear the wind or the beat of the rain on the leaves. Was she floating? She was beginning to feel as if she were weightless, drifting slowly up into the heavens. And the sky around her had turned a bright, fierce blue.

Warm fingers touched her clammy cheek, drawing her back to earth, to harsh, forbidding reality. She did not want to return.

The fingers pressed into her flesh, insisting, demanding. She tried to open her eyes in response, but her heavy lids refused to move.

'Where am I?' Though the words formed in her throat, no sound came out. She was so weak. So tired. Sleep. She longed to sleep again. To float away.

'Wake up, woman! You cannot stay here. Come. Open your eyes.' A man's voice. Strong, deep, educated. Forceful. Pulling her back.

Then a hand gripped her shoulder and shook it. Pain seized her, huge waves of pain in her shoulder and in her head. Pain that shattered her floating dream. She screamed.

'Dear God! You are hurt. Let me help you.'

She opened her eyes at last. Darkness. A single light, from a lamp, low down. She was lying on the ground. Was she badly injured? How had she come here? How had—?

More agony as the man slid his arms under her body and lifted her. She groaned aloud, partly from pain, partly from loss. She did not want to leave her floating refuge.

He laid her on the open ground in the freezing rain. Instantly, the cold was attacking her again, intensifying the pain. He lifted the lamp to her face and stared at her. She lay still, transfixed by his gaze.

The lamp was moved away. 'Trust me, ma'am. I will see you safe.' A moment later, he was stripping off his heavy coat and wrapping it round her helpless body. The smell of warm wet wool engulfed her. And the smell of man.

'Forgive me,' he said abruptly. 'I need a free hand for the lamp.' Without another word, he picked her up and slung her over his shoulder. Pain scythed through her. And then the blessed darkness returned to claim her.

She seemed to be dreaming his voice. Words, questions. Sometimes soothing, sometimes sharp. But never strong enough to pull her back from the cocoon of warmth that now surrounded her and held her safe. She felt she was floating away all over again, this time for ever.

And then her cocoon was gone!

She was alone with her suffering. She forced her eyes open. She was propped up in a curricle. By the dim light of its lamps, she saw that the horses were hitched to a fence. Was there a house beyond?

'You are come back to us, ma'am.' His tall figure reappeared from the darkness. He had not deserted her. Perhaps she could trust him, after all. 'Come, let me carry you in.'

This time, he was more mindful of her hurts, lifting her carefully into his arms and cradling her close to his body. She let herself relax into his reassuring strength. The scent of man and horse and leather surrounded her. For a moment, he stood still, gazing down at her with concern in his dark eyes. Then his jaw clenched and he started towards the house.

She saw a winding path through dark, dripping shrubs. Then an open doorway filled with light and warmth and welcome. And a small round man in clerical garb, hovering anxiously.

As her rescuer hurried towards the doorstep, a little old lady in a lace cap appeared from the depths of the hallway, followed by an even smaller maidservant. 'Why, Master Jonathan! You are welcome, as always. But who is this you have brought us?'

'Mrs Aubrey! Thank goodness!' He shouldered his way past the old man and into the hall. 'I have never seen her before, but I believe she is a lady. I rescued her from the woods by the old oak. She is hurt. And almost frozen to death.'

The old man gasped. 'Dear God. Poor child. And at Christmas, too.'

His wife stepped forward in order to smooth back the wet hair and peer into the new arrival's face. 'What is your name, my dear?'

That came like a blow, worse than all the pain that had gone before. It was a terrible, terrifying realisation. 'I...I do not know.'

Chapter One

'Beth, dear?'

Beth. Sometimes, it still jarred. Was that truly her name? 'Dear Beth' had been the only legible words on a soggy, much-folded note in the pocket of her threadbare gown. They had found no other clue to her identity. All their discreet enquiries had yielded absolutely nothing more. So, after more than six months, Beth was still in Fratcombe with her benefactors, and still the woman of mystery she had been on the night Jonathan rescued her. It nagged at her that she might not even be 'Beth' at all.

Mrs Aubrey had appeared in the doorway. 'Yes, ma'am?' Beth said brightly.

'Do you think you could fetch me some ribbon from Mr Green's when you finish at the school today?'

'Yes, of course,' Beth replied immediately. 'What do you need?'

Mrs Aubrey brought out a length of dress fabric, and they

spent a comfortable few minutes discussing the style the old lady planned to stitch.

'You have chosen a delightful shade, ma'am. Not quite purple and not quite garnet red, either. The only difficulty will be finding a ribbon to suit such an unusual colour. But I promise I will do my very best.'

'You will have time?'

'Oh, yes. Mr Green's will be open for at least an hour after the children have gone home. If it takes me longer than that to find your ribbon, Aunt Caro, I shall be a failure indeed.' She smiled down at the little old lady. Beth had come to love Mrs Aubrey like a mother, for she was kind and generous, as well as surprisingly full of fun and mischief. Neither Mrs Aubrey nor the rector cared that Beth had no history before her arrival in the village. Her educated speech and soft hands proved her a lady, the Aubreys said, and so, over Beth's guilty protests, they had insisted she remain with them. Indeed, the rector's wife had let it be known from the first that Beth was a distant relation, come to make a long stay in Fratcombe. Most of the village had accepted it without question. As the months passed, even Beth had come to think of herself as Miss Elizabeth Aubrey, one of the rector's family. It was a warm, comforting feeling, one she treasured. But it could not quite overcome the guilty fears that sometimes gave her nightmares. What might she have done in the past? What could be so bad that her mind refused to let her remember?

Gathering up her basket with the lesson materials she had prepared, Beth dropped a kiss on Mrs Aubrey's cheek and made her way out into the bright morning sunshine. The rectory stood next to the Saxon church at one end of the village. The school had been set up in a vacant house near the middle of Fratcombe alongside the main shops. It was an easy walk, though the day promised to be very hot later.

Beth smiled up at the clear blue sky. A Spanish sky would be a darker, deeper blue, she supposed, nearer the colour of Jonathan's eyes, as far as she could remember it from that single, pain-hazed meeting. She had never even had a chance to thank him. The morning after the rescue, he had left Fratcombe Manor in response to an urgent summons from Horse Guards. There had been an apologetic farewell note to the rector, as good manners required, but he had taken the trouble to include good wishes for Beth's recovery as well. That thoughtfulness still warmed her heart, though it saddened her that she had not seen him again. It was the life of a soldier, she supposed. Apart from that one fleeting spell of home leave, he had been in the Peninsula for years, fighting the French.

She had not thought it her place to ask questions about her rescuer. That would have been vulgar. But, by listening to others, she had learned to admire him even more. His name was Jonathan Foxe-Garway. And although the Aubreys had known him as a boy and still referred to him as 'Master Jonathan', he was in fact the Earl of Portbury, a man of rank and great wealth. He was the rector's patron, of course, but he was also a man the Aubreys valued for himself. They spoke of him often, telling tales of outrageous childhood escapades at the Manor, and amusing pranks when he had first gone up to Oxford. No doubt he had also done things that the rector judged unfit for a lady's ears but, if so, his sins were far outweighed by his devotion to duty and his bravery on the battlefield.

Whatever the rector might say about duty, it seemed strange to Beth that an earl should have chosen to join Lord Wellington's army, to face the hardships and dangers of campaigning. Did he not have a greater duty to his name and his estates? He could not possibly be managing them from a windswept tent in Spain.

She was unlikely to discover the truth of that. The Aubreys' tales were entertaining and sometimes revealing, but never indiscreet. In any case, it was not her concern. However, it was impossible for Beth to forget Jonathan Foxe-Garway. He was her rescuer. The passage of time could not change that, even though his image was a blur. No wonder, for she had been barely conscious. She had little more than a vague impression of height, and strength, coupled with penetrating blue eyes and that reassuring voice as he carried her up the rectory stairs and laid her on a warm, soft bed. Sometimes, in her dreams, she saw him clearly, but only there. Once, she had even dreamt he was galloping towards her, clad in silver armour and mounted on a white charger, like a knight in a fairy tale.

That, she knew, was quite ridiculous. She was a grown woman. She must be at least twenty-four or twenty-five. A woman of such advanced years should certainly know better than to cling to childish fantasies. Yet the sound of his voice kept haunting her dreams. She imagined it would be so until the day she died, a schoolmistress, and an old maid.

One of her pupils, a little boy called Peter, came racing up, bowling a hoop. 'Miss Aubrey! Oh, Miss Aubrey, look at my hoop!' At that moment, he lost control and it toppled into a patch of nettles by the lane. Before Beth could stop him, he had dived in after it. He cried out in pain.

Poor Peter. He was only five and knew no better. Beth lifted him into her arms and wiped away his tears with a gentle finger. 'You are a brave boy, Peter. Come, let me set you down and we will find something for that sting.' She carefully retrieved the hoop with her gloved hand. 'Hold that for me, while I look.' She used the handle of her parasol to brush aside the lush greenery of high summer. 'See this, Peter?' She pointed to a dock plant. 'For nettle stings, the sovereign remedy is dock leaves. Let me show you.' She picked a few, stripped off her gloves and began to rub the leaves on the reddened patches on his skin. Then she wrapped some larger leaves around his injured arm. 'Hold those against the sting, Peter, while I take your hoop. It will soon stop hurting.'

'Stopped hurting already, miss.' He sounded much cheerier.

'Well done. You are very brave, and you will be able to teach all your friends about avoiding nettles, and curing their stings, won't you?'

He grinned cheekily, showing missing front teeth. Still, he was a clever boy, one who would make something of himself if Beth had her way, even though he was only the son of a farm labourer. In fact, his father had a cottage on the Fratcombe Manor estate. Jonathan's estate.

Everything kept coming back to Jonathan.

This was a matter of the future of a child, she told herself sternly. If Jonathan—if Lord Portbury ever returned to Fratcombe, she would ask him to take an interest in Peter. She was quite sure he would not begrudge his help to a bright lad who had grown up on his own estate.

They had reached the school. Peter, mindful of the manners Beth had taught him, bowed neatly to her before racing away to show off his scars and his new hoop. The other children gathered round him, exclaiming excitedly in piping voices. There were only ten of them, six boys and four girls, but Beth was proud of what she had achieved with them in just a few short months. The village, and the rectory, had given her shelter. It was right that she should repay them with her labour, the only thing she had to offer. Besides, doing good for others helped to lessen her ever-present guilt at what might be hidden in her missing past.

She checked her watch. It was almost the hour. She laid aside her bonnet and gloves and lifted the handbell to call the children into class.

It took no time at all to select a ribbon from Mr Green's vast range, even though Mrs Aubrey's silk was such an unusual shade. Beth stowed the tiny parcel in her basket and stepped out into the afternoon heat, grateful for her parasol and straw bonnet. Mrs Aubrey would not be expecting her for at least another half hour. She had some time for herself.

She looked around a little apprehensively, wondering whether anyone from the gentry families might appear. They often drove by in the afternoons. Such an encounter would quickly spoil her sunny mood.

In spite of the care the Aubreys had taken, it had been impossible to prevent some gossip. The wealthy ladies of the district had descended on the rectory to inspect the new arrival as soon as she left her bed. Unfortunately, Beth's vague answers to questions about her background and family aroused suspicion among these eagle-eyed mamas, who lost no time in issuing instructions to their offspring. Their sons might ogle pretty Beth Aubrey from a distance, but they would never ask to be introduced. Just one young man had approached Beth—Sir Bertram Fitzherbert's eldest son— but his only interest was in a quick grope behind a hedge. He had not succeeded, and his fumbling attack had taught her to be extremely wary of all the young sprigs of fashion. None of them had Jonathan's honour and integrity where an unprotected female was concerned. He was a shining knight; they were arrogant young puppies. Or worse.

Not surprisingly, most of the society invitations arriving at the rectory were pointedly addressed to the rector and Mrs Aubrey alone. Mrs Aubrey had been minded, at first, to confront such appalling rudeness. But the mere suggestion had reawakened all Beth's guilty fears. She knew the rector could not afford to offend the great families, especially when Jonathan was not in England to take his part. Her nightmares had returned, and the sick headache that often followed. She had pleaded desperately for the insult to be ignored, and dear Mrs Aubrey, much affected by Beth's distress, had finally agreed.

Not all the families shunned her, however. In two of the

grand houses—houses with no unmarried sons—Beth had actually become quite well acquainted with the younger daughters. Beth's eye for fashion was particularly valued; the girls often sought her views on the trimming of a bonnet or the important business of changing a hairstyle. Beth enjoyed it all, although she had no place at the side of young heiresses, for she knew she was nothing of the sort. Nor had she ever been one. No heiress would have owned the dowdy clothes that Beth had been found in. They were fit only for a gypsy, or a tramp.

Beth glanced up and down the village street one last time. It was safely deserted. There was no one to see which way she went.

Instead of turning right, in the direction of the church and the lodge gates, she turned left. If anyone should question her, she would say she was going to call on old Mrs Jenkinson, who lived in the last house at the far end of the village, just before the sharp bend in the road. From there, it was but a step to Beth's goal.

Walking at a very brisk pace, she soon reached the woods, though she was uncomfortably hot by then. The turn in the road now concealed her from the village itself. And since it was highly unlikely that anyone would pass this way, she was at liberty to indulge herself. Just a little.

She put her basket and parasol on the ground behind a fence-post and leaned on the rail, gazing round at the clearing. This was where it had all begun. This was where Jonathan had found her.

There was nothing in the least unusual about it. It was

simply a clearing at the edge of a wood, surrounded by thick evergreens and with a single, venerable oak where the clearing joined the main path. She smiled up at the branches of the tree, now green and youthful where, before, they had been black and bare. On an impulse, she ducked under the rail and started across the grass. In spite of the hot weather, it was still quite spongy underfoot. There was a stream close by, which never dried out. No wonder everywhere had been so muddy that night.

She made her way across to the overhanging shrubs and lifted the long branches to peer underneath. The heaps of leaves were still there, blown in, year after year, and too dry to rot. She was grateful for that. If she had lain down on wet leaves, soaked as she was, she would probably have died long before Jonathan could find her. His arrival was like a miracle.

She picked her way across to the path by the oak and stroked its wrinkled trunk. She had come here so many times, looking around, walking along the path, trying to retrieve some memory of what had gone before. It had never succeeded, and this time was no different.

Beth sighed. She had been here quite long enough. She must hurry back to the rectory. Mrs Aubrey must not have cause for worry.

It was only when Beth came out from under the shade of the oak tree that she realised how dark it was. In the space of only a few minutes, the sky had become almost black. There was going to be a fearsome storm. And she was here, far from shelter, with no protection at all!

She started to run across the clearing, back to where she

had left her basket, but she had forgotten the treacherous ground. Her ankle turned, she lost her balance and fell her length. She swallowed the urge to utter a most unladylike curse and tried to brush the grass from her pale muslin gown. She made to get up, wondering all the while whether Mrs Aubrey's maid had a remedy for grass stains.

'Ouch!' The moment she put her right foot to the ground, a pain shot up her leg. She closed her eyes in frustration. Now what was she to do? She was out of sight of the village, she had sprained her ankle, and a storm was coming on. This time she did curse. Vehemently.

First and foremost, she must get away from these trees. She glanced up at the sky again. Huge black anvil clouds promised thunder and lightning, as well as rain. She *must* get away from the trees.

She hobbled slowly back to the fence and leant on it to catch her breath. Her parasol would act as a makeshift walking-stick, she decided. Her basket could remain where it was.

But not Mrs Aubrey's ribbon! That must not be soaked by the storm. Beth tucked the little parcel safely into the bodice of her gown. Then, gritting her teeth against the pain, she ducked under the fence and started back along the lane to Fratcombe.

It had felt like no distance at all on the way here, but now the bend seemed miles away. Beyond it was Widow Jenkinson's house, where Beth would be able to ask for shelter. She hobbled awkwardly along, leaning heavily on her parasol. It was not strong enough to bear her weight. The handle snapped after just a few yards. Fate was definitely against her.

She stood on her good leg gazing down at the pieces of broken parasol. 'Oh, fiddlesticks!' She hurled the useless handle to the ground.

'May I be of assistance, ma'am?'

Beth whirled round so quickly that she forgot about her injury and put her weight on her sprained ankle. She cried out in pain and almost fell.

'Good God, ma'am! You are hurt.'

That voice had not changed. It was Jonathan.

She had been so intent on cursing the flimsy parasol that she had not heard the sound of his arrival.

'Go to their heads.' This time, he was not alone. A groom jumped down and ran to hold the horses. Jonathan sprang to the ground at the same moment and reached Beth just as she managed to regain her balance.

Her pain was forgotten. It was Jonathan. He had returned. He had returned to save her, all over again.

'Let me help you into my curricle, ma'am.' He offered his arm. 'Lean on me. You should not put any weight on that ankle.'

She accepted gladly. Even with only one good leg, she felt as if she were floating, buoyed up by his touch, but when they reached the carriage step, reality intruded. She stopped, uncertain of whether she could mount.

'Allow me.' With a single, swift movement he picked her up in his arms. Her mind was instantly full of the scent of him, long familiar from her dreams, but before she could relax into his embrace, he had deposited her on the soft leather seat and stepped back. She felt bereft. 'Shall I fetch your parasol for you?' He pointed back to where it lay on the ground.

'If you would be so good, sir,' she said demurely, trying to avoid those penetrating eyes. She needed a few moments to collect her thoughts and regain control of her soaring emotions. This was no time for the stuff of dreams. He was bound to have questions. Her stomach lurched alarmingly. He would want to know what she had discovered about her past. How could she ever explain that there was nothing to tell?

He was back in a trice, offering her the broken parasol. When she shook her head, he dropped the pieces on to the floor and sprang up to take his seat beside her. 'There is a storm coming. My horses can smell it. I need to get them under cover before it breaks.' Without waiting for orders, the groom ran to swing himself up behind, while Jonathan started his pair into motion. He was giving them all his attention, keeping them under rigid control. There must be a danger that they would try to bolt when the lightning came. She found she was perversely glad of it. No questions yet awhile.

She tried to keep her eyes on the road, but she could not stop herself from stealing greedy sideways glances at Jonathan. This time, she would fix every detail of his image in her memory. His face was extremely brown. Too dark and leathery for a gentleman's complexion, of course, but only to be expected in a man who had served for so long under the burning sun of the Peninsula. There were flecks of grey in the dark hair around his temples and behind his ears. She could make out fine white lines at the corner of his eyes, too. Laughter lines, perhaps? Or simply the result of screwing up his eyes against the brilliant light? She was not at all sure that he had been laughing much. His expression seemed harsh, and there was a stern set to his jaw. He looked…he looked intimidating.

She guessed—no, she knew, by instinct—that her gallant rescuer had been changed by his years in the army, and that his experiences had not softened him. No doubt he had been involved in bloody battles. He must have suffered. He had probably lost comrades, and friends. Beth had read the lists of casualties in the rector's newspaper, always with her heart in her mouth lest the Earl of Portbury be among them: She knew his regiment had taken heavy losses, particularly at the siege of Badajoz, only months before.

They had almost reached the bend that led to the village. Jonathan was slowing his horses for the turn, his gloved hands pulling back on the reins. They were lean, strong hands, but sensitive, too, as Beth knew from experience, both then and now. His hands had touched her skin and—

She forced herself to push the image aside and to smile politely. A real lady would never permit such wanton thoughts!

They had completed the turn and were speeding up once more. 'And now, ma'am, I pray you will tell me where I may set you down.' He glanced across at her face, his eyes widening with what might be admiration. Her heart began to race, all over again. Was it possible that he—?

He turned back to his horses. 'You are a lady of remarkable fortitude, to smile through the pain of your injured ankle,' he said, with studied politeness. 'I know it is not quite the thing, but I hope you will permit me to introduce myself, for it is seldom that a man has the pleasure of meeting a lady with such courage.'

Beth's smile faltered. Great waves of pain broke over her whole body. He had forgotten her completely.

Chapter Two

The introductions were brief and rather stilted, but Jon did not waste valuable time in enquiring what suddenly ailed his passenger. He sprang his horses along the empty village street and hauled them to a stand at the rectory gate. A quick glance up at the louring sky warned him that the storm would break at any moment. Polite niceties would have to wait.

Leaving his groom to mind the horses, Jon leapt down and hurried round to Miss Aubrey's side. 'There is no time to lose, ma'am. The storm is coming. Pray put your arm around my neck and I will carry you in.' He ignored her shocked gasp and her chalk-white face. This was no time for displays of missish modesty. He slid one arm round her back and the other under her knees, hefted her into his arms and raced up the path to the rectory door.

'Would you be so good as to ply the knocker, ma'am?'

It seemed to take her a moment or two to realise what he was asking of her. Was she slow-witted? No, surely not. He was being too hard on her. Perhaps the pain in her ankle had worsened? In addition to her strange pallor, she was also biting her lip.

The door was opened by a very small maid. 'Oh, miss!' she cried.

'Open the door wide, that I may carry Miss Aubrey inside. Hurry!' He almost pushed his way into the hall. He carried her through the first available door, into the small parlour at the front of the house. It was deserted. 'Fetch the rector or Mrs Aubrey. Quickly now!' The maid was still standing in the hall, open-mouthed. Jon knelt to slide Miss Aubrey on to the sofa and then rose again, frowning. He took one angry step towards the girl, who gasped in fright and took to her heels.

Jon turned back to the invalid. 'Forgive me, ma'am, but I must get my horses under cover before the storm. Perhaps you would give my regards to Mr and Mrs Aubrey? I—'

'Master Jonathan!' Mrs Aubrey was standing in the doorway.

Jon spun round and sketched a quick bow. 'As I was saying to Miss Aubrey, ma'am, I must see to my horses before the storm. Miss Aubrey, I fear, has sprained her ankle, but now that you are here, I know she will be well taken care of. I shall call again, as soon as may be.' He strode to the door and smiled down at the old lady's puzzled frown. 'We shall be able to talk more comfortably then.' He bowed again. 'My compliments to the rector.' Then he hurried back to the front door.

The timid little maid was nowhere to be seen, so Jon let himself out and ran down the path to his curricle. 'Right, Sam. Let's see what kind of speed we can make to the

Manor. If this pair are going to bolt, I'd much rather they did so on my own land.'

'You poor child, you are shivering. It must be the shock. Let me find you a shawl.' Mrs Aubrey tugged hard at the bell. 'Brandy. The rector always says it is the best remedy. Oh, if only he were here.' She was talking as much to herself as to Beth. 'Ah, Hetty. Go upstairs and fetch down Miss Beth's heaviest shawl. And then bring me the decanter of brandy from the rector's library. Quickly now. Miss Beth is injured.'

The little maid bobbed a curtsy and disappeared.

Beth neither moved nor spoke. She could not. Her teeth were chattering. Her body felt as if it had been doused in freezing water. She could not feel any of her limbs, not even her injured ankle. She was totally numb. Her shining champion was nothing of the kind. She had been looking for his return for months now, while he had completely forgotten that she existed. She had been conjuring up castles in the air, like one of the tiny children in her schoolroom. She was an utter fool!

Mrs Aubrey set a chair by Beth's feet and pushed aside the grubby muslin skirts. 'Oh, dear. That is very swollen.' She began to ease off Beth's shoes. She was trying to be gentle, but pain shot up Beth's leg, pulling her sharply back to the real world. She was unable to suppress a little groan. 'Aye, my dear. I know. It does look very painful.' Mrs Aubrey ran her fingers very gently over Beth's foot and lower leg.

Beth gritted her teeth. She would not allow herself to make another sound. She might have behaved like a silly schoolgirl over Jonathan, but she was not such a faint heart as to scream over a turned ankle.

'I am almost certain that it is only a sprain, my dear, though once the storm has passed, I shall send the boy for the doctor. Just to check.'

'Oh, ma'am—' Beth could barely find her voice.

'Hush, child. Ah, Hetty. Excellent. Here, give it to me.' Mrs Aubrey helped Beth to sit up a little further and wrapped her warmly in the shawl. Then she slid extra cushions behind her, for support.

Before Beth could say a word of thanks, Hetty reappeared with the decanter and two glasses.

'Put it down there.' Mrs Aubrey pointed to the small piecrust table near Beth's hand. The old lady was in her element, for she loved caring for invalids. 'Now fetch me a basin of cold water, some cloths, and towels. We must put cold compresses on this ankle before it swells any more.'

The little maid nodded and disappeared again.

'First, a little brandy.' Mrs Aubrey poured out a small amount. She hesitated and then poured the merest film of liquid into the second glass. 'I have had two shocks this afternoon. First, your sprained ankle, and then Master Jonathan's unexpected return. He has put off his regimentals, too. I wonder…?' She paused, staring at nothing. Then, recollecting herself, she pressed the fuller glass into Beth's hand and raised her own. 'To your speedy recovery, my dear. And poor Jonathan's also.'

Jon dropped gratefully into the huge leather chair and stretched out his legs. What a day!

His valet, Vernon, pulled off Jon's boots with gloved hands and exaggerated care. Then he padded off to the dressing room where he had already hung up Jon's wet coat.

Jon sighed as the door closed between them. There was no noise inside the bedchamber now, apart from the hiss and sputter of the newly lit fire. He let his head fall back on to the leather. For a moment, he stared vacantly at the ceiling. Then he let his eyes drift closed and forced his shoulders to relax. Peace at last.

It was good to be back at Fratcombe. Here he would be spared his mother's tart reminders of his duty, and his brother's annoying company, too. Here he could visit his good friend, the rector. That last visit to Fratcombe seemed an age ago now. It had been so short—less that twenty-four hours, all told—that he had barely spoken to the Aubreys. Before he could even unpack, Jon had been summoned to London and sent back to Spain where—

He shook his head vigorously. He did not want to think about Spain.

A question began to nag at the edge of his brain. He had been so busy trying to escape the storm that he had pushed it aside till now. Who on earth was Miss Elizabeth Aubrey? The Aubreys had no children, Jon knew. Nor had there ever been any mention of brothers on the rector's side. So, probably not a niece or great-niece either. She must be some very distant relation. But why had she never been mentioned before?

Intrigued, Jon decided that he would pay a call at the rectory first thing in the morning. A few polite questions would soon solve this little puzzle. Besides, the lady herself was quite attractive, as far as he could recall. He had been too concerned for his horses to pay much attention to her—until he carried her inside. Lifting her into his curricle was one thing, but carrying her the length of the rectory path and into the little parlour was quite another! He might be unsure of the colour of her eyes, but he certainly remembered the feel of her curves through her thin summer muslins. A tallish lady, and slim, but rounded in exactly the right places to fill a man's hands.

It was interesting that she was unmarried, for she must be at least two- or three-and-twenty. Lack of dowry, probably. But at least she was old enough to have passed the simpering stage. He was surprised to find he was actually looking forward to becoming better acquainted with the mysterious Miss Aubrey. Perhaps he should invite all three of them to visit the Manor? Nothing at all improper in that, not when he and the Aubreys were such old friends. Yes, he would pay a call tomorrow, and if the lady proved to be amiable—as he fully expected any relation of the rector's to be—he would issue the invitation. It was too long since he had been in company with real ladies, of the kind who could converse sensibly with a man. By comparison with the insipid schoolgirls that Jon's mother favoured, Miss Aubrey might be a refreshing change. Just the kind of pleasant diversion he needed during this brief visit to Fratcombe Manor.

Thunder rattled the windows. The storm was now raging immediately overhead: blinding flashes of lightning, followed almost instantly by drum rolls of thunder. Between them, Mother Nature and Father Zeus were showing what they could do.

Behind the closed door of the dressing room, Jon's valet was probably still tutting over his ruined hat and coat, or muttering about the mud on his boots. Jon did not give a fig for the man. An earl's consequence required a tonnish manservant, and Vernon was certainly that, but he had little else to recommend him. Jon should have chosen with more care on his return to England, but he had been too world-weary to bother with such a chore.

He had of course ensured that Joseph, his army batman, was properly recompensed and given a comfortable annuity for his years of devoted service. Joseph planned to set himself up in a small public house, he said. He might even find himself a wife.

A wife?

Jon groaned and rose to put more logs on the fire. At this moment, he really longed to see cheerful flames. One of his good and abiding memories of his years in Spain was sitting round the camp fire, sharing the local brandy with his comrades, and laughing together at the very silly tales they told each other.

The valet might be new to Jon's service, but he had at least thought to provide a decanter of brandy in the master's chamber. Jon smiled wryly and poured himself a large measure. He was minded to toss it down in a single swallow, but he did not. Once or twice in Spain, he had allowed himself to get very drunk when the pain of loss was almost unbearable. Returning to England's damp countryside did not justify seeking oblivion in drink. It would insult the friends who had been left behind in baked Spanish earth.

Jon took one large mouthful, savouring the flavours.

The dressing room door opened. 'Is there anything else I can do for your lordship?'

Jon shook his head and waved the man away. He was too punctilious by half. Perhaps if Joseph had not yet spent his money…? No, that would not do. Joseph was a batman, not an earl's valet. Besides, he wanted more than a business of his own. He wanted a wife, and perhaps a family. If he returned to serve Jon, what woman would have him? Let it be.

Jon sat down again and took another slow sip of his brandy.

A wife. Everything always came back to a wife. Particularly in his mother's eyes. Jon had barely had time to kiss her cheek before she started on the subject. Since Jon's first wife had been dead for well over a year, he should be looking about him for another. The matter was urgent, the Dowager maintained. And this time, he *must* set up his nursery.

Her ideas of duty—an earl must make a dynastic marriage and produce at least an heir and a spare—were much the same as his late father's. And just as blinkered. Jon's wife, Alicia, had been a duke's daughter, but their marriage had been a total disaster. Even his mother would admit that now. And yet, she wanted him to do it all over again, to select a bride of rank from among the simpering debutantes on the London marriage mart. It would not cross her mind that an age gap of well-nigh twenty years might be unbridgeable. How was he, a man of thirty-five, to take charge of a green girl just out of the schoolroom? He need not spend much time with her, of course—except for the inescapable duty of getting an heir—and he would certainly hold himself aloof, as his rank required, but still, the prospect of all that empty-headed gabbling was more than he could stomach. That was the kind of marriage his father had made, and his grandfather before him. But neither of them had been to war or watched friends die. War changed what a man valued in life…

Beth felt a bit of a fraud, leaning on a walking stick. It was not as if she had done any real damage. On the other hand, it was extremely painful to put her full weight on her injured ankle. So, for the moment, the walking stick would have to stay. The most difficult part of life was coping with the stairs without a strong man to help her. The rector was much too old to carry Beth. If he had offered, she would certainly have refused.

If Jonathan had offered to take her in his arms…

Beth's insides were melting at the mere thought of his hands on her body. She shook her head, cross with herself for allowing his image to intrude, yet again. She had been trying so hard not to think about him. Sadly, the more she tried, the more he filled her mind and confused her rioting senses. And the more her guilt returned to haunt her.

She stood at the top of the stairs, looking down to the hall. It seemed a very long way, but she would conquer it. With her walking stick in one hand and her other hand on the baluster rail, she started carefully down.

Hetty appeared when Beth had reached about half way. 'Oh, Miss Beth. Let me help you.' She started up the stairs.

Beth paused, balanced carefully and shook her head.

'Thank you, Hetty, but I am quite well enough to manage. I must learn to use my cane and, in any case, you have better things to do than to act as a crutch for me.'

'Well, if you say so, miss. But you will not go out of the house, will you? I can bring you anything you need.'

Beth finally reached the hallway. She was a little out of breath, but she was proud of herself. 'No, Hetty, I will not go out of the house. Though I must say that I am glad that it is not a school day. The children would have worried if I had failed to turn up for their lessons.'

'Mrs Aubrey said she would take over while you were poorly. She's looking forward to it, she says.' Hetty grinned knowingly.

'Does she now?' Beth smiled back at the maid. It sounded as if Aunt Caro intended Beth to remain an invalid for several more days. Well, Beth would see about that. The rector's wife had responsibilities enough. She could not be expected to become the schoolmistress as well.

Beth made her way slowly into the little parlour at the front of the house so that she would be able to see the comings and goings in the street. She might even be able to see Jonathan's curricle. 'Oh, for goodness' sake!'

'Did I do something wrong, Miss Beth?' Hetty sounded hurt.

Beth realised she had spoken aloud. 'I am sorry, Hetty. I was berating myself, not you.' She shook her head. 'This leg of mine refuses to do what I tell it.' That was not the cause of her outburst, but it would do.

'Mrs Aubrey said as you was to sit on the sofa with your leg up. And I was to bring you anything you needed.'

Beth gave in and subsided gratefully on to the sofa by the window. Before she could even draw breath, Hetty was lifting her bandaged leg on to the cushions. 'There, miss. Now, what may I fetch you?'

'If I am to lie here, like a pampered cat basking in the sun, I had better do something useful. If you would fetch me the mending, Hetty, I will make a start on that.'

Hetty returned with the mending basket. Beth, mindful of her latest resolution, selected the most difficult piece of work she could find. That should keep her mind occupied until Aunt Caro returned from her visiting. Being alone, and having time to think, was too dangerous. The last thing she needed was one of her sick headaches on top of a sprained ankle.

She had barely completed her first neat darn when Mrs Aubrey bustled in, removing her bonnet. She handed it to the maid. 'Would you fetch us some tea, Hetty? I am sure Miss Beth would enjoy a cup.'

'You are very good, ma'am, though I fear I have not earned it. Look how little I have done.'

'You are an invalid, child. You should be taking your ease, with nothing more than a romantic novel to amuse you. Invalids do not mend shirts.'

'This one does!' Beth replied pertly, but with an affectionate smile.

Mrs Aubrey chuckled and sat down opposite Beth. 'I have visited Widow Jenkinson this morning. She sends her best wishes for your speedy recovery. She was sad to learn that you had not been brought to her house to escape the storm.'

'It would have given her food for gossip for a month, especially if she had seen Jo—if she had seen his lordship carrying me up the path.' Mrs Aubrey might have leave to use Jonathan's given name, but Beth did not.

Mrs Aubrey chuckled again. 'I made a quick visit to the lodge also, as I was passing, although Master Jonathan was not at home.'

Beth raised her eyebrows, feigning surprise. Mrs Jenkinson and the lodge were at opposite ends of the village.

'Now *that*, young lady, is a most impudent look, I must say.'

Beth raised her eyebrows even higher.

'Oh, very well. No, I was not passing, as we both know. I went there deliberately, to find out about how long he means to remain at Fratcombe, that kind of thing. The least we can do is invite him to take dinner with us. Once you are well enough, of course.'

The thought of seeing Jonathan again, and of the difficult exchanges that might ensue, made Beth's head pound dangerously. 'I had best remain upstairs, ma'am. His lordship and the rector will have much to discuss. To have me hobbling about would be an unwelcome distraction.'

'Now that is a whisker, if ever I heard one.' Mrs Aubrey shook a mittened finger in mock reproof, but her eyes were twinkling. 'I shall pretend that I did not hear it at all.'

Hetty appeared with the tea tray and placed it carefully on the table in front of Mrs Aubrey. Just at that moment, someone plied the knocker, with considerable force.

Mrs Aubrey started. 'Goodness, who can that be, so early in the day? Hetty, go and open the door. Slowly.' Mrs Aubrey grabbed the mending out of Beth's fingers, bundled it into the basket and pushed the basket under a chair in the darkest corner of the room. Then she scurried back to resume her seat, clasping her hands demurely in her lap.

Beth was hard put to keep her face straight.

'The Earl of Portbury,' Hetty announced, bobbing a curtsy. He seemed much too large for the small family parlour.

Mrs Aubrey rose and dropped a tiny curtsy in response to her visitor's elegant bow. 'Master Jonathan! How kind of you to call. Will you take tea with us?' He nodded. 'Hetty, fetch another cup, if you please.'

He took a couple of paces into the room and bowed, separately, to Beth. She was suddenly so weak she could not even start to rise. Her body was remembering the feel of his arms around her, and softening, as if in anticipation. 'Forgive me, my lord, I cannot—'

'Pray do not attempt to move, Miss Aubrey. I am sure it took quite enough exertion for you to make your way downstairs this morning.' He paused, frowning suddenly. Then, turning back to Mrs Aubrey, 'Would you permit me to send over one of my footmen to help while Miss Aubrey is recovering? He could carry her up and down the stairs. And you could use him for any other convenient chores.'

'Master Jonathan, I should not dream—'

He waved a dismissive hand. 'You would be doing me a favour, ma'am. There are far too many servants at the Manor and, with only myself in residence, they do not have nearly enough to do. I cannot abide idleness.'

'Well…'

'Am I not to be consulted in this project of yours, my

lord?' Beth's voice sounded sharp in her own ears, for she had overcome her weakness by stoking her anger against him. He was treating her like a parcel. She would not allow that.

He turned to look down at her. The very faintest tinge of redness had appeared on his cheeks. 'I beg your pardon.' His voice grew quieter. 'It was not my intention to impose on you.'

She softened again, instantly. He had sounded arrogant, but he surely meant well. She had no right to let her inner turmoil betray itself in bad temper. 'Your offer is most generous, my lord, but it is not necessary. My ankle is mending extremely well and the more I exercise it, the sooner I shall be fully recovered.'

'Very well, ma'am.' He made to sit down beside Mrs Aubrey.

'And I would suggest,' Beth continued, feeling increasingly in control of this unequal encounter, 'that if your servants are underemployed, you should put them to work in the village. I am sure Mrs Aubrey can provide you with a long list of chores and repairs which need to be done.'

'Beth! You go too far!'

'No, ma'am. Miss Aubrey is quite right. I noticed yesterday, in spite of the storm, that some of the houses need urgent work. My agent has been most remiss in allowing such dilapidation. The repairs will be put in hand today.' He took a cup of tea from Mrs Aubrey and rose politely to carry it across to Beth. 'However, I fear I must disappoint Miss Aubrey. I doubt that my footmen have the inclination, or the skills, to carry them out.'

Beth took her tea with a demure nod and pursed lips. Was he roasting her? She hoped so. Strangers did not tease. But he had kept a totally straight face so she could not be sure. Until she was, she certainly must not laugh.

'Do you remain at Fratcombe long, Master Jonathan?' Mrs Aubrey poured his tea and handed it to him.

'Not on this occasion, ma'am, though I expect to return again quite soon. It is a huge change, from the army in Spain to the English countryside, I may tell you. There, our duty was simple—to fight the enemy. Since my return, I have been reminded of my other duties. To my various estates, for example, and to my position in society.' His voice grated, as if he was finding duty a hard taskmaster. Then, quite suddenly, he smiled warmly at the old lady in a way that transformed him. His face was softer, younger, and his eyes were dancing. 'Here, at the rectory, I know that I am welcomed as just an unruly lad who happens to have grown up. A little.'

Mrs Aubrey nodded, trying not to return his smile, but she could not conceal her fondness for Jonathan.

Beth swallowed. A knot of anxiety formed in her stomach. He had had the run of the rectory when he was a boy. Did he intend to visit often, to renew his intimacy with the Aubreys? Oh dear. When he was relaxed like this, he was much too attractive. Soon, she would be dreaming of silver-clad knights again, and she must not! She could so easily betray herself. She must find some way of avoiding his company. It was the only solution.

Mrs Aubrey cleared her throat. 'Perhaps you would tell us about your time in Spain?'

A sudden shadow crossed Jonathan's face. 'If you will

forgive me, ma'am, I would prefer not to speak of it. Much of it was not…er…pleasant, particularly of late.'

'I understand,' the old lady said quietly. 'We know that you were at the siege of Badajoz.' They knew, too, that he had been mentioned in dispatches for his part in the final assault, but Mrs Aubrey would not embarrass him by mentioning it. 'We read about the shameful outrages after the battle.'

He said nothing, but his face had assumed a very stern cast. Beth could not begin to imagine what he had experienced, or what he had seen, in that terrible siege and in the sack of the town which had followed. The casualties in the assault had been enormous, and the soldiers' conduct in the town afterwards had been utterly sickening.

The awkward silence stretched between them. Jonathan did not even move to drink his tea, though his jaw and his throat were working. He was remembering terrible things, Beth was sure. She tried desperately to think of something to say, to distract him from his obvious pain.

Mrs Aubrey was before her. 'So, Master Jonathan, what do you think of your lady foundling now? She has improved a good deal, would you not say, from the drowned stray you carried across our doorstep last Christmas?'

'What? *Miss Aubrey* is the lady from the clearing?'

Chapter Three

Shocked, and embarrassed, Jon moved in his seat to stare directly at the injured woman. 'I beg your pardon, ma'am,' he began, the words tumbling out in his haste to apologise. 'I had completely forgotten the incident until Mrs Aubrey mentioned it just now, because you look so—' He stopped just in time and cleared his throat.

Yesterday, he had assumed Miss Aubrey was a true lady, even if only a poor relation. But she was not an Aubrey at all. The bedraggled woman he had rescued could be anything, even a woman from the gutter! He recalled thinking at the time that she *might* be a lady, but still…

She was really very attractive, now he took the time to look at her. He let his gaze travel slowly from her curly red-brown hair and perfect complexion down the slim curves of her body, finally coming to rest on her bandaged ankle. 'Forgive me, but you look considerably more like a lady than you did then.' It was no more than the truth. But it was too stark. He had spoken without sufficient thought. Again!

What on earth was the matter with him? Coupled with his brazen scrutiny, his words were almost an insult. She had turned bright scarlet.

Recollecting his manners at last, and the wisdom of silence, he busied himself with his teacup while he tried to gather his wits.

After a long pause, he turned to Mrs Aubrey and said, in a polite but neutral voice, 'So our foundling has been here with you all this time? And with the name Aubrey? You did not discover her true identity?'

'We did everything possible, including advertising— discreetly—in the newspapers for a missing woman by the name of Elizabeth. But none of it produced any informa- tion at all. It is as though poor Beth had emerged out of nothing, like a phantom.'

Jon turned back to 'poor Beth'. Her heightened colour had drained away completely. 'I am heartily sorry that nothing could be done, ma'am. And you have had no memory at all, not the least flash of anything, in all these months?'

'No, my lord. Nothing.' Her response was very swift, and very definite.

Jon could not help wondering whether he should believe her. He had heard of cases where unscrupulous people had preyed on their benefactors by pretending to have lost their memory. Might that have happened here? Was Beth Aubrey a fraud? Perhaps that was why she had turned so pale? The Aubreys were a generous couple who would never look for such duplicity. 'It is very strange, I must say.

Has Dr Willoughby nothing to suggest on the matter? You have consulted him, I assume?'

'If we had consulted him about Beth's memory loss, it would have become common knowledge. Besides, what does a country doctor know of such things? So we—the rector and I—we allowed ourselves a little white lie. We gave out that Beth was a distant relation who had come to stay with us for a while, having no remaining close family of her own.'

'I see. Then no one hereabouts knows how Miss Aubrey was discovered?'

'Some of the gentry families suspect that Beth is not quite what she seems. I am sorry to say that some of them forget their Christian duty, and treat her like a servant, rather than a lady born and bred.' Mrs Aubrey shook her head sorrowfully. 'It is not what we would have expected of them.'

'Nor I, ma'am. When I stayed here as a child, I was always struck by the kindness and generosity of all the great families of the district.'

'That might have had something to do with the fact that you were heir to an earldom, sir.' Miss Aubrey sounded waspish. Not surprising, perhaps, especially if her plight was genuine.

Jon looked assessingly at her and was struck by the direct way she met and held his gaze. She certainly had the air of a true lady. 'As it happens, ma'am, I was not the heir then. That was my elder brother. But I do agree that my being the son of an earl might have coloured their judgement a little. And I am disappointed to learn that you have not always been accorded the respect due to a lady. The rector's sponsorship should be enough for anyone, however high their status.'

Yet again, he regretted his words the moment they were spoken. After all, the rector's word had not been enough for *him*. Guilt pricked Jon's conscience. He was responsible for this. He was the one who had rescued Beth; and the one who had foisted her on the Aubreys, even though he had not expected her to remain with them for long. If she was genuine, it was now Jon's duty to ensure she was restored to her rightful place, however lowly that might be. And if she was a fraud, it was his duty to expose her. She was not to be a welcome diversion after all. She was just one more irksome duty to be discharged.

Mrs Aubrey laid a hand on his sleeve. 'If *you* were seen to accept Beth, the other families would follow your lead, I am sure. As Earl of Portbury, you outrank them all.'

That was true, but was he prepared to do what she asked? Was it not his duty to satisfy himself, first of all, that Beth Aubrey was worthy of his support? He was still trying to decide how to reply when the sitting room door opened.

'Lady Fitzherbert has called, ma'am, and asks if—'

The little maid was not allowed to finish. Lady Fitzherbert, resplendent in rustling purple silk and feather-trimmed bonnet, pushed the girl aside and marched into the room. She paused barely long enough to drop a disdainful curtsy to Mrs Aubrey before launching into an angry complaint. 'I have come to consult the rector on a matter of urgent business, but your servant here tells me that he is not at home to callers. I must protest, ma'am. Why, I am—'

Jon had risen at the same time as Mrs Aubrey but did nothing else to draw attention to himself. He waited to see what would happen next.

'There has been some misunderstanding, I fear,' Mrs Aubrey said simply. 'The rector cannot see you because he is not at home. However, I expect him to return within the hour. Perhaps you would like to—?'

'Why, Lord Portbury! How delightful to see you safely returned!' Lady Fitzherbert abruptly turned aside from her hostess and sank into a very elegant curtsy.

Jon prepared himself for the worst kind of toadeating. Sir Bertram Fitzherbert and his detestable wife were relative newcomers to the district, but held themselves to be above everyone but the nobility. The Fitzherberts were bound to be among those who had slighted Beth Aubrey, for she was a nobody, with no social standing at all in their eyes.

In that instant, Jon decided their behaviour was an insult to him, as well as to the lady herself. Miss Aubrey was *his* foundling, after all. The rector's word *should* be good enough for such upstarts as the Fitzherberts. This harpy needed to be taken down a peg or two.

'Sir Bertram will be so pleased to learn that you are back in residence at the Manor,' Lady Fitzherbert gushed. 'There is so little truly genteel society hereabouts.'

'Country society can be a little restricted, to be sure,' Jon said, as soon as she paused to draw breath. 'But you have several families within easy driving distance. And during my absence from Fratcombe, you have had the rector and Mrs Aubrey. And Miss Aubrey, also.' He stepped aside so that Lady Fitzherbert would see Beth lying on the sofa behind him. 'You are already acquainted, I collect?'

'I…er…' Lady Fitzherbert's nostrils flared and her lips

clamped together. For several seconds, she stared down her long nose at Beth Aubrey. Then she half-turned back to Mrs Aubrey and drew herself up very straight. 'Excuse me, I may not stay longer. Pray tell the rector, when he returns, that Sir Bertram is evicting that band of dirty gypsies who are trespassing on our land. Sir Bertram wished it to be understood that they should not be given shelter in the district. Not by *anyone*.'

Mrs Aubrey's eyes narrowed dangerously, but her voice was soft. 'I am surprised that your husband did not come himself to deliver so important an instruction.'

Lady Fitzherbert tittered. 'Oh, Sir Bertram would never think to *instruct* the rector. Certainly not. Just…just a word to the wise.'

Jon had heard quite enough. 'I am sure the rector will be properly grateful, ma'am. But as it happens, Sir Bertram's warning is a little late. The gypsy band has leave to camp on my land at Fratcombe Manor.'

Lady Fitzherbert gasped and turned bright red. Then she swallowed hard. 'Since the rector is not here, I shall not trouble you further, ma'am. Lord Portbury.' She dipped another elegant curtsy to Jon, inclined her head a fraction to Mrs Aubrey and hurried out, without waiting for a servant to be summoned.

'Well, I declare!' Mrs Aubrey let out a long breath. Then she frowned up at Jon. 'Since when has Fratcombe Manor offered hospitality to gypsies?'

'It has never yet done so. I—'

'My lord, I pray you will not allow Sir Bertram

Fitzherbert to run them out of Fratcombe. He will not care what damage is done to their caravans and their horses. And there are so many helpless children—'

Jon stopped Miss Aubrey with a raised hand. His foundling was bringing him yet another problem. Now, she was prepared to plead for people who were truly outcasts from society. 'I have said they may use my land. For a week or two, at least. I will not go back on that.'

Nor would he, unless they broke his trust. He would instruct his workers to keep a sharp eye out for thieving or damage. At the first sign of either, the gypsies would be turned off. He was cynical enough to expect it within days.

'Thank you, my lord. I will impress on them that there must be no mischief.'

'*You?* You have dealings with the gypsies?'

She coloured a little but raised her chin defiantly. 'I am the Fratcombe schoolmistress. I teach all the children in the district. Whoever they are.'

'Master Jonathan, Beth goes to the gypsy camp when she can and gives lessons to the children. Just simple lettering and stories from the Bible. Even gypsies are God's creatures.'

'Yes,' Jon admitted grudgingly. The rector had often preached about the Good Samaritan. Now was Jon's chance to show that he had listened. 'Yes, you are right, ma'am. As long as they respect the law, they will not suffer at my hands. I do not persecute waifs and strays.'

Mrs Aubrey smiled at Jon and then very warmly across at Beth. 'No, you do not. Indeed, you rescue them. You brought us the daughter we never had.'

It was worse than he had imagined. If Beth Aubrey was a fraud, he could not expose her without hurting Mrs Aubrey. He knew he could never do that. The old lady had been like a mother to Jon when he and his brother had been at Fratcombe as boys. She had comforted Jon when his brother died. Her support had helped him to face the grief-stricken father who thought Jon a worthless replacement for his dead heir. How much had she understood of a young boy's desperate striving to win his father's esteem? It had never been spoken of. But she and the rector understood human failings. They would have seen how hard Jon tried, and how little he succeeded.

According to Jon's father, an earl's heir had to be brought up to understand his duty from the cradle, or he would never be more than a poor second best. Not that it stopped the old man from trying to thrash Jon into the mould he sought—duty, and distance, and distrust of everyone. He had almost succeeded, but he could never undermine Jon's trust in the Aubreys. They were truly good people, probably the only ones Jon knew. And if they loved Beth…

He turned back to the sofa. 'Has Lady Fitzherbert ever acknowledged you, ma'am?' he asked sharply.

She coloured and looked down at her clasped hands, shaking her head.

So that insufferable woman really was trying to usurp Jon's place in society. A set-down over the gypsies was not enough. There must be public retribution. It would be fitting to make Beth Aubrey his instrument.

'I have a mind to hold a splendid party at the Manor, to

which I shall invite all the gentry families. If you, Mrs Aubrey, would do me the honour of acting as my hostess, with your adopted daughter by your side, we shall teach all our stiff-rumped neighbours to treat Miss Aubrey with proper respect.'

'Oh, but you cannot,' Beth breathed.

'I can. And I will, if Mrs Aubrey agrees. Do you approve, ma'am?'

Mrs Aubrey twinkled at him. 'I do, Master Jonathan. It will succeed, I am sure, for there is not one great house that would turn down an invitation from the Earl of Portbury. Even if the price is to acknowledge Miss Elizabeth Aubrey.'

He took the old lady's hand and raised it to his lips. 'We have a bargain, then.'

The conspiracy was sealed between her benefactress and her rescuer. Beth had had no say at all. It seemed she was still to be treated like a parcel. 'I may develop a most inconvenient headache on the day of this party, my lord,' she said tightly.

'I pray you will do no such thing, ma'am.' He rose to fetch a hard chair from the wall by the door, and set it down by the head of the sofa where Beth lay. Sitting down, he took her left hand in both of his. His clasp was gentle and reassuring. She felt calluses on his palm from riding and fencing. This was no sprig of fashion but a man of action. 'Perhaps you could think of it, not as revenge on petty coxcombs, but as a favour for Mr and Mrs Aubrey? They have sheltered you, and accepted you as if you were a member of their own family. It is an insult to *them* that some of the local gentry have cut you. By agreeing to this, by attending my party and showing your strength of character, you will be repaying something of what you owe the Aubreys. Can you not see that?'

Beth could now see precious little. Her vision was blurry, as if she were trying to see through a howling gale. The touch of his skin on hers was flooding her whole body with heat, making her heart swell and race. She was terrified by his proposal, yet at the same time she felt light-headed, as if she might float away. When she tried to speak, no words came out.

'Miss Beth? Will you not agree? For Mrs Aubrey's sake?'

She had no choice. 'I will do what you ask,' she said, in a rather strangled whisper.

'Thank you, Beth.' He raised her hand and kissed it, just as he had kissed Mrs Aubrey's.

But Mrs Aubrey could not have felt the surge of heat that travelled through Beth's fingers and up her arm. It was not quite pleasure, and not quite pain, but she almost cried out in shock. She sat quite motionless, trying to recover her wits. He had kissed her hand! And he had called her by her given name! She must be back in one of her unfathomable dreams.

Jonathan, it seemed, had noticed nothing. After a second, he laid her hand back in her lap, replaced the hard chair by the door and resumed his seat by Mrs Aubrey. 'Excellent. I must look to you to oversee the arrangements, ma'am, for I am promised to King's Portbury for the next few weeks. But before I leave Fratcombe, you and I shall put our heads together and decide precisely who is to be invited. Oh, I am going to enjoy this!'

Mrs Aubrey was beginning to look a little prim. 'They shall be punished for their lack of Christian charity, Master

Jonathan, but do not forget your own, in the process. For-giveness is a virtue, you know. You must not enjoy yourself too much. That could be a sin.'

He nodded. 'I will try to suppress my baser instincts. And with you as my partner in this enterprise, ma'am, I am sure that generosity and forgiveness will prevail.' Laughter burst out of him like ginger beer from a shaken bottle. 'They will prevail, I promise you. Eventually.'

'What will?' The door had opened without a sound. The rector stood there, looking puzzled. 'Do I take it that you and my lady wife have been conspiring together, Jonathan?'

Jonathan leapt to his feet to bow politely. 'Your wife has most generously agreed to act as hostess for an evening party I plan to give at the Manor next month, sir. I hope you do not object?'

The rector's cheery countenance suddenly became bleak. 'Of course not. I appreciate that entertaining must be quite awkward for you now. I…we heard about the death of your wife, Jonathan, and we were very sorry. It must have been hard on you, hearing such sad news when you were so far away. Please accept our very sincere condolences.'

Jonathan's face had turned ashen. 'Thank you, sir.'

Beth could barely recognise him. The mention of his dead wife had turned him grey and gaunt. It was as though he had aged on the spot, by at least ten years. He must have loved his late wife a great deal if his grief could do that. The fact that he had been in Spain, and unable to leave his post, would have cut him to the quick. No doubt, his countess was long buried by the time the news finally reached him. Poor, poor man.

'Your wife died of a fever, I collect?' As he always did, the rector was being kind to the bereaved, giving them an opportunity to talk about the person they had loved and lost.

Jonathan drew himself up very straight and tall. He seemed to have sucked in his cheeks. His nostrils were pinched. 'I am grateful for your sympathy, sir. If you will forgive me, I prefer not to discuss my late wife's passing. It is well over a year ago now, you understand.'

The rector coloured. 'Yes, of course, my boy. Of course.'

The easy companionship in the little parlour had evaporated. Jonathan bowed to Mrs Aubrey and then, very sketchily, to Beth. 'If you will excuse me now, ladies, I have a great deal of business to attend to before I leave Fratcombe.' He bowed again to the rector. In a trice, he was gone.

Beth flung herself out of bed and just managed to reach the basin in time. It was months since she had suffered one of her sick headaches, but yesterday's encounter with Jonathan had brought back all her guilty fears. She had been tossing and turning all night. Now she had a pounding head, and sickness, as well.

She felt for her towel, dipped it in the cold water in the ewer, and wiped her face. Then she crawled back to bed, and lay there, panting. No point in trying to light her candle. At this stage in her headache, she would barely be able to see. It would be like standing in a dark, narrow tunnel, with occasional pulses of painfully bright light striking into her eyes like arrows.

She tried to push aside her fears, to blank her mind, but

the ideas kept on drumming like a nasty refrain. She had agreed to take the place of honour at a Fratcombe Manor dinner. She would have to suffer all those pointing fingers, all those whispered insults. She deserved them, for she was a nobody, perhaps even a fugitive. But she had agreed. She could not escape.

The nausea gripped her again and she raced for the basin. This time she carried it back to the bed and laid it carefully on the floor. This was going to be very bad. Usually, her headaches lasted only an hour or two, at most. Usually, she managed to conceal her pain from the Aubreys and even from Hetty. But usually there was no sickness. Sickness was impossible to hide.

For a long time, she lay on her back, eyes closed, trying to control her body. She was shivering as if it were winter rather than midsummer. She tried to breathe deeply, to think of innocent, beautiful things, like summer flowers and laughing children. Eventually, the shaking stopped and she dozed a little.

She was in a grand dining room. It must be Christmas, for the room was decked with holly and ivy. One moment she was sitting at table in the place of honour, the next, all the guests were attacking her, pointing fingers, screaming abuse, throwing branches of greenery into her face. She put up her hands to ward them off and was smeared with the waxy film of mistletoe berries. There was no one to defend her, not even the Aubreys. She shrank from her attackers. In her dream, she knew them all. In her dream, she knew that she was to be cast out. She struggled against the hands that were trying to grab her—

'Miss Beth! Miss Beth, wake up!'

She screamed.

'Miss Beth, wake up!' A cold cloth was put to her brow and held firmly.

She groaned and tried to open her eyes. Hetty was hovering anxiously, mopping Beth's face. It was after dawn. There was light coming through the shutters, blessed light that Beth could see. The tunnel had gone.

'You have one of your sick headaches,' Hetty said flatly. 'I will tell Mrs Aubrey and then I will make your peppermint tea.'

'Hetty, don't tell Mrs—'

Hetty straightened and shook her head. 'I have to, Miss Beth. You can't possibly teach the children when you are in such a state.' She nodded towards the basin on the floor. 'I know you sometimes hide it when it's only the headache, but you can't hide this. Mrs Aubrey will want you to stay in bed until the sickness has gone. And you know it's for the best.'

Beth tried to protest. She began to push herself up, but it was more than she could manage. The nausea threatened to overcome her again. She sank back on to her pillows and willed her stomach to behave.

'Lie still and breathe deeply,' Hetty said gently. 'I'll be back with the tisane in two shakes of a lamb's tail.' She tried to smile encouragingly and then whipped out of the bedchamber.

Chastened, Beth did as she was told. She had no choice. Until this attack subsided, she was not going to be able to do anything. Except think.

She had promised Jonathan she would do it. For the Aubreys, he had said. But when he was holding her hand, when they were touching, skin to skin, she would have agreed to anything he asked. She was being a fool, all over again. She had berated herself before, for thinking of him as her silver knight. Now she was thinking of him as a man—a living, breathing, desirable man—which was even more idiotic. He could be nothing to her. He was a great nobleman. She was a foundling with no past, not even a name of her own. If the terrors of her dreams were even half true, she had done something wicked in her past life, and her present sufferings were probably a just punishment.

Perhaps the dinner at Fratcombe Manor was part of that punishment, an ordeal she had to undergo in order to be cleansed? That thought was oddly calming. The pounding in her head was even beginning to recede. It was a sign.

She was going to have to find a way of meeting, and enduring, the trial to come. It was her only hope of over-coming the demons that haunted her.

It was late afternoon when Jon strolled into his mother's sitting room in the east wing of Portbury Abbey, his principal estate. She always sat here in the afternoons, to avoid the sun, she said, which was ruinous to a lady's complexion. Since Jon had returned from Spain as brown as a nut, she had stopped adding that the sun was ruinous to a gentleman's complexion, too.

'Jonathan! At last! I had almost given you up!'

He came forward to kiss her hand. 'Good afternoon, Mama. I hope I see you well?'

'Tolerably so, my dear.' She patted the place by her side,

but before he could sit down, she said, 'Have you ordered tea? No, of course you have not. Ring the bell, would you, dear?'

Nothing had changed. His mother was well-intentioned, but she did have a lamentable tendency to treat her sons as though they were still in short coats.

He crossed to the empty fireplace to pull the bell. How long would it be before she drove him to distraction, all over again? He had told her he planned to remain at the Abbey for three weeks, to deal with estate business, but he had barely set foot in the place before he was wondering whether he might need to create an urgent summons back to the peace of Fratcombe. It was yet another reminder of the duty he had been trying to ignore. If he wanted to reorder this house according to his own lights, rather than his mother's, he had to find himself a wife. This time, however, he was determined that the wife would be a lady of his own careful choosing. He planned to take his time. Eventually, he would install a new countess at the Abbey, and his mother would move back to the Dower House. Eventually, he would have peace.

The door opened. Jon ignored it. It was his mother's role to give instructions to the servants.

'Oh, forgive me!' It was a young and educated voice, not a servant's.

Jon spun round. Standing in the doorway was possibly the loveliest young woman he had ever seen, with guinea-gold curls framing a heart-shaped face and eyes the colour of bluebells. Damn it! His mother was matchmaking again! Just how many beauties had she installed here to tempt him? Had she turned his working visit into a house party on the sly?

The young lady dropped Jon a very elegant curtsy and then came into the room. 'Forgive me, ma'am,' she said again. 'Had I known you had company, I should not have intruded.'

'This is not company, this is my son, Jonathan, home to do his duty as host. And about time, too.' His mother rose. 'You will permit me to present him to you?'

The girl blushed the colour of overripe strawberries.

'Lady Cissy, I should like to introduce my son, the Earl of Portbury, lately a major with the army in Spain. Jonathan, make your bow to Lady Cissy Middleton, second daughter of the Duke of Sherford.'

Jonathan swallowed his ire and bowed courteously. It was not the child's fault, after all, that his mother was overstepping the mark yet again. As a dutiful son, he could not possibly respond in kind.

Lady Cissy sank into a deep curtsy. When she rose, she offered him her hand with practised elegance. 'I am delighted to meet you at last, my lord,' she said, looking up at him through thick golden lashes and then opening her eyes very wide, as if she were beholding something amazing.

'Practised' was definitely the word, Jon decided, with an inward groan. Why did his mother always choose rank and artifice over principles and honesty? He found himself remembering Beth Aubrey's sharp retorts with more admiration than he had felt at the time. She told the truth. She defended the weak. And she did not flirt. Unlike Lady Cissy.

He helped the girl to a seat beside his mother. He had a feeling this was going to be a very tedious afternoon.

Three sentences from the lady's lips confirmed his worst

fears. She was as empty-headed as most of her ilk. What's more, she had a high-pitched giggle that would drive any sane man to drink.

Chapter Four

Jon ignored his brother and ate his breakfast in silence. His house party ordeal was almost over. Three interminable weeks, just as he had feared. Escape had been impossible, of course, for what reason could he possibly have given for deserting a houseful of his own guests? He had been trapped by his own good manners. At least, none of the resident beauties had trapped Jon into proposing, in spite of the underhand tricks that one or two of them had tried. The rest were either so shy that they were struck dumb in his presence, or so empty-headed that their conversation bored him to death. They all had rank or beauty, to be sure, but that was no compensation. It was a relief that they would all be gone on the morrow. There was not one restful woman among them.

The door opened to admit an unexpected visitor.

'Miss Mountjoy! How splendid!' Jon's brother, the Honourable George Foxe-Garway, sprang up and stepped forward to bow over the lady's hand. Then he waved the butler away and pulled out a chair for her.

Jon also rose and bowed, distantly. From their very first meeting, a week before his wedding to Alicia, he had instinctively distrusted Louisa Mountjoy, who was Alicia's long-time companion and bosom bow. He had discovered soon enough that his instincts were right.

In the early weeks of their marriage, Alicia had played the loving, doting wife, in public and in private. For Jon, it was a glorious liberation from his father's emotional tyranny. He dared to have feelings again, and even to show them. Until the day of his twenty-first birthday, when he came upon Alicia cavorting naked with her lover—Louisa Mountjoy!

He had instantly seen how he had been manipulated, but he could say and do nothing, for fear of scandal. He had realised he would remain bound, until death, to a woman who would play the part of his wife in public, but would never again share his bed. His only solace was to vow that no one—and especially no woman—would ever have the power to humiliate him again. His father was clearly right—feelings made a man vulnerable. Only a fool trusted anyone but himself.

Now, all these years later, Jon was free of Alicia at last. He was not free of Louisa Mountjoy, however. Under the terms of Alicia's will, he had been required to provide an annuity for the Mountjoy woman so that she might enjoy financial independence for life. Jon had been sure she would be gone from King's Portbury when he returned from Spain. Unfortunately, she had taken a cottage in the village and was a frequent visitor to the Dower House instead. It was much too late now for Jon to tell his mother the real truth.

George, Jon's only surviving brother, was talking animatedly to their visitor. Judging from his expression, George thought at least as highly of Miss Mountjoy as his mother did. That was surprising, given George's tastes in women: he frequented low-class brothels and thought nothing of attacking defenceless servant girls. Not in Jon's house, though. Not any more. On the last occasion, Jon had almost broken George's jaw. And he had made it clear that if George repeated the offence, he would find himself booted into the gutter, and penniless.

If George had the run of the estate, no woman would be safe. And none of the tenants, either. George had no idea of duty. He believed the purpose of an estate was purely to provide money to fund the owner's pleasures. In Jon's absence, George had 'persuaded' the agent at Fratcombe to advance him considerable sums against his expectations as Jon's heir. The results were disastrous, as Jon had discovered for himself during that one brief spell of home leave. He knew Portbury would have been next. In the end, Jon had had to sell out and come back to England to prevent his brother from doing irreparable damage.

He turned to their visitor. 'To what do we owe the pleasure of this visit, ma'am?' he asked, silkily. It was a peculiar time for her to pay a call. Most of the lady guests were still asleep; any that were awake would be breakfasting in bed.

'Oh, nothing of importance by contrast with the great affairs of running an estate. Merely a receipt that I promised to your lady mother.'

A receipt? The Dowager had never in her life concerned herself with receipts. Cooking was to be left to cooks. Jon bit the inside of his lip to stop himself from laughing aloud at Miss Mountjoy's ridiculous attempts at deception. In his experience, this woman had a calculated motive for everything she did.

'I'm afraid my mother is still in her bedchamber,' George put in quickly, 'though I imagine she will be down quite soon. Perhaps you would take some coffee while you are waiting? Or chocolate?'

Miss Mountjoy shot an assessing glance at Jon's stony expression before she replied. 'Thank you, sir, but I have errands that cannot wait. I shall walk back to the village.' She stood up and reached for her gloves.

The two men rose. Jon held out his hand, palm up. 'If you care to give me your receipt, ma'am, I will ensure it is delivered to my mother.'

'I— No, I— Thank you, my lord, but I should prefer to deliver it myself. There is no urgency and it requires…er…a little explanation. I—'

George intervened before Miss Mountjoy could tie herself in even more knots. 'No need for you to involve yourself, Portbury. I will mention it to Mama. I am taking her driving later this morning.'

'I am sure that dear Lady Portbury will find that quite delightful, sir. You are such an excellent whip,' said Miss Mountjoy.

George preened a little. 'As it happens, ma'am, I was just about to take my pair for an airing, to take the edge off them before I drive out with my mother. She prefers placid horses, you know. Perhaps I could drive you to the village?'

'Why, Mr Foxe-Garway, that would be such a treat!'

Jon kept his face impassive. He bowed and watched as the pair walked out into the hall, arm in arm. He could have sworn that the woman whispered something in George's ear as soon as they were beyond the doorway. Was something going on between them? No, impossible. Mountjoy had no interest in men. Yet that encounter had been much too neat. Might they be conspiring together to drain money from the estate?

Jon would need to be even more on his guard. Against his own brother. He sighed, for such suspicions were not new. He stared into space, his coffee cup half-way to his lips. There was no point in agonising over George's failings. He had become totally set in his selfish, spendthrift ways. He would do almost anything for money. Even the Dowager had stopped making excuses for him.

'Good morning, Jon.'

Startled, Jon put his cup down with a clatter and sprang to his feet. 'Good morning, Mama.' As Jon helped her to the seat next to him, the butler disappeared to fetch her usual pot of chocolate. 'May I ask what brings you down so early?'

'As hostess, it is my duty to see to the welfare of our guests. Besides, George is to take me out driving this morning. Is he down yet?'

'Ages ago, Mama. He's just...er...driven out to take the edge off his horses. He knows you are a nervous passenger.'

'Nothing of the sort. But I do like to drive behind well-schooled horses. George persists in buying unruly beasts. "High-couraged", he calls them.' She snorted in disgust. They both knew that George bought horses he could barely handle because he fancied himself as good a whip as Jon. It rankled with him that he was not.

The butler returned with the Dowager's chocolate. She dismissed him with a nod. 'I will ring if I need anything more.' The man bowed and left the room, closing the door silently behind him.

Jon looked up from his plate. Her face was set. He resigned himself to what was to come.

'Jon, I need to talk to you. About…about things.'

He reached for the coffee pot to pour himself a refill. It proved to be empty, but he did not ring for more. Instead, he sighed and leaned back in his chair. 'I am listening,' he said, in a flat voice.

'Jon, I have filled the house with the most eligible young ladies of the *ton*. You have played your role as host impeccably, as always, but I have not seen you—' She sighed impatiently. 'Does none of them take your fancy? What about Miss Danforth? Now, there's a delightful girl. And Lady Cissy, too. Even you will acknowledge that she is a glorious creature.'

He stared at the ceiling for a moment. Then he picked up his cup and began to turn it in his fingers, admiring the fineness of the porcelain. 'Mama, they are both pretty, beautifully behaved, and without a single interesting thought in their empty heads. After all those years in the schoolroom, you would think they would have learned something. But apparently not.'

'That is because they are young, Jon. They are only just out.' She laid a hand reassuringly on his arm. 'A young wife can be moulded by her husband,' she said stoutly. 'In a few years, you can make exactly what you want of her.'

'Can I?' His father had been all in favour of moulding, too. Brutally, on occasions. Jon would never follow such an example. He wanted a restful woman, but a woman of principle—her own principles, too, not a straitjacket of her husband's design. 'Mama, these chits are young enough to be my daughters. I can't take a child to wife.'

She was clearly shocked by his words, but she kept her tone level. 'In that case, when we return to London, I shall arrange a few select evening parties at Portbury House. I can invite some of the…er…more mature single ladies. There are one or two widows also, of impeccable reputation, who might interest you if—'

He was shaking his head vehemently even before she had finished speaking. 'No, Mama. I thank you, but no. When our guests leave tomorrow, I shall return to Fratcombe.'

'Fratcombe? But why? There is precious little society there.'

'It is not society I need, Mama, but useful occupation. George has drained that estate in my absence and it needs— Oh, pray do not look so distressed. You could not have known what he was about.'

She could not meet his gaze.

'It will require several months of work to restore Fratcombe. I find I relish the challenge there. I cannot be doing nothing, Mama, as I do here.'

'But you are not doing nothing! You have guests, you—'

'I am doing nothing useful, ma'am,' he snapped. He had never used such a tone with her before. 'Engaging in frivolous entertainment with house guests is not what I have been used to, these last few years,' he explained, rather more gently.

'I knew the army would be the ruination of you,' she muttered.

He lifted her hand to his lips in an uncharacteristically gallant gesture, in apology for his bad temper. 'Poor Mama. I must be a sad trial to you. I know that you mean well. It is just that we do not see eye to eye on what I need out of life.'

'You need a wife and a son,' she retorted. 'Surely we are agreed on that?'

He started back and began to breathe deeply, holding himself in check. With anyone else, he would have lost his temper at such gall, but a gentleman could never do such a thing with his mother, no matter what she did.

She hastened to apologise. 'I promise I will stop meddling,' she finished, trying to smile. 'But if there is anything you wish me to do, you have only to ask. Will you be content with that?'

'More than content. Thank you, Mama.' He leaned forward to kiss her cheek.

The Dowager was surprised into a blush. And rendered speechless.

The door opened. 'Why, Mama! Good morning. I must say you are down in excellent time, and looking quite splendid for our outing. Is that a new walking dress? Very dashing.' George strolled forward and bent to kiss her cheek, just as he did every morning. They all knew it was an empty gesture.

Now that George had arrived to keep her company, Jon rose. 'If you will excuse me, Mama, I must attend to some estate business this morning, but I will be free later to hear all about your expedition. Take care George does not overturn you,' he added mischievously. 'It would not do to get mud on that delicate fabric.' He touched a finger to the Prussian blue silk of her sleeve. 'You look as fine as fivepence. There is a matching hat, I presume?' He grinned suddenly, and she made to reach out to him. Then she let her hand drop. Jon was relieved to see that she had not forgotten how much he detested public displays of affection.

Jon pulled Saracen to a halt at the top of the hill. They were both blowing hard after the climb but, from here, he could see the whole Portbury estate and miles beyond. It was a good place to be alone to think.

He dismounted, leaving the reins loose on the big bay's neck. The horse was too well trained to wander far.

Jon strolled across to lean his back against an aged hawthorn, bent sideways by the prevailing wind that scoured this ridge in winter. Fratcombe. He knew in his bones that he had to return there, though it had come to him only as he spoke the words. He needed work to occupy him. After army life, he could not return to the wasteful ways of before. He had tenants, and workers, and dependants. As Earl, he had a duty to them all. Surprisingly, that duty no longer felt like a burden. Was that the rector's influence? He did not know, but, for some reason, he was eager to return. He would try to look after his people as he had looked after his soldiers; he would seek to make their lives a little better, educate their children. Yes, even the gypsy children that Miss Beth defended so stoutly.

Beth Aubrey. Unlike the gang of simpering misses his mother had gathered here at Portbury, Beth was a woman of decided character, a clear-headed, practical woman who tried to do good in the world. She had not an ounce of the guile that had surrounded him, these past weeks at King's Portbury. He could see that clearly now. But the fundamental question remained—could he really be sure she was not a fraud?

He took a deep breath of the clean air of the hilltop. He would be arriving back at Fratcombe just a few days before the evening party at the Manor. He would visit the rectory, he decided—he had the ready-made excuse of consulting Mrs Aubrey about the party arrangements—and he would use the time to judge Beth Aubrey's character, once and for all. If his foundling was as upright as he suspected—and, he admitted, as he hoped—he would use his rank to establish her position in Fratcombe, and with it, his own. After that, no one would dare to accept a Fitzherbert's judgement over the Earl of Portbury's.

Mrs Aubrey's little maid answered Jon's knock, as usual. At the sight of him, her eyes grew as round as saucers. She stood rooted to the spot, making no move to admit him. Impudent wench! It was not for a mere servant to have opinions on how often Jon chose to call.

'Is Mrs Aubrey at home?' he asked sharply.

She nodded and showed him directly to the parlour, without first seeking leave from her mistress. Almost as if he were one of the family.

'Why, Jonathan! Three visits in three days! We are

honoured.' Jon did not miss the hint of laughter in Mrs Aubrey's voice as she rose from her work table and dropped him a tiny curtsy. It was only yesterday that he had finally persuaded the old lady to use his given name, as her husband always did. It felt right. He was truly glad of it.

Beth—Miss Aubrey—would do nothing so intimate. She too had risen from her place, laying aside her pen. Her curtsy was a model of decorum. It showed off her slim figure and upright carriage, too. Somewhere she had been well schooled. 'Good afternoon, Lord Portbury.' Her voice was low, almost husky. He persuaded himself it sounded a little strained. Could she be worrying about tomorrow's party?

He smiled down at her. 'You have been working too hard again, ma'am. You have ink on your fingers, I fear.' He was hoping to make her laugh as readily as on the previous afternoons.

Instead, she looked horrified. She lifted her fingers to stare at the dark stain as if some monster had settled on her skin. 'Oh, dear. I shall never get it clean in time. What shall I—?'

Mrs Aubrey stepped forward and clasped her wrinkled old hands over Beth's smooth ones. 'Stop worrying, my dear. I have a remedy for that, I promise. You shall be as white as snow when you don your new evening gown.'

Beth resumed her seat, but her eyes were still wide and apprehensive, Jon saw. It had not occurred to him before now that she might worry about appearing at his party. She seemed so confident in everything else she did, in the school, with the villagers, with servants, even with him... She was a lady, but she was still a nobody, and about to be foisted on to a group of haughty gentlefolk who most definitely did not wish to accept her as an equal. Of course it would be an ordeal. Why had he not seen that? In the long run, it would make her life easier, he was sure, but that was little consolation today. Even a true lady could be afraid of confrontation.

He hastened to reassure her. 'In any case, you will be wearing evening gloves, and—'

'Jonathan!' Mrs Aubrey interrupted sharply, adding a warning shake of her head. 'Will you take tea with us?'

Now, why…? Oh, yes, of course. The ladies would remove their gloves at the dinner table. Stupid of him. His wits had gone a-begging. He was not helping Beth at all. He smiled his agreement to the old lady and set about restoring poor Beth's peace of mind.

He joined her on the sofa. 'You seem incredibly busy, ma'am.' He gestured towards the pieces of card spread across the table. 'Is this for my party, too?' He picked one up. The name 'Sir Bertram Fitzherbert' was written in a very elegant hand.

'Place cards for your dinner table, my lord. We remembered them only this morning.'

'Ah, yes. Yet another of the hostess's duties. I had not realised quite how many burdens I was putting on Mrs Aubrey's shoulders when I asked her to take this on.' He glanced across at the old lady who was standing in the open doorway, giving instructions to her maid. 'It must be much more difficult for a hostess who does not actually live in the house.'

Beth shook her head. 'It could be, but your butler is extremely competent. And we had weeks to prepare while you were away…' Her voice tailed off. She threw him an enigmatic sideways glance and then quickly looked away.

Was that an accusation? That he had decreed this grand party and then fled the field? If only she knew! Those three weeks at King's Portbury had been more dangerous than any battlefield. If he had not been awake to the matchmakers' scheming, he might have found himself forcibly leg-shackled to a chit he could not abide. Fratcombe was a peaceful refuge by comparison. Here he could relax and be himself. Here, no one was scheming.

Except himself, of course!

He laughed aloud at that subversive thought.

'My lord?' She sounded hurt. She still did not know him well enough to realise he would never laugh at her.

'Forgive me, ma'am.' On impulse, he reached out to cover her ink-stained fingers with his own and patted her hand reassuringly. She froze instantly. Good God, what was he doing? He drew in a quick, horrified breath, but forced himself to give her one last friendly pat before nonchalantly dropping his hand back into his lap, as if he had done nothing in the least improper. 'I was laughing at the picture you painted…of myself.' He grinned down at her. 'Far too top-lofty to involve myself in anything as mundane as *work*. And absconding from the scene to ensure I could not be called to account. Very remiss, I agree.'

'Oh, no!' She was blushing now. The tints of rose on her cheeks merely served to highlight her perfect complexion.

There was colour on her neck, too, though it was partly hidden behind her high collar. Under her muslins, he had no doubt that even her bosom was delicately pink and—

She pulled another card towards her and busied herself with carefully writing the name. Just as well that she was not looking at Jon. She might be a single lady, but she was almost certainly old enough to recognise sensual awareness in a man's face. He had no right to allow himself to stray into such thoughts. She was a nobody, a protégée at most. It was beneath his dignity to dally with her.

'Oh, bl—!' Her nib had broken and blotted the card. 'Bother!' she corrected herself quickly. When he did not react, she threw him a mischievous look. Unlike the simpering debutantes, she was sensible enough to realise that his touch had been a mistake. And to be forgotten at once. Yes, sensible, but delightful company, too, as he had learned since his return. Her eyes were now dancing with mischief. 'You will permit me to observe, my lord, that your *supervision* of my work is not helping.'

Excellent. She was back to her normal quick-witted self. Easy with him, and more than ready to take him to task. He much preferred her that way.

He allowed himself a sheepish grin. 'I will take myself further off at once, ma'am.' He rose and crossed the room to Mrs Aubrey's side. 'It is clear that Miss Aubrey finds my presence a burden this afternoon. However, my intentions were of the best, I assure you. I knew there were bound to be last-minute chores and, since it is my party, I thought I should offer my services. Is there any way in which I can help?'

Mrs Aubrey smiled, shaking her head. 'No. Apart from the place cards, everything is done. Unless you wish to help with those?'

He snorted with laughter. 'If you had seen my handwriting, ma'am, you would not ask.'

She laughed, too. 'I thought as much. It tends to be the way with gentlemen. No, you may sit and converse with me over the teacups, so that Beth is left in peace to finish her task. We are treating you as a friend of the family, you understand, rather than an exalted visitor who must become the centre of everyone's attention.' She paused. Jon thought he saw a fleeting shadow cross her face. 'After all these daily visits, it could hardly be otherwise.'

Was that a warning? Had he overstepped the mark?

'But we do appreciate your help and advice,' the old lady went on quickly. 'However, I warn you that you must not call tomorrow, Jonathan. Both Beth and I shall be fully engaged with gowns and curling tongs. Male company will definitely *not* be welcome.'

He nodded an acknowledgement, trying to keep his face straight. 'I shall wait with…er…interest to see the results of so much female industry. I dare say I shall not recognise my hostess and my guest of honour when they cross my threshold.'

Mrs Aubrey's eyes were sparkling wickedly now. That was too much for Jon, who laughed aloud. In a moment, Mrs Aubrey was laughing, too.

For some reason, Beth did not respond at all. Clearly she was too absorbed in her work to have heard another word he said.

★ ★ ★

Beth touched slightly shaky fingers to her lips and then, even more tentatively, to her hair. It was a splendid confection, but much too elaborate for a woman with no name. Could she go through with this? She closed her eyes. She really did not want to look at the woman in the mirror. That was not Beth. That was some other person, a fine lady, the kind of lady who could go into society and hold her head high.

She swallowed hard. She had promised Jonathan that she would do this. She had repeated the promise during one of his recent visits. But he did not know who Beth was or where she came from, any more than she herself did. When she was with him, talking and laughing as they had been doing over these last three days, she had begun to feel calm, almost serene. He treated Beth exactly as he treated Mrs Aubrey. Like a lady. But was she a lady?

It was true that she had not been a menial. Her soft hands proved that. But she could just as well have been a lowly companion, or in some other inferior position in a household. The fact that she enjoyed her duties as the village schoolmistress, and that she was apparently so good at it, suggested she might have been some kind of teacher, or governess. That would make her a lady—of sorts—but not one whose position in society allowed her to sit at the right hand of an earl.

Her eyes flew open in horror. She stared at her reflection. She had turned stark white at the thought of sitting in the place of honour at Jonathan's table. He was going to insist upon it. He had said so, and Mrs Aubrey had readily agreed. According to the printed invitations, the select dinner, followed by a larger evening party, was 'to introduce Miss

Aubrey'. Therefore, she would have to take the place of honour on the host's right, no matter how high the station of any other of the lady guests.

Beth cringed inwardly. How could she possibly do this? She had promised not to develop a convenient headache. Unfortunately, she was beginning to develop a real one.

She rose and began to pace up and down her bedchamber. The skirts of the beautiful new evening gown floated about her caressingly. Oh dear. Mrs Aubrey had gone to so much trouble, and so much expense, for this. The gown was a very elegant affair of delicate white gauze over pomona-green silk. It had a low square neckline and vandyking on the sleeves and hemline, to show off the gleaming colour beneath. Much too fine for a foundling.

The bedroom door opened. Hetty was back. Her excited chatter would begin all over again. Beth was not sure she could bear it.

'Mrs Aubrey sent these.' The maid opened a flat leather case with exaggerated care.

Beth stopped and gazed. 'Oh,' she breathed. The jewel case contained a single strand of exceedingly good pearls, with matching ear drops. Perfect.

'Sit down, Miss Beth, and I will put the necklace on for you.'

What choice did she have? The whole household was determined that, like Cinderella, she should go to the ball. But, unlike Cinderella, Beth could never be worthy of this prince.

Hetty quickly clasped the pearls around Beth's neck and helped her to hook the earrings in place. Beth straightened her shoulders. There was no going back now. She had promised them all, and so she must do everything in her power to play her part in this…this charade. She pinched her cheeks and bit her lips a little. That was better. There was colour now, in both. She rose again and shook out her skirts. She could do this. She would.

She forced herself to smile as she drew on her long gloves and took up her matching fan and reticule. 'Thank you, Hetty, for the hairstyle.' On an impulse, she put her gloved hands on the girl's shoulders and dropped a kiss on her cheek. 'You are a wonder.'

Hetty blushed to the roots of her hair. And then she dropped a curtsy. 'Miss Beth, I— Oh, ma'am, thank you.'

Beth could not tell which of them was more overcome. Not wishing to embarrass Hetty further, she patted the girl's shoulder and left the room.

At the foot of the stairs, the rector and Mrs Aubrey were waiting. Mrs Aubrey had fashioned that wonderfully unusual red-purple silk into a most flattering evening gown. She had garnet drops in her ears, and a matching aigrette in her hair.

'Oh, ma'am!' Beth stopped halfway down the stairs. 'How fine you look. His lordship could not have a more splendid hostess at his side.'

Mrs Aubrey preened a little and touched her grey curls. She too had had the benefit of Hetty's clever fingers. 'Thank you, child.'

'May I say,' the rector intervened, 'that both my ladies look extremely fine.' When Beth reached the hallway, he shook out her evening cloak and placed it gently on her shoulders.

Mrs Aubrey leant forward to tie it for her, straightening

the folds so that the deep green velvet would hang beautifully. 'You look radiant, Beth. Exactly how a guest of honour should be. Come now. Since his lordship has kindly sent his carriage to fetch us, we must not keep his horses standing any longer. What time do you have, James, my dear?'

The rector checked his silver pocket watch. 'If we leave now, we will have at least a quarter of an hour before any of the other guests arrive.'

Unless they are truly bad-mannered. What if they arrive early, in order to ogle Cinderella before she has learned how to walk in her glass slippers?

Beth could not silence that unruly voice in her head. There were certainly some of the guests who were capable of such rudeness. Beth could imagine Sir Bertram and Lady Fitzherbert doing so. Lady Fitzherbert would give that tinkling, tittering laugh of hers, place her beautifully manicured fingers on Jonathan's sleeve, and gush that she 'must have mistaken the time'.

I will not let them embarrass me. They shall not look down on me. Whoever I was, I am now Miss Aubrey. If the rector and Mrs Aubrey are prepared to treat me as a lady, everyone else shall do so, too. Jonathan believes in me. Surely that is enough?

Chapter Five

Jon paced up and down in his library, waiting for the butler to appear, to warn him that the carriage was coming up the drive. For some reason, he was a little nervous. He could not understand why. He was only preparing for an evening party, not an assault with bayonets fixed and guns blazing.

The butler entered silently and bowed. 'Your lordship's carriage will be at the door in a few moments. Shall I show the guests into the crimson saloon?'

'No, Sutton. Mrs Aubrey is my hostess, and Miss Aubrey is the guest of honour. I shall meet them at the door myself.' He strode out into the hallway, past the thin-lipped butler. The man clearly did not approve of such condescension to a mere rector and his family.

The footman had already thrown the great door wide. Mrs Aubrey led the way into the house, followed by the rector, with Miss Beth on his arm. Mrs Aubrey let her cloak slip from her shoulders into the footman's waiting hands. Then she curtsied in response to Jon's deep bow. 'Good evening, Jonathan.'

Jon smiled broadly and returned her greeting. It still gave him a warm feeling to hear her use his given name.

He turned to greet the rector. 'Good evening, sir, and welcome.'

The rector was too busy removing Miss Beth's cloak to reply. He took her hand and led her forward. 'Good evening, Jonathan.' He bowed briefly. 'May I present your guest of honour, Miss Aubrey?'

There was only time for a single glance before she sank into a deep curtsy, a curtsy fit for a queen, not a mere earl. When she did not rise immediately, Jon stepped forward and took her hand to raise her himself. His eyes had not deceived him. She looked utterly radiant, as beautiful as the dawn. His breath caught. For a second, he could not find any words. How did you tell a woman that she had been transformed into a vision out of a fairytale?

Mrs Aubrey was gazing at Beth with pride in her eyes and a slight smile on her lips. But it was the rector who broke the silence. 'Fit to grace any man's table, I'd say. Wouldn't you agree, my boy?'

Jon found his voice at last. 'Rector, I have no doubt that your ladies—both your ladies—will outshine any in the county.'

By the time the guests were seated at the dinner table, Jon had more or less recovered from the revelation of Beth's astonishing beauty. How had he failed to see it before? Had he stopped using his eyes once he decided she was a foundling in need of rescue? It was possible. In Spain, after the siege of Badajoz, many women had been attacked by drunken British soldiers. Jon and his fellow officers had been unable to save them from molestation, and worse. That failure still haunted him, so much so that he had sworn he would always defend a lone woman in distress. That was part of the reason he had made common cause with the Aubreys to support Beth, though it had suited his other purposes, too. Had he been so intent on securing his own place in Fratcombe society, that he had failed to understand she was not just a cause, but also a living, breathing woman?

He knew it now. The living, breathing body beneath that filmy gown was the stuff of a man's dreams.

His heart was still beating faster than normal but he fancied he had hidden his physical reactions pretty well. He had even succeeded in escorting her to the dining room without betraying himself. She had rested her hand so lightly on the sleeve of his dress coat that he had had to check it was actually there. It was, but even then he was not totally convinced. Her fingers could easily have been hovering a fraction of an inch above his arm. Was she as aware of his body as he was of hers? He could not tell. But he must not allow himself to lust after her. She was far beneath him, but she *was* a lady. It was his duty to treat her as one.

The dinner was for a very select group—the Aubreys, Beth, Jonathan and the other couples who had done most to turn Beth's stay in the district into a severe trial. Worst among them were the Fitzherberts, of course. Rank dictated that, while Jon had the pleasure of seeing the beautiful Miss Beth on his right hand, he had to suffer the gushing Lady Fitzherbert from his left.

The dinner progressed relatively smoothly. Knowing that Lady Fitzherbert was listening to every word, Jon began the first course by trying to draw Beth out on innocuous subjects such as books and music. Her responses were polite but unforthcoming. He could not blame her. What lady would want to offer up her opinions to Lady Fitzherbert's vinegar-soaked tongue?

After Beth's third murmured monosyllable, Jon began to feel thoroughly frustrated. What had happened to the girl who had even dared to sharpen her quick wits on him? He was beginning to think he preferred the rather dowdy poor relation, if the price of her physical transformation was to be the cowing of her spirit. Beauty, as he had discovered to his cost with his late and unlamented wife, was no guarantee of character.

'Mrs Aubrey tells me you have made excellent progress at the village school. Perhaps I may pay a visit and see your teaching for myself?' When that produced no response other than a rather startled glance, he continued calmly, 'Do you have many pupils this year?'

It was like opening a sluice gate. She had hesitated to speak of herself, but the colour returned to her cheeks as she spoke more and more enthusiastically about her charges. 'The most promising child is Peter. He has a bright, enquiring mind and is already reading very well for one so young. His figuring is good, too.'

'So you foresee a golden future for him?'

She dropped her gaze to her plate and began to push some of the uneaten food around with her fork.

Something was troubling her about this child. After a moment's pause, Jon said, 'In my experience, the cleverest children are often the naughtiest. One of my cousins—I shall not name him, to save his blushes—was just such a one, always into mischief, and leading all the others astray.'

'Oh no, Peter is extremely well behaved in school, and no more boisterous than the other boys outside. It is just that he—' She took a deep breath. Her lush bosom rose alluringly against her tight décolleté. Jon tried to keep his eyes from straying. He must remember his role as host.

'I must tell you, sir, that his father is only a labourer. As soon as Peter is strong enough to work on the farm, his father will take him out of school.' She sighed. 'It is his right, of course. The family has many mouths to feed.'

They both knew it was not her place to interfere, however good her motives. It was no business of Jon's, either. He should turn the subject. To his surprise, he heard himself asking, 'Where does the father work?'

Her silence was eloquent, as was the look she gave Jon. She had huge, and very beautiful eyes, the colour of rich chocolate. Eyes to drown in. One more entrancing feature of an entrancing girl.

'Ah. Do I take it that he is employed by one of my tenants?'

'Er, no.' Her voice was barely audible. 'He works on your home farm.'

Jon almost laughed. Had the man been employed by one of Jon's tenants, it could have been awkward, even improper, to make special arrangements for the family. But for a home farm labourer, the solution was in Jon's gift. He would give the boy a future, in return for one more approving look from those beautiful eyes. 'Estates need good men at all levels, Miss Aubrey. My agent will arrange it. If Peter continues to excel at his lessons, a place can eventually be found for him in my estate office. He will learn a good trade. Will that content you?'

She nodded to her plate. Then, when he said nothing more, she raised her head. Her peach-bloom complexion was glowing and the smile on her lips was beyond mere politeness. And her shining eyes were glorious. 'Thank you, my lord. I had not thought that you could be so— Thank you.'

Jon started to reach for her hand. He wanted to show her that he truly approved of her motives. At that very moment, the butler ordered the footmen forward, to clear the first course. Jon's hand dropped back to the table.

Just as well. What on earth had possessed him to do such a thing? And with Lady Fitzherbert watching, too? He must keep himself under tighter control. He must not allow himself to be beguiled by a pair of fine eyes.

Beth had begun conversing with the gentleman on her right, while Jon would now have to endure Lady Fitzherbert's incessant chatter. He consoled himself that his penance could not last too much longer. Eventually, the cloth would be removed and he could turn back to Beth. With rather more care, this time.

The conversation round the table got louder and louder during the second course. No doubt, Jon's excellent cellar was lubricating the guests' throats, particularly those of the gentlemen. He listened with half an ear to Lady Fitzherbert's boasting of her eldest son's prowess on the hunting field.

One lesson had not been enough to keep the confounded woman in her place, it seemed.

'Very commendable,' he said with a nod and a half-smile. Then he raised his voice a little, to be sure most of the other guests could hear, and asked casually, 'I fancy Fitzherbert is not a common name. Are you, by any chance, related to Mrs Fitzherbert, ma'am? The Prince Regent's former...um... *friend*?'

One or two of the guests gasped aloud. Lady Fitzherbert's eyes goggled. She became so still she might have been stuffed. Eventually her mouth worked as she tried to speak, but no words came out.

Beth Aubrey's clear voice broke the strained silence. 'Is it possible your years in Spain have led you into error, my lord? Perhaps you were not aware that Mrs Fitzherbert is a Roman Catholic?' She turned to fix big, innocent eyes on Jon, though there was nothing innocent in her neat defence of Lady Fitzherbert. Why on earth should Beth do such a thing for a woman who had wronged her?

Because, unlike Jon, she was kind, even to her enemies. Beth had absorbed the Aubreys' goodness in a way that Jon, to his shame, had not. He suspected he must be looking a little self-conscious now. In an effort to recover, he said quickly, 'You are right, of course, Miss Aubrey. My mistake. The Fitzherberts of Fratcombe are pillars of the established church.'

When he turned back to Lady Fitzherbert, he found she was glowering across the table at Beth, as if the insult were Beth's doing rather than Jon's. No sign of Christian charity there. But it was his duty to show that he had a little, at least.

'I ask your pardon, ma'am, if my thoughtless remark has disturbed you in any way.' He raised his eyebrows, waiting for her acceptance.

Lady Fitzherbert simpered and inclined her head, before pointedly changing the subject back to her children's achievements. Their little spat was over. Unfortunately, her ladyship seemed to be even more set against Beth than before. Was that because Beth was an easy target, while Jon himself was not? In the early part of the meal, Lady Fitzherbert had been watching Beth like a cat eying a captive mouse, but Beth's behaviour had been impeccable. Jon suspected that perfect manners had been bred in her from a very early age. Everything was done correctly and without a moment's hesitation. There was nothing in the least ill-bred about the delicious Miss Aubrey, however much the sight of her might stir a man's blood.

Beth was a lady. He had absolutely no doubt of that now. Her ravishing appearance this evening, coupled with her faultless and unselfish behaviour, was serving to prove that. No one should have cause to snub Miss Aubrey after this. And once Jon had carried out the final part of his plan, even the Fitzherberts would have to toe the line he had drawn.

The servants were waiting to remove the cloth. Soon the ladies would leave for the drawing room.

The moment was now. He nodded to the butler to refill the wine glasses. Then he rose in his place.

'Ladies and gentlemen, it is my great pleasure to welcome you to the first dinner party that I have given here for many years. When I was here as a boy, I found Fratcombe to be one of the friendliest and most generous parts of England. I have always remembered it with fondness. It is to return some of that generosity that I have invited you here, for you are the first families of the district.'

There was a great deal of preening around the table. Most of the guests were smiling rather smugly. Two feather head-dresses were nodding vigorously.

'My other reason for this dinner party, as you will know, is to welcome Miss Aubrey into Fratcombe society.' Out of the corner of his eye, he could see that she was beginning to blush and was staring down at her tightly clasped hands. No matter. This had to be done. Honour demanded it. 'Miss Aubrey is a distant relative of our good rector.' Jon smiled at the old man sitting half-way down one side of the long table. 'Since she came to stay at the rectory, she has done immense good for all of us, by volunteering to be school-mistress to all the children of the district. She shows the same selfless nature as Mr and Mrs Aubrey, and I am sure you will all agree that the whole district is beholden to her.'

He paused, letting his gaze travel slowly round the table, resting on each guest in turn until they nodded in agreement. Good.

'Miss Aubrey will be remaining at the rectory since, sadly, she no longer has any other family of her own. However, that is Fratcombe's gain, and we are fortunate indeed to have her here among us. I therefore propose a toast. To Miss Aubrey, a most welcome, and valued, member of Fratcombe society.'

Jon raised his glass. There was a scraping of chairs as all the gentlemen rose, some more willingly than others, but with Jon's eye on them, they had no choice. The toast was repeated and drunk.

Glad that his stratagem had worked, Jon tossed the contents of his wine glass down his throat in a single swallow. Then he let out a long breath and smiled round at his guests, before resuming his seat. On his right hand, Beth had not moved a fraction. Her colour had risen, but she was still staring at her clasped hands. He knew she was embarrassed and would not wish to speak to him now. She probably would not even wish to look at him. Understandable enough, in the circumstances, for he had given her no hint of what he intended. But he would miss those glowing eyes.

He glanced at Mrs Aubrey and gave her a tiny nod. It was now up to her how this little melodrama would play out.

Barely ten minutes after the cloth had been removed and the dessert and decanters set upon the polished mahogany, Mrs Aubrey took a last sip of her wine and rose. 'Ladies?' Though it was earlier than normal, her tone was commanding. She gazed round, as if daring the ladies to object.

Lady Fitzherbert whispered something, quick and low, to the dinner partner on her left. Jon did not catch it all, but he was sure he heard the word 'impostor'. For a second, his hands clenched under the table. He clamped his jaws together. He must not give any hint that he had heard. He must trust Mrs Aubrey to deal with Lady Fitzherbert's venom.

Jon and all the other gentlemen rose to help their partners from their chairs. But Beth seemed quite unaware that the ladies were about to leave. Jon moved quickly behind her, put his hands on the back of her chair and bent forward until his lips were only an inch or so above her curls. He could smell lavender—and hot, wild hillsides. 'Miss Beth,' he whispered, forcing himself to ignore the subtle scent of her and the tempting pictures it conjured up in his mind. 'The ladies. Courage!'

She started in her place, but recovered almost instantly. She rose gracefully and turned to smile a little shakily at Jon. 'Thank you, sir. And for your kind words. I shall treasure them.' As she spoke, she looked directly into his face. Her eyes were wide and glistening. Not tears, surely? She had shown such self-control since the moment she arrived.

'Courage,' he said again, in a lower but more meaningful voice. He took her hand and placed it firmly on his sleeve. There would be no hovering this time. He led her to the door and opened it himself, for, as guest of honour, she must leave first. 'We will join you soon, Miss Beth,' he murmured and reluctantly let her go.

He watched as she made her way to the stairs. She had drawn herself up very tall; her spine was ramrod straight. Even from the back she looked like a soldier preparing for battle. In the drawing room upstairs, she would face the claws of the harpies.

Beth was halfway up the stairs, still stunned by Jonathan's immensely flattering words, when she was dragged back with considerable force. She cried out in shock, grabbing for the baluster rail. Someone had trodden, hard, on the hem of her gown.

'Oh, I am so sorry.' It was, of course, Lady Fitzherbert.

'Have I torn your gown, child? What a pity. It is such a pretty, girlish confection, too.'

Beth did nothing to betray the fact that she knew the damage was intentional. That would be a victory for the woman which she did not deserve. Instead, keeping a firm grip on the wooden rail, Beth turned her shoulder enough to smile sweetly into the older woman's face. 'If you would be so kind as to remove your foot, ma'am, I shall see what may be done to repair the damage.'

Lady Fitzherbert whipped her foot away as swiftly as if she had stepped barefoot on to burning coals. 'I do apologise. Such a silly accident. I am not usually so clumsy.'

'I am sure you are not, ma'am,' came Mrs Aubrey's tart voice from the hallway below. There was a tightness about her pursed lips, too. She clearly knew, just as Beth did, that the incident had been deliberate. If Beth had not had the presence of mind to grab the rail, she could well have tumbled all the way to the foot of the stairs.

The other ladies were twittering helplessly. Mrs Aubrey frowned up at them. 'Come, ladies. Let us settle ourselves in the drawing room for coffee. Then Beth and I will see to the repairs.' Mrs Aubrey ushered the stragglers on.

'Thank you, Aunt Caro,' Beth said quietly. She lifted the fragile white gauze so that the ripped portion would not trail on the stairs. She doubted that Lady Fitzherbert would try the same trick again, but it was safer to give her no opportunity for further mischief. Beth hurried up the remaining stairs and waited for Mrs Aubrey to join her. 'Thank you,' she said again, 'but I am sure that there is no need for both of us to leave the guests. With a maid's help, the damage can be quickly repaired.'

Mrs Aubrey nodded. They both knew it would be best not to leave the other ladies to their own devices in the drawing room, where they could pick over Beth's reputation like vultures. Lady Fitzherbert was quite capable of acting as the malicious ringleader, given half a chance. Under Mrs Aubrey's gimlet eye, she would not dare. Probably.

The gentlemen would join them very soon, Beth was sure. Jonathan had almost said as much. He was being so very attentive, doing so much for Beth's comfort, that this dinner party was proving rather less of a trial than she had feared. Where the other guests were concerned, at least... With Jonathan himself, it was much more difficult—conversation, and compliments, and touching... There had been too much dangerous touching.

It had taken Jon longer than he expected to lure the gentlemen away from the decanters. Predictably, Sir Bertram Fitzherbert had been the worst. He insisted on proposing toast after toast, on ever more ridiculous subjects, culminating with the hunter he had recently bought. That had been the final straw and too much for even the rector's good nature.

As host, Jon brought up the rear when they mounted the stairs. Sir Bertram, in the lead, was definitely swaying. With luck, he would drop into a comfortable chair and fall asleep. That was certainly better than leering at the ladies and repeating the kind of suggestive remarks he had made over his port. It was also the best that Jon dared to hope for. The Fitzherberts were truly a disgrace to their class. Jon's firm intention was never to permit them to cross his threshold again.

He dawdled on the stairs, reluctant to join the noisy, self-satisfied group above. In half an hour or so, the guests for the evening party would arrive to swell the numbers to more than thirty. There would be several younger ladies and gentlemen among them, so the noise level was bound to grow even worse. That prospect irked him greatly. He had endured too much horrendous noise in the last few years.

He needed peace. And peace of mind.

Yes, of course! *That* was what he longed for. Now, he understood. He wanted the comfort of a home of his own, a place where he could build his life again. Perhaps there could even be a gentle, smiling wife who would understand and share his desire—his need—for a calm, quiet refuge? A woman of principle who would do good in his name?

He did not require love, or passion. In his experience, they did not exist. Even if they had been attainable, they were not for a man of his class. Love gave a woman power she should never be permitted to have. But a comfortable room, a glowing fire, a patient partner sitting opposite, and children playing at their feet. Was that so much to ask? Surely he could find such a restful woman, such a companion, somewhere in the Upper Ten Thousand?

His decision was made without a qualm. As if he had always known what he should do. He would remain here at Fratcombe for a little longer, restoring his strength of mind in the quiet of his park. He would be able to enjoy his own company, now that he knew what he wanted from life. It was all remarkably simple.

Soon he would begin searching the *ton* for a placid, restful bride.

He took a couple of deep breaths, relishing these moments of quiet on the deserted stairway. Now that he knew his own mind, he could endure the hubbub, however bad it became. He straightened his shoulders and continued up to the drawing room.

The relative hush surprised him. He had expected chatter and laughter, but there was neither. He was shocked to see that Mrs Aubrey was sitting at the open instrument and Beth was standing next to it, looking a little flushed. It seemed they had only just finished performing. Beth must have been singing. But how could that be? She had no memory of what had gone before. How could she possibly remember music? Or how to sing?

'Bravo, my dear!' That was the rector. The guests began to clap. Even Lady Fitzherbert was applauding, though without much enthusiasm.

What on earth had Jon missed?

He tried to slide into the room without being noticed, but he did not succeed. The rector came across and clapped him on the shoulder. 'A host's duties are never done, eh? Such a pity you missed Beth's song.'

'Perhaps, if I asked her, Miss Aubrey would sing another?' Jon had not meant to say any such thing, but the words were out now, and sounding very particular. He cursed his unruly tongue. In that same instant, he caught an exchange of knowing glances between Lady Fitzherbert and her husband. That confounded woman would still make mischief if she could. Jon fervently hoped it was not too late to recover the situation. From now on, he would be wise to ensure his relationship with Beth was a model of propriety, especially in public. After all, that was the fact of the case, was it not?

Of course it was.

He found himself waiting by the door to see what would happen next. There was a lingering stillness, an atmosphere that he could not quite account for. He felt as if he were intruding into a private realm, and was there only on sufferance, even though this was his own house. The rector spoke quietly to his wife, and then to Beth. At first, she looked rather embarrassed, but she nodded at last and began to confer with Mrs Aubrey in a low voice. The rector was beaming as he resumed his seat.

She would sing again. In response to Jon's too particular request.

He decided to remain where he was, detached, and as far as possible from the performers. He leaned against the door jamb and let his head fall back on to the wood so that he was gazing at the ceiling. His guests might assume he had had too much wine, but he did not care. He did not want to be near any of them while Beth sang. He did not want to have to look at their hypocritical faces, either.

At the first notes of the accompaniment, he allowed his eyes to drift closed. It was not a piece he recognised, but it was gentle, and soothing. Mrs Aubrey had chosen well for Jon's mood.

Beth had not forgotten how to sing. Perhaps one never did? She had the voice of an angel, sweet and caressing. Jon felt the music rippling through his body like a cleansing cascade, washing away his troubles and leaving him refreshed. And consoled. Consoled? He did not understand it, yet it was true. Through her song, he was finding a degree of peace that had been lost to him for years.

Chapter Six

Jon groaned aloud and forced his eyes open. He was drenched in sweat, as usual, but he was accustomed to that now. He dragged his pillows back into place and pushed himself upright. The chill night air raised gooseflesh on his naked torso as he reached for his tinder box.

By the light of his candle, he checked his watch. Nearly four o'clock. Little more than an hour till dawn and blessed daylight. Anything was better than the dark, and the ghosts it brought.

He would not think about them. Nor would he sleep again. In sleep, he too often fell prey to emotions he could not control. It was laughable, really. All those years when his father had been trying to school him to be cold and calculating and distant. The old man thought he had succeeded, too. Even Jon thought he had succeeded. But he had not reckoned with the ghosts.

He must not give in to such weakness! Cross with himself, he set the bedclothes to rights and lay back, hands clasped behind his head, staring up at the silken bed canopy and forcing his mind to go over the evening's events, to focus on images he could control. He was quite proud of what he had done to the upstart baronet and his wife. The Fitzherberts would know their place in future. And they would not dare to cut Beth again, he was certain. The Aubreys might not approve of Jon's methods, but they would surely approve of the result. Jon had done it for them, because of the immense debt he owed them.

He had *not* done it for Beth Aubrey. Indeed, he had barely thought of her until a few hours ago. Not as a woman, at least. She had been a foundling, a possible fraud, and a source of irritation to his ordered life.

It was impossible to think of her in those terms any more. Her memory loss must be real; he was convinced of it. Besides, she was beautiful, and desirable, and when she sang…

He could not fathom his reaction to her singing. It had been as soothing as waves on the sea shore, gently caressing the sand. Sadly, the effect had not lasted long enough. He might have felt peace and consolation in his drawing room, but here in the darkness of his bedchamber, nothing had changed.

That reminded him, uncomfortably, of his need for a woman in his bed. He had been celibate for months since his return from Spain. At first, even the thought of coupling had disgusted him, but now, with the passage of time, he was becoming whole again, as his thoroughly masculine reaction to Beth's ravishing appearance had proved. Unfortunately, she was the adopted daughter of the people he admired most in the world! It was shameful to want to bed her.

He forced himself to go logically through the facts of her case. He had rescued her last Christmas, and deposited her with the Aubreys like a half-drowned kitten. She had no memory of her past life, but she was certainly a lady—last night's dinner had proved that, even by Jon's exacting standards—and almost on a par with the Aubreys for goodness and generosity of spirit. She had precious little standing in life, but she cared for those who were even worse off than she was.

He must not lust after her as if she were a lightskirt! It would be dishonourable to debauch a lady, especially one who was in the care of people who trusted him. His options were stark: keep away, or marry her!

Where on earth had *that* thought come from? The Earl of Portbury could not possibly marry a woman with no past and no family. It was unthinkable, no matter how desirable the female. Nor could she become his mistress. So she could not be anything at all.

Perhaps she could be a friend?

That subversive thought came as a shock. Friendship led to attachment, and attachment was dangerous. And yet…and yet something might be possible, provided he could behave like a gentleman. The answer to misplaced desire was to keep his distance from Beth Aubrey. If he avoided her for a while, the urge would subside. That was the answer. Perfectly logical.

He would spend a week or two alone, supervising improvements to his estate. Hard work would divert his mind and tire his body. Then he would invite the Aubreys, and Miss Beth, to spend the day at Fratcombe Manor. He would treat her as a guest and prove to himself, in the process, that his hard-earned lessons in detachment still held sway. His father had surely been right. A nobleman had to be cold and unemotional; his position required it. Feelings led to weakness that would always be exploited. Jon had buried them all, long ago.

Outside in the courtyard, a dog barked.

It sounded just like Caesar. Horrified, Jon screwed up his eyes against the memory. It was not buried after all. His father, the gun, the boy and his beloved dog. A gundog that was gun shy. There had to be a test, his father had said. If Caesar was gun shy, he must be shot so that he could not breed. The first barrel had proved it beyond doubt. Caesar had been shivering with fear. The second barrel had ended his life. Jon, at ten years old, had been forced to pull the trigger. And then to fetch a shovel and bury his best friend. He had never had another.

The Aubreys were friends, surely?

No. The Aubreys treated him almost like a son—and they called each other 'friends'—but Jon had never granted them the intimacy of true friendship. They knew how much he had mourned for his dead brother, but they knew nothing else. Once Jon became his father's heir, he had never confided in anyone. The burdens of his childhood and his marriage were his to bear. As were the horrors of war. He would bear them alone.

'Forgive me, Miss Beth, but I am curious. You have no memory of your life before you came to Lower Fratcombe and yet you do remember how to sing. Quite beautifully, too. How does that come about?'

They were in company again for the first time since that dinner party in her honour. In the intervening two weeks, they had not exchanged a single word. She had thought about him, dreamt about him constantly, but since he seemed determined to maintain a certain distance, she had had to comply. At church, they had merely bowed. Now, walking across his park and with a chance to converse at last, the first thing he did was to question her about her singing?

Beth sensed increasing suspicion. Jonathan was wondering whether her lack of memory was a fraud. Deep hurt settled in her gut, where it began to eat away at the fragile self-esteem she had worked so hard to build. He had lauded her in public, at the dinner. Now, in private, he was set on cutting her down. She had been wrong to hope he trusted her. He was not her champion at all.

He was waiting for her answer. He looked implacable. Like an inquisitor.

'I cannot explain it. I must have been taught, I suppose, at some time in my past life. Like…like learning to read. Or to write. I can still do both of those, but I have no memory of how or when I learned. You do not find it strange that I can read and write. Why should singing be different? It is simply one more basic skill.' When he still looked doubtful, her pent-up feelings overcame her and she rounded on him. 'I see that you do not believe me, sir. That being so, I shall relieve you of my presence.'

She turned on her heel and began to march back towards the Manor and the safety of the Aubreys' company. She could see them in the distance, strolling contentedly around the flower garden by the house. She would join them. Unlike Jonathan, they did not doubt her honesty.

She had gone barely half a dozen steps when he caught her by the arm and forced her to stop. His fingers were almost biting into her flesh through her fine Norwich shawl. She froze, refusing to turn to look at him. 'Please release me, sir.' Her voice was a low, angry hiss. How could he do such a thing? This—their very first touch since the party—was neither friendly nor gentle. This was nothing like the touch she had longed for. She needed to get away from him. In a moment, her head would start to pound.

He relaxed his grip a little, but he did not let her go until he had moved to stand directly in front of her, blocking her path. Then he dropped his hand. 'I apologise, ma'am, both for my words and for my actions just now. It was not my intention to insult you.' He raised his hand and stood gazing down at his cupped fingers as if they belonged to someone else, as if they had chosen, of their own volition, to seize Beth so roughly. After a moment, he shrugged and dropped his arm. He seemed perplexed.

She could not begin to understand him. He had been so intent on using that party to restore her to her rightful place in society, but then he had spent two whole weeks practically ignoring her. The change dated, she realised with a start, from the moment he had heard her sing. Without a shred of evidence, he had apparently concluded, there and then, that she was a fraud. And to be shunned.

Had he invited Beth and the Aubreys to visit the Manor this afternoon so that he could question her in private? She had assumed, naively, that it was a kindness to the Aubreys, because the sun was shining for the first time in a fortnight. Was he so very devious?

'Miss Aubrey.' His voice was low, almost inaudible.

Beth was staring at the lush grass beneath her boots and refusing to look at him. She dared not think about him, either, lest her body betray her yet again. She focused instead on the salutary effect of two weeks of rain on the growth of grass.

'I will escort you back to the house if that is your wish, ma'am. But may I not tempt you to walk with me as far as the lake? You must be feeling the want of exercise after so many days of rain. I admit I do myself.' He paused. His voice softened even more. 'May we not call a truce?'

It was a real apology this time, not just mere words, Beth decided. She raised her head and looked into his face. His eyes were troubled and he was frowning. Conscience, perhaps? Well, she would show him that she was not to be cowed, no matter what he might say of her. She was not such a poor creature. 'If you continue to frown so blackly at me, sir, I shall not accept your escort at all.' He blinked in surprise, but his frown disappeared on the instant. That made her smile. 'Much better. I accept your offer of a truce. Let us talk of nothing in the past, neither mine nor yours. Shall we agree on that?'

A fleeting shadow crossed his face. Then he, too, smiled. 'I am only now coming to understand how wise you are, ma'am. Will you allow me to say that I have missed our conversations these last weeks? You have such a refreshing way of seeing the world.'

Beth felt herself beginning to blush. This would not do at all. 'Just at this moment, sir,' she replied a little tartly, 'I should like to be refreshed by walking up to your lake so that we may discuss the…the—' she scanned the rolling parkland, desperate to light on an innocent topic of conversation '—the rearing of sheep,' she finished triumphantly.

He threw back his head and laughed heartily.

Beth found herself laughing, too. Her absurd remark had served to break the increasing tension between them.

He offered Beth his arm. He was still grinning. 'Let us walk then, ma'am, and I shall do my best to enlighten you on the subject of…er…sheep.' When Beth hesitated a little, wary of his touch, he took her arm—gently this time—and tucked it into his. 'There. That is much better.'

To her surprise, it was. For once, her insides were not churning simply because her fingers were on his arm. She refused to let herself dwell on the strength of the muscles beneath that elegant sleeve. She would concentrate solely on the scenery. Surely she had enough self-control for that?

They began to walk towards the distant lake. Beth noticed that he was matching his stride to hers. He was again the considerate companion.

He managed a couple of extremely general sentences about the size of his flock. 'And of course, warm weather and rain make the grass grow strongly which is, in turn, good for the sheep. More wool and more meat.'

Beth waited politely for him to continue. He did not. They walked on for another twenty yards. Still nothing. Now it was Beth's turn to burst out laughing. 'Have you imparted the full extent of your knowledge of sheep, sir? That they do better when they have good grass to eat?' She could not stop laughing. 'I do believe that the five year olds in my school-room could have told me that. You, sir, are a fraud.'

He shook his head in mock contrition. 'Yes, I fear I am. Sadly, I spent too much of my youth dreaming about the army. I was not the heir, you see, so there was no point in my learning to manage the estates. I—'

Beth stopped him by the simple expedient of laying her free hand on his arm. 'Nothing of the past,' she said softly. Then, after a short pause, she began brightly, 'Tell me, sir, do you have many trout in your lake?' She waved her free hand in the general direction of the water. It was much safer than leaving all her fingers in contact with his warm, tempting flesh.

She had lit on a subject he did understand. He spoke at some length about his love of fishing and of the fine spec-imens that had been taken from the lake over the years. 'Do you fish, Miss Beth? Many ladies do.'

'I…I don't know.' There was no point in racking her brains over it. If there was a memory, it would refuse to show itself, as always. Perhaps, if he put a rod in her hand, she would do it automatically? Perhaps the body remembered such things all by itself, just like writing or singing?

He laid his free hand over hers for a moment in a brief gesture of reassurance. 'Forgive me. That was clumsy of me. And in breach of our agreement, besides. But if you would like to learn to fish, I should be more than happy to teach you. I—' He stopped dead, struck by some sudden thought. 'Ah, no. Not this year. What a pity.'

The shock of his words numbed her senses as surely as a cascade of icy water. He must be planning to leave again soon. She was going to lose even those brief chances to feast her eyes on him. Beth's throat was suddenly too tight for speech. Her silver-armoured knight had delivered her to safety and now he was about to ride off in search of new adventures, perhaps to rescue some other lady in distress.

If there had been anguish in her face, he had not noticed it, for he continued, as if thinking aloud. 'Riding, now, is a different matter. That can be enjoyed all year round. I wonder, Miss Beth, if you ride? No, do not tell me that you do not know. Tell me instead that you are willing to give it a try. Let me mount you on my most biddable mare and then we shall both see whether you know what you are doing in the saddle.'

'I—'

'If you do, then we may ride around the park together. What say you, ma'am?'

Was he planning to leave, or was he not? The question was hammering at Beth's brain, forcing out all other notions. She shook her head, trying to clear the fog of confusion.

'Oh.' His voice sounded flat. Was he disappointed? 'I assure you there is nothing improper in my proposal. I would ensure we were accompanied by a groom at all times.'

He had misunderstood her. No wonder, for she herself was mightily confused. 'I did not mean— I beg your pardon, sir, I was not refusing your offer, merely—' She closed her mouth firmly. This was no time for gabbling like an excited school-child. She took a deep breath. 'I do not know whether I have

ever learned to ride, sir, and I agree that it could be…um…
interesting to find out. However, I cannot accept your word
that your proposal is not improper. Perhaps you will allow me
to take Mrs Aubrey's opinion on that before I decide?'

He was having trouble concealing his smile. 'Whatever
else your memory may conceal from you, ma'am, your sense
of propriety is very much to the fore.'

Beth was not at all sure that was a compliment. Before
she could work it out, he continued, 'And, if you will permit
me, I shall take it upon myself to persuade Mrs Aubrey to
chaperon you. I am sure she will agree that the exercise
would be beneficial.'

Beth had no choice. She nodded her agreement and fixed
her eyes on the smooth water of the lake. Something disturbed the glassy surface. Ripples were spreading from a
point about thirty yards from the bank. 'Oh, is that a trout?'

'Possibly.' He shrugged his shoulders.

'I am surprised at your reaction. You said you were a keen
fisherman, sir. Will you not be fetching your rod in order
to catch him?' He smiled down at her then. Rather indul-
gently, she fancied, as if he were dealing with a small and
ignorant child. Temper overcame her earlier turmoil. She
straightened her shoulders and glared at him. 'May I ask why
you are laughing at me, my lord?'

He tried to school his features into a serious expression
but he failed. He was laughing at her. Beth wrenched her
arm from his and spun round so that she was presenting
Jonathan with her back. She would rather not talk to him
at all if this was how she was to be treated.

'If that is a trout, ma'am, it will be a miracle. No laughing matter, in truth. In my absence, the herons have had all the fish. I need to restock.'

She let out a long breath. 'Oh.' The light dawned. She turned round to face him again. 'So that explains why you said— Um.' One day she would learn to think before she opened her mouth. She was careful and measured with everyone else. So why was it that she behaved like a fool with Jonathan? And only with him? From now on, she must keep her emotions under the strictest control.

He had stopped laughing. Perhaps he had recognised her embarrassment? He held out his hand invitingly. 'Now that we are both agreed on the subject of riding and fishing—'

'And sheep,' Beth put in pertly, recovering a little of her composure and determined not to let him best her again.

'—and sheep,' he agreed with a smile that could only be described as slightly sheepish, 'I suggest that we return to the house to consult Mrs Aubrey on the subject of propriety. Will you take my arm again, Miss Beth?'

Jon relaxed into the hot water and closed his eyes. It had been a perfect day. He could not remember when he had last enjoyed himself so much. The simplest pleasures were certainly the best, and riding round his own park, in company with Beth Aubrey, was most definitely a pleasure.

She might not know how to fish, though until they tried it, there was no way of knowing that for certain, but she had certainly been taught to ride. Well taught, too. It had been obvious from the first moment he had thrown her up into

Becky's saddle. She sat tall and secure, controlling the old mare easily with whip and heel.

She was definitely a lady. Well educated, cultured, musical, good in the saddle… So who on earth was she? And why was it that no one was searching for her? She had spent the best part of a year at the Fratcombe rectory and there had been not the slightest hint of who she was or where she came from. A mystery. A truly baffling mystery.

He began to soap his limbs. Was Beth doing the same at this very moment? Her muscles must be aching after riding for so long. Mrs Aubrey had smiled benignly and waved them off into the park, with the obligatory groom trotting behind. It had been such a glorious, liberating day that Jon had allowed his pleasure in her company to overcome his common sense. He knew perfectly well that, if Beth rode too long, she would suffer for it. She had made no complaint, of course. She was too much the lady to do so. And, he fancied, she had been enjoying Jon's company too much to give it up.

He threw the soap into the water in disgust. What a coxcomb he was becoming! Beth Aubrey was his lady guest, nothing more. If she had been enjoying his company as they rode together, it was not to be wondered at, for she had precious little recreation time. She occasionally visited the Miss Alleyns and Miss Grantley, but apart from that, she spent her time as unpaid schoolmistress to the village and unpaid helper for all Mrs Aubrey's charity projects. Beth would maintain that she was more than content, that she was merely repaying the Aubreys' generosity, but Jon was far from convinced. She was a young woman still, and she should have at least a little time to herself to enjoy a young woman's pleasures. Such as riding.

With him?

He was suddenly glad that he was leaving Fratcombe in a few days, for Beth Aubrey was much too tempting. He could not take her riding again, much as he might wish to. That would start the worst kind of gossip. However, as an acknowledged friend of the Aubreys, he could make provision for Beth to ride the old mare in his absence. His grooms had little enough to do. He would instruct them to make the mare ready every day and to accompany Miss Aubrey whenever she wished to ride out. She would have free rein over the whole of his park which was the least he could do. Once her muscles were used to riding regularly, she would enjoy the exercise, he was sure. And she would have no need of Jon's company.

He realised, with a start, that he would miss her. With Beth, he did not have to mind his tongue. Indeed, she seemed to understand what he was going to say before his words were out. They laughed together. They talked of anything and everything, without restraint. And they shared the simple joys of nature and fresh air, and a love of the land. It was a pity Beth was not a man. A man could perhaps have become a friend.

He would miss her company, but it was wise, he knew, to avoid her. He had assumed that a little distance would subdue his desire to possess her delectable body. It had not. And now, in addition to desire, there was something more, something deeper—admiration, and liking, also.

With a groan, he dug into the cooling water for the soap and began to scrub at his legs.

'I've brought your hot water, Miss Beth.' It was Hetty, carrying the large brass can across to the dressing table.

'Goodness, I have overslept! How could I have—?' Beth made to sit up and throw back the covers. 'Argh!' She could hardly move. Every single muscle was shrieking with pain. With a supreme effort, she rolled on to her side and forced her legs out of the bedclothes so that she could push herself up with her hands. 'Good grief! I feel as if someone has pounded me all over with a…a cricket bat.'

Hetty set the can down and came across to help Beth to stand. 'I did warn you, miss, but you wouldn't listen. You should have had a long hot bath and some of that embarkation rubbed into your muscles.'

Beth laughed. She stopped pretty sharply though, for it hurt. 'Embrocation, Hetty.'

'Whatever. You shouldn't have gone riding for so long, miss, when you're not used to it. No, not even at his lordship's invitation. He should have known better, an' all.' Of late, Hetty had become extremely forthright with Beth who valued the maid too much to correct her ready tongue.

'Besides, there ain't no point in you learning to ride all over again, when you'll be stopping just as quick. You can't go riding out on your own, after all, can you? You'll have had all this pain for no gain, as they say.' Hetty swung Beth's wrap over her shoulders and helped her into it.

Beth winced. She had forgotten that Jonathan would be

leaving soon to go to one of his other estates. He had not said which one. He had several, he had explained, and all of them needed the master's careful supervision. That was his duty as Earl.

He took his duties seriously, of course. But he had a lighter side, too, and she was glad to have discovered it. She wanted him to be a...a friend, the kind of person with whom she could share everyday pleasures like riding out with the sun on her back, or walking for miles across lush meadows and shady country paths. The kind of friend who would share her wit, who could tease her until she was doubled up with laughter, and who could subside into easy silence when they were both content to commune with nature and their own thoughts. One day, perhaps, they might come to be all those things together. She must not hope, or dream, of anything more.

She would miss him when he left, but friends parted. It was the way of the world.

'The groom said as he's leaving Fratcombe on Monday morning.'

'Monday?' Beth choked and began to cough, in an attempt to cover up her shock. Monday? That was the day after tomorrow. Was she to see him at church and then never again?

Hetty poured a glass of water and handed it to Beth, who gulped it greedily.

'Well, Sam—that's the groom, miss—said it would definitely be Monday. Unless his lordship changes his mind again.'

'Again?' Beth croaked.

'Aye. Apparently he were all set to leave last week, but

decided he wanted to stay on a bit. To enjoy the fine weather and the peace, Sam said.'

'That sounds rather strange. Are you sure, Hetty?'

'Oh, yes, miss. When he's at his main estate, it's just one long round of parties and entertainments, Sam says, with house guests all the time. Sam reckons it's because his lordship's mama is determined to get him married off again, so she fills the house with pretty girls. Can't see it m'self. I'd say his lordship is too much his own man to be governed by his mama, or any other lady. Don't you think so, Miss Beth?'

Beth swallowed the rest of her water and muttered something that could have been agreement. Hetty might be right about Jonathan's character, but the maid did not understand the demands of his position in society. He had been a widower for a considerable time. He had no son. He would not need his mother's urging to understand that it was high time he married again and set up his nursery. No doubt he was returning to King's Portbury, to look over yet more candidates to be his new countess.

So much for friendship, and simple shared pleasures.

Chapter Seven

Fratcombe Manor had been a peaceful refuge but Lorrington was utter bliss. Jon had forgotten how wild and remote it was here. George had never visited, probably because the Lorrington estate was too poor to provide him with any ready money. And the place was blessedly free of women, too, for there were no gentry families for miles. Jon was spared the plaguey females that always bedevilled him at King's Portbury.

After two weeks of riding the land and speaking to all his tenants, Jon was ashamed of what he had allowed to happen here. It was his smallest estate, to be sure, but he had failed in his duty to those who depended on him. Their farms were ramshackle and their livestock was scrawny, barely surviving on the thin hill land. There was some good land, but it was not productive, for the farmers had no money for seed or new tools. He would change all that. Some of the surplus from King's Portbury would be invested here. Lorrington would never be rich, but his people's lives would be improved. He was determined on that.

Until now, he had paid them no heed. But Spain had changed him. War had changed him. Among his soldiers, there had been men from the land, good men who had taken the King's shilling because their families could not afford to feed another mouth. He had seen those men fight, and he had seen some of them die. In the depths of the Spanish winter, he had seen what hunger could do to a man. He would not allow it to touch any of his lands. Never again.

It was a matter of honour, for those who had died. And a matter of duty.

He would discharge his duty here at Lorrington and then he would take a wife. He had delayed for long enough now. There must be no more excuses. Surely there was one lady of rank, somewhere, who was not simply out for herself, simpering and blushing in her efforts to snare a rich husband?

If such a one existed, he had not set eyes on her.

He sighed and reached forward to run his gloved hand over his horse's glossy neck. As far as he could tell, debutantes were all the same. It was enough to give a man permanent indigestion. Why could none of them be like Beth Aubrey?

He swore aloud. She was intruding again! He kicked his horse into a gallop and began to race across the grass to the foot of the gorse-covered hill. He would make his way to the top for a final check of the Lorrington estate. He might see something he had missed, some out-of-the-way farmstead where the children were barefoot or unable to go to school. It was his duty—he was happy to accept that now—to ensure that all the children on his estates had a better chance in life.

That reminded him that he had promised Miss Beth he would do something for that young protégé of hers. Peter, was it?

Yes, Peter. Jon would speak to his agent about the child as soon as he got back to Fratcombe. He did not want to see the disappointment in Beth's fine eyes if she discovered that he had failed to live up to his promises. Why had she not challenged him on it before he left?

Because she trusted him to keep his word. She trusted him, and confided in him, as a friend.

He could not return that trust—he confided in no one—but he could rely on her word. He knew that, without a shadow of a doubt, because of the remarkable person she was.

He would rather spend an hour with her than whole weeks among the carp and cackle of the ladies of the *ton*. Unlike them, Beth was an eminently restful woman, now he came to think about it. Had he been so taken with her luscious curves that he had failed to see that? And value it?

He hauled his horse to a stand and threw himself out of the saddle so that he could make the rest of the steep climb on foot. Beth was the only woman in England who came near to being the kind of wife he wanted, and needed. Yet she was a woman he could not have. Why was fate so determined to laugh in his face?

He plodded on. Somewhere in the back of his mind, a beautiful voice began to sing, softly at first, and then more clearly, so that the bitter fury of his thoughts was calmed. It was Beth Aubrey's voice, as if from far away. And it consoled him.

Why could he not marry her?

Because he was the Earl of Portbury and his duty required him to marry a lady of rank. Duty. It had driven him for years, but what had it brought him, apart from hardship and heartache? Surely a man could be more than the sum of his duties? Jon was a man of rank and wealth. An earl. An earl did not need to play by the rules of lesser mortals. Nor did he have to pay heed to anyone else's opinion. Not even his father's. Not any more. An earl could decide for himself where his duty—and his own best interests—lay.

Jon's decision was made. He would call at the rectory as soon as he was back at Fratcombe Manor.

Beth was glad when her solo ended and she could resume her place in the rectory pew. Glad, too, that Jonathan had not returned, to hear her sing and to wonder yet again if her memory loss was some kind of fraud.

If only it were! Then she might have some certainty about who she was. There were those dreams—nightmares, sometimes—in which she saw bits and pieces of memories, of places, even of people, but none of it made any sense at all when she woke up.

But last night's dream had not been like that. It had been full of colour and scent, almost more vivid than life itself. Because of him. Because of Jonathan. She had been dreaming about Jonathan.

'Let us pray.' The rector's voice recalled Beth to her devotions. She knelt and began to pray, fervently, for deliverance from the man who was haunting her. The man she had not dared even to address as her 'friend'.

The service passed more quickly than usual. Beth knew she had made all the responses, though she could remember none of it. But it was over. The rector was standing in his normal place outside the door, exchanging kind words with everyone, asking after missing parishioners, the sick and the old. From inside the church, he was only a dark silhouette. Beth watched from the far end of the aisle, waiting for her turn to leave. He was such a good man. No wonder the whole district loved him.

'I think we may go now, Beth, dear,' Mrs Aubrey said at last, nodding towards the empty doorway. 'I wonder if the rector has invited any guests?' she added, as an afterthought. After divine service, he made a habit of inviting needy souls to eat in the rectory kitchen. It was part of God's charitable purpose, he always said, and his wife did not disagree.

For once, there seemed to be no unexpected guests waiting around when the two ladies emerged, though it was difficult to see clearly. Beth blinked and screwed up her eyes against the sudden dazzle. It had been overcast when they went into church, but now the sky was a bright, clear blue and the slight breeze was warm from the early autumn sunshine, contrasting with the cool airiness from which they had come. Beth let her shawl drop, closed her eyes and turned her face up into the warmth.

'Beautiful, is it not?'

That was not the rector's voice. Jonathan! He had returned!

Beth stepped back so quickly that she almost tripped over her skirts.

A strong arm held her up. 'You must take more care, Miss

Beth, or you will fall. Wait until your eyes are accustomed to the light before you start prancing about.'

He was still holding her arm. She could feel the strength of his fingers through her muslin sleeve. And the warmth of his body—

'Miss Beth? Is anything amiss?'

She forced herself to turn to look at him. Jonathan. The face from her dreams. This time, he was not surrounded by vibrant colour but starkly outlined against the venerable grey stone of the church. And still he was beautiful.

'Lord Portbury,' she said softly, trying to withdraw her arm from his clasp without seeming to struggle. 'We did not look to see you in Fratcombe again so soon.' That sounded suitably polite. And distant, too.

'I'm afraid I arrived too late to attend divine service this morning. I was apologising to the rector, but he will have none of it.'

'Do you tell me, Jonathan, that you have been travelling on the Sabbath?' Mrs Aubrey wagged a finger at him. 'Fie on you, sir. I hope the rector has reproved you soundly.'

'Unfortunately not, ma'am.' He was grinning like a naughty schoolboy.

'No, indeed,' the rector put in, 'for what good would it do? But you may take him to task yourself, Caro. I have invited him home to dine with us.'

It was almost over. He must go soon, surely? He seemed to be taking an inordinate length of time to drink a single cup of coffee.

Beth concentrated on listening to the rector's words. And trying to avoid Jonathan's eyes.

At last, he rose from his place by the rector and crossed to the table where Beth sat over the tea and coffee pots. He was simply doing her the courtesy of returning his empty cup. Now, he would certainly go!

He seemed a little hesitant. He stood over Beth, but made no move to put down his cup. He half-turned to glance at Mrs Aubrey, and then back to Beth. His behaviour was most disconcerting, and it was making Beth's inner turmoil even worse. She had known and admired him as a decisive man. What had happened to him during his absence from Fratcombe?

The thought settled around her like a shroud. He was going to announce that he was about to marry again. Yes, that must be it. It was common knowledge in Fratcombe that his mother had been inviting all the most eligible young ladies of the *ton* to visit King's Portbury. Even a duke's daughter, according to the lodge-keeper. Beth told herself it was only what he deserved. He had an ancient title and needed a wife of suitable rank. A duke's daughter would suit admirably.

Beth tensed her muscles, held her breath and waited for the words she was dreading. She was resolved that she would not betray, by the slightest blush or blink, that his news was a disappointment. For who was she, the supposed Elizabeth Aubrey, to believe she had any claim on such a man? She was, as he said, a foundling. A nobody. Not even high enough to be a friend.

'Mrs Aubrey, you and the rector have given me the friendliest possible welcome on my return, by inviting me to your table. I am truly grateful. But I wonder if I might impose on you even more? I should very much like to take a turn round your garden before I return to the Manor.'

What on earth was he talking about? Walking round the garden? At the beginning of October?

'I could not help but notice that some of your trees are looking very fine in their early autumn colours. Especially in the late afternoon light.'

'I did not have you down as a garden lover, Jonathan,' the rector said with a hint of laughter in his gentle voice. 'But even if it be a recent conversion, I will not deny you.' He made to rise. 'My dear, will you—?'

Mrs Aubrey shook her head, settling herself more comfortably.

Jonathan quickly raised his hand. 'Forgive me, sir, Mrs Aubrey, I did not mean to impose my whims on you. Pray do not disturb yourselves on my account.'

The rector nodded and sank back gratefully into his seat. 'I am sure Beth would welcome a chance to take a stroll, after sitting for so long listening to an old man prosing on.'

'Come, come, my child,' the rector said, when Beth began to protest, 'we cannot let our guest wander our shrubberies without escort. Spare my old bones, if you would be so good.'

Beth knew she was about to lose. She threw one pleading glance at Mrs Aubrey, in hopes that the old lady would change her mind and accompany them, but Mrs Aubrey was gazing at the rector with concern.

'I am a little tired, Caro, that is all. Sunday is not a day of rest for the clergy, you know.' He chuckled. 'I am saving my strength for evensong.'

Mrs Aubrey seemed to be reassured, for her features softened. She turned to Beth instead. 'And you, my dear. Do make sure you take a wrap with you. The afternoons soon grow chilly at this time of year.'

Beth nodded and looked around for her shawl. She had had it earlier, but in the confusion of the moment, she could not remember where she had laid it down. Before she could move an inch, Jonathan came forward with it in his hands and stroked it round her shoulders without even asking leave. His touch was so caressing that her skin began to burn. Her mouth was suddenly too dry to say a word, even though she knew she ought to upbraid him for taking such a liberty.

He was smiling down at her. 'Shall we, ma'am? Before the sun goes down and we lose the last of the warmth?'

She gave a tiny nod. It was the most she could manage. Together they strolled out through the French windows and into the garden.

They had gone the length of the shrubbery path before Beth forced herself to break the silence. 'For a garden lover, sir, you are paying remarkably little attention to the turning trees.' She had not meant it to sound like an accusation of bad faith, but it did. She could not help herself. She was barely in control.

His voice, when it came, was strained. 'Miss Aubrey. Miss Beth. I was hoping for a moment's private conversation with you. My excuse was clumsy, I am afraid.' He stopped dead.

Beth had no choice but to do the same. He took a sideways step so that he was standing in front of her. 'There are… er…things I need to say to you.'

Beth's heart began to beat very fast. He was going to do her the courtesy of confiding his plans in private. That was more than she had looked for. He really was treating her like a friend. A tiny spark of warmth flickered around her heart but quickly died. This friendship would be doused as easily as an uncertain flame.

He was gazing out over Beth's head towards the trees and the graveyard beyond, but he was focused on nothing. 'I…er…I have decided that I must remarry. It is essential, given my position in society. There needs to be a Countess of Portbury. And…er—' He glanced down into Beth's face at that moment. She saw the hint of embarrassment in his eyes, though he was not blushing.

Beth's emotions might be in confusion, but she was not fool enough to mistake his meaning. He needed a wife, and then a son.

'I have considered carefully. I find I do not hold with these new-fangled notions of love.' He was trying to sound matter of fact and uncaring. Perhaps, when it came to marriage, he was both of those? 'I do not believe in such things. A man must choose a partner who suits him in every way—a lady who will grace his table and take charge of his household, a lady who will create a comfortable, restful home, a refuge where a man can take his ease.'

A refuge? It was clearly of huge importance to Jonathan. Beth was not quite sure why that should be. Perhaps it was to do with his time in Spain? It was strange that such a strong man could also seem so vulnerable.

He took a deep breath. It would be now. He was going to tell her the name of the lady he had chosen to share his peaceful refuge. 'I can tell from your face that I am making a mull of this. Forgive me. It is not often a man puts such thoughts into words. I was trying only to describe…to set out what I seek. I would not, for the world, mislead you about my motives.' Abruptly, he took both her hands in his. It was a gesture of kindness, the gesture of one friend to another. But now he was silent, waiting for her to speak.

Beth gulped. 'I…I never doubted your intentions, sir,' she said. It was a rather bald reassurance, but it was the most she could manage.

'No, you would not. You see good in everything, and everyone.'

Beth felt the beginnings of heat on her neck. Such a simple compliment, but she was blushing. He was still holding her hands in his. She looked down at them, just as he gave her fingers a tiny squeeze. That was a shock. Beth jerked her gaze up from their clasped hands to his face.

'Beth, will you do me the honour of becoming my wife?'

Her mouth fell open, but no words came out. Her head began to spin. Soon she was swaying on her feet. *I am going to faint. But I never faint.*

He caught her by the shoulders as she staggered, and then he steered her to the bench beneath the massive beech. Its leaves were beginning to turn brown, but most of them still clung to the parent tree. He guided her onto the seat and unceremoniously pushed her head down between her knees. 'I have shocked you. It was not my intention.'

After a few moments, she straightened. Her eyes were very wide, and very dark in her ashen face. 'It is unkind of you to make a may-game of me, sir.' Her voice cracked. She looked away.

Good God! She did not believe he meant those words, the most difficult for any man to utter. Jon had been standing over her, watching her, worrying. Now, he threw himself on to the seat beside her and seized both her hands. He was not about to let them go until he had received his answer.

'Beth, I value your good opinion far too much to do any such thing. We are friends, surely? Friends do not… Beth, I would never mock you. My proposal is utterly sincere. You are the most restful woman of my acquaintance. I know it is a rather bloodless union that I am offering you, but there must be honesty between us. I will not attempt to dupe you with false protestations of love. For you are not an empty-headed chit who takes her notions from the pages of the latest romantic novel. You are sensible, and practical. I had hoped that my offer would tempt you: a home of your own where you could be mistress; a proper station in society. It would give you certainty, Beth. You would have your rightful place. Will you have me?'

She jerked her hands out of his with a sound that could have been a strangled sob. She surged to her feet as if she were about to flee, but at the last moment, she turned back to him, holding up one small white hand to prevent him from rising. 'There can be no certainty for me, my lord. I am nothing, nobody. I have no name but the one the Aubreys were kind enough to lend to me. I am no fit wife for any gentleman. And certainly *not* for the Earl of Portbury. It is wicked to suggest otherwise, but I will forgive your ill-conceived jest. Let us forget the words were ever spoken.'

She had become as rigid as the beech trunk at Jon's back. He realised he had been clinging to a vision of his comfortable life with her. He had seen Beth there by the fireplace, sitting quietly opposite him, but he had never once considered that she might not share his longing for a peaceful refuge. In truth, he had not considered her at all. He scrutinised her features carefully now, for the first time in a long while. She was holding herself together by sheer force of will. She was affronted by his proposal, and deeply hurt. In a moment, she would regain enough strength to flee. Unless…

Ignoring her still outstretched hand, he stood up and put his arms around her. Since she did not believe a word he said, he had best try something other than words.

He kissed her.

It was Jon's first real kiss in a long time. He brushed his lips over hers, very lightly, unsure of how she might react. Her lips parted, and he felt the warmth of a tiny sigh on his skin, as if she had been waiting for his touch, holding her breath. And yet her response was hesitant, the response of an innocent girl. She did not have the way of kissing.

A strange feeling surged through Jon, an unfathomable mixture of pride and possession. He was almost sure that Beth Aubrey had never been kissed before. And yet she was trying to respond to him. Her head might be telling her that Jon's proposal was a wicked jest, but her warm body and her soft mouth wanted to reach for him. Jon stopped trying to analyse her reactions and gave himself up to the simple pleasure of kissing her. He wrapped her even more snugly against his body and put a hand to the back of her head, holding her still so that he could explore. He feathered tiny kisses along her bottom lip. She tasted of coffee, and sweetness. He risked a bolder touch, putting the tip of his tongue to the tiny sighing gap between her lips. This time it was no sigh, but a groan he heard, from deep within her. That was too much.

He deepened the kiss. Now she truly did respond. Her hands slid up his chest and around his neck. She opened her lips to welcome him in. Desire swept through Jon's body. There could be something between them after all, more than mere companionship. They would sit restfully together by the fire, no doubt, but he fancied the getting of an heir could be pleasurable for them both.

It was as if her body were relaxing into a bath of warm, scented water, which lapped over her limbs and caressed her flesh. She was floating. Yet she had never been so alive. Her skin, all over—from her cheek to her throat to her breasts to her belly—was awake, reaching and yearning. She wanted him to touch her. Everywhere.

She drove her fingers into the thick hair at the back of his head and pushed her body closer into his embrace. She could feel the strength of him, held in check, restrained so as not to alarm her. But it was there, none the less, a warm, reassuring strength. She could feel that what had begun as a simple kiss was turning into something much more demanding. He desired her.

That sudden awareness brought her back to grim reality as surely as if he had scrubbed handfuls of snow on to her naked skin. She pulled her hands down to his chest and pushed hard, with balled fists. She tore her mouth from his. The moment her lips were free, she cried out. 'No!'

The reaction was instantaneous. His hand had been in her hair, holding her steady for the exploration of his lips and tongue, but he did not try to restrain her. He dropped his hands to his sides and took a very deliberate step away from her.

Beth clasped her hands together very tightly. She refused to let them shake. 'My lord, you—'

'Jonathan. My name is Jonathan.' He did not move to close the space between them, but his gaze softened and the merest hint of a smile curved his lips as he looked down at Beth. 'Jon,' he said, in a deeper, warmer voice.

He was asking her to use his given name? She shook her head vehemently, trying to clear her thoughts. He had proposed. He *was* proposing. To her! And it seemed it was no jest, after all. She could not think straight. That kiss… Oh, heavens, that kiss had turned her bones to butter. Her body was burning hot and icy cold, all at once. She was quivering. Would she melt altogether? Or freeze?

'Beth?' He was uncertain, too. She could hear it in his voice. He raised his right hand, palm up, and offered it. 'Beth, will you have me?'

She dared one look at his face, but she could not read his expression. Whatever his emotions, he was managing to conceal them. All she knew was that his proposal must be sincere. 'It is impossible!' she burst out. 'You know it is so!'

He was standing as still as the statues in his park. His outstretched hand had not moved even a fraction.

'Oh, you ridiculous man!' She let anger bury the hurt. 'You must know it is impossible. You are the Earl of Portbury and I am nobody. I have no past, no family, not even a name. You insult me by suggesting you would take me to wife.' That spurt of anger had saved her. She was back in control. She had even managed to bury the delicious sensations that his kiss had brought to the surface and that had been threatening to overwhelm her. She would not think of those. She turned abruptly and began to march along the path towards the rectory. That was where her refuge lay. That was where she could be free of this torment.

He caught up to her after three paces. He did not touch her. If he had, she might have cried out, so tense were the feelings consuming her. No, he just strode past her and planted himself like a rock on the path, as if a landslide had suddenly blocked the way. Heavy, impenetrable, dangerous. He was not smiling. He held up a hand, not an offering this time, but a command.

She stopped. She had no choice.

'You *would* have a name. My name. You would be the Countess of Portbury. My wife. Your position in society would be alongside mine. No one would dare to question that.'

He was very sure, and absolutely wrong. 'Of course they would,' she retorted, trying to swallow the pain that was gripping her heart. 'You have no idea what black deeds there

may be in my past that led me to flee. Have you never thought
that my memory is shuttered because of what lies hidden
there? The Earl of Portbury cannot risk discovering that his
wife is a fugitive. Or worse. What would society say then?'

'No one would dare to accuse my wife of *anything*,' he
retorted, with a dismissive wave of his hand.

His tone was so arrogant that Beth was stunned into
silence. He frowned down at her for a moment, and then
said, in a more thoughtful voice, 'You are a truly good
woman, Beth. If you fled, it was from someone else's
wickedness, not your own. I believe—I know that to be true.
No one would dare to suggest otherwise.'

'Of course they would,' she said again, though less forcefully. 'They would say that the Earl of Portbury had taken
leave of his senses, in marrying such a woman. They would
obey the outward forms, no doubt, but the gossip, the sly,
sneering comments, would be made at every turn. Not only
about me, but also about you! Can you not understand that,
Jonatha—? My lord?' She winced. His stony expression had
softened at the sound of his given name. The moment she
retracted it, he had begun to frown again.

'I understand no such thing. What's more, I would not
care a jot about society gossip. I do not seek to marry for
society's sake, but for my own. I do not seek to cut a fine
figure in this world of theirs. I do not give a fig for that.
And I had thought that you would not, either. Beth? Beth,
do you care for such things? I thought you would wish to
live retired from society, as I do. Let the tabbies say what they
will of us. We have no need of them, and their stiff-rumped

opinions. Our life together will be peaceful, and content. As far from society as we wish to be. It is a delightful prospect, is it not?'

It was more than delightful. It would be paradise. But she could not possibly answer with the truth. Nor could she lie. She just stared at him.

He cleared his throat. 'I can see that I have shocked you with my proposal. It is no wonder, for you are a gently bred lady.'

At that, her head came up even more. He did not know— He *could* not know anything about her upbringing. She herself did not know.

'But I beg you to understand that my proposal is sincerely meant. You would do me the utmost honour if you accepted me. Will you not at least take a little time, a day, to consider what I am offering?' He took half a step towards her. 'Please, Beth. Do at least consider.'

She felt an almost overpowering urge to raise her fingers to his face, to stroke away the tension that was so evident in his frown and in his narrowed eyes. She clasped her hands together once again, forbidding them to stray.

She had to stop him, to save him. She must not let her feelings overcome her principles. She fixed her gaze on the ground at her feet, knowing she dare not look at him for this. 'I suggest that *you* consider, my lord. Has it not occurred to you that you are proposing to a woman who may be married already?'

Chapter Eight

She had planted him a facer.

Jon had been boxing for too many years to give in just because he had been floored once. He refused to quit, especially when his goal had suddenly become so much more important.

'Look at me, Beth,' he said, as gently as he could, reaching for her tightly clasped hands. She tensed for a moment, but then she yielded enough for Jon to take them in his. He did not attempt to pry her fingers apart. He simply lifted them to his lips and dropped a featherlight kiss on her skin. She was still staring at the ground, however. She seemed determined to resist him. Was she afraid, perhaps? 'There is no need to be anxious. I know you for a strong woman who is afraid of nothing, and no one. I am your friend, Beth. Please look at me.'

It seemed the word 'friend' was able to reach her, where his touch had not. Without moving her hands in his, she slowly raised her head and her gaze joined with his. She was as white as her tucker; her eyes were huge and dark in her pale face. She made no move to speak, but she did not need to, for her emotions were written in her brilliant eyes. His proposal had injured her. Even if she now accepted that Jon was not mocking her, she was certainly not convinced that there was any kind of a future for them as man and wife. She thought Jon was too high, and she—a woman with a shadowy past and no memory—was much too low.

'I can assure you, Beth, that you are wrong about marriage.'

'I…I know I am not wrong about this one. It is impossible.'

'I understand your reluctance, but I cannot agree with you. Will you allow me to explain why?' He drew her arm into his—she had stopped resisting, he was glad to see—and escorted her back to the bench under the beech tree. He had a chance now, though perhaps not for long. He was going to have to be truly silver-tongued, for she was clearly set against him.

He took his seat beside her, still holding her hand tucked into his arm, but he did not sit too close. 'I must ask you first, Beth, if you still think I am trying to play a base trick on you with my proposal?' He had to know that she would listen.

She coloured a little and shook her head.

'Good. That is a start.' He patted her hand, just the lightest of touches. It was too intimate, it seemed, for she flinched. He felt the tightening of her muscles through the layers of clothing. He let his free arm drop back to his side. One more false move and she might run.

'You think you may already be married. I can see why you would think that. For a lady, it is a logical assumption but, as a man, I can tell you that you are certainly…er…un-

touched.' No married woman would have responded so innocently to Jon's kisses. He was not mistaken there.

'Untouched?' She blushed, like a white rosebud caressed
by the first rays of the early morning sun.

Jon cleared his throat. That had not been a good choice
of word. There were some aspects of marriage that one did
not discuss with a gently-bred, single lady. 'Beth, you think
you are not good enough to become a countess. To become
my countess. Will you not permit me to be the judge of that?
Believe me, your lack of memory does not matter. You are
a lady, bred in the bone. It is clear in every word you say, in
everything you do, in every step you take. No one doubts
it. My wife must be a lady, I admit that. But you fulfil the
requirement admirably.'

When she began to protest, he shook his head and continued without allowing her to speak. 'Beth, I have had my
fill of ladies of rank. My first marriage—' He swallowed
hard. 'Normally, I would not discuss the failure of my first
marriage, but you are entitled to know. My late wife was a
duke's daughter, with all the accomplishments her position
entailed, but she brought me nothing. Another dynastic
marriage to a chit out of the schoolroom could easily be just
as bad. I want— I *need* a wife who will be a companion and
a friend, a woman I can esteem, not an empty-headed child
whose world revolves around balls and bonnets. You, Beth,
are a truly remarkable woman. You care for others. You look
to do good in the world. As my wife, you would be able to
use my wealth and position to achieve all that you desire.
Think what you could do.'

There was a small, sharp intake of breath beside him. Then silence.

'My rank would protect you. And we would be comfortable together, I am sure of it. Imagine how our life could be.' Jon waited. Had he said enough to persuade her? Would she at least consider his offer?

She withdrew her hand and clasped her fingers in her lap once more. Not a good sign. Was she going to refuse him again?

'If I do not accept you, sir, what will you do?'

Another facer. 'I would—' His answer began automatically, but then he stopped short, trying to collect his thoughts. He owed her a considered response on something so important.

That was when he realised that he had no answer to give her. He had not the faintest notion of what he would do if she turned him down.

The silence stretched between them. Jon found that it was surprisingly comfortable to sit in silence with Beth, even when he was trying to decide how to reply to her searching question. It was just as he had supposed: she was a restful woman and an estimable companion. She was exactly the wife he needed. He could not afford to lose her. He must not.

That sudden urgency had started his mind racing, as if he were back facing the enemy. He was going to have to fight— and fight harder—to convince her to accept him. His tactics so far had failed. He needed—

A new idea exploded in his rioting thoughts. Now, at last, he knew how to begin. 'I have a bargain to offer you, Beth.'

'A bargain?' Her voice had become hoarse. 'I don't understand.'

He grinned at her, feeling himself regaining control at last. 'I have made you a sincere proposal of marriage. You have asked, reasonably enough, what I will do if you refuse me. I will answer you, and truthfully, but not now, not here. Tomorrow, if you agree, I shall call at the rectory to take you out driving. I will dismiss the groom as soon as we reach the park, so all our conversation will be quite private. Then, I promise, I will answer your question. And perhaps you, in turn, will give me your response to my proposal?'

'I…I should not— You will not take my answer now?'

He shook his head. He allowed his self-assured grin to subside into a wry smile as he looked down at her, but he could see that her resolve was weakening. If he could make her wait, make her reflect, then all hope was not lost. 'If you want to hear my answer before you speak, Beth, you will have to drive with me tomorrow. Do we have a bargain?'

She sat immobile for a long time, staring vacantly across the garden. Jon waited. The longer she thought, the better his chances, he decided. He would wait until darkness fell if that would help his cause.

Beth rose quite suddenly, in a single graceful movement. A well-bred lady's movement. This time she did not stop him from joining her on the path. 'Perhaps we should go in?' she said, in what Jon could only describe as her company voice. 'It is beginning to get a little chilly out here and Aunt Caro will be wondering what has happened to us.'

Without waiting to be asked, she tucked her arm into his. It was a confiding gesture, Jon thought. And hopeful.

They began to stroll towards the house. 'Let us hope that

the fine weather continues for a few days yet.' She glanced up at the sky. 'It looks to be set fair.' She smiled at nothing in particular and twisted her head to look up at him. 'At what time do you plan to call for me tomorrow?'

Beth began to pace up and down in the small free space between the end of her bed and the window overlooking the shrubbery.

Untouched. The word was echoing in her head like a drumbeat in an empty hall. *Untouched.* How could he know for certain? Surely he might be mistaken?

But did it matter, provided he really wanted Beth to wife? He said he did. And it was more than wanting. It seemed that he needed her. Beth had been wrong to believe he had loved Alicia. In fact, his first marriage had been a failure. He had no son. And she sensed that he was very lonely. He wanted a companion and a friend more than he wanted a wife. He had almost said as much.

Could she really be that woman? Wife to an earl? Would it be such a sin for a woman with no past to accept him?

It would be a sin to condemn him to loneliness. And it would be worse to condemn him to another marriage like his first. Perhaps he would prefer no wife, and no heir, to marriage to a woman he could not esteem? He did esteem Beth, for all her lack of family and history. He said there could be nothing truly wicked in her past, that he knew her well enough to make a judgement about her character. He was so sure of it that she had begun to believe him. But did *she* know *him*?

Yes, of course she did. He was a fine man, a man of integrity who cared for his tenants, and for all those who depended upon him. When he returned from Spain and discovered what his brother had done to the Fratcombe estate, he had set about putting matters to rights. The repairs had been done, the workers had received fair prices for their labours, and he had paid for the children to be sent to school. Yes, he was a good man. He did need an heir, certainly. Unless he married again, and produced a son, his heir would remain his younger brother, George, the man who had tried to bleed Fratcombe of every penny it would yield.

It had been so simple to refuse him when he first proposed. His offer had come as a shock, and her answer had been automatic. But it was not simple any longer. Was Beth truly the only woman he could bear to think of as a wife? She would not know the answer to that until tomorrow. If he said it was Beth or no one, would she accept him? She refused to think about that. Jonathan was a man of the world. He knew he had to marry. If Beth refused him, he would find someone else, surely? He would not marry a girl out of the schoolroom. That was abundantly clear. But there must be other women, other ladies, who were older, more knowledgeable. A widow might suit him, perhaps. Yes. A widow of rank.

Beth's pacing had brought her back to the window yet again. She stopped. The sun was setting. The red–gold light was shining through the leaves of the huge beech, making them glow like amber jewels. In a few weeks, its branches would be bare. It was nearly winter. This golden autumn was a joy, but short-lived.

She pressed her palms to the panes, leant her forehead against the wood and closed her eyes. She tried to visualise Jonathan sitting in comfort by his fire, his new wife on the opposite side, calmly reading a book of sermons. The new countess's face was hidden from Beth's view. She was wearing a fine silk gown in a deep shade of red, her hair concealed by an expensive lace cap and her head bent as she concentrated on her reading. Was she reading aloud? It appeared not.

And Jonathan? What was he doing? He seemed to be leaning back, staring at the fire. His hands were resting on the carved wooden arms of his chair. He looked…he looked…

Beth could not decide. His expression was rather vacant. It was not happy, not even content. He was somewhere else entirely. And his wife, the high-ranking widow he had married, was quite oblivious of it.

'Oh, it is wishful thinking!' Beth exclaimed, exasperated at her own wilful daydreaming. 'You want him. That is the truth of it. You have always wanted him. And you are looking for reasons to persuade yourself that he needs you, that you should not refuse him. You are a fool, Beth Aubrey, or whatever your true name is. You are a fool!'

But what if he really does need me? Just as I need him? What then? What if he might come to love me, as I love him?

Those forbidden words. She had spent so long trying to banish them from her thoughts. And now they had ambushed her. Did she really love him? She took one last look at the glowing golden tree and sank to her knees on the floor, pillowing her head in her hands. Of course she did. She wanted him in her heart, and in her bed. She wanted more than that one spell-binding kiss. And she wanted to spend her whole life trying to make him happy, to ease the loneliness and hurt from which he was suffering. Perhaps one day, he might even confide in Beth about what had happened when he was in Spain.

He had never said a word in her hearing, but she was sure that something he had done, or something he had seen in his time there, was at the root of what troubled him. The man who had carried a shivering foundling to the refuge of the rectory was a man who needed a refuge of his own. He seemed to be sure, in his own mind, that Beth was the woman who would provide the sanctuary he was seeking. Why deny him and, in so doing, deny her own deepest longings?

Because you have no right to inflict a nameless wife upon him, no matter how much you may love him. If you really loved him, you would not do so. Who knows what there is in your past? Who knows what men you may have known? Whatever he says, Jonathan cannot know that you are untouched.

That was surely the cause of her recurring guilt. Some-where in her past, she had lost her virtue, perhaps even colluded in her own disgrace. No wonder her memory was blank. She deserved to be a nameless outcast. If she had done such a wicked thing, she was no fit wife for any man.

The dream had come so close, yet now it was floating away again like a soap bubble borne aloft on the tiniest breath of air. She could not do it. She must not. The Countess of Portbury must come to her husband untouched, and unsullied.

Beth could not swear to be that woman. And without

that, she had no choice. She wiped the back of her hand across her eyes. It was no weakness to allow a single tear, or even two, for the man she loved and would have to refuse.

Beth could not sleep. It was not surprising, for her mind was full of tomorrow, what she would say, how much he would be hurt. She rolled over yet again and punched the pillow.

She was going to look a fright when he appeared to escort her to his curricle. Perhaps that would be some consolation to him. However estimable he thought her, he would not wish to marry a woman with black circles round her eyes and quivering limbs.

She pushed the coverlet down to her waist. It was remarkably hot considering that it was already autumn. Should she open the window? A little fresh air, even night air, would do her no harm. She could shut it again before Hetty appeared to berate her for doing something so foolish.

She crossed to the window to push the curtains back a little and then eased the sash up an inch or two, working slowly and carefully to avoid any squeaks that might disturb the rest of the household. There was a sliver of moon just behind the beech tree. Where earlier its leaves had been golden and glowing, they were now dark, cold shadows. There was no movement, no wind. The great tree was holding its breath, waiting for the embrace of winter, making ready to fall asleep. As Beth should sleep.

If only there were a way... If only...

From the fields beyond the glebe, the sheep were bleating. Strange, for the lambs were long gone. Was the ram back in the field to ensure next spring's crop of lambs? The ewes would be ready, for they could certainly not remain untouched. That was the way of nature.

She shook her head. What a strange pattern of thought. She yawned. Good. At last she should be able to sleep.

Beth took one final breath and pulled the curtains closed, resolving she would rise early to shut the window again. She was sure she would sleep better with the sweet night air around her. She climbed back into bed, pulled the covers up over her shoulders and closed her eyes.

The last thing she heard was the bleat of the ewes beyond the glebe.

'Miss Beth, you *never* slept with the window open?'

It was Hetty with her hot water. So much for Beth's good intentions. She sat up with a jerk and put her hands to her hair, sensing something was amiss. Her plaits had come undone in the night. Her hair was a mass of tangles and her nightrail was all bunched up above her waist. The bed-clothes, too, seemed to have tied themselves in knots. She—

Heavens, she had been dreaming about Jonathan! Again! This time, she had been in his arms while he covered every inch of her skin with passionate kisses. Every last inch. Her whole body had been hot and alive. And willing. It had been blissful. It was a wonder she had not torn off her nightrail along with the fastenings of her hair. In her dreams, she had been so very sure, so—

In your dreams, you were wanton. You should be ashamed.

Beth forced herself to ignore the warnings of her conscience. He would arrive soon. 'Hetty, would you bring me a large jug of cool water please? I seem to have become very hot in the night. It would be best if I give myself a sponge bath before I dress.'

'You've caught a fever, Miss Beth. On account of the open window.'

Beth shook her head. Her fever was not of the kind Hetty meant. Hetty's fevers could be cured. 'I am not ill. But I am going driving with his lordship this morning and I must be looking my best. Make haste with the water, if you please. It is going to take you an age to comb the tangles out of my hair.'

Hetty paused a moment, looking mutinous, but then she obeyed.

Beth breathed a sigh of relief and jumped out of bed, allowing the rumpled nightrail to fall back to her ankles. She was decent again. Outwardly. A quick glance in the mirror showed her that her skin was still flushed, especially where the ribbon ties had come undone to expose her throat and breasts. Yes, he had kissed her there, too. And she had gloried in it.

In her dreams, she was not untouched.

And in her dreams, she had discovered what she must do.

It was a beautiful morning, more like late August than early October. The sky was blue and cloudless, and the slight breeze was warm. Only the turning trees betrayed how late in the year it was. Soon their crisp leaves would be heaped in the gutters and under the hedgerows, offering winter hiding places to small animals and rich food for worms and beetles.

Beth refused to think about the dead leaves that had saved

her from oblivion, long ago. Better to think about her rescuer, the man who now sat beside her in the curricle, his lean hands guiding his matched pair along the curving path through Fratcombe Manor park. She and Jonathan were easy enough together, even though he had spoken barely a word beyond the normal courtesies. She was starting to wonder if he felt as tongue-tied as she did.

He had promised to tell her what he would do if she refused him. And she—heaven help her!—had promised to respond to his proposal.

She could not bring herself to ask him to begin. Once he did, she would have to speak, too. This was one confrontation she could not run from, no matter what was said. She had to trust him. She did trust him.

He spoke at last. 'I thought I would drive you to the far side of the park this morning. For once, the track is dry enough to take a carriage.' His voice sounded remarkably normal. How did he do that? Could he feel none of the confusion that was threatening to overwhelm her?

'Usually the ground is too marshy for wheeled vehicles. Pray do not upbraid me, Miss Beth,' he added hastily, with a hint of humour in his tone. 'I do intend to drain that land as soon as I can. I am fully aware of my duties there, I promise you.' He turned slightly. Beth saw that he was smiling.

She found herself smiling back. She could not help it. He was in control of this encounter and, strangely, it made her feel…protected. He was deliberately teasing her into relaxing with him once more. 'Have I been such a termagant, sir? It was not my intent to badger you.'

'No?' He chuckled. 'No, I am sure your reproofs were kindly meant. Such as when you told me to look to the repairs of my tenants' houses. And to ensure that travelling gypsy bands could camp unmolested.'

'Oh!' Yes, she had done both of those. 'I apologise if I overstepped the mark, sir. My intentions were of the best. I was trying to—'

'You were trying to take care of others, to do good, as you always do, Beth, which is one of the reasons why I admire you so much. And why I want you to be my wife.'

Beth's heart clutched in her breast. She could not breathe.

'But before I press you for your answer, I owe you mine. A promise is a promise, especially between friends. Do you not agree?' He waited a beat. When she said nothing, he continued, airily, 'I have decided that, if you refuse me, I shall keep repeating my proposal until you accept. In other words, you might as well accept me at once.' His voice dropped a little, to a deeper, more serious tone. 'Will you marry me, Beth? Please?'

Beth had been screwing up her courage for this since the moment she awoke from that beckoning dream. She lifted her chin, focused on the horses' ears and launched into her prepared answer. 'I will accept your proposal, sir—'

'Beth, that is wonderful—'

'—but on one condition.'

'Ah. Name it.'

She took a deep breath. 'On condition that you prove to my satisfaction, and to your own, that I am still a virgin *before* you lead me to the altar.'

The noise he made sounded to Beth like the growl of a furiously angry bear, beset by slavering dogs.

'If I am a virgin, I cannot have been married before. And I…I would not be dishonouring you by accepting your proposal. My plan provides the only sensible solution.'

'And how do you propose, sensible Miss Aubrey, that I should establish your virginity? I take it you have a plan for that, too?' His voice was very hard, very cold.

Beth shivered at the sound, but she would not give up now. She was mortified enough and already scarlet to her hairline, she knew. She had nothing more to lose. 'I believe the only reliable method is the…the natural one. I…I will come to your bed and let you…let you—'

His string of curses included mostly words that Beth did not recognise. 'I beg your pardon,' he said at last, recovering his control, though not his colour. He was sheet white under his tan. 'You are proposing that I should deflower you in order to prove you are fit to be my wife? What kind of cold-blooded devil do you take me for?'

'If you do indeed discover that I am a virgin, then I will marry you. But if you do not, if I am already…er… *deflowered* as you call it, I will not marry you, for that could be bigamy. It seems simple enough.'

'Simple?' He was having even more trouble controlling his temper now. That one word was a howl of rage. 'Has it not occurred to you that, as a result of this *plan* of yours, you could end up carrying my child? Virgin or no, would you marry me then?'

'I…I…' In for a penny, in for a pound. 'I am not totally

ignorant of such matters, sir. I know how children are got. I do not know precisely how they are prevented, but I have heard that there are ways of...of ensuring that—' She stopped and swallowed hard. She knew she had to go on with this, no matter what. She mustered all her remaining courage and dared to meet and hold his stormy gaze. 'I know you to be a man of the world. I assumed you would know the way of it. Was I wrong?'

Chapter Nine

At that moment, Jon could have strangled Beth Aubrey, even if he had to swing for it. Luckily for her, his hands were fully occupied in controlling his horses. They had sensed his anger and were becoming extremely restive. He must calm them, or they would probably bolt.

It took more than five straining minutes to ensure that his pair—and his unruly temper—were back under control. He did not dare to speak until they were. In fact, he did not dare to speak at all. What an extraordinary proposal, from an innocent young lady. And yet…

And yet her logic could well be less flawed than Jon's. How could he truly be sure she was unspoilt on the basis of one single kiss? Beth's test was a surer touchstone than Jon's. How much courage it must have taken for her to propose such a thing. And to go further, to speak of preventing pregnancy… It was utterly outrageous.

It was one of the bravest things he had ever heard.

It appeared she was indeed willing to accept Jon, but only

if there was no risk to his honour. His honour, not hers! As if she cared more for Jon's honour than he did himself.

He risked another quick sideways glance. Beth's shoulders had not drooped even a fraction from her normal upright carriage, and she was staring down at her gloved hands. She was implacable. He could see that in every line of her tense body. Either he accepted her offer—her extraordinary plan—or she would be lost to him. That must not happen. In the course of this summer and autumn, Beth Aubrey had become the woman he wanted. He would not part with her. He needed her beside him. And so he was going to have to accept her terms.

She would come to his bed and let him—

Poor Beth. She had been unable to say the word. Yet it had taken courage to go as far as she had. She was as brave as any comrade he had served with.

She would come to his bed…

Oh dear. He laughed aloud, his black doubts disappearing with the sound. Poor Beth, indeed. Her carefully constructed plan was going to be her undoing.

'You find my question amusing, my lord?' Her tone was frosty.

'No, Beth. Forgive me. I was not laughing at you, but at the extraordinary predicament in which we find ourselves.' He slowed his horses for the sharp bend in the track. The right fork led round the back of the stable block to the furthest parts of his land. The left fork led to the lake and the tamer parkland beyond, where the folly lay hidden. 'You asked me about…er…prevention. Yes, I do know how it can be done.'

'Good.' She nodded. 'Then there is nothing to stop us from following my plan, is there?'

The die was cast, by her own hand. Jon turned his horses towards the lake.

She glanced sharply up at him, her eyes questioning, but she did not speak. Unlike most of her sex, she would be content to wait in silence.

'Your plan, ma'am. I think it needs to be…er…fleshed out a little. You said you would come to my bed. Believe me, I am honoured by your offer. Might I ask, though, how you were…um…planning to manage it?' He was having trouble keeping the laughter out of his voice. His mind was filled with the ludicrous image of his butler announcing Beth at his bedchamber door. *Miss Aubrey is here, my lord. To be deflowered.*

Beth gave a gasp of horror and began to cough, trying to cover her acute embarrassment. If he had not seen it with his own eyes, he would not have believed a lady could turn that particular shade of vermilion.

Yes, the die was cast. And the play was his.

Jon relaxed and let the horses have their heads up the gentle slope. The path was clear. Beth would have her assignation. On Jon's terms.

'Someone is living here!'

The folly consisted of a single square room. Beth would have expected it to be empty, or to contain a few chairs, at most, where guests might sit to recover after the long climb up from the house and past the lake. Instead, it looked like the cluttered living quarters of some rich young buck with an extremely idle servant. There was a fireplace, with a kettle suspended, but the fire had burned down long ago, and the ashes had spilled out over the small hearth. In front of it were comfortable chairs and a table strewn with used plates and glasses. There was at least one empty wine bottle on the floor.

Beth turned away. She had seen quite enough. The only part of the room that was not at sixes and sevens was the desk, where a neat row of books stood propped against the wall. Next to them were several leather-bound notebooks, a pile of writing paper and an inkstand. The desk was so tidy, it could have been in the rector's study. But the rest—!

'No. Not living.' He gazed round, apparently trying to view the chaos as Beth had just done. 'I use this place from time to time for…er…my own pleasure. It is totally private. The servants are not permitted to enter, even to clean and restock it, without special leave. And as you can see—' he waved a hand in the direction of the tumbled cushions and the dirty plates '—I have not yet given them leave today.'

'You were here last night?'

'Yes, I was here. I prefer solitude when I want to think. Besides, it was a splendid night.'

She frowned. A splendid night? What on earth did he mean? Glancing round again at the mess and at what, she now realised, was a kind of bed in the far corner, she decided that she did not wish to know.

He was smiling down at her. It was the kind of superior, knowing smile that made her want to slap him. He was waiting for her to ask. Well, she would not. Whatever his *splendid* nocturnal activities might be, he could keep them to himself. 'Might I ask why you have brought me here, sir? It is barely minutes since you said you would drive me to the marshes. The marshes you have promised to drain,' she added, with emphasis. That wiped the superior smile from his face, she was glad to see.

From mocking to serious in an instant. 'I brought you here to make plans. I understand now—forgive me, I did not understand before—how strongly you feel on the subject of our...er...possible union. I understand, too, that the condition you have laid down is absolute.' He took her right hand in his, holding it lightly. 'But I think you must now realise, Beth, that meeting your condition will be far from easy. I cannot simply walk into your bedchamber, nor you into mine.'

Beth felt herself colouring yet again. It seemed she had done nothing else since the moment he had arrived at the rectory door. But he was right that she had been a fool. Society, especially in villages like Fratcombe, was arranged precisely to prevent such carnal assignations.

Jonathan led her across to the desk and invited her to sit. There was only one chair. Once she was seated, he let go of her hand and leaned nonchalantly against the corner of the desk. 'Our meeting cannot be at the rectory, clearly. Nor at the Manor, for there are too many servants with prying eyes and long noses. Did you imagine you could come there, alone, and be admitted by my butler?'

'I...um...' Beth fixed her gaze on the tooled leather of the notebook.

'I have a better plan to propose. First, you must be conveyed from the rectory to our meeting place. You cannot be expected to go on foot, alone, in the dark. I suggest you slip out and wait behind the beech tree. At the appointed hour, I will meet you and bring you to our rendezvous. You have only to leave the rectory without being seen. And to return again before first light, of course. Do you think you can do that, Beth?'

'I...I...' This was no time for missishness. Jonathan was providing a practical plan that would allow the condition— Beth's own condition—to be met. 'Yes. Yes, I can do that.'

'Beth.' He reached for her hand again and held it in a strong clasp. 'Are you sure you want to do this? It is not necessary, believe me. I really do want to marry you, and I require no such demonstration of your virtue beforehand. What's more, I am sure you would be easier if our first love-making took place when we were already man and wife.'

'No,' she declared stoutly. 'That cannot be the way of it, for the reasons I have given you. I will not risk bigamy. Nor your honour. Unless we fulfil my condition, there will be no marriage.'

He shook his head. 'You are a stubborn woman, Beth Aubrey. Very well, it shall be as you wish. You may leave all the arrangements to me. Apart from one thing. You must be sure to be warmly clad and sensibly shod, for I will not be able to bring a carriage for you. That would attract too much attention, even in the dark. I shall come for you on horseback.'

She could see the sense in that. She nodded. 'Do I need to ride, too?'

'No. Saracen is more than capable of carrying us both.'

He was going to take her up before him and ride with her in his arms, close against his powerful body. The prospect sent a delicious frisson down her spine. Especially as it would be followed by… Oh dear. A virtuous lady should not be thinking of such things, but she could not help it. She wanted him so. 'Will you bring me here?' she asked quietly, trying not to dwell on the sensual images that were invading her brain. She glanced round the room. Unfortunately that added even more wanton thoughts, for the room had an air of wild abandon.

'Yes. For it will be quite private.' He grinned ruefully. 'I will have it set to rights before you arrive. There will be nothing to offend your delicate sensibilities, I promise you.'

Nothing except what they were going to do in this private place!

Jonathan's eyes were twinkling with mischief. Her face must have given her away, yet she could not bring herself to be angry with him this time. After all, the condition was hers. And he had found a way of making a reality of it. If he was teasing her a little in the process, she would not object. Better to respond in kind. 'I should hope so, indeed, sir,' she said brightly, reaching out to run a gloved finger along the window sill behind the books. She examined it closely, shaking her head in mock disgust. That window had not been dusted for some time. 'A lady likes to meet her…um… A lady likes to go to an encounter with a gentleman knowing that all her needs will be met—warmth, comfort, *and* cleanliness.'

He chuckled. 'I promise you that all your requirements will be met.' He raised her hands to his lips, kissing each in turn. 'All of them. Now, if you are content, ma'am, I suggest we continue our drive.'

How very matter of fact he was about such a momentous thing. Yet those kisses on her hands had not been matter of fact, or even necessary. She sensed they were his way of sealing their very special bargain.

She nodded. She would try to sound as normal as he had. 'Yes. By all means. Let us view your marshes.'

He tucked her hand into the crook of his arm and started for the door, stopping there for a last swift glance back at the room. 'It will be transformed, I promise you, Beth. Meet me behind the beech tree at a quarter to midnight and you shall see for yourself.'

Tonight? It was for tonight?

He was smiling down at her. It was not a leer, nor anything like. It was a smile of encouragement, the kind of smile Beth often used in the schoolroom when a child was facing a new and daunting task. 'Courage, little one,' he said softly. 'A quarter to midnight.'

She met his gaze bravely. 'A quarter to midnight? So be it.'

The big bay stopped by the entrance to the folly. The whole park was in darkness except for a single candle glowing through the slit window alongside the door. In the silence, a long shiver passed down Beth's body. Jonathan must have felt it, for he pulled her a little more closely against his body. He made no comment. He had made clear from the outset that this condition of hers did not need to be met. He had repeated it as he pulled her up before him and settled her into his arms. She had only to say the word, at any stage, and he would return her to the rectory.

She did not say the word now. And he did not hector her. He was paying her the compliment of treating her like an equal, able to make her own decisions. If she changed her mind, he was trusting her to say so.

'You are chilled,' he murmured against her ear, his breath caressing her cheek. 'You must go in to the warm.' He dismounted and helped her down, holding her close against his side. Then he led her to the door and reached for the handle. 'Go in. Make yourself comfortable. And warm. I will join you in a moment, once I have seen Saracen safely bestowed.'

Beth glanced back at the horse which stood motionless, waiting patiently. 'He looks as though he would stand there all night.' She was trying to inject a degree of lightness into her voice.

Jonathan chuckled. 'Aye, he would. But I think he deserves a net of hay, and to be rid of the weight of the saddle on his back.' He opened the door for Beth and pushed her gently inside, closing it behind her.

The room was transformed. A few hours earlier, there had been chaos and abandon. Now everything had been set to rights; it was warm and welcoming. Indeed, as a venue for an illicit tryst, it seemed a little tame. A good fire was burning in the hearth and the kettle had been swung close enough to sing, though not to boil. The fire, an oil lamp on the desk and that single candle by the door provided the only illumination, although several branches of new, unlit candles had been set around the room.

Beth risked one quick glance at the bed in the far corner. It had been piled high with cushions so that it looked more like a sofa than a bed. Almost unthreatening.

She shivered again. She must be cold. There was no other reason for it. She was not being forced. Everything that took place now would be by her own choice and her own will. Crossing to the fire, she stripped off her gloves to warm her hands. Ah, delicious. It was only then that she noticed a tea tray standing ready on a low stool by the hearth. Tea? After midnight? And at an assignation?

She began to laugh. If she had been afraid, even a very little afraid, she was so no longer. She was here, tonight, to be in the arms of the man she loved. It was a time for anticipation, not for fear.

In that moment she knew that, whatever the outcome of this encounter, she wanted it. More than anything. Even if they parted after this one night, she would cherish every second of it, for the rest of her life.

Jon gave Saracen one last pat and left him contentedly munching hay in the lean-to behind the folly. The big horse was well used to being left there at night, while Jon enjoyed the peace and isolation of the place.

Jon slowly made his way round to the front. He could see through the small window that Beth had not lit any of the candles inside. What was she doing? Would she now finally realise what a momentous step she had chosen to take and change her mind? He hoped so.

And yet he hoped not. The thought of making love to Beth Aubrey—the woman he fully intended to marry—was an arousing one. She was everything a sensible man could want in a wife: kind, generous, thoughtful, dedicated to doing good in the world. She was restful, and beautiful, too. She would grace his arm and his bed. God willing, they would make fine children together, children a man could be proud of. It would be a solid, reassuring union. As a woman, she could never be a trusted confidante, of course. Such was the reality of life. In public, they would have to be distant and formal, as their rank demanded, but in private they could be comfortable companions. It was more than he had dared to hope for in a wife.

Just at this moment, however, his body was telling him that a comfortable companion was not what he sought. His purpose now was to introduce Beth—his innocent Beth—to the joys and delights of lovemaking.

At the door he paused to look up at the night sky. No wonder it was so cold. There was not a single cloud. The great upturned bowl, the colour of deepest indigo, was spattered with the points of light he knew so well. This picture was eternal. These same stars would blaze down on Beth and Jon's children, and on their children's children. Nothing would change.

And yet, tonight everything would change. Children… He had told Beth that he knew the way of preventing conception, but she had not asked him to promise to use it. If Beth were not a virgin, she would never agree to marry him, so he was duty-bound to ensure that no child resulted from what they did together this night. He owed her that. But what if he found that he was holding a virgin in his arms? He fully expected it to be so. What then? She had promised to accept his proposal if there were no risk of bigamy. And the purpose of marriage was children, was it not?

He shook his head. High above, the dog-star seemed to wink at him. 'Yes, I know,' he murmured, gazing up at it. 'I am trying to find an unselfish reason for following my own selfish desires. And yet, the risk of pregnancy could make matters easier, later.' He shook his head again, trying to clear his thoughts. This was no time for logic-chopping.

He allowed himself one last glance up at the star-mapped sky. 'I will make it good for her. I promise.' He turned and opened the door.

She had put back the hood of her cloak and was kneeling on the rug in front of the hearth. Even across the full length of the room, he could see that her shoulders were shaking. Poor girl, she must be terrified. And he had been communing with the stars?

He closed the door quietly, not to frighten her, before setting down his hat and whip and striding across the room to kneel beside her. 'Oh, my poor Beth,' he began gently, putting a comforting arm round her shoulders.

The face she turned up to him was not stricken, not in the least. It was alight with laughter.

'Beth?'

'Tea!' The single word was barely a croak. She was laughing too much to be able to control her voice.

He looked down at the tea tray he had ordered. It was unusual, to be sure, but it had seemed a good idea. Comforting, unthreatening.

'Tea!' she said again, on a throaty chuckle.

He was trying very hard to keep his face straight, but he knew he was not really succeeding. 'I thought you might be glad of it, after our cold midnight ride.'

'And indeed I am, sir. See, I have set the kettle to boil.' She had swung the kettle fully over the fire. 'But I must tell you that this was not quite what I was expecting.'

'Oh?' He raised an eyebrow.

'I had imagined champagne, or something equally decadent.'

'You may have champagne, or brandy, if you wish. I have both here. I could even make you hot rum punch if you had a fancy for it.'

She shook her head, trying not to smile.

'No, I thought not. Remember that we are friends, Beth. After this night, we will soon be man and wife. And still true friends.'

Her expression became more serious, but she did not protest. They both knew the condition. There was no point in belabouring it.

'True friends enjoy each other's company and seek to provide for each other's comfort. In your case, tea seemed to be the ideal solution.'

Beth touched her hand to Jon's arm. 'You are a good friend, sir.'

'No. No, I will not permit that. Not when we are alone. You will not call me "sir" as if you were an inferior. You are to be my wife, my countess. My name is Jon. Jonathan if you must, but I should prefer Jon.'

Her eyes widened and misted for a moment. 'Jon,' she said slowly, lingering over the sound as if testing it, tasting it with her tongue. 'For this night at least, it shall be as you wish.'

Chapter Ten

The orange and red of the fire was vividly reflected in her wide, glowing eyes. Her laughter had been infectious, and good to hear, for it meant that she was not afraid. She was doing what she wanted. And with a full heart.

He took both her hands in his—as he had done so many times before—and gently raised her. But this time, there was no chaste kiss on her white skin. This time, he raised first one hand and then the other to his lips and took finger after finger into his mouth, sucking greedily. Reaching her second index finger, he began to nibble her flesh, too.

She gave a little yelp of surprise. Then it mellowed into a sigh of acceptance, and pleasure.

By the time he came to the ring finger of her left hand, he was desperate for more than this. He swallowed it to the first knuckle, and the second, then slowly pulled his mouth away again, in a long drawn out kiss, revelling in the trail of heat and desire he was leaving behind him. On this finger, she would wear his ring. He paused, holding the very end of her ring finger lightly between his lips and stroking its fleshy pad with the tip of his tongue. She tasted wholly delicious.

She groaned, deep in her belly. It was the sound of willing surrender. At last. Jon pulled her into his arms and began to plunder her soft, yielding mouth. She was almost as eager as he, though her lack of experience was just as obvious as on that first occasion. She wanted him. She wanted *this*, but she certainly did not know the way of it.

Jon told himself to go slowly, to take her with him every step of the way, to show her how to relish the moment, the touch, the feelings that they would enjoy together. He would make it beautiful for them both.

He drove his hands deep into her hair. From far off, he heard the tinny sounds of metal—hair pins?—clinking on the hearth as her hair tumbled and settled in silken waves around her shoulders. He was holding her head steady for his kiss, but she was avid for him, too. She dug her hands under his waistcoat and round to his back where her fingers gripped and tugged at the fine linen of his shirt, trying to reach his skin.

This was not the slow, gentle seduction he had intended. He forced himself to break the kiss and take a pace back, dropping his hands.

'Jon?' His abrupt movement had loosed her frenzied grip on his flesh. Her face was glowing in the firelight, but with far too much colour now. She was embarrassed again, poor girl. She thought… He did not know what she thought, but he did know he must reassure her.

'We go too fast, Beth.' He spoke softly, stroking the back

of his fingers soothingly down her cheek. 'You are very lovely, but I fear my desire is driving me faster than is wise.'

She swallowed hard, but when she looked up at him again, her eyes were defiant. 'You forget, sir—' she began proudly. 'Pray do not forget, Jon,' she repeated, rather more gently, 'that I am a willing partner here.'

Partner. The word had a good, solid sound to it. He liked it. 'Yes, we *shall* be partners. But, for this first time, our partnership should blossom a little more slowly.' He smiled down at her and, with careful fingers, began to untie the strings of her cloak. Behind them, the kettle had begun to boil. With barely a sideways glance, Jon hooked it away from the fire with his boot. This was definitely not a moment for tea.

By the time he had removed her cloak and turned to lay it aside, Beth's breathing had become fast and shallow. Not fear, but desire. She might be innocent—he was sure of that in his own mind—but even an innocent could be overtaken by the human body's natural urges. Jon's task was to fan those flames. The slightest mistake on his part could damp her natural fires and ruin this night for her. That must not happen.

When he turned back to her, he saw that she was starting to undo the neck of her simple gown, in the sort of practical, matter-of-fact way that he had come to associate with Beth Aubrey.

'No,' he whispered, laying his fingers over hers. 'Pray allow me. This gift you are offering me needs to be unwrapped very, very slowly. It would be generous indeed if you permitted me to do this. Please, Beth.'

'I— Oh.' She coloured again until her skin was like a ripe

peach, its luscious flesh concealed beneath the dark bloom, inviting a lover's bite.

'But if you keep looking at me like that, my dear girl, I shall find myself hard put not to simply tear off your gown.' That was nothing less than the truth, for she looked good enough to eat.

'Oh,' she said again, but this time with a knowing glint in her eye. Her beautiful blush was fading, and her mouth was starting to curve into a shy but eloquent smile. She slipped her fingers out from under his, teasingly stroking his palm as she did so. She was beginning to understand this game of theirs. And, he suspected, to enjoy it very much.

Jon slowly removed the pins that fastened the front panel of her gown. It fell forward, revealing the simple white chemise beneath and the ties of her skirt. His eyes widened—she wore no corset. There was only a single layer of lawn between his fingers and her breasts.

She read his reaction immediately. 'I…I had to be able to dress myself without help,' she whispered.

Practical as ever. She could hardly summon Hetty to lace her into her stays at midnight. And yet she was shy of the fact that she had come to meet Jon while less than properly clad. He put his hands to her face and kissed her gently, full on the mouth. Her response surprised him. Her lips opened under his and her sweet breath invited him in.

He moaned and deepened the kiss. At the same time, he dropped his fingers to the ties of her skirt. One single tug, and they were undone. Using touch alone, he pushed the gown off her shoulders so that it slithered down her body to pool at her feet. It made almost no sound, for the fabric was old and soft. One day, Jon would dress her in the finest silks and satins, fabrics that would rustle luxuriously when he peeled them away to reveal the glories beneath.

Glories they were. He could not resist stepping back to admire her. Somewhere, she had kicked off her shoes, for she was now clad in only a chemise and stockings. That thin chemise did nothing to conceal her breasts—small, pert and the delicious colour of cream ripening in the skimming pan. Under Jon's appreciative gaze, her nipples rose and darkened, straining up towards him. It was the most erotic vision he had ever seen.

Jon's body reacted instantly. Shocked at his own callow response, he heard himself groan aloud.

'Jon? Is something wrong?'

Absolutely nothing was wrong. Nothing at all. Except that, if he did not put his lips to those perfect pouting nipples, his body might explode.

He threw off his coat and waistcoat and glanced towards the bed in the corner. No, not there. Here, in the warmth. Here, where every inch of her skin would glow.

He set his hands on her bare shoulders. A fleeting touch. 'How beautiful you are there, lit by the flames. Give me a moment.'

She frowned, puzzled, though she did not move from her place. But her frown melted away, as she watched him pull off his cravat and then drag the bed out from the corner and into the space in front of the fire. He had tumbled the colourful cushions into a heap in the middle.

'Will it please you to sit, my lady?' He waved a hand towards the bed. Then he held it out to her with exaggerated courtesy.

Beth's stomach lurched. The bed was only two steps away, the two most important steps of her life. She hesitated for a fraction too long.

'Beth?' He sounded uncertain, troubled.

Beth hesitated no longer. She placed her fingers in his and squeezed gently. 'I swear that is a throne you have prepared for me,' she said lightly, nodding towards the piles of silken cushions.

It was the reassurance he seemed to need. He did not give her a chance to move. He just swept her up into his arms and laid her down on the bed, arranging the cushions for her head and back. She allowed her body to sink deep into the unaccustomed luxury. 'Ah, that is wonderful,' she sighed, turning her face against the silk and breathing deeply. It had a fragrance of its own, of exotic places where the sun shone fiercely and the sky was too blue to be captured by any painter's palette. She was in a dream. She must be. Such bliss could not be real.

He was still standing, staring down at her, watching her every movement. She stroked the fingers of one hand over the velvet coverlet and purred like a contented cat. 'Mmm. How comfortable this is. But a little lonely, I would say. Do you think there is room for two?' She lifted her naked arms invitingly.

'Aye, provided we snuggle together a little.' His voice seemed to have become lower than normal.

'That sounds…er…a most practical approach.' Beth gave

a nervous giggle. Enough! She could not bear to wait any longer. 'Would you care to try the experiment? Jon?' She stretched her arms even more towards him.

In a second, he was lying beside her, pulling her close. She could feel the heat of him through the layers of his shirt and her chemise. His heart was thrumming. Or was it hers? It felt like the pulse of a drum, linking their two bodies. But not close enough.

She pushed at the fabric of his shirt where it opened at the collar, exposing the deeply tanned skin of his neck and upper chest.

'There *are* buttons, you know,' he said throatily, putting his fingers to them. 'How shall I explain to my valet if they are all ripped off?'

Beth had just enough sense left to appreciate the risk he described. Her gown must not be torn; nor must his shirt. She took a deep breath and applied herself to his buttons. Unfortunately, her fingers seemed to have forgotten their role. They would not obey her.

Jon laughed and raised one of her hands to his mouth. A kiss, and then the nibbling began again. Beth felt as if her insides were melting, and glowing fit to outdo the fire.

'Let me,' he said softly, laying her fingers against his neck while he found and undid his shirt buttons. 'And now, what is your will, my lady?'

His shirt was open to the waist and free of his riding breeches. The invitation was obvious, but he was going slowly, out of concern for Beth. He was allowing her to set the pace she wanted.

Oh, how she loved this man! And how she wanted him! Desire was driving her now. All thoughts of missish propriety were long forgotten. With one delicious movement, she slid her fingers into the gap, then stroked up across his chest and shoulders, to push the shirt from his body. 'Ah.' The single word emerged as half-sigh, half-groan. He was beautiful. And in the firelight, his body was glowing with a golden warmth. Her knight, her golden knight. He would be hers, at last.

His mouth came down on hers, seeking, probing, gently at first, but once she began to respond, he became more demanding. He sucked at her lips and then he nibbled them, just as he had done her fingers, though the sensation was even more arousing on her mouth. Beth closed her eyes and gave herself up to her other senses. Emboldened by the darkness, she touched the tip of her tongue to his and felt an answering groan rippling through his body and into hers. She gasped his name, but it made no sound at all, for he swallowed her very breath and deepened the kiss yet more. Their tongues began to touch and tangle. They were united, in taste, in touch, even in the air they breathed.

When, at last, Jon broke the kiss, they were both gasping like drowning men pushing up to the surface of the sea. But if this was drowning, Beth would gladly give herself up to it. Her whole being was soft and molten, and as pliable as potter's clay. She felt as though Jon's kisses had dissolved her bones, leaving her formless, ready to take some exquisite new shape under his hands. She wanted to be enfolded in his arms once more, to fill the space that his gentle embrace would create.

The silence lengthened. He had gone from her. Reluctantly, apprehensively, Beth opened her eyes. 'Jon?' Her voice quavered.

'I am here.' He was over by the window. Beth moved just in time to see him extinguish the oil lamp. The candle by the door had already been snuffed out. 'Forgive me,' he said softly. 'I did not mean to alarm you, but I thought you might prefer the dark. Now we have only the glow of the fire. Does it trouble you? I can screen it if you prefer.'

Without light, Beth would not be able to feast her gaze on her golden knight. 'No, it does not trouble me.' She swallowed and then added, greatly daring, 'Though your absence did.' Shocked by her own forwardness, Beth closed her eyes and tried to force herself to relax into the cushions. After a moment, she felt the bed dip as Jon sat down. She thought she could hear him struggling with his boots. And she was sure she heard a muttered curse. She giggled nervously. She could not help it.

'It appears I am quite useless without a valet to pull off my boots.'

There was laughter in his voice. 'I could help you, if you wish?'

'Good God, no!' he exclaimed, still laughing. 'I could not cope with the sight of you kneeling at my feet. It is difficult enough as it is.'

'Perhaps you should buy boots that do not fit quite so snugly?'

'I may tell you, ma'am, that it is not the snug fit of my boots that is troubling me at this precise moment.'

Beth half-opened her eyes and then shut them again hurriedly. Jon was removing his tight riding breeches. In a moment, he would be completely naked. In a moment, he would be stretched out beside her. The tension grew, first in her neck and shoulders, and then spread down through her torso to her stomach.

'Beth.' He was beside her again. She could feel his warm breath fluttering across her cheek. 'Beth, open your eyes. Please.'

She could not resist that pleading note. And when she looked, she saw his face above her, half in shadow, and half glowing red in the firelight. Yet, in spite of the glow, his eyes seemed to be completely black, like fathomless pools. She longed to drown in them.

'Beth. My beautiful Beth. Will you permit me to remove your chemise so that I may see you? All of you?' When she hesitated, he continued hurriedly, 'I know you are shy. I ask too much. Forgive me.' He stroked his hand down the side of her body, smoothing the chemise into place as if he were trying to restore, rather than remove it.

But that was not at all what Beth wanted. She understood that, even while his fingers slithered over her hip bone and started down her thigh. She wanted him to smooth his hands over her skin. Without the intrusion of petticoats. She laid her hands on his cheeks and ran them gently down over the line of his jaw, his neck, and the taut muscles of his chest. She could go no further, for his body was resting on the bed beside her. She pushed against him with the flat of her hands. 'I…I want to see you.' Her whisper was barely audible, even to her own ears. 'And for you to see me.'

He took a deep breath and touched his mouth to the side of her neck, below her ear. 'It shall be exactly as you wish,' he whispered against her flesh, the words vibrating through her whole being. He kissed his way up to her ear lobe and began to nuzzle there. At the same moment, with featherlight touches, he was untying the ribbons of her chemise and pushing it carefully from her body. Soon, she was completely naked, apart from her stockings. A gentle hand lifted away the chemise and began to stroke up the side of her calf, teasing at the weave of her stocking and sending shivers through the flesh beneath.

Beth groaned out his name. He responded with a sound, low in his throat. She had never heard the like before, but she recognised it as male satisfaction, and anticipation. And then his questing fingers reached the naked flesh above her garter. That single touch was electrifying. He stroked his hand round to her inner thigh and let it rest there, while his lips nuzzled a path across her cheek to find her mouth.

'Oh, Beth. You are so very desirable.'

Her own desire for him was becoming almost impossible to endure.

He kissed her, deeply, on the mouth and then continued to kiss his way across her cheek and along her jaw, down her neck to the little indentation at the base. He paused there to flick her skin with the tip of his tongue. Then on, down, to the valley between her breasts. He took one breast in each hand, weighing them reverently, rubbing his thumbs back and forth across her aching nipples until they rose, hard and proud against his touch.

'Mmm.' Beth felt the low rumble against her flesh. Then he was rolling one nipple between his thumb and forefinger while he sucked the other with such force that she felt the pull all the way down to her womb. She gasped aloud at the strange, elusive pleasure of it.

Jon raised his head from her breast and murmured something she could not catch, before transferring his mouth to her other breast. This time the sensation was even stronger, as if her womb was contracting in response to his sucking mouth. Was this what it was to be loved by a man? It was almost more than she could bear.

Then Jon was kissing his way down her body, from the crevice between her breasts to her navel, and on, and on. She thought she cried out, but he hushed her and returned his wicked fingers to her breasts, pushing and rolling the nipples until they rose even more.

'Ah! Jon!' He had pushed himself down her body until his head was resting between her legs. She could feel the beginnings of his stubble against the tender skin of her inner thighs. And then… Heavens! He was kissing her. There! Oh! It was too much. Building, building, in great waves of feeling that she could not control. It was going to overpower her. She let out a long scream and tumbled into darkness.

Jon dropped one last kiss on her damp curls and pulled himself up to cover Beth's motionless body with his own. He settled himself into the cradle of her hips, making sure he was taking his weight on his elbows so as not to crush her slight form. He found himself gazing anxiously down at her flushed skin, luminous in the firelight. At the moment of ecstasy, she had fainted away. That was almost proof enough that she was still a virgin. Almost, but not quite. Beth herself would never accept it.

For one fleeting second after she had lost consciousness, Jon had been about to take her, to spare her the pain of first penetration. But he had not done it. He could not. He had to allow Beth the chance to refuse him, even now. Anything else would be a violation.

He bent to kiss her parted lips and then the purplish shadows on her closed eyelids. His taut flesh was straining towards the hot, moist entrance to her body, but he would not yield to its clamouring. There would be no union between them unless Beth herself decreed it should be so. No matter what it cost him. He kissed her mouth again and ran the tip of his tongue along the length of her lower lip. 'Beth. Come back to me, little one.'

It was like a fairy charm. Her eyes opened. She stared up at him, unfocused at first, and then all too knowing. 'Was that…?'

'No. No, my sweet Beth. That was ecstasy for you alone.'

'Not for you?'

'No, my dear. That was for you, to let you feel what love-making can become.'

'But it proved my virginity?'

He shook his head and touched a finger to her cheek. 'I wish— No, Beth. It was not proof.'

'But—' She was trying to shake her head. 'Jon, that was not our bargain.'

'You still wish that?'

'Yes.'

He took her mouth then, plunging deep, and insistently, until her response became more and more frenzied, and as feverish as when he had taken her, all alone, to the heights. Only then was he sure that she was ready for him.

'Beth.' He pulled his lips from hers and raised his head. 'Look at me, Beth.' She opened her eyes in response. 'Do you trust me?'

She gazed up at him, wide-eyed. 'Yes.' A whisper, but determined.

Jon drove into her with one long, powerful stroke. It was exactly as he had known it would be. The barrier of her virginity broke before his thrust. A sob rose in her throat and her face contorted in pain. Shocked, in spite of himself, he held himself very still within her, waiting, wishing he could absorb her suffering.

At last, her anguished face relaxed enough for her to look up at him. Even in the dim light, he could see that her eyes were sheened with tears.

'Oh, my poor Beth.'

'No. It is done. It is proved. And the pain will never come again, I know. Kiss me, Jon.'

He obeyed her, gladly. But as his lips and tongue moved on her mouth, so the rest of his body moved too, driven by ungovernable desire. It was impossible to prevent it, and yet he did not want to hurt her again. He should withdraw. He must.

But it seemed that Beth had other ideas. She wrapped her stocking-clad legs around him and began to kiss him even more passionately. It was too much. His driving thrusts became stronger, until they were both gasping for breath and Beth was bucking against him.

He could not. Oh, God, he must not! In a moment, it would be too late. With his last ounce of conscious control, he pulled himself from her embrace.

One moment, she had been soaring. The next, she had plummeted back to earth. Her body felt like an overwound watch spring, brittle enough to snap at a touch. 'Jon? I…I don't understand. Why—?'

He took a long shuddering breath, rolled on to the bed alongside her and drew her into his embrace. She felt his hand on her breast and his lips on hers. Skilful fingers trailed down her belly and began to stroke the innermost folds of her hot flesh. She groaned aloud. In an instant, she was soaring again. Soaring. She could see a bright light. Distant. But coming closer.

And then it exploded.

Chapter Eleven

When Beth opened her eyes, she was alone on the bed. How long had she been asleep? She had no idea. But she had clearly been dead to the world for some time, since her naked body was now warmly wrapped in the padded velvet bedcover. The crackle of a branch drew her eyes to the hearth. The fire had been made up and was burning fiercely. Where the folly room had been comfortably warm before, it was now becoming rather too hot.

'Jonathan?' He must be here somewhere.

The only response came from the fire, spitting like a snake as it consumed the dry logs. Beth began to shiver uncontrollably, as if she had been drenched in icy water. She was alone. Jon had taken his pleasure. And then he had left her.

At least he took the trouble to ensure you would not be cold as well. Her cynical internal voice pecked at her conscience like a vulture.

That single thought was enough. She refused to lie helpless like a victim. She was her own mistress, and she would take responsibility for everything she had done. Even this. The slight ache in her belly was real enough, a reminder of her own complicity. She would not regret it. After such bliss, she could not. But her reputation must not be lost along with her virginity. She must be safely back at the rectory before first light.

The prospect of making her way across the expanse of Fratcombe Manor park in the dark was daunting. She would have only starlight to see by, for there was no moon. Still, it could have been worse. If the sky had been clouded over, there would have been no light at all.

She sat up, struggling to free herself from the velvet folds. She must find her clothes. Thank goodness she had had the sense to dress warmly.

As Jon had warned her to do. Had it been his intention, from the first, to leave her to walk back to the village alone? Was he so callous, so calculating?

'Beth.' A draught of freezing air swept across the room, turning the flames bright orange.

He is still here. As I should have known he would be. He asked me to trust him and, faint-heart that I am, I failed to do so. I shall not do so again.

'I did not think you would wake so soon.' He was beside her on the bed, pulling her into his arms, caressing her hair.

Beth tried again to free herself from the bedcover. She was desperate to return his embrace, to prove to him—and to herself—that she trusted him completely. 'Oh, bother, I—' She growled in frustration.

Jon responded by tightening the covers around her, pulling her even closer, and kissing her very thoroughly. Yet he was laughing at the same time. 'You must not get cold, my dear,' he murmured as he broke the kiss.

'But you——' It was only then that Beth saw he was fully clad. He was even wearing those confounded boots!

She turned her gaze to the fire. 'Is it time to leave?' she asked quietly. She could feel the colour rising on her neck. The thought of returning to the rectory, even with Jon's careful help, was reminding her of just how far she had strayed from the path of propriety.

'No, not yet. There is something I wish to show you first.'

Beth whipped round to look at him. He looked more relaxed, more at ease, than she had ever seen him. The fine lines on his face seemed to have been smoothed away and there was a slight curve about his mouth... Not a smile, exactly, but a sign that he was content, at peace with his world. Was she, Beth, responsible for that?

He stood up and, in a single powerful movement, lifted her into his arms. Wrapped as she was, she could not resist. In truth, she had no desire to. She did try to free her arms, for she needed to touch him. Very much.

'Don't fight me, Beth. It is too cold for that.' He dropped a kiss on her forehead and started for the door.

Beth was too astonished to say a word. Jon shouldered the door open and carried her out into the night. He had been right about the cold. Under the cloudless sky, the air was almost freezing. If Beth had not been so warmly held, she would have shivered. As it was, she sank deeper into Jon's arms. She did not care where he was taking her. It was glorious simply to be held so.

He carried her round to the back of the folly. She heard noises, scuffling movements on the ground, and whiffling. Saracen, of course. He must be stabled somewhere near. To Beth's surprise, Jon ignored the horse and started to climb some stairs. She had not realised they existed.

'Where are you taking me?'

'On to the roof.'

'Why?'

They had reached the top of the stairs. Jon strode across to the middle of the roof and planted his feet firmly so that he could adjust Beth's position in his arms. 'Look up, and you will see.'

She leant her head back on to his shoulder. 'Oh. Oh, how beautiful it is.' The sky was not black, as she had expected. It was a deep rich colour, somewhere between darkest blue and purple. And the stars were strewn across it like daisies in a meadow—except that these daisies were twinkling and they would never fade and die, as mere flowers did.

'Have you never gazed at the stars before, Beth?'

'N…not like this.'

He laughed, low in his throat, and tightened his grip. 'It is a little unusual, I admit. But when we are married, we can do it again. Only if you wish it, of course,' he added, sounding apologetic.

'Is that why you come here? To look at the stars?'

'Mmm. In the wilds of Spain, the night sky always seemed

immense, and magical. So I had the folly refurbished as an observatory. I come here at night. And not for the nefarious purposes you suspected yesterday, Miss Prim.' His white teeth flashed. He was trying to make his grin look like a leer, but it was not working. He was laughing too much.

'Fie on you, sir! To call me "Miss Prim" when I am here in your arms and we have—' She stopped. Even with their new-found closeness, she could not quite say the words.

Jon's reply was to carry her over to one corner of the roof where he sat down on a wooden bench and settled Beth on his lap. 'From here, you may see most of the park, as well as the stars.' He gestured towards a fine telescope and a small stool behind it.

Beth snuggled against him. Was this what their life together would be? He had talked of companionship, but she had never imagined it could be so close, so warm, so trusting. She was right to love this man, even if he would never be able to love her in return.

The back of her head was on his shoulder. His arm was around her, holding her snugly, safely against his body. Then he rested his cheek against her hair so that she could feel his breath on her skin. She closed her eyes to savour the moment. She wanted to remember this for ever.

'I'm afraid that gnarled old tree rather spoils the panorama.'

His prosaic comment shattered Beth's reverie. She opened her eyes and followed his pointing finger. 'You could always cut it down, if it offends your notion of perfection,' she said, a little sharply.

'Oh, no, I could never do that. It is the only tree on the

whole estate with mistletoe growing on it. I never saw a single sprig of it in Spain.'

'Mistletoe?' Beth suddenly felt very, very cold. It made no sense. She was as warmly wrapped as before, and just as secure in Jon's arms.

'It is my childish fancy, I fear, but I know you will not betray my weakness. An earl is not supposed to feel affection for such things. But, when I was a little boy, mistletoe seemed to be the symbol of Christmas. It was a truly happy time for all of us, especially for Henry and me, as we were so close in age. We played such games together! We— Sadly, he died, and I became the heir. Nothing was quite the same afterwards. George and I—'

Jon's bleak grimace was telling. In her sudden concern for him, Beth pushed the image of mistletoe from her mind.

'He is a great deal younger than me and we…we have very little in common,' Jon said in a low voice. 'You will meet him soon, of course.'

Jon's brother was bound to attend the wedding, however quickly it took place. 'Shall you invite him here?' She could not bring herself to mention the wedding itself. If she dared to assume it was going ahead, some demon might appear and snatch it from her fingers.

'No!'

Beth could not believe how much anger there was in that single word. Did Jon have reason to hate his brother?

'No. George does not come to Fratcombe Manor.' He kissed her hair, breathing deeply. When he spoke again, his anger was leashed. 'You will meet him—and my mother—

at King's Portbury. But only after I have made you mistress of it. Which requires a wedding. A very *private* wedding. As soon as I can arrange it.'

'You mean here?'

'Why, yes. I assumed you would wish the Reverend Aubrey to perform the ceremony? Was I wrong?'

She shook her head. Her throat was too tight for speech and she could feel the beginning of tears in her eyes. To be married to Jon, and by the dear man who had protected her against so much pain and loneliness… It was much more happiness than she deserved.

'Excellent. I shall speak to him tomorrow. Or rather—' he glanced up at the sky, but it was still quite dark '—later this morning.'

'What if he will not agree? What if—?'

'He will agree, I promise you.'

'But—'

Jon silenced her protests by putting his lips to hers and kissing her hungrily. Soon passion was beginning to consume them both, just as before. For Beth, everything else was forgotten.

She tore her mouth from his at last. 'I need to touch you.' She was wriggling within her velvet. 'I don't care if I freeze in the process.'

'But I do,' he said, on the thread of a laugh. He rose easily to his feet and started across the roof, still holding Beth securely wrapped. 'Let us return downstairs where it is warm. We have hours yet before I must take you back. A long, long time, Beth, in which I promise I shall let you do exactly as you wish.'

★ ★ ★

Jon strode so quickly along the hallway that Mrs Aubrey's little maid was left a long way behind. 'I will announce myself,' he called over his shoulder. Better to have this done quickly. He rapped on the library door and threw it open, without waiting for the rector to respond.

'Jonathan!' Mr Aubrey had been sitting behind his desk, quill in hand, gazing vacantly out of the window. He threw down his pen and started to his feet, smiling broadly. 'What brings you to see us so early?'

Jon paused in the open doorway to bow politely, before closing it quickly and coming forward into the small book-lined room. A good log fire burned in the grate, warming the library against the autumn chill, just as Jon had warmed the folly room last night…

'Jonathan?' The rector's smile had become a little uncertain.

Jon dragged his wandering thoughts back to the business in hand. This should be a straightforward interview, a matter of plain dealing between two men who knew each other very well. So why did memories of sweet-tasting skin and sighs of ecstasy keep trying to intrude and divert him from his purpose?

Because this was more than a business transaction now. Those last blissful hours holding Beth in his arms, uniting their bodies till they were sated with loving, and yet still yearning for each other… In one night, Jon had learned that their physical union could be more satisfying than he would have dreamt. *Could be?* Rather, it *would* be, for both of them, provided there was no impediment now.

'Good morning, sir. I have come to ask your permission to marry Beth.'

The rector's mouth dropped open. He stared. No wonder. Jon had blurted out his request like a panting, love-sick boy, rather than a grown man. What had become of the Earl of Portbury's hard-won self-control?

The rector cleared his throat and straightened his shoulders. 'It is perhaps a little early in the day,' he said carefully, 'but I think I should welcome a glass of Madeira.' He crossed to the little table where the decanters stood. Stopper in hand, he half-turned back to Jon. 'You will join me, I hope, my boy?'

Jon forced himself to respond as if this interview were the most normal thing in the world. 'Thank you, sir. With pleasure.'

By the time the rector had set down the glasses and resumed his seat behind the desk, they had both had time to collect their thoughts. Jon took the visitor's chair opposite the rector's and allowed himself a small swallow of wine. It was only Madeira, but it burned its way down to his empty stomach. After returning to the folly to remove every last trace of Beth's presence there, he had stopped only long enough at the Manor to change his clothes.

The rector set his elbows on the desk and steepled his fingers. 'You are asking my permission to marry Beth?'

'Yes, sir. As soon as may be. We hope you will perform the ceremony, too. If you agree, I plan to post up to London for a special licence.' He had not said as much to Beth, but it was the only sensible way to proceed. She would accept that. She was nothing if not sensible.

'Jonathan, I... My boy, I do not see that I can give you

what you seek. Beth lives here as our adopted daughter, it is true, but I have no authority over her, especially not in something as important as this. She is a grown woman and her own mistress.'

Jon nodded. 'I am aware of that, sir. And I am proud to say that she has already accepted my proposal of marriage.'

'Indeed? You surprise me.'

Jon bristled. 'May I ask why?'

The rector laid his hands flat on the desk and leaned forward, frowning. 'Beth has great common sense, and great delicacy, too. She knows—as you and I do, also—that she is a lady born and bred, but a lady with neither name nor family. A nameless female cannot marry a peer of the realm. I cannot believe that she would have agreed to such a thing.'

Jon swallowed his surging temper. This old man was his friend, and Beth's protector, to boot. If he could not be brought round to see the advantages of the match, no one else would, either. 'Beth has your name, sir, and that is quite honourable enough for *this* peer of the realm. Allow me to be open about this. I may be an earl, but I do not seek another great match, for I have learned how disastrous they can be. What is more, I have seen the available candidates. Believe me, sir, I could not abide any of them for even a week.' He forced himself to relax a little, and tried to smile winningly. 'Beth and I have an understanding. She will bring me the peaceful, comfortable home I have been longing for and—God willing!—the children I need to carry on my line. In return, I will give her my name and the position she has lacked since her unfortunate accident. Once she is the Countess of Portbury, no one will dare to question her past.'

The rector's eyebrows rose but he said only, 'So it is not a love match?'

Love? Jon shook his head vehemently. 'Love is for hot-headed young bloods and simpering misses just out of the schoolroom. No, sir, this is to be a union of wiser heads than that. I esteem Beth greatly. She is a woman of sterling qualities, as she has amply demonstrated during her time here at Fratcombe. She will make me a splendid countess on the public stage. And in private, we shall enjoy the quiet companionship we have both come to value.'

'I see.' Mr Aubrey sounded a little sad. He was staring down at his hands, avoiding Jon's gaze.

In the end, it was Jon who broke the tense silence. 'Will you agree to perform the ceremony, sir? It is Beth's dearest wish.'

The rector slowly raised his head. His eyes had lost their usual brightness. They were rheumy, as if he had suddenly aged ten years. 'I am sorry, Jonathan. It is impossible. You must see that, surely?'

Jon drew himself up. 'No, sir. I do not.'

The rector sighed. 'I have to know that the couple are free to marry. You are a widower, but Beth… Jonathan, she could be anything, even some other man's wife.'

Jon took a deep breath. He was going to have to be extremely frank and trust to the old man's discretion. 'I can assure you that Beth has not been any man's wife, sir.' He held the rector's gaze, waiting for a sign that the full import of his words had been understood. It came sooner than Jon had expected. The rector's eyes widened a fraction, and his sharp intake of breath echoed in the silence. 'I see that you take my meaning, sir. To put the matter beyond doubt, I should perhaps add that there is now every reason to carry out the marriage ceremony as soon as it may be arranged.' It was a little underhand to lead Mr Aubrey to believe that Beth might be with child, but Jon found he was prepared to go to almost any lengths to achieve his purpose. Nothing else mattered.

The rector downed the rest of his wine in a single swallow, got to his feet and began to pace. There was precious little room in the tiny library. He had to turn after every three or four steps.

Jon remained perfectly still, watching. There was nothing more he could do until the old man had finished struggling with his conscience.

'You leave me with no choice,' the rector said at last, in a weary voice. 'You assure me that Beth has been no man's wife, and I must accept your word. Though I must tell you, my lord, that I deplore what you must have done to establish your proofs of that. I would not have trusted you alone with Beth if I had suspected you might fail to behave as a gentleman should.' He glowered at Jon. 'It seems my judgement of you was wrong.'

Jon had risen when the rector began to speak. Now he clamped his lips tightly together. He could say nothing at all in defence of his own honour without impugning Beth's. That he would not do.

'If there is a risk that you have got her with child…?'

Jon looked the rector in the eye but made no other

response. He had done enough to hurt the old man. He would not tell him a direct lie.

The rector shook his head sadly. 'If she was a virgin when you took her, there is at least no risk of bigamy.'

Jon allowed himself a tiny nod.

'And as there must now be a risk that she is with child, I have no choice but to ensure that this…er…irregular union of yours is sanctified in church. You have forced my hand, Jonathan, as I have no doubt you intended.' He frowned up at Jon. 'Go to London. If you return with a special licence, I will marry you both.'

Jon let out a long breath. 'Thank you, sir. I…I ask your pardon for the—' His voice trailed off. He could not think of an appropriate word.

'Deception?'

Jon flushed like a guilty schoolboy caught in some childish mischief. 'You have every right to be angry, sir, and I admit that my behaviour has been…er…less honourable than you had the right to expect. For that, and that alone, I apologise unreservedly. I hope that I may, one day, regain your trust.' He raised his chin. 'However, I cannot apologise for what has been done, since there was no other route that could have led to marriage between myself and Beth. That I could never regret, even if it were to lead to a rift with you. Needless to say, I fervently hope that it will not.'

The rector's eyes had lost their rheumy cast. They had become thoughtful instead. He nodded slowly, twice. 'I doubt there will be any rift, provided… Jonathan, I have one question for you. Tell me the truth of it, on your honour. Was Beth a willing partner in this?'

The question twisted in Jon's gut. The rector was asking if he had taken Beth by force, to ensure she could not refuse him. How could a Christian gentleman think such a thing?

Because he does not know what to think of you now, Jon. The voice of Jon's conscience was strong. He had given the rector every reason to doubt his honour. He must reassure the old man now. But he must not betray Beth. After a pause, he said only, 'Beth was a willing partner. Yes.'

The rector sighed. With relief, Jon supposed. 'Since I have every intention of forgetting what has passed between us this morning, you may be easy now, Jonathan.' The harshness of tone was gone. 'I shall say nothing to my wife. Or to Beth. Other than to offer my congratulations, of course.' His warm smile lit up his eyes. He might disapprove of what they had done, but he was glad for them both, or for Beth, at least.

'You are very generous, sir.'

'Thank you, my boy. Shall you live here at Fratcombe, do you think?' It sounded like the most natural enquiry possible. The inquisition was done, and forgotten.

'For some of the time, I am sure,' Jon replied, relaxing at last. 'Beth will want to keep an eye on her school and on the progress of her little ones. I shall endow it on her behalf, of course, so that you may employ a replacement teacher. But I imagine we shall spend much of the year at King's Portbury, my principal seat. May I hope, sir, that you and Mrs Aubrey will visit us? I am sure that Beth will join me in issuing the invitation, the moment we are settled at Portbury Abbey.'

The rector cocked his head on one side and narrowed his eyes, though his smile did not falter. After a moment, he said, 'That is very generous of you, Jonathan. Mrs Aubrey will be most gratified, I am sure. And speaking of Mrs Aubrey—' he crossed to the fire to pull the bell '—I think it is high time we gave her this momentous news. She will wish to congratulate you both.'

He turned to smile wickedly at Jon. 'I have not seen Beth yet today. I wonder how she will look? I imagine—don't you?—that she will be blooming like a rose, now that she is…er…betrothed.'

Chapter Twelve

Jon gazed at the dying fire as he savoured the last of his port. Supper had been something of a trial, even though he had dismissed the servants. Beth had seemed subdued, even anxious. Jon could not understand it. Now that they were married, her position was secure. No mere Lady Fitzherbert could harm her. Surely she could not be fearing her wedding night? They both knew that their lovemaking could be glorious.

She would be in her bedchamber now, their private realm. Jon felt his body stirring in anticipation and swore at the flames. He could not endure the thought of backstairs gossip about the master's feelings for his wife. If he was to avoid that, he would have to pay particular attention to keeping a proper distance from Beth. Cool formality was required between an earl and his countess. He had seen it between his parents, even without servants present. It was a lesson Jon had learned very young. It should not be difficult to put it into practice now.

He glanced at the clock. Too soon yet to join her. He would drink another glass of port. Slowly.

He began to make plans for the journey from Fratcombe to London, hoping that it would divert his thoughts from the night's pleasures to come. Gentle, prolonged lovemaking was what they needed, for the early days of their marriage. Unfortunately, travelling so late in the year would not make that easy.

Tomorrow, he would tell his steward to organise Portbury horses at all the staging posts. That would make the journey more comfortable for Beth, and quicker, too. The sooner Jon had her installed at King's Portbury, the sooner their comfortable union could truly begin. And then his mother could take over the task of instructing Beth in her duties.

His mother would welcome Beth with open arms, he was sure. He could not promise her an heir yet, but he fully intended to do his best to get one. With Beth, he would enjoy the intimate side of their life. Perhaps, one day, he might even be able to tell her about—

No! There were some things that a gently bred lady should never hear, even from her husband. In that dark moment, Jon realised that he would not be able to sleep in Beth's bed, however much he wanted to hold her in his arms. He could not take the risk. He must always leave her to sleep alone.

This was not a bedchamber, Beth decided. It was paradise.

'Happy, my dear?'

Beth forced her heavy eyelids open. Jon was leaning over her, gazing down into her face. 'Mmm.' The tiny lines around his eyes relaxed but otherwise he did not move a fraction. He was waiting for her to say something a little more…er…meaningful. 'When we were…um…together at the folly,' she began shyly, 'it was wonderful. I did not think that anything could be— But here, in our marriage bed, it was utterly blissful.'

'Ah.' He sank back on to the bed beside her and pulled her into his embrace. After a second or two, his fingers began idly playing with a lock of her hair, pulling it straight and watching it spring back into a tight curl. 'You have beautiful hair, Beth. I cannot tell you how often I have longed to do that.' He repeated the gesture and laughed at the simple pleasure of it.

She was, without doubt, the happiest woman in the world. She had married the man she loved and, while he did not love her in return, he must care for her a little. How could their physical union be so glorious if he did not? He was very formal and reserved in public—too much so for Beth's taste—but that might change. And, even if it did not, she would have moments like these, when he held her in his arms and they could talk about anything, and nothing. They had all the rest of the night in front of them.

'Will you teach me about the stars, Jon?'

'If you wish it. But that cannot be until we return to Fratcombe, next year.'

'Oh.' Beth had dreamt of being carried up to the folly roof again, safe in Jon's arms. But perhaps it was for the best. It was truly winter now. They could wait until the summer, when the weather would be warm enough to dispense with clothes altogether. Goodness, what an outrageous thought! It must be the effects of all the wanton things that she and

Jon had been doing together. She snuggled a little closer and tried to stifle a yawn. It had been a long, tiring day but she was not yet ready for sleep. Not when Jon's naked body was so tantalisingly close.

He dropped a kiss on her hair and rested his cheek against it. 'After London—where our visit must be very brief—we shall be at King's Portbury until after Christmas. In January, I shall have to be in London when Parliament reassembles, but there is no reason for you to leave the Abbey until just before the Season starts. We probably shan't be able to return to Fratcombe until the summer. Can you wait until then for your lessons?'

'I...' He had her life all mapped out. And large parts of it seemed to involve leaving her alone in a house where she knew no one, except Hetty Martin. Thank goodness Beth had had the strength to insist that Hetty should serve as her lady's maid.

Jon stroked a finger down her neck and over her breast. His touch was magical. Her body took fire instantly. She reached up to pull his mouth down to hers. 'The lessons I need, husband,' she said huskily, 'are here and now.'

Jon lay motionless until he was sure that Beth was sound asleep. She was a wonderful bedmate, so generous, so passionate. He would never have believed that a virgin could turn into a seductress in such a short space of time. But she had. If he were younger, and less conscious of his position, he would remain in her bed for a week, at least. But that would shame them both before the servants. He could not do that to Beth. Their intimacy must be reserved for the hours of darkness.

He allowed himself to drop one last kiss on her curls and slipped out from under the covers. His heavy silk dressing gown was as he had left it, draped across the chair by the bed where he could easily lay his hand on it in the dark. He let it slide over his body. The silk felt cold and stiff compared with Beth's soft, caressing touch, but he fought down the urge to return to her.

He padded barefoot to the connecting door. The way was clear, for he had been careful to ensure there was nothing he might trip over. He had even counted the steps.

He left Beth's bedchamber without looking back.

Beth was finding London something of a trial. Since Parliament was not sitting, most of the great families were on their country estates, slaughtering birds. Jon had taken rooms at Grillon's Hotel, in order—he said—to avoid opening up Portbury House. He was also avoiding any formal announcement that the Earl and Countess of Portbury were in residence in town, and ensuring that Beth could go about the business of acquiring a new wardrobe without having to receive calls from sharp-eyed town tabbies, eager to find new material for tittle-tattle.

Unfortunately, Beth's shopping expeditions had been lonely ones, for Jon would not accompany her. A man was worse than useless on such occasions, he maintained; besides, he had business affairs to attend to. Beth was prepared to accept that his business might be more important than his new wife's wardrobe, but did it really have to occupy every waking hour? Did he have to be so distant?

After three days with only Hetty for company, Beth concluded her husband was avoiding her. There was no other possible explanation. Why, they had dined together only once, and he had left again immediately, without a word of excuse.

On the fourth day, she woke with a pounding headache and the old familiar nausea. Her nightmares had returned to point accusing fingers at her guilty past. Had she been wrong to let Jon persuade her into marriage? He had been adamant that her past did not matter, that his great position would place his wife beyond criticism. Yet he himself was now avoiding her. Was he having second thoughts about his hasty proposal and their even hastier wedding?

She tried to push the drumming guilt away. She had not deceived him. She had refused him. But he had ignored her objections and then used wicked—wonderful—persuasion to change her mind. He was still doing so every night.

He could not make love to her with such tenderness if he regretted their marriage. She would not believe that. He was distant because…because he was always so, with everyone. She refused to believe that he might be ashamed of her. But he certainly wanted to establish her at King's Portbury, and with his family, before they entered London society as a newly-wed couple. Was that also why he planned to return to London alone, in the New Year? He must know that she was haunted by guilt about her mysterious past. He had thrown the protective cloak of his rank around her, but that would not stop the whispering, malicious gossip. Was it to save Beth from wicked tongues that he was leaving her behind?

But no, that could not be the way of it. He had announced his intentions on the very day of their wedding. It was not out of concern for Beth's sensitivities that he planned to go to London without her. He had not considered Beth's preferences at all.

She was being unfair, and she knew it. Jon was not callous in that way. He simply stood aloof. He was sure of his own judgement and consulted no one before making decisions. He was convinced that Beth would soon find herself very much at home at King's Portbury. Why should his wife wish to exchange such a comfortable situation for the cold and clamour of London in early January? The weather would no doubt be foul, and the roads quite appalling. It would never occur to him that his wife would gladly endure hours of freezing travel, and damp posting-house beds, in return for just a few hours a day with the husband she loved.

He did not know, he would not ask, and she could never tell him.

The private parlour was heaped with packages. Poor Hetty was trying to unwrap and arrange the contents in piles suitable for packing, but even so, there was barely space to sit down.

'Good Gad, ma'am! More purchases?'

Beth spun round. Jon was leaning against the door jamb, surveying the chaos through narrowed eyes. A thread of anxiety began to uncoil in her stomach but, this time, she refused to let it grow. She was awake, and in control of her doubts. This was Jonathan, her husband, the man who came to her bed and took her to paradise. He was not hostile to her, and he did not seek her humiliation. His public manner was only a mask he wore, to protect them both from the barbs of the gossips, inside or outside their household.

She had learned one way of cracking his mask during these last few days in London. 'I have a confession to make, my lord.' She bowed her head meekly. 'I think I may have bankrupted you.'

He roared with laughter and started towards her. Hetty, eyes demurely downcast, sidled out behind him and closed the parlour door.

Beth raised her head again, and gazed at Jon. When he had first appeared in the doorway, she had thought he looked worn, but now he seemed alive again, almost carefree. 'This is the last of them.' She gestured towards the piles of expensive clothing he had urged her to buy. 'We may leave London as soon as you wish.'

'Excellent.' He reached out a hand to stroke her cheek, but pulled it away hurriedly before it could touch her skin. He flushed very slightly, as if embarrassed by what he had almost done.

Beth held his gaze unwaveringly. She had finally come to accept, reluctantly, that he never made gestures of affection, even when they were alone. It was as if he expected an interruption at any moment. In her bedchamber, it was different, but only there. And he never, ever, stayed with her till morning.

'Everything is ready for our journey,' he said. 'Tomorrow,

I think. I have arranged for Portbury horses at all the staging posts, so we should not be delayed.'

Beth tried to keep her expression neutral. She disliked travelling in such pomp, with servants bowing and scraping at every turn. She had been surprised that Jon chose to do so. At Fratcombe, he unbent a little, at least with the Aubreys. The moment he left it, he donned this starched-up, aristocratic manner with everyone. Sometimes, she was not sure what kind of man she had married.

He was spelling out the route they would take. 'We will travel light. Any extra baggage may follow on behind.'

'Hetty will take care of it.'

'No. Your maid will travel with you, ma'am, in your carriage. The Countess of Portbury does not travel alone.'

'You…you do not accompany me, sir?' Beth did not quite manage to control the tremor in her voice.

'But of course. However, I plan to ride. I have taken far too little exercise while we have been here in London.'

He was avoiding her company, even more than on their journey from Fratcombe. It must all be part of that con-founded mask he would not discard. But why? What could he possibly be hiding from?

'We shall reach King's Portbury in a few days, if the weather holds. Then, at last, we will be able to settle down to that comfortable, companionable life I promised you, Beth. You will learn to run my household—my mother will instruct you in your role there—while I deal with the business of my estates, and my duties to Parliament. I have neglected both, I fear, since my return from Spain. In the evenings, we will be able to sup together, as a family, and sit by the fire. It is a delightful picture, is it not?'

It was not delightful at all. It appeared that the Dowager would be living with them, as well as *instructing* Beth. That sounded daunting enough. Worse was that Jon clearly wished to avoid being alone with Beth, except in her bed, which was simple necessity, for the getting of an heir. She had thought he valued her, as a trusted friend. She was beginning to wonder if she had been wrong.

'Ah, Jon. Punctual as ever.' His mother was beaming at him without a trace of artifice. 'Do come over to the fire. I know how chilly you find it, here in England.'

Jon took his stance in front of the roaring fire and let it warm his back. He glanced round at his mother's cosy sitting room. Soon, she would return to the Dower House and Beth would take over this room. In the spring, he decided, he would offer to have it redecorated for her, in any colour she wanted. She might like new furniture, too. There was no reason why she should have to keep what Alicia had chosen. The memory of his dead wife sent the usual shudder down his spine.

'There, it is just as I said. You are still frozen to the marrow. I cannot imagine why you chose to ride when you could have travelled in your comfortable carriage, with hot bricks for your feet.'

'I needed the exercise, Mama.' A half-truth. After London, he had known it was wisest to avoid Beth's company. 'Spain can be cold in winter, too, you know,' he quipped.

'I'm sure it can, my dear.' She glanced towards the door.

'Is your wife not planning to join us? I thought we might have tea, just the three of us. We have had no time for real conversation since you arrived.'

'Beth is tired after travelling all day, Mama. I told her to rest before dinner. I knew you would understand.'

His mother gave him a very quizzical look. 'If she is fatigued, then she must certainly rest. Pull the bell, Jon, if you please.'

The butler arrived almost instantly with the tea tray. As was her wont, Jon's mother sat silent and immobile until Goodrite had bowed himself out. It was partly from her that Jon had learned the importance of protecting his privacy. Gossip, whether from servants or gentry, could be the very devil.

The Dowager calmly poured tea and handed Jon his cup. She had remembered exactly how he liked it. She had always been a consummate hostess. Beth would be learning from the best possible teacher.

'If you are warmer now, perhaps you would sit down? I find that looking up so far creates a pain in the neck.'

Jon gave a snort of laughter, but he did as he was bid.

'Your wife seems a delightful girl, Jon. You met her at Fratcombe, I collect?' When he nodded, she continued without a pause. 'I see now why you were so eager to return there. You said, if I recall correctly, that you were returning to meet a challenge you relished. If Miss Aubrey was the challenge in question, I can quite understand your haste. She has a…a certain quality that would draw a man.'

Jon started back, took a deep breath through his nose and let it out very, very slowly. He did not dare open his lips, lest he insult his mother by telling her precisely what he thought of her tasteless remark. Was she actually daring to suggest that Beth had led him on in some vulgar fashion? That she was a practised seductress?

His silent fury must have been obvious, for she quickly became contrite. 'Forgive me, I did not mean to say anything in her dispraise. She is, as I said at the outset, a delightful young lady. I would not, for the world, pry into the details of your courtship, Jon. It is enough for me that you are married, and content.'

'Thank you, Mama.' He must have mistaken her meaning, he decided. She would never malign the wife he had chosen. And she would help Beth to find her feet at Portbury, too. 'I hope that you and Beth will soon become like mother and daughter. After all, you never had a daughter of your own, did you?' Alicia did not count. She had been a failure as a wife, and also as a daughter-in-law.

'No, I did not,' she said, with a slightly tight smile. 'If your wife becomes like a daughter to me, I should be more than glad.'

It irked him suddenly that his mother would not call Beth by name, even though she knew it perfectly well. 'Her name, Mama, is Beth.'

'Elizabeth?'

'She prefers Beth.'

'Then so it shall be.' She leant towards him a little, smiling broadly. 'By the way, I sent out all the Christmas invitations in the normal way. I knew your wife—I knew Beth would not arrive here in time to do them.' She preened a little. 'The first guests will arrive in about a week.'

Jon swore inwardly. The Portbury tradition of holding a grand Christmas house party was the last thing he wanted to continue. He should have told his mother to cancel it this year, but he had totally forgotten about it. So he could not blame her for what she had done. Indeed, she had been trying to be helpful. He managed to exclaim as if he were delighted. 'I had no right to expect such exertions from you, Mama, especially now that I have a wife at my side to act as hostess.'

'As I said, there would not have been time. If the invitations had been late, there would have been gossip.' She sniffed. She detested gossip about her family. 'I was happy to do it. And Miss Mountjoy helped. In fact, she has made some remarkably useful suggestions.'

Miss Mountjoy. He should have guessed. No doubt, her suggestions had served to increase the guest list and lengthen their stay. The Mountjoy woman was both clever and dangerous, with a slyly malicious tongue, but as long as she was his mother's confidante, there was nothing Jon could say, not even to Beth.

Hetty slipped into Beth's bedchamber and crept across to the bed.

'I am not asleep, Hetty. I feel much refreshed and my headache has gone.' That was a blessing, since she had misled Jon, saying only that she was weary.

'Miss Mountjoy is here, m'lady. With a message from her ladyship.'

'Miss Mountjoy? Here? How very strange. I will come at

once.' Miss Mountjoy had been introduced by the Dowager as a neighbour from the village, yet here she was, running errands as if she were a menial. Moreover, although she did not live at Portbury Abbey, she clearly knew the house intimately. Beth was at a loss to understand what was going on, but good manners prevailed; she slipped her arms into the wrapper Hetty was holding and followed her maid into the sitting room that divided her bedchamber from Jon's.

Miss Mountjoy's eyes widened as Beth came into the room. She stared for several seconds too long, before dropping a brief curtsy. For some reason, it made Beth uncomfortable to be meeting this odd woman when so informally clad. 'I am a little cold, Hetty. Fetch my shawl, please.'

'Hetty?' Miss Mountjoy said as the maid disappeared. 'What a curious name for a lady's maid.' She clapped a hand to her mouth to cover a high-pitched titter. 'Oh, pray forgive me, my lady. I did not mean to sound impertinent. But I thought— That is, her ladyship said you would be bound to engage a high-class dresser while you were in London. Seeing someone so…er…young and small was something of a shock.'

Miss Mountjoy might be the Dowager's bosom bow, but she was certainly not going to be Beth's! Insufferable woman! How dare she?

Beth waited for Hetty to wrap the heavy Norwich shawl around her shoulders and return to the bedchamber before she spoke. She was the Countess of Portbury now. She would not be outfaced by a woman like this. 'My maid said you had a message from her ladyship. It was not, I collect, about my choice of dresser?'

Miss Mountjoy's nostrils quivered for a second. Then she smiled too broadly. 'No, indeed, my lady, I— His lordship's lady mother was concerned to learn that you were so fatigued after your journey, especially after travelling in such extravagant comfort. We thought you might perhaps be…er…ailing. She knows I have some knowledge of attending to ladies when their health is…er…delicate.' She raised her chin proudly. 'That was before I came to King's Portbury, of course. If there is anything I might do to assist your ladyship…?'

Good grief! Jon's mother was sending this…this toady to enquire if Beth was breeding. It was beyond insult. It was utter humiliation. Was this how her life was to be at King's Portbury?

'Hetty!' The maid appeared instantly. She must have been just behind the door.

'Thank you for your concern, Miss Mountjoy, but I shall not be needing your assistance.' Let her make what she would of that! 'Hetty, show Miss Mountjoy out.' Without so much as a nod to her unwelcome visitor, Beth turned on her heel and marched back into her bedchamber.

'How much of that did you hear?' Beth demanded when Hetty returned.

'I…I beg your pardon, m'lady. I wasn't trying to eavesdrop, but I knew I should be on hand in case—'

Beth cut off the excuse with a wave of her hand. 'We will not discuss Miss Mountjoy's insinuations about my…er… state of health.' She swallowed hard, determined to master her emotions, even though only Hetty was there to see. 'But her comments about you are another matter.'

Hetty reddened and stared at the floor.

'Hetty?' When the maid did not reply, Beth began to suspect there was something more at work than Miss Mountjoy's vitriolic tongue. 'We have been here less than a day. What has happened to upset you?'

Hetty did not move or look up. At last, she whispered, 'Countess Alicia had a very superior French dresser, according to the housekeeper.'

'I see. And she implies that you are not equal to the task?'

'Not in so many words, m'lady. No one does. There are just…er…looks and whispers. And I might have imagined those.'

Beth was fairly sure that Hetty had not been mistaken. And if the servants were gossiping behind Hetty's back about the new mistress's choice of maid, what were they saying about the mistress herself? For Hetty's sake, Beth would find out the truth of all this. And then she would nip such rebellious behaviour in the bud.

'Ignore them, Hetty. Remember that you are maid to the mistress of the house, if you please. For now, it's probably best for you to remain rather aloof. Just as a superior French maid would do.' Beth smiled encouragingly down at her maid.

'I'll do just as you say, m'lady. Your ladyship chose me to serve you and I am proud of the fact, no matter what Miss Mountjoy may say.'

'Miss Mountjoy? Has she been sowing mischief below stairs? But how? She is not a servant.'

'She used to be, after a fashion. She were Countess Alicia's paid companion for more than ten years, so I were told, m'lady. Now she lives in a fine cottage in the village. His lordship gave it to her, they say.'

'Whatever they *say* about his lordship, Hetty, you will *not* repeat.'

Hetty blushed an even fierier red than before. 'No, m'lady. Begging yer pardon, m'lady.' At Beth's nod of dismissal, she fled back into the bedchamber.

Beth began to pace up and down the sitting room. Jon had bought a cottage for his late wife's companion? Why on earth would he do that? She was clearly a mischief-maker of the first order. Sly, too. No doubt the mean backstairs gossip about Hetty had started with her. Beth would have to find a way of countering that.

But in the meantime, she had to understand about Miss Mountjoy and Jon. Years ago, before he went to Spain, the woman might have been an attractive armful for a man with a roving eye. Had she and Jon been lovers, perhaps? Jon was a passionate man. If he could not bed the wife he hated, would he bed her companion instead? Was the cottage given by way of compensation?

It was a hateful thought. Had Jon thought to resume his liaison with her on his return from the wars? Even if that had been his intention, surely he would not pursue it now that he had remarried?

But Miss Mountjoy had a proprietorial air that disturbed Beth a great deal. As if she had power in this house. As if she knew secrets.

Chapter Thirteen

The Dowager smiled complacently. 'The first guests should arrive tomorrow, Jon.'

He was struck by a sudden uncomfortable thought. 'I take it they do not include the young ladies from your summer party, Mama?'

Her haughtily raised eyebrows were eloquent. No duke would allow his unmarried daughter to attend a house party where there were no eligible male guests. George, even if he deigned to attend, was far from eligible, for he was only an impecunious younger son, and had a reputation as a rake, besides.

'Beg pardon, ma'am. I should have known better than to ask.'

Mollified, his mother began to list names, while Jon made mental notes of what he needed to say to Beth about her house guests. Some of them, sadly, were much too high in the instep to be good company.

The butler appeared in the doorway. 'Your ladyship asked to be informed when the countess returned from her drive.'

'Ask her ladyship if she will be good enough to join us.'

Before Goodrite could bow in response to the Dowager's instruction, Jon was on his feet and making for the door. 'No need. I will do it,' he said curtly.

In the entrance hall, Beth was in the process of removing her heavy pelisse and bonnet. She turned at the sound of his step. Her cheeks were flushed from the chill wind, but her eyes were sparkling. He had clearly been right to send her out to take the air, to restore her bloom after several days of sitting at the Dowager's feet, being tutored in her new role.

She smiled up at him. 'Good afternoon, my lord,' she said formally, though there was nothing in the least formal about the way her gaze softened when she looked at him. It reminded Jon, much too forcefully, of the way her eyes locked with his when they were making love.

One unwary memory, and desire was thrumming through him. He tried to say something innocuous, but he could not find the words. To cover his confusion, he took her hand and bowed over it, hoping that his extravagant gesture would make up for the words of polite greeting he could not utter.

She must have sensed something, for she ran her middle finger across his palm in a teasing caress. The unexpected touch rippled through his whole body. What on earth was she doing? It was the middle of the afternoon, and they were standing in the hallway, watched by the butler and two footmen. He dropped her hand like a hot coal and hurriedly stepped back.

'That will be all, Hetty,' she said, calmly nodding dismissal to her maid. 'You wanted something of me, my lord?'

Oh yes! I want to carry you up to your bedchamber and ravish you until we are both mindless with passion!

Shocked by his own reactions, Jon assumed the haughty manner he always adopted when he was at risk of betraying his inner feelings. 'My lady mother is waiting for us in the saloon. Will you join us, ma'am?' As custom required, he offered Beth his arm, willing his flesh to remain totally numb. He was determined that there would be nothing for the servants to remark upon.

There was something very knowing about the way she smiled and laid her hand on his arm to be escorted to the saloon. For a woman who was only lately wed, she had learned extremely quickly how to drive a man to madness. Was that what it was? Or was he imagining it all?

'How well you look, my dear.' Jon's mother smiled in welcome and waved them to the seats opposite her. Behind them, the butler closed the door without a sound.

Jon led Beth to the seat opposite his mother, but he did not take his place beside her. Better to observe her from a distance, he decided, throwing himself on to the far end of the Dowager's sofa and trying to appear more relaxed than he felt.

Beth held out her hands to the blazing fire. 'We had a delightful drive, ma'am. There was a sharp wind, to be sure, but the sun was shining and the sky was absolutely clear. The park was quite beautiful, even though the trees were bare.' She turned to Jon, raising her eyebrows a fraction. 'Perhaps, when your business is less pressing, my lord, you might be able to join me, to show me more of the estate? I should so like to know about all the features here. At one point, I thought I saw an old stone building, half hidden by trees. Do you have a folly here, too?'

Minx! Her confidence was clearly growing by the day. She was roasting him. And in front of his mother, too! He ought to be cross with her, but he was finding it increasingly difficult to maintain his austere mask. In truth, he wanted to laugh aloud. And then to kiss her till she begged for mercy. He was going to have some very strong words with the new Countess of Portbury. Later, when they were safely alone.

'Jon and I have been discussing the arrangements for the house guests,' the Dowager put in tartly. 'If the weather continues fine, Jon will be able to entertain the gentlemen with outdoor pursuits. I imagine some of the ladies might like to join them. I recall that some of the younger ones are excellent horsewomen.' She turned to Jon, who nodded rather absently. 'I imagine that you will prefer to rest quietly here at the house, Beth. In the circumstances.'

Beth blushed rosily and turned away to stare at the fire.

'I see no reason why Beth should not go riding if she wishes to,' Jon said, rather more harshly than he had intended. 'She is a fine horsewoman, too, and she may have the pick of my stables.'

'Thank you.' Her response was very low and directed at the hearth.

'Hmmph. I should tell you, Jon, that one of a hostess's duties is to ensure that her guests are entertained. Beth may of course go riding, but only if all the other lady guests are doing so. If some of them choose to remain at the house, as I would expect, their hostess cannot desert them. We are agreed on that, are we not, Beth?'

Beth raised her head and turned to look directly at the Dowager. 'None of our guests will have cause to fault the hospitality in this house, ma'am. Your lessons will not go unheeded.'

The Dowager nodded slowly twice, as if accepting due homage from an inferior. Jon found himself wondering just what had taken place during the last few days when his mother was supposedly helping Beth to assume her duties as mistress of Portbury Abbey. Was there a degree of friction between the two of them? He had blithely told Beth that, once she was his countess, no one would dare to malign her. But his mother, a dowager countess and the daughter of a wealthy and powerful family, had no need to mind her tongue. If she disapproved of Beth, she could certainly turn her life into a trial.

Jon stared across at his wife, trying to read her expression. Poor Beth. She was still far from secure in her new position. She was haunted by fears that ghosts might appear from her past to accuse her of wicked crimes. Sometimes, those fears had become so strong that she suffered appalling sick headaches. They were less frequent since her marriage, she said, but if his mother—

'I must say that you seem to be quite an apt pupil, Beth,' the Dowager said loftily. She ignored Beth's sharp intake of breath and turned to Jon. 'Your wife may have come to us with little knowledge of how to run a great house, Jon, but she is certainly trying to learn. I have no doubt that she will do extremely well. Eventually. Once she has had a chance to put my lessons into practice.'

That was exceedingly barbed, and quite unnecessarily hurtful. Jon looked at his mother with new eyes. He had thought her the pattern card of ladylike behaviour, but this…? What on earth did she have against Beth? His mother was a great lady, but she clearly lacked Beth's kind heart and generosity of spirit. Beth did not deserve to be the butt of his mother's sour tongue.

'Beth, you are beginning to look rather pale,' the Dowager continued, in slightly friendlier tones. 'Are you sure you are quite well? Miss Mountjoy told me that she found you laid upon your bed last week. She had concerns that your health might be…er…delicate. She is quite experienced in such matters, of course.'

In the space of seconds, Beth's slight pallor had changed to a fiery blush. She made to speak, but no words came out.

Jon was shocked and angered by his mother's sly hint that Beth was not in robust good health. Apart from the occasional headache, she was blooming. He would not permit his wife to be tormented by Miss Mountjoy's malicious insinuations, even at second hand. Equally, he could not rebuke his mother in front of his wife. 'I am surprised to learn that Miss Mountjoy took it upon herself to venture up to my wife's bedchamber. She is no longer employed here. As a visitor, she does *not* have the run of my house,' he finished firmly, looking directly at his mother.

The Dowager raised her chin a fraction and glared back

at him. 'I understood that Beth had invited Miss Mountjoy upstairs.'

Jon did not believe that for a moment.

Beth was shaking her head. 'I fear you have been misinformed, ma'am. I did no such thing. Nor would I,' she added, with unusual vehemence. 'Miss Mountjoy told me that you yourself had sent her to offer me the benefit of her…er…experience.'

The Dowager clamped her lips together. Her eyes were flashing angrily.

Jon knew exactly where to place the blame. Miss Mountjoy was capable of almost anything in pursuit of her hatred for Jon. This time, he would certainly have to deal with her, but first he had to prevent a rift between his mother and his wife. 'Beth, my dear,' he said gently, crossing to where she sat and raising her to her feet, 'I am truly sorry there appears to have been a misunderstanding over this. But Mama is right, you do look a little pale. May I suggest you rest this afternoon? You have been working so hard, preparing for the house party. And you will have precious little time to yourself once the guests start arriving.' He clasped her hand firmly and led her to the door. She did not resist, of course. She was too well bred to argue with Jon in front of his mother.

'I will deal with this, I promise,' he murmured into her hair, as he ushered her into the hall and stood watching while she made her way towards the stairs. He tried to ignore the sway of her hips, but the motion was exceedingly attractive to the eye. It was partly his own fault, since he had encouraged her to buy that expensive velvet carriage dress. Its every movement reminded him all too vividly of the body concealed beneath.

He was shaking his head when he returned to the saloon. He must stop enjoying his wife's attractions and start thinking about how to deal with his mother's apparent antipathy to her. What on earth could be the cause of it?

'Was there something in particular you wished to discuss, Mama?' he began innocently, taking the seat that Beth had vacated. 'In relation to the guests?'

His mother seemed to have relaxed now that Beth was no longer in the room with them. 'No, nothing in particular. I merely wanted to impress on your wife how important it is for this house party to pass off well. It is, after all, her first experience of acting as hostess since she became your countess. She has some rather…er…quaint notions of how to go on.'

Jon swore inwardly, but schooled his features into neutrality. 'Indeed? I'm afraid I must have missed those, for I have seen nothing amiss. As a mere male, of course…' He allowed his words to hang in the air, like a fly dancing on the surface of the water for the fish to bite.

His mother rose to the bait. 'No, you would not. Men never do, I'm afraid. Your father was just as bad.' When Jon said nothing, she continued, a little hesitantly, 'I am hoping that your wife will come to appreciate the difference between her guests' dressers and her own maid. I do not see that a chit from the workhouse, or wherever that girl came from, is at all appropriate to serve as lady's maid to a countess. *You* understand what is needed. Your own new man knows exactly what an earl's consequence requires.' The Dowager was starting to sound much more confident. 'I wish your wife would take her cue from you and engage a proper dresser.'

Jon nodded curtly. 'Thank you for your advice, Mama. I will ensure the matter is dealt with.' He paused a moment to bring his seething anger under control. First Miss Mountjoy, and now this! 'Was that the only thing you wished to discuss with me, ma'am?'

His mother looked for a moment as though she were about to make some other comment, but there must have been something in Jon's expression that warned her to take care, for she pursed her lips and shook her head.

Jon smiled tightly. 'I must thank you for all the help you have given Beth since we arrived, Mama. I am sure that, thanks to your tuition, she will do very well in her role as mistress of the Abbey. I know that you have found it irksome to be acting as my hostess over all these months, but I am very grateful. I imagine you will wish to return to the peace of the Dower House now that you have helped Beth to settle in?'

'I…er…' There was just a hint of a flush rising on the Dowager's neck. She swallowed. 'That is very considerate of you, Jon,' she said tightly, 'but I think it would be unwise for me to leave your wife alone quite yet. I am sure she will appreciate having a more experienced female at her side to act as…er…co-hostess. After all, she has had no chance yet to practise everything I have taught her.'

'Quite so, quite so,' Jon said, nodding. 'And there will be other benefits of having two ladies to act as hostess. For example, you will be able to remain here at the house to entertain the older ladies, while Beth rides out with the younger ones, will you not?'

'I—' For once, the Dowager looked nonplussed.

Jon leaned across to pat his mother's hand. 'It is very good of you to do this, Mama, and I know Beth will appreciate the extra freedom you are giving her. As do I.'

His mother nodded. She was clearly outmanoeuvred, but she was much too proud to say a word.

Jon rose and bowed. 'I must ask you to excuse me, Mama. I have urgent letters to write and some other business that must be discharged today.' With his jaw set, he made his way out into the hall where the butler was hovering. 'Have a message sent to my land agent, Goodrite. I will see him here, in one hour.' Without waiting for an acknowledgement, Jon made for the stairs. Dealing with his agent was important, but there was something else that had to be done first.

When Jon entered the sitting room that he shared with Beth, he was surprised to find it empty. There was no sound at all, not even the crackle of a fire, but the door into Beth's room stood partly open. He paused, wondering. He knew Beth was quite sharp enough to have understood the meaning underlying her mother-in-law's words. Would he find her weeping in her bedchamber?

He stole forward and peeped round the half-open door. Beth was lying on top of the bed, fully clad, but with her eyes closed. The maid, Martin, was sitting alongside, stroking Beth's face and— No, the girl was bathing Beth's forehead with lavender water. The subtle scent was unmistakable.

And it meant Beth had the headache again. No wonder, perhaps, after that nasty confrontation downstairs. Jon took a silent step into the bedchamber.

The little maid must have sensed his arrival. She looked over her shoulder and frowned at him. Then, pert little madam, she dared to put a finger to her lips and motioned to Jon to leave!

Jon's first impulse was to reprimand her for her impudence, but one more look at Beth's peaceful face choked the words in his throat. If she was now sleeping, he should let her rest. He could deal with the maid without waking his wife. He would simply retreat to the sitting room and wait.

After a few moments, Martin emerged, closing the door very quietly behind her. Only then did she remember to curtsy. 'Her ladyship is asleep, my lord.'

'So I saw. Is she…?'

'She had the headache, and a little nausea, my lord, but she was quite determined that no one should be aware of it. She…she made me promise not to tell you.'

'And if I had not seen, you would have said nothing?'

'No, my lord. I…I could not betray my lady's trust. I…I am sorry.' She looked up at him, unafraid, in spite of the implicit challenge in her words. Hetty Martin might be still very young, but there was no doubt of her devotion to Beth. Love was shining in her eyes. Love for Beth.

Jon's few remaining doubts evaporated on the spot. That sort of devotion more than made up for any lack of dressing skill, or French genius with ointments and potions. He doubted that any of the top-lofty dressers arriving with his mother's guests would show even a fraction of Hetty's loyalty and commitment.

'I would not wish you to do so, Hetty,' Jon said quietly, noting how the maid's eyes widened at his use of her given name. 'You are her ladyship's dresser and personal maid. Your loyalty must be to her. And only to her.'

Hetty curtsied again.

'I am truly sorry that my wife is unwell, Hetty. I think I know the cause, on this occasion, and I will deal with it. However, if…if she should be upset in the future, or…or afraid, I should like you to come and tell me. Will you do that?'

Hetty stared at the floor, shaking her head.

'What do you mean, no?' Jon snapped. 'If my wife needs help, who should provide it but I?'

The maid was still shaking her head. 'I could not betray my lady's confidence,' she whispered. 'Not even to your lordship. Not to anyone.' She continued to stare at the floor, like a prisoner waiting for sentence.

No wonder Beth had braved the Dowager's disapproval to keep her own maid by her. This girl was a pearl beyond price. 'I am not asking you to betray your mistress, Hetty,' Jon said, more gently. 'I only ask you to use your common sense. If my wife should need help, should need a friend, please encourage her to come to me. Or come to me yourself.'

She glanced up, surprised. For a moment, she seemed to be considering his words. Then, at last, she nodded.

'And whatever should happen, I thank you for your devotion to my wife.' With that, he nodded her dismissal and strode into his own bedchamber.

'Is there anything I can do for your lordship?' Vernon, the valet, slipped into the room, soft-footed as ever. Did he feel a fraction of the loyalty that little Hetty was showing to her mistress?

'No. I shan't need you until it is time to dress for dinner.' Jon glared balefully at Vernon until the man bowed himself back into the dressing room. Then Jon sat down at the small desk under the window to make the most of the remaining light. He would not know for a few days whether his plan was going to work. All would depend on the response to this letter.

He pulled out a sheet of his embossed writing paper and dipped his pen in the standish. It took only a few minutes to complete the short letter and seal it. Devotion was worth more than rubies. And this would prove whether he had earned it, as Beth had.

With a shrug of his shoulders, he rose and made his way downstairs, dropping the letter on the silver salver in the entrance hall. He would have to be patient until a response could come. And in the meantime...

Jon smiled to himself and strode down the corridor to his library. By now, his agent should be waiting for his new instructions.

Beth woke early and lay staring up towards the silken canopy. She could see nothing in the gloom. And she was alone again.

Jon had been a little hesitant about coming to her bed this last time. He had enquired, obliquely, if she wished to sleep alone. Of course, she did not! She wanted to sleep in his arms all night, but she could not tell him so. The most she could do was to encourage him to come to her, even if only for an hour or so.

Instead of ignoring the Dowager's hurtful remarks, Beth had stupidly let them prey on her mind. So the headache had been her own fault. She must simply accept that her mother-in-law did not like her, or trust her. But the Dowager's power in the household would diminish, as Beth became more secure. She must do what she could to hasten the process. She had managed to respond with spirit, on occasion. She would cling to that. The Countess of Portbury must not cower, or flee.

She strained her eyes towards the shuttered windows. Soon it would be dawn. She thought she could already hear the servants stirring. This late in the year, they could not wait for daylight to begin their chores, especially as the first guests were to arrive soon. To her own surprise, Beth found she was not at all anxious about dealing with Jon's friends, or even the Dowager's. Beth had learned during her time with the Aubreys to handle all sorts of people, from the highest to the lowest. And in the weeks since her marriage, she had even begun to learn how to deal with her husband.

She smiled up into the darkness. She was beginning to understand him. A little. In public, he was the essence of the aristocrat—distant, austere, mindful of his duty, and polite to a fault. Some of it was assumed, though not his concern for his duty. He had inherited that from the old earl, who had valued duty and rank above all else. Beth fancied he had not been a loving father to Jon. There was no doubt, however, that even though the Dowager did not approve of her son's choice of second wife, she did love Jon very much. For that alone, Beth would endure any insult that her mother-in-law might voice.

Beth shrugged against the pillows. There was precious little she could do to remedy the Dowager's poor opinion. Jon had married Beth out of hand, without introducing her to anyone first. Had he been determined to have his ring on Beth's finger before his mother could object to a penniless woman of no family? Had he—?

'Oh, fiddlesticks!' she said aloud. She was the Countess of Portbury now, and Jon was her husband. It was up to her to make this marriage work. And that included the task of running this vast mansion. Beth was sure she would have the measure of it soon. Somewhere in her past life, she imagined, she must have been taught the way of managing servants, for it came naturally enough. Beth fully intended to demonstrate just how much she had learned from the Dowager, too. If she could make Jon's mother proud of her, it might ease the tension between them. She would make Jon proud of her, too, if she could.

If only he would stay with her at night. If only he would spend more time with her in the day. Sometimes, she was sure he was deliberately avoiding her company. But why? He did not come to her bed merely for the getting of an heir. Beth might have been an innocent before that astonishing night in the Fratcombe folly, but she could tell that the passion they shared was very special. Jon could not make love to a woman he did not esteem. His first wife had repelled him. With Beth, there was desire, and passion, and rapture for them both.

She laughed softly, remembering. Each time was different, and yet the same. He still explored her body with a sense of wonder, as if he were uncovering something magical. That reverence almost made up for being left to sleep alone.

Almost, but not quite. There must be a way to persuade him to stay, if only she could find it. If she continued to tease him, in private ways that only the two of them understood, he might eventually unbend.

Had his mother noticed that second of shock on his face when Beth had asked about a folly at Portbury? That tiny flicker of response had been utterly delicious. She hugged the memory to herself. Teasing him in public, ever so subtly, was the way to ensure he remained aware of his wife. All the time.

It was a good plan. And she would use it again. She had half expected to be well scolded once they were alone together, but Jon had been too concerned about her to do any such thing. He was a truly considerate man. And, heaven help her, she loved him to distraction! If only he—

She shook her head, vehemently. Jon did not love her. Perhaps he had never loved any woman? Perhaps he never could? She had seen precious few signs of attachment to anyone, or anything, apart from his duty. It would have to be enough that Beth loved him without reserve. One day, God willing, she would put a son into his arms and see him gazing down, with love, on a child of their joined flesh. Perhaps that would be enough.

In the meantime, she would do everything in her power

to prove that she was fit to take her place by his side. Let the Dowager judge as she would. Beth was going to show Jon that she could be a worthy countess.

Chapter Fourteen

A fine carriage was bowling down the drive towards the house. Beth automatically took half a step back from her sitting room window, even though she knew that the passengers could not possibly see her up here. She did not know which guests these were, and she could not go downstairs to find out. The Dowager's instructions had been absolute on the point. Her house guests expected to be shown to their bedchambers, so that they could refresh themselves and change their dress before they came down to greet their hostess.

Beth moved closer to the window in order to see down to the sweep where these first guests were about to alight. She had to stand on tiptoe and crane her neck to catch even a glimpse of what was happening.

As she stretched, warm breath shivered across her taut skin. The scent of horse and leather and warm man surrounded her, creating vivid, sensual pictures in her mind. Her body came alive instantly, tingling at the prospect of being touched. She felt herself softening, waiting.

'Good morning, my lady,' Jon said softly, his breath caressing the back of her neck. He was standing just behind her, almost kissing her skin with his words.

Beth took a deep breath, reminding herself sternly that Jon would not be feeling any of the excitement that was coursing through her veins. Outside her bedchamber, he was always perfectly correct and infuriatingly distant. She fixed a polite smile on her face and turned. 'Good morning, my lord. I did not hear you come in. Did you enjoy your ride?'

Her movement forced him to take a step back. 'I…' There was something in his eyes, a hint of sparkling mischief, that Beth had not seen before, but his smile was as polite as her own. 'Yes, it was splendid, thank you. The weather is remarkably fine for so late in the year. Indeed, you could—' He stopped short.

Had he been going to ask Beth to ride with him? Her heart began to beat even faster.

A noise from below caught his attention. He ushered her closer to the window so that they could both see down. 'Your first house guests, my dear.' His voice was neutral, matter-of-fact. As it always was in public.

A small, rotund gentleman climbed down from the carriage, and turned to help an even smaller, rounder lady. They made for the door without waiting for the third passenger, a much younger lady who stepped down and stood for a moment, gazing round her. She was tall, but she lacked the elegance of movement that Beth always associated with tall ladies. In fact, there was even something a little awkward about her.

'Sir James and Lady Rothbury, and Miss Rothbury,' Jon murmured.

'They have only the one daughter?'

'Yes, but there is also a son. Rather wild. He declined the invitation. I will admit that I was glad to hear it. As it is, we must make do with the daughter who is not, I fear, the sharpest needle in the box.'

Beth stifled a shocked giggle. Goodness, he was becoming quite free with his opinions, even thought it was broad daylight and they were standing in the sitting room. Was this progress at last?

'Look!' Jon pointed down the long drive. In the distance, a second carriage could just be seen. 'More guests, thank goodness. At least you will not have to entertain only the Rothburys, my dear. On their own, they can be something of a trial. They—' He stopped to clear his throat. 'Well now, if I am to help you to greet them all, I had better go and change my dress.' He bowed slightly to Beth. 'Excuse me. I shall be down to join you shortly.' He strode through the door into his own bedchamber and closed it behind him. The confidences were at an end.

Beth hesitated for a moment. Should she wait for Jon? No, best to go downstairs so that she was already waiting in the drawing room when the first guests came down. The Rothburys might be the kind who could get changed in just a couple of shakes. It would not do for them, or for any of the guests, to find their hostess missing from her place.

She walked calmly into her bedchamber to check her appearance in front of the glass. Yes, she looked very well in her elegant silk morning gown. Jon had not commented upon it, but Beth knew the simple style suited her. Was that what had brought that stray sparkle to his eyes? Impossible to tell. She shook her head at her reflection, picked up her brightly patterned shawl and made her way along the corridor and down the sweeping staircase to the entrance hall.

Her timing was as wrong as could be. She arrived in the hallway just as the latest guests were shown into the house. How on earth had they arrived so quickly? They must have sprung their horses all the way down the drive. For a second, she stood stock still, horrified, searching for an avenue of escape. There was none.

'My woman will direct the unloading of the luggage and— Oh!' As the butler moved aside, the new arrival caught sight of Beth, marooned at the foot of the stairs. This rather gaunt lady lifted her chin, narrowed her eyes, and looked down a very long nose at Beth before dropping the smallest of curtsies. 'Lady Portbury, I presume?'

Beth returned the newcomer's tiny curtsy. She added a polite smile, too, since this unknown lady was her guest. 'Welcome to Portbury Abbey, ma'am. I shall not attempt to detain you, for I am sure you will wish to rest after your journey. Goodrite will show you to your chamber.'

'Thank you, my lady. We shall be—' The newcomer frowned suddenly and pursed her lips. 'How strange! Forgive me, ma'am, but have we met before? I was told not and yet… You seem familiar, somehow.'

It was all Beth could do to maintain a semblance of composure. Did this woman come from her past? If so, what did she know? Beth forced herself to glide forward a few steps and to smile condescendingly. 'I think not, ma'am. I hope I should not have been so impolite as to have forgotten you if we had.' She shook her head a little, to complete the effect.

'Er…um, no. Of course not. Forgive me, I was clearly thinking of someone else. Pray excuse me, ma'am.' She hurried towards the stairs.

Goodrite turned to one of the footmen. 'Bring Mrs Berncastle's valises to the yellow bedchamber,' he said deliberately, ensuring that Beth would hear the lady's name. 'And be quick about it.'

Beth walked along the corridor to the morning room, trying not to look as though she were escaping. Berncastle. An unusual name, to be sure, but it seemed totally unfamiliar. Oh, why could she not remember? And what did Mrs Berncastle really know?

Quite possibly nothing at all, for where would Beth have met such a rich society lady? Beth had certainly been poor before she arrived in Fratcombe. Poor women did not mix with the likes of Mrs Berncastle.

Should she warn Jon? No, she would say nothing of this to anyone, for even if Mrs Berncastle had some lingering suspicions, she would never embarrass her hostess by giving the least hint. Such an insult could lead to a speedy departure for the guest in question, and a scandal, besides. Mrs Berncastle had come to enjoy a Christmas house party. She would never take the risk of being asked to leave.

Beth resolved to put the encounter behind her and to spend the rest of the day concentrating on welcoming more of her guests.

★ ★ ★

'Your ladyship, I have such news!' Hetty gasped the next morning. She dumped the ewer of hot water by the basin and turned, her face full of animation.

Beth straightened the wrapper over her nightrail and assumed a stern expression. 'Do you mean *news*, Hetty, or gossip? You know that you are forbidden to spread gossip in this house.'

'No, truly it *is* news, m'lady.' Before Beth could say a word more, Hetty burst out, 'His lordship has given notice to Mr Vernon.'

Beth tried to frown the girl down. What, after all, was so exciting about the departure of Jon's top-lofty valet? Now that almost all the guests had arrived, Hetty should have better things to do. Beth certainly did.

'But that is not the *real* news, m'lady. His lordship has sent for his old army batman to take Mr Vernon's place. I'm told that her ladyship—his lordship's lady mother, I mean—is fit to be tied.'

'Now *that*,' Beth said sternly, 'is definitely gossip.' It was, indeed, but Beth recognised that it was also likely to be true. She had found out that on Jon's return from Spain, the Dowager had urged him to take on a top-o'-the-trees valet. Jon must have shared her view, for he had paid off his army batman, and engaged Vernon. It seemed that he had now changed his mind. But what did it mean?

No doubt the servants knew, but Beth could not possibly question Hetty, not after giving the girl such stern warnings about the evils of gossip. Did she dare to ask Jon himself? Well, why not? They were man and wife, after all, and he had asked Beth to run his household. He should have told her that he had engaged a new valet. He should have told her.

Since it was still very early, he would be downstairs in his library, working. Later, once the guests' breakfast was over, he would be spending his time entertaining the gentlemen, but for the moment he would be alone.

She would finish dressing and then she would go downstairs to Jon's library and ask him what he had done. And why.

The weak morning sunshine was struggling to illuminate Jon's library. If his desk had not been near the window, he would have needed candles in order to work. At least there was not much correspondence to deal with. Possibly the last two days' bad weather had delayed the post?

The door opened to admit the butler. 'Miss Mountjoy has called and begs the favour of an interview with your lordship. She is waiting in the yellow saloon.'

So early? Jon continued to write. 'Let her wait. In fifteen minutes' time, you may invite her to join me here.' He glanced up just in time to see a flicker of surprise cross the butler's face. No, it was not how the Earl of Portbury was wont to treat a lady guest, but Jon was not at all sure that Miss Mountjoy deserved either title. He hurried to finish the instructions for his steward at Fratcombe. There was still much to be done there to remedy the damage done by his brother. George had a lot to answer for.

After some minutes, Jon sanded and folded the paper ready for dispatch. He checked the time by the long case clock. Any moment now.

Seconds later the door opened. 'Miss Mountjoy to see your lordship,' the butler intoned.

Jon rose politely but did not acknowledge his visitor. Instead, he held out the letter. 'See that this is sent to my steward at Fratcombe Manor immediately, Goodrite. That will be all.'

As the door closed, Jon turned to Miss Mountjoy and favoured her with a cursory bow. 'There was something you wished to discuss, Miss Mountjoy?' He waved her to the chair opposite him. With a swift curtsy, she crossed the floor in an angry swish of silken skirts and took her seat. Jon leaned back in his chair, calmly steepled his fingers and set his facial expression to bland. Then he waited.

'I imagine, Lord Portbury, that you were expecting me to call? In the circumstances.'

Jon raised an eyebrow. Otherwise, he did not move. The loud tick of the long case clock was the only sound to be heard in the room.

'I have come to tell you, Lord Portbury, that I will not be abused and manipulated in this outrageous fashion.'

'Outrageous, is it?'

'You know very well that it is. When you settled that annuity upon me, and gave me the cottage to rent, it was in response to your wife's last request. It was a sacred trust, yet now you would renege upon it.'

Jon allowed his hands to drop softly to the desk. 'I have reneged on no promise, Miss Mountjoy,' he said carefully. 'Your annuity remains in place. Your cottage, however, was a mistake, about which I was not consulted. It is worth a rather higher rent than you are paying. Therefore, as my agent informed you, the rent will increase from the next quarter day.'

'To a level which you know I cannot afford!'

'That, ma'am, is not my concern. You have your annuity. You may always move to cheaper accommodation.'

'You have ensured that there is none available, Lord Portbury. You take me for a fool, but I know you intend to force me to leave the district.'

'If you know it, ma'am, why are you here?' Jon said silkily.

'I have come to tell you that I have no intention of quitting King's Portbury,' she snapped, 'or the cottage I am renting from you. If you try to force me out, I shall fight you. I am not without ammunition, as you should be aware.'

Jon leant forward a little and allowed a sardonic smile to curl the corner of his mouth. 'Indeed? Perhaps you would enlighten me? I do *own* your cottage, after all.'

'I cannot stop you from evicting me, but I can ensure that your reputation, and that of your house, is destroyed if you do. If you proceed against me, I shall tell the whole world about your first wife's preferences and why the Earl of Portbury was unable to sire an heir.'

Jon leaned back once more and sighed theatrically. 'What a fascinating piece of gossip that will make, especially once your own role, as my late wife's *paramour*, is made plain to all. I fancy your reputation might suffer at least as much as mine. Do you imagine you would be received after that?'

'It is a price I would gladly pay for a victory over you, my lord. After all, I could always remove from the district later, perhaps even change my name. You, the great Earl of Portbury, have no such escape route. Once the world learns that Alicia preferred me to you, you will be the butt of every scandal-sheet in the land.'

Jon nodded slowly, as if considering her threat. 'Do tell me about this escape route. If you move to another district, precisely what will you live on?'

She smiled then, for the first time, a confident, knowing smile. 'Unlike the rental of my cottage, you cannot change my annuity, my lord. It was my deathbed gift from Alicia, a token of her regard. You merely executed her wishes. I find it gratifying that, even if I ruin your reputation, you will still be obliged to maintain me.'

'Ah, I see. You believe your annuity renders you invulnerable.' He pushed back his chair and rose. With one fleeting sideways glance at her, he strode across to the window and stood staring out at the garden with his hands clasped behind his back. 'You know, Miss Mountjoy,' he said evenly, 'you really should read legal documents with more care.' He heard her sharp intake of breath, but he did not turn. 'If you had done so, you might have noticed the character clause I inserted in your annuity. It states, quite clearly, that if the beneficiary should lose her character, whether by criminal conviction or otherwise, her right to any payment will cease. I would wager a considerable sum that a woman who admitted to having a lewd relationship with the late Countess of Portbury would forfeit her character in the process.' He turned slowly. 'Shall we put the matter to the test?'

Miss Mountjoy's hands had become claws, gripping the

arms of her chair. Her face and neck had turned grey. In the space of moments, she had shrunk from a handsome woman to a desiccated husk. 'You are a devil! I hope you rot in hell!'

'And you are—' He gave a snort of mirthless laughter and shook his head. 'No, we will not discuss that. So…what do you propose to do now?'

'What choice do I have?'

'None.'

'You wish me to leave King's Portbury?'

'I do.'

'Very well. I will go. I will leave before the next quarter day.'

'That seems an eminently sensible solution. And the other matter?'

She seemed to shrink even more. 'I will say nothing. You leave me no choice.'

'Quite so, ma'am. Let me add, however, that if any rumours should arise, from any quarter, about the conduct of my late wife, the annuity payable to Miss Louisa Mountjoy—wherever she is and whatever name she may trade under—will cease on the spot. Do I make myself clear?'

'Yes,' she said, in a small, crushed voice. 'There will be no rumours, and no gossip. I shall not trouble you again.'

Jon crossed to pull the bell, but thought better of it. His first marriage had been a disaster, largely because of Louisa Mountjoy's liaison with his wife. But, even so, he could not parade her defeat before the servants. 'You are distressed, ma'am, which is understandable.' He could not help his icy tone. The woman would have ruined him if she could. 'I will leave you here to regain your composure. My butler will return in a quarter of an hour to show you out. I suggest we do not meet again.' With a curt nod, he strode to the door and left her.

In the corridor outside, he almost fell over his wife. 'Beth! I…I did not expect to see you down so early.' She was looking remarkably alluring, in a gown of palest pink trimmed with flounces. Another one of those expensive fripperies he had encouraged her to buy in London. They all became her much too well.

She dropped him a curtsy. 'Good morning, my lord. I wonder if I might have a word with you?' She sounded un-usually determined.

Jon wondered what had caused her change of mood. Last night, when they had been together in her chamber, she had been so soft, so yielding… Not at all like this stern young matron.

'Might we go into your library? Where we may speak in private?'

That pulled him up short. 'Er…no. Not the library. It is not— That is to say, Miss Mountjoy is in there.'

Beth stiffened and grew a little pale.

'We were discussing a…a matter of business. She will be leaving in a few moments, once she has recovered—' This would not do. He was tying himself in knots, and for no good reason. He refused to feel guilty about what he had just done to Miss Mountjoy. She deserved it all, and more.

Jon smiled down at Beth and tucked her hand under his arm. 'The library is too gloomy this morning. Let us leave it to Miss Mountjoy. We can be private in the conservatory, and make the most of the light, besides. Madam, will you walk?'

Beth held herself a little apart as they walked through the house to the conservatory. She did not remove her hand from his arm—that would be much too confrontational—but she certainly could not relax into his touch.

Miss Mountjoy! He had been alone in his library with Louisa Mountjoy! What on earth had they been doing at this time of the day? And why did she have to be left alone there? To recover? From what?

The pictures racing through Beth's imagination were far from comfortable. Although she had no reason to suspect that Jon and the Mountjoy woman were lovers now, she could not banish the suspicion that they might have been lovers once. Had she come to see him this morning, by appointment, before any of the guests was about? Before his wife was about? It did not bear thinking of. Beth fancied Miss Mountjoy was capable of anything, even seducing a married man.

In total silence, they walked through to the conservatory where Beth let Jon usher her inside. He had been right. By comparison with the rest of the house, it was full of light. It was warm, too, but the myriad of green leaves made it seem cool, and very restful to the senses. Jon pushed aside some of the overhanging branches and led her through to a small clear space where they could be private. There was a white painted bench to one side, but he did not invite her to sit. He simply stopped and faced her.

Now that they were alone, and the moment had come, Beth felt her courage ebbing away. How had she ever thought she could challenge Jon? She struggled to put a simple sentence together, but no words came.

'You asked for a private word?' His tone was gentler than she had expected. Was that because he was guilty about Miss Mountjoy?

The thought of that obnoxious woman in Jon's embrace gave Beth a degree of courage that surprised her. 'I understand you have engaged a new valet, sir.' The words came out in a rush. 'As mistress of your household, I should have preferred to learn of such a change from you, rather than from the servants.'

He flushed. 'Good God! First my mother, and now my wife! Since when do I need permission from the women of my household to decide upon my own manservant?'

He was angry. Yet Beth was beginning to know him well enough to suspect that this show of temper was partly a cover for his embarrassment. He must know he was in the wrong over this.

'Might I ask why you have decided to make the change, sir?' Beth asked innocently.

Her tone had its effect. He took a deep breath and, when he spoke again, his anger had been replaced by gruffness, as if he were explaining a lesson to a rather stupid child and working hard to control justifiable impatience. 'I no longer have need of Vernon's skills. He should serve a single man, the kind of employer who wishes to cut a figure in society. All well and good when I was just returned from Spain, but no longer.'

He reached for Beth's hand and, to her surprise, raised it to his lips for a gallant kiss. Was that by way of apology for his show of bad temper?

'Now that I am married, I plan to spend more time in the country.' His voice was almost normal again. 'There is much to do here, and at the other estates. A country gentleman has no need of a man like Vernon. Joseph's skills will be more than adequate, even when I am in town.'

'You call him "Joseph"?' Beth said, surprised into betraying herself. Was Jon's relationship with Joseph as close as Beth's with Hetty?

He shrugged. 'We spent a long time together in the Peninsula. For some reason, everyone there used his given name. I fell into the way of it. I accept that it is improper, but— Well, let us see what happens once he has arrived.'

Jon watched the play of emotions crossing Beth's expressive face. She was clearly intrigued by what he had done and would want to learn more of his relationship with Joseph. What would she think if she learned he had done it for her? His mother had taken it almost as a personal insult. She had even accused Jon of abandoning his station in life. But Jon's plan had worked. The Dowager was now training her fire on Jon rather than on Beth. Her disdain for Beth's choice of lady's maid had been forgotten in her anger at her son's deliberate flouting of the standards she had instilled in him.

Jon allowed himself an inward smile. He had promised his mother he would deal with the situation. And he had.

At that moment, he became aware that he was still holding

Beth's hand. Shocked at his own weakness, he dropped it. Too abruptly.

Beth flinched as if from a blow. 'Is Miss Mountjoy ailing?' Beth's voice was cold. 'Perhaps I should offer my help if she is feeling unwell.'

'I am sure she will have recovered her composure by now.' That was the truth, but it was not enough to restore Beth's confiding mood. If he wanted that, he would have to unbend a little. 'I must tell you frankly, Beth, that I do not think she would welcome an offer of assistance from either of us.' There, it was done.

Beth's eyebrows rose and her eyes widened in apparent disbelief.

In for a penny... 'I do not wish to malign the lady. She was Alicia's friend and they had...um...a great regard for each other. However, I find Miss Mountjoy's continued visits here excessive.'

Beth glanced up at him in surprise and then quickly looked away. Strange. Surely Beth did not actually like the woman? There had been no sign that she did. Given the woman's history with Alicia, Jon would much prefer to keep his wife and Miss Mountjoy as far apart as possible.

He drew himself up and said, 'Miss Mountjoy will be leaving King's Portbury before the next quarter day. I— She has decided that this area is no longer to her taste.' He had betrayed himself, he realised. There had been too much venom in his voice.

But perhaps not? Beth's shoulders were no longer so tense, and there was the beginning of a smile on her delicious mouth. The temptation was just too much, especially in a place like this where they could not be observed. Jon dragged her into his arms and began to kiss her.

She stiffened, but only for a second. Then she melted into his embrace and returned his kiss with more skill than he had thought she possessed. This was not the innocent nymph of the Fratcombe folly. His wife had become a practised and eager seductress.

He knew he should break the kiss, put her from him so that they could resume their proper, public relationship, but her response was so passionate that he could not. Just a little longer exploring her luscious mouth, stroking her hair, her skin, the curve of her breast… Just a little more of the scent and taste of her…

She groaned from deep in her belly and put her hands to the waistband of his pantaloons, fumbling for his buttons. In a moment, there would be no going back.

'No, Beth.' He did not recognise his own voice as he pulled away from her. Since the day of their marriage, he had been telling himself to keep his distance from her. Closeness made a man vulnerable, and weak. And closeness to a woman was the most dangerous of all.

She had blushed scarlet. The fingers that had been trying to undress him just a moment ago were now twisting together in embarrassment. She was mortified by what had happened between them.

It had been his mistake as much as hers. 'Sit down, my dear,' he said, as gently as he could.

She crossed a little unsteadily to the bench and took her

seat. She looked up at him expectantly. Did she think he was about to join her? Poor Beth, marriage had taught her much, but she did not fully understand what drove a man.

He smiled and shook his head. 'No, best if I stand,' he said, keeping his tone light. He would focus on practical things until this interview was over. And then he would avoid Beth for the rest of the day.

'Now that all our guests are here,' he began, but stopped when she shook her head. 'I beg pardon. I thought that—'

'The Reverend and Mrs Aubrey will not arrive for a few days yet. Do you not recall? The rector wanted to be sure that his curate was not taking on too much of the Christmas burden.'

Jon had completely forgotten the Aubreys. Extraordinary that he should have done so, when he owed them so much. His preoccupation with his wife must be affecting his brain. He took a deep breath and began again. 'Now that *almost* all the guests are here, we can direct the servants to bring in the greenery to decorate the rooms. The Yule log will wait until Christmas Eve, of course, but there is plenty of mistletoe to amuse the younger guests.'

Mistletoe. The word hit Beth like a blow. It registered vaguely in her mind that Jon was still talking to her, but she could no longer hear what he was saying. *Mistletoe.* The word was pounding in her head like the crack of doom. With mistletoe in the house, something terrible would happen. She could not explain it, but she knew, for a certainty, that it would be so.

She sprang to her feet and ran for the door.

'Beth? What on earth is the matter? Beth!' Too late. She was gone in a flurry of pale pink skirts. Jon slumped on to the bench where she had been sitting just moments before and tried to piece together what had just happened. He had been talking about the Christmas festivities, the Yule log, the mistletoe. He had warned her that he would be avoiding the mistletoe. Their kisses could easily become too passionate for any room but a bedchamber. It had happened here, only moments ago. If it happened in front of their guests, everyone would be mortally embarrassed.

Had she run from him because he refused to kiss her in public?

Chapter Fifteen

From her place near the centre of the drawing room, Beth let her gaze travel round, counting heads. It was almost six. Nearly all the guests were assembled for dinner. Only the Berncastles were not yet down. For the first few evenings, they had been just a small party and conversation had been rather difficult. But tonight there would be twenty people sitting down to dinner. With so many guests, they should make a merry party, surely? And better still once the Reverend and Mrs Aubrey finally arrived.

Beth was trying to avoid looking up at the chandelier in the middle of the room and the large sprig of mistletoe that hung there. It seemed to draw her eye, even while it horrified her. It was full of sinister pearl-white berries. Their pallor was waxy, like the skin of a corpse. The very sight of them made her feel nauseous, and strangely guilty. But why should she feel guilty at the sight of mistletoe? What did it mean?

She shivered a little and backed away a step, straight into a man's arms. She knew immediately, without turning, that this was not Jon. This man's touch, and his scent, were repellent.

The man was not about to let Beth go. 'A kiss under the mistletoe, sister,' he cried gleefully, pulling her under the chandelier. It was George, of course, Jon's disreputable brother. Beth tried to slide out from his embrace without seeming to struggle, but it was useless. He was quite determined on his prize. His mouth descended on Beth's, his lips thick and wet. Where Jon's every touch was wonderful, George revolted her.

She began to struggle in earnest, but George was holding her so tightly that she could not even pull her mouth away from his. Then his tongue tried to force its way between her lips. She clamped her jaws and teeth together as tightly as she could. She would not allow this...this beastly invasion.

At last, defeated, he let her go.

'A great institution, mistletoe,' he said with a lascivious grin. 'Gives a man—and a gel—a chance to see what they have been missing.'

Beth could not suppress a shudder.

'I think you should perhaps ensure your partner is willing before you indulge in such activity, brother.'

Beth whirled round. Jon was standing in the doorway. He was white with anger. For once, he had ignored the presence of the other guests. He was challenging George directly.

But George was not in the least put out by Jon's rebuke. He casually reached up to pluck a berry from the sprig of mistletoe. 'Plenty more where that came from, eh, sister? And plenty more kisses for us both to enjoy, too, I'd say.' He dropped his voice to murmur in Beth's ear. 'You don't want to give 'em all to my prude of a brother, you know, m'dear.'

Beth gasped.

Ignoring her reaction, George turned to face Jon. 'The ladies will have kisses a-plenty, for I have rarely seen mistletoe with quite so many berries. It is an invitation to Christmas mischief, and merriment for all.'

For a moment, Beth fancied that Jon was going to plant his brother a facer. There was a stunned silence in the room. But then Miss Rothbury broke it, stepping under the chandelier and reaching up to pluck mistletoe berries, one after another, counting them into her hand. 'Look, Mama.' She beckoned to Lady Rothbury who was standing by the fire, slack-jawed in astonishment. 'They are just like jewels. I do like jewels so much, don't I?'

Her mother rushed forward to grab her daughter's hands and hold them still. 'Enough, my dear, enough. The berries are to be picked one at a time, one for each kiss. And when they have all been picked, there can be no more kissing under the mistletoe. That is the tradition, you know.'

'I may not pick them?' Miss Rothbury sounded like a small child, deprived of a favourite toy.

Beth stepped forward to join the pair. 'I am sure we can find plenty more sprigs of mistletoe if you like them,' she said gently. 'Shall we put a sprig in your bedchamber?'

Miss Rothbury's beaming smile was all the answer Beth needed. She nodded to the butler, standing impassively just inside the door. Goodrite would see to it. For now, Beth needed to distract her guests from these odd happenings until dinner should be announced. She sensed Jon's large, reassuring presence only a few paces behind her. Yes, she could do this.

'Ladies and gentlemen, shall we decide now on what we wish to do after dinner? Since it is Christmas, his lordship—' she nodded towards Jon '—has a predictable fancy for telling ghost stories, but we would be happy to accept more energetic suggestions. Charades, perhaps?'

With a feeling of relief, Beth shepherded the ladies along the corridor to the drawing room. The dinner had gone remarkably well, helped by Jon's excellent and plentiful wine. One or two of the older ladies were swaying a little and would probably soon be asleep in their chairs. No matter. The younger ones could play games at one end of the room while the older ones dozed.

How long would it be before the gentlemen joined them? Beth rather hoped they would not play charades after all, for drunken gentlemen could be difficult during such games. George had been downing bumper after bumper. That kiss under the mistletoe had been bad enough. What might he do now?

She told herself that Jon would ensure his brother behaved. If necessary, Jon would throw him out until he had sobered up. At least, she hoped he would.

When Beth entered the drawing room, she saw that Mrs Berncastle was holding forth from the centre of the room. She too had taken rather a lot of wine. She was not drunk, of course. No lady was ever drunk. But she had certainly become more and more talkative and uninhibited as the evening wore on. Some of her earthy comments had put Beth to the blush.

At Mrs Berncastle's side, Miss Rothbury was giggling, pointing up at the chandelier. Beth tried to ignore them and especially the mistletoe she so dreaded. Surely Goodrite would bring in the tea tray soon?

'Mistletoe is lovely,' Miss Rothbury crooned. 'The berries are just like the finest pearls, don't you think, ma'am?'

For a moment, Mrs Berncastle looked thunderstruck. 'Mistletoe! Of course, *that* was it!' She spun round and pointed accusingly at Beth. Her arm wavered slightly, but her voice was steady enough and full of outrage. 'I *knew* you were familiar! I recognise you now. Under all that finery, you are nothing but a dirty little thief! You are that Clifford woman, who was companion to my great-aunt Marchmont. You stole her priceless mistletoe jewels, and then you fled the county to avoid being hauled off to gaol and hanged, as you deserved.'

Beth stood like a statue, transfixed by that accusing finger. Clifford! The name pounded in her brain. The barrier cracked. Her name was Clifford. Of course it was.

The room and everyone in it seemed to melt into a hazy, indistinct blur. She felt she was floating, revolving in a cloying mist. It was a mist of memories, and guilt, and unbelievable pain. A moment later, the mist dissolved as if drenched by a shower of sheeting rain.

She remembered it all now, every last mortifying moment of it. She could feel the shivers convulsing her body as if she were still ploughing on through that freezing, howling gale. She closed her eyes for a second, but when she opened them again, nothing had changed. She was still freezing, still shivering. And the house guests were still staring at her as if she had sprouted devil's horns.

Near the open doorway, Jon stood frozen, his face ashen. He must have heard it all. He had learned he was married to a thief, and the revelation had shocked him to the core. Such an honourable man would surely never touch her again. Beth could not blame him. She was to be an outcast. All over again.

Pain engulfed her. The familiar tunnel began to close in. She picked up her skirts and fled from the room while she could still see.

The headache had lessened but Beth had not slept.

She swung her bare feet to the floor and crept across to the window to peep out. Still much too dark. In half an hour or so, perhaps. At least she would not have to climb out of the window this time, as she had done from old Lady Marchmont's house. This time, the key was on Beth's side of the locked door. For the moment, she was still in control of her life.

She returned to the bed, checking yet again that everything was ready. She had laid out her simplest, warmest clothes. Her stout boots were on the floor alongside. And her little valise contained the few essentials she would need. She could dress in these clothes without Hetty's help, and she would be gone long before anyone in the house was aware of it. Hetty would mourn, of course, and not only for the loss of her place. The girl had tried so hard to help and console Beth last night, even though she had not understood the cause. She would understand everything by now. The news of the mistress's disgrace must have spread like wildfire below stairs.

And Jon? What was Jon thinking?

It had been cowardly to lock him out of her bedchamber, to refuse to see him or speak to him. But truly, Beth had been unable to bear the thought of it. Jon had been plainly horrified to learn that his wife was a fugitive from the law. By now, his horror would have turned to disgust, perhaps even hate. Beth knew she could not remove the slur from her name. Nor could she undo their marriage. The most she could offer him was her absence, in hopes that, eventually, the scandal would die down and the gossips would leave him in peace. He would remain bound to her, however, and the brother he distrusted would be his heir. He would blame Beth for that. Rightly. She was guilty of so much.

But she had not known! She would never have married him if she had known the truth of her own past! She had tried so hard to warn him, but he had refused to listen. He had been so sure that the rank he offered was enough.

She dropped her head into her hands, but the cold metal of her wedding ring jarred accusingly against her skin. Why was she wearing it? She was taking almost nothing that Jon had given her. Her fine clothes remained in the dressing room, and her jewels were in their cases. He would have no cause to reproach her there. She would take a little money, but only just enough for her journey. Her wedding ring, however…

She turned it on her finger. Last night, she had taken it off and laid it aside, but then she had put it on again. She had told herself that, if she was claiming to be a poor widow, she would need a wedding ring to prove her status to the world. But of course that was not the whole truth.

She twisted it off once more and laid it by the letter she had written to him. She had asked him not to follow her. But why should he want to, after all she had done? More likely that he would be glad to be rid of her.

There was no time now to start composing another letter. This one had taken hours, and many tears. With a sigh, she picked up the ring and slipped it back on to her finger. She could not leave it behind. It was the only thing she would have from him.

Time to dress now. Soon, it would be time for her to go.

'Could you please cease this pacing, Jon? You are making my head spin.'

Jon sank on to the end of her *chaise longue*. 'I am sorry, Mama, but I have to talk to someone about all this, and there is no one else but you. Beth has locked herself in her bed-chamber. She refuses to admit anyone. I have been pacing my own floor for hours and it is driving me to distraction. I cannot think straight.'

His mother sighed. 'You saw what happened, my dear. We all did. Beth fled from her accuser, without saying a word in her own defence. That had all the appearance of guilt.'

Jon ground his teeth. He had come to ask his mother's help for Beth, not to hear yet more condemnation. He believed—no, he was certain—that his wife was innocent and good, but everything was so confused that he was incapable of working out how to defend her. 'Mama, I—'

'In the end, it may be for the best,' his mother continued quietly. 'Indeed, you would be better off without her, were it not for the child. You could—'

'What do you mean *child*, ma'am?'

'There is no need to play the innocent with me, Jon. I know that she is breeding, and I know that she used it to entrap you into marriage. It is a sorry business, and if the child should prove to be a girl after all…'

For a moment, Jon was struck dumb. Then he began to laugh. He laughed until his whole body was wracked with pain. His mother looked by turns indignant and then hurt. Jon ignored her. At last, when the pain became too much, he dropped his head into his hands. His laughter cracked and stopped dead.

Jon felt the brush of his mother's silken wrapper against his leg. Her soft hand reached out to cover one of his. 'Jon?' Her voice was low, the thread of worry clear. 'I do not understand. It is as if you were bewitched.'

Jon flung himself to his feet and began to pace again. He could not endure her touch. There was only one touch he needed now.

'Jon?'

He stopped abruptly and turned to face her, planting his feet firmly and his fists on his hips. 'You are wrong, ma'am. You could not be more wrong. You tell me that Beth is breeding, that she seduced me into marriage.' He gave one last shout of bitter laughter. 'If only you knew the lengths I had to go to, in order to persuade her to accept me.'

'I do not understand.' Her usual confidence seemed to have left her.

'Beth did not entrap me into marriage, Mama. What made you think such a thing? It seems you have a very low opinion of my character.'

'I am sorry, Jon. All the physical signs pointed to pregnancy—her tiredness, her sickness. Miss Mountjoy was quite sure of it.'

Jon clamped his jaws together. Miss Mountjoy again! But she was dealt with. He would not lecture his mother about her now.

'And the fact that you, who are so very conscious of your position in society, should have rushed into marriage with a woman with no name and no family... How else could I explain it, but by your need for a legitimate heir?' When Jon did not reply, she swallowed hard and added, in a small voice, 'I have tried to like her, Jon, but I found it impossible to overcome my disgust of what she had done to you. Except that now you tell me it was not so?'

'No, Mama, it was not so. She refused me.' The Dowager frowned up at him. 'Twice,' Jon added, with deliberate emphasis. 'And when she was finally persuaded to accept me, she added onerous conditions that I had to fulfil. If there was entrapment, ma'am, it was my doing, not Beth's.'

The Dowager let out a long breath. 'Then she is not breeding?'

'She was certainly not breeding when I took her to the

altar, ma'am,' he responded stiffly. 'The symptoms you mentioned are a great embarrassment to her. She feels—felt guilty about her missing past. That, and open hostility, can bring on the headache. Sometimes, she can barely see, and she has to take to her bed. That, not the guilt you thought you saw, is why she fled. I am sure of it.' He held his mother's gaze for a moment before turning away to stare out of the window. .

'Your ladyship!' The Dowager's dresser rushed into the room without knocking, followed closely by Hetty. 'Miss Martin says—!'

The Dowager's gasp of outrage was drowned by Hetty's anguished cry. 'She has gone, my lord! In the dark! She will die out there, my lord!'

Jon spun round. He ignored the tears coursing down the girl's pale face. 'How long ago did she leave? Where is she going? Tell me what you know, Hetty. Quickly now.'

The girl seemed bewildered, and Jon's barked questions were not helping. He would have to coax the information out of her. He forced himself to curb his impatience and ask one careful question at a time. Her mistress, Hetty offered at last, must have fled at some time during the night. She had taken only a small valise. She had left everything else behind—clothes, jewels, money, everything. And a letter.

Jon dismissed the two servants with a stern warning about discretion. Without even a glance at his mother, he turned his back and tore open the letter. It was barely three lines. She was leaving him in order to purge the stain on his honour; she would never return; and Jon should not try to seek her out. That was all. There was not a word about her guilt or innocence.

He crumpled the sheet in his fist and stared out into the darkness. There was no moon, but the sky was clear. It wanted more than an hour till sunrise and, even then, it would still be exceedingly cold. Beth was alone, somewhere, fleeing in order to protect Jon's honour. She had nothing, and no one, to protect her. She might freeze to death out there, without ever knowing how much Jon loved her.

The realisation shuddered through him. What a fool he was! What an arrogant fool! He had been in love with her almost from the first, but he had convinced himself that she was simply a friend, a restful companion, a willing participant in their mutual passion. Because of Jon's failings, she might die, out there in the dark. Alone.

He groaned aloud. A red–hot blade was twisting in his gut. He deserved every shred of the pain that knifed through him.

A gentle hand touched his upper arm. 'Jon? What is it, my dear?'

'I love her. And I have driven her away.' The words were torn out of him against his will, as if they had a power all their own. In that moment, staring vacantly into the far distance, Jon understood that he loved Beth more than life itself. If he did not find her, if he did not bring her back, warm and alive, his own life would be worthless.

He glanced down at his mother. He wanted to shake off her restraining hand, to berate her for the mischief she had done. But one look at the pain in her face chased all those angry notions from his mind.

She stroked her fingers gently down his arm and dropped her hand to her side. 'Will you go after her?' When he nodded, she said crisply, 'Let me deal with your guests. And with everything else here. What matters is that you should bring your wife—your Beth—back safely.' She was trying to smile encouragingly.

Jon's mind was tumbling, racing, planning for action. 'Make sure that none of the guests leaves while I am gone, Mama. And no letters, either. There must be no scandal-mongering. As for this wicked accusation against Beth, I will deal with it when we return. In the meantime, let no one know we are gone.'

His mother nodded. 'If I may be allowed just one word of advice before you go…'

Jon pulled himself up very erect and frowned forbiddingly. He did not want any advice from his mother. Her coldness and hostility had led Beth to believe she was friendless in this house.

His mother's eyes were glistening. 'When you find her, tell her that you love her,' she said hoarsely. 'It will make you vulnerable, like baring your breast to the sword and saying "Strike here". But love cannot be demanded, it can only be offered. If you want to win Beth's love, you will have to risk your own.'

Jon was shocked into immobility. His own mother, the starched-up Dowager Countess of Portbury, believed in love?

She laid her hand on his arm once more. This time, she pushed him towards the door. 'Please bring her back, Jon.' There was a catch in her voice. 'When you do, I promise that I will welcome her as the daughter I never had.'

Jon needed no urging. He already knew he had not a second to spare. He must ride out after Beth, the woman he loved. He must bring her home.

It was cold. So very cold.

Beth bent her body into the wind and trudged on. This time, there was no sheeting rain to soak her. This time she was more warmly clad, and better shod. And this time there would be no knight in shining armour to rescue her from the beckoning darkness.

There must be no rescue at all. Jon was noble enough to come after her, but he must not find her. He would expect her to walk the eight miles to Broughton to board the coach for the first stage of her journey. He would assume that she was making for Fratcombe. He would be wrong.

In truth, she had no idea where she should go, except that it must not be Fratcombe. The Aubreys could not be asked to harbour a thief. Besides, they would be bound tell Jon where she was. No, she must go somewhere she was not known. Bristol, perhaps, or even Cornwall.

The wind was whipping at her skirts. Did she dare to follow the second part of her plan? To her left was the long flat road that would bring her, eventually, to Broughton and the coach office. To her right was the two mile path up over the moor. There was light enough now for her to see her way. And no one would think to look for a countess there.

Beth's little valise had been getting heavier. She transferred it from one hand to the other and began to climb the lonely path. The slope was easy enough, at first, though the air swirling around her seemed to become colder with every step she took. She continued doggedly. She could endure worse than this. Before Fratcombe, her life had been very hard. As Lady Marchmont's companion, she had been no better than a menial, wearing cast-off shoes and gowns that even Jon's servants would have rejected. Lady Marchmont was exceedingly rich, but her household lived like paupers while she hoarded her money and her jewels. Especially her jewels. That mistletoe clasp—intricate, heavy gold for the stems and leaves, and berries made of priceless pearls—had been the old witch's pride and joy. Until the day it vanished.

Lady Marchmont's maid had claimed to have seen Beth sneaking into the mistress's bedchamber. On such flimsy evidence from a jealous servant, Beth had been pronounced guilty by Lady Marchmont and all her guests. Including the Berncastles. If Beth had not climbed out of that locked room, she would probably have ended up on the gallows.

The path seemed to stretch for ever, steeper than she recalled. No matter. It was only the first of many challenges she would have to face. At least the wind seemed to have dropped. It was no longer cutting through her cloak and biting at her skin. She tried to smile up at the sky. She would cling on to her innocence, and to her love for Jon. She was doing this for him. She would cherish the memories of their times together, of how he had held her, and kissed her, and loved her. Nothing could deprive her of those.

She plodded on with even greater determination, clutching the memory of him like a talisman. She might find another village that needed a schoolmistress. She would be

Mrs Clifford, the poor widow of an army captain tragically killed in the French wars. There were many such. One more would not be noticed.

She was shivering again. It was not the wind this time, but cold, penetrating damp. She glanced up at the sky. Was it starting to rain?

She could not tell. She could not see the sky. Suddenly, there was ghostly grey mist swirling all around her. It had come out of nothing. But it hid everything. She could see barely a yard in front of her feet.

She refused to allow herself to panic. She had no cause. The path over the moors was straight enough. She had only to keep going and she would soon reach Broughton. She must not allow herself to be afraid.

She stretched her free hand out in front of her, just in case there might be some obstacle in the path, and continued to walk into the forbidding grey wall, though she could not prevent her steps from becoming shorter, and rather timid. Surely she had already passed the halfway point? She must reach her goal soon.

The path was becoming much more uneven. She stumbled to a stop and strained to make out the way ahead. Were there loose rocks here to make her lose her footing? She must take care. If she were injured here, no one would find her.

The mist had become so thick now that she could barely see her own feet. She took a few steps more, but stopped. She could see nothing. She was no longer sure she was on the path at all. Perhaps she should sit on the ground and wait until the mist lifted? But if she did so, she might freeze.

Besides, she would lose precious time. She must reach Broughton, and catch that first stage before anyone from Portbury discovered her flight. She dare not delay. She must keep on, in spite of the mist.

Taking a deep breath of the thick air, she made to stride out again.

A hand caught her waist from behind. She screamed. The sound was swallowed up in the swirling mist. Then another hand clamped across her mouth. She was pulled sharply backwards into a man's body. It reeked of sweat. The hand on her mouth was so filthy she could taste it. She fought to free herself, trying to kick and stamp with her heavy boots.

Her captor was too wily to be caught by such feeble female struggles. He held her fast and dragged her backwards into the enveloping mist.

Chapter Sixteen

Jon had succeeded in leaving the Abbey without being seen by any of the guests. The grooms were quite another kettle of fish. They had stared, goggle-eyed, at the pistols holstered by his saddle, and the extra rolled-up cloak tied on behind. They had not dared to ask questions, of course, and the grim set of Jon's jaw should have warned them not to gossip.

He would make everything right again, once he had brought Beth home. But where was she now? He slowed Saracen to a walk while he checked the time by his pocket watch. He had covered barely two miles of the Broughton road. Beth had several hours' start on him and, even on foot, she would probably reach the town before he could overtake her. A stage was due to depart in less than half an hour from now. What if Beth was on it? Whatever he did then, he was bound to create a scandal. And he could hardly demand they stand and deliver his wife.

Saracen sidled a little, nostrils flaring in response to the wild scents of the moorland. 'You want a gallop, boy. And you are right. If we go this way, we can save at least four miles. We might even reach Broughton before Beth's stage leaves.' He turned the big horse towards the moors and cantered up the slope.

What if Beth had come this way, too? What if she had already caught the first stage out of Broughton?

He shook his head in exasperation. Surely it was much too dangerous, especially at this time of year? But she had done dangerous things before and nearly died in the process. That thought worried him so much that he turned Saracen on to a side path after only half a mile. The diversion would not take him long. And he had to know. He eased the big horse down the slope until he could make out the fallow field at the edge of his own estate. Yes, the travellers from Fratcombe were still there. But would they be able to tell him anything of value?

Jon covered the remaining distance at the gallop and put Saracen at the wall. The big bay cleared it easily and cantered across to the cluster of caravans at the far side. From nowhere, a shrivelled old man appeared and held up a commanding hand. He must be the leader here. Behind him, curious faces peeped out from painted doors and windows. Dirty tousle-haired children crawled out from behind wagon wheels to stare at this latest arrival.

'What d'ye want?' The old man scowled up at Jon.

'I am the Earl of Portbury and you are on my land. By my leave.' The man's scowl softened but he still did not allow Saracen to pass. 'I have come to ask for your help in— Good God! Beth!'

He was sure he was not mistaken. He had glimpsed Beth's face in the window of the furthest caravan. She was here, with the gypsies. Had they taken her by force?

He snatched a pistol from its holster and levelled it at the old man. 'You have my wife. Give her to me, or I swear I will shoot you down.' Slowly and deliberately, he moved his thumb to cock the weapon.

Before he could do so, the pistol was struck from his hand.

A merry laugh broke the sudden silence. Jon half-turned to see a darkly handsome young gypsy lounging against the side of the nearest caravan. He was holding another throwing knife loosely in his hand. Judging by his success against Jon's pistol, he knew exactly how to use it.

'What right have ye over this woman?' the old man demanded. 'We rescued her from death at the Devil's Drop. She do belong with us now.' He glanced over his shoulder. Beth had emerged from the caravan and come to stand just behind him. She was dirty and dishevelled. Her cloak was torn and her boots were thick with mud. She was the most beautiful woman in the whole world.

Jon gazed longingly at her. 'I rescued her from death, too, a full year ago now. So her life was always mine.' Beth nodded warily, as if to confirm the truth of Jon's words. Another tiny sign. It gave him hope.

'She be safer here. In your household, she be cried a thief. Leave her where she be valued. Or was you wanting to deliver her up to the noose?'

'Of course not! Even if she were a thief, I would still defend her, with my life if needs be. She is my wife!'

The old man shrugged. 'So we do both have a claim on her. But my son here do hold the knife. Why should he give the woman to you?'

Jon let his hands drop, displaying empty palms. 'Because I love her,' he said simply.

Beth's gasp echoed round the camp. The young gypsy hurled his knife, point first, into the earth, just as Beth started to run towards Jon. In what seemed like only a second, Jon had thrown himself from Saracen's back and his precious wife was in his arms.

'You love me?' She was gazing up at him with wide, glowing eyes.

'More than life,' he groaned, and began to kiss her.

They clung to each other, oblivious of everything. Their bodies seemed to melt together, while their lips sought and their tongues danced. When at last they broke apart, gasping for breath, they found they were alone but for Saracen, cropping the grass by the half-buried knife.

Jon bent to draw it out of the ground. He ran his thumb along the blade with a grimace. It was wickedly sharp.

Beth clasped her own cold hands round his to hold them still. 'I am no thief, Jon. I swear it.'

Jon freed a hand to cup her chin and gazed deep into her eyes. 'I know that. You are the essence of honesty and goodness. You could never have been a thief. Together, we will find a way of proving it. But first, we must go back and face them down. Can you do that, my love?'

'With your love to strengthen and support me, I can do anything.'

He threw the knife back into the ground and picked up his pistol. 'Come then.'

'Wait!' The young gypsy had appeared again, as if by magic. He retrieved the knife and offered it to Jon, hilt first. 'Take it. Use it on the black heart of any man who would harm your woman. She be worth a life.'

Jon stared. Then he took the knife and tucked it into his boot. 'Thank you. And be sure that, as long as I am Earl of Portbury, your band will always be welcome on any of my estates.'

Beth leaned in to Jon's beloved body. Even through the heavy cloak he had wrapped her in, she could feel the heat of him reaching out to her. He loved her. He loved her! She sighed out a long breath and allowed herself to relax even more. They had not ridden together since that night in the folly. That memory made her insides glow even hotter.

Jon nuzzled her ear. 'What on earth were you doing at the Devil's Drop, love? It's nowhere near the Broughton path.'

She shuddered. 'I must have wandered from the path when the mist came down. That young gypsy pulled me to safety, though I didn't realise it at the time. I kicked him quite hard.' Jon's deep chuckle vibrated against her cheek. 'They said that, if I needed sanctuary, I could have it with them. I...I was going to stay.'

His arm tightened round her. 'But you changed your mind.'

'Yes,' Beth whispered. 'Because you said you loved me.'

'I did. I do,' he replied earnestly. 'Though I did not realise it until I thought I had lost you.' She felt him swallow hard. 'Beth, do you—?'

She reached out from her cocoon to press a finger to his lips. 'You know, for a leader of men, you are remarkably unobservant.' He tried to catch her finger in his teeth, but she was too quick for him. That was for later. 'I have loved you since that first time you lifted me into your arms.'

'Ah. At the folly.'

'No, you noddy. When you rescued me from the storm.'

His eyes widened. He shook his head a little, as if trying to cope with a momentous new idea. Then, after a long silence, he said, on a choke of laughter, 'I can see that I have a great deal of catching up to do. May I say, ma'am, and darling wife, that I expect it to be a pleasure?'

Jon leaned back against their sitting room door and let out a long sigh of relief. Beside him, Beth put her hands to her burning cheeks. She must have been terrified she would be caught, stealing back into the house looking like a grubby gypsy!

He could smile now the danger was over. 'Chin up, my sweet. We are safe now. Only Hetty and my mother knew you were gone, and mama will have made sure that no one suspected a thing. You may trust her, you know. She has promised to support you. So hurry and get changed into something appropriate for a top-lofty society hostess.'

'Your mother will support me? Are you sure, Jon? She does not like me above half. And if she—'

He stopped her worries by the simple expedient of kissing

her again. 'My mother's mind was poisoned against you, I am sorry to say, by Miss Mountjoy. She detests me, and would do anything to injure me.'

'Because she is your discarded lover?'

'Good God, no!' he exclaimed, though her new-found daring delighted him. 'What made you—? Ah, Beth, you could not be more wrong. In truth, Miss Mountjoy... er...loved Alicia very much and blamed me for her unhappiness. Now that Alicia is dead, the Mountjoy woman seizes every opportunity for mischief-making. But she is leaving Portbury soon. She will not trouble us any more.'

'Poor woman. She must be very unhappy.' Beth was shaking her head sadly. 'And lonely, too, without Alicia,' she added.

'She is your enemy and yet you think kindly of her?' He was thunderstruck. He had known Beth was generous, but this...?

'Of course. Ask the rector when he arrives. He will tell you that we are to love our enemies.'

Jon stared at her in stunned silence. She was right. He would never be able to match her goodness. And he did not deserve such a treasure. 'You must hurry now, love,' he said gruffly, leading her towards her bedchamber door. 'And while you are preparing to face your guests, I shall have an interview with Berncastle. I guarantee that his wife will be begging your pardon before the day is out. She will admit she mistook you for a woman named Clifford. Since she was foxed at the time, you will graciously forgive her, will you not?'

She let out a gasp of embarrassed laughter.

He used the moment to pick up her left hand and touch the

ring. 'You left everything behind but this. It gave me hope.' He kissed it reverently. Then he patted her on the bottom and pushed her through the door before he changed his mind.

There was tension in the atmosphere of the drawing room. Although Mrs Berncastle had publicly avowed her mistake and apologised to Beth in front of everyone, Beth knew perfectly well that not one of them believed it. Soon the tale-bearing letters would go out, and the gossip would start. Poor Jon. How would he bear it?

Beth forced herself to ignore that horrid thought and threaded her way through groups of laughing young men and formidable dowagers to join Lady Rothbury by the fire. She smiled down at her. Poor woman. The high-waisted fashions were far from flattering on her, for she was as round as an apple. 'Your daughter is joining us, I hope, ma'am?'

'Oh, yes, Lady Portbury. Indeed, she says she plans to surprise me this evening.' She cocked her head on one side, like a fat, black-eyed robin. 'I fancy she is going to come down to dinner in her new evening gown.'

'That will be splendid,' Beth said kindly.

'Why, Miss Rothbury!' Mr Berncastle exclaimed at the same moment. 'How fine you— Devil a bit!' He rocked back on his heels and grabbed a chair to recover his balance. 'I mean, beg pardon, but that is the missing mistletoe jewel!'

The whole room gasped as one and turned to stare at Miss Rothbury. She was dressed in figured white silk. And on her shoulder she was wearing a huge clasp of wrought gold and pearls in the shape of a bunch of mistletoe.

She smiled round innocently at the company and straightened the folds of her skirts. 'I told you I should surprise you, Mama. Is it not beautiful?' She stroked a finger over each of the pearls, and then down the golden stalk.

Lady Rothbury rushed forward to grab her daughter by the shoulders. She was almost weeping with embarrassment. 'Child, child, what have you done? Where did you get this?'

Miss Rothbury looked confused. 'I think I have always had it. Have I not, Mama? You know I have always loved pearls.'

Mrs Berncastle pushed her way to the front. 'You must know, Lady Rothbury, that this jewel belongs to my great-aunt, Lady Marchmont. It was stolen from her last year.' She glanced along the line of astonished faces and paused, like an actress. 'We were both in the house at the time, as I recall. As was your daughter.'

Beth was gripped with boiling fury. How dare the woman make such accusations against a poor simple girl? There was no malice in Miss Rothbury, none at all, but Mrs Berncastle was clearly determined to have her revenge for that humiliating public apology. Well, Beth would not allow it. She strode across the room to stand between Miss Rothbury and her accuser. 'Mrs Berncastle, I am sure you would not wish there to be *another* misunderstanding over this. Would you?'

Faced with the grim challenge in Beth's face, the woman paled and took a step back. After a moment, she shook her head.

'Miss Rothbury must have picked up the jewel by mistake,' Beth said flatly, daring Mrs Berncastle to contradict her. 'She is fond of such trinkets and would not have thought it wrong. I am sure her mama will see that it is returned to Lady Marchmont with a suitable apology.'

'Quite right, my dear,' Jon said firmly, taking his place by her side and dropping an arm round her waist.

Bless him. Just when she needed him. They had their proof now, but at the cost of poor simple Miss Rothbury's reputation. It felt so wrong. 'I hope,' Beth began, fixing each of her guests in turn with a stern glare, 'that I may rely on everyone here to say nothing at all about this incident?'

'I am sure they will not, my dear,' the Dowager put in quickly, smiling warmly at Beth. 'For it would be such a shame if there were to be no more invitations to Portbury Abbey, would it not? And all because of a little scurrilous gossip with no foundation. No foundation at all.'

Miss Rothbury was still looking bewildered and stroking her pearls. Then, seeing the Dowager's encouraging smile, she began to laugh.

Slowly at first, and then with increasing mirth, the rest of the Portbury guests joined in, until the room was ringing with laughter.

Jon was not laughing. Instead, he squeezed Beth's waist and pulled her into the centre of the room. He was looking down at her in a very serious way. Had he changed his mind? Was he thinking she had done wrong to support Miss Rothbury?

'It is Christmas,' he said, not attempting to lower his voice. 'And at Christmas, a man may kiss his sweetheart under the mistletoe.'

Beth's gasp of astonishment was caught in a long, delicious kiss that went on and on, until her head was swimming and her legs were like jelly. Her distant, austere husband was content to kiss his wife before all the world. Under the friendly mistletoe. Love was truly a wonderful thing.

'The Reverend and Mrs Aubrey!'

At the sound of the butler's announcement, Jon broke the kiss. Beth fancied he did so reluctantly. For herself, she would not have cared if it had gone on for ever.

'My, my,' the rector said, coming forward with both hands outstretched. 'Now *that* was certainly worth travelling all this way to see!'

Jon pulled out the last pin and watched with obvious satisfaction as Beth's hair tumbled down. He stroked a curl back from her cheek. 'You know, you are a remarkably good woman, Elizabeth Foxe-Garway. I swear you do not have an unkind fibre in your whole body.'

'I—' She could feel herself blushing all over. It was not helped by the fact that she was wearing nothing but a pair of silk stockings and her unbound hair. Jon had the advantage of her, for he had not yet removed his dressing gown.

She tried to make a dash for the bed, but Jon caught her up into his arms and stood, looking down at her with very male appreciation. She wriggled, but he held her fast. 'You will be allowed to hide under those sheets later, my dear Elizabeth. For the moment—'

'But my name is not Elizabeth!' she burst out. For a second, she thought he was going to drop her, but he strode across to the bed and set her down. She squirmed between the sheets. That was better. She could not think straight if he was gazing at her with so much desire in his eyes.

'Explain, please,' he said curtly. Suddenly, he was frowning.

Oh dear. She should have told him before, when they came back from the gypsy camp, but they had had no time alone. And then the furore over the mistletoe clasp—and that very public kiss—had pushed all other thoughts from her mind. 'My name is—was Bethany de Clifford. I was always called Beth. Don't you see, Jon? They were searching for a missing Elizabeth. It is no wonder that they never found a missing Bethany.'

He shook his head and then he laughed. 'And you remember everything now, do you? Parents, a family? Now I think of it, I seem to know the name, de Clifford.'

She nodded. 'Sir Humphrey de Clifford was my father's grandsire. Papa was a younger son with no prospects. When he eloped with my mother, who was only a poor curate's daughter, the baronet cast him off. Lady Marchmont always told me I was lucky to have any position at all, after they died, for I was barely a lady.'

'You are more of a lady than she could ever be.' He leaned over her and ran his fingers through her hair. 'And now that you are a countess—*my* countess—you are above censure. You may do exactly as you like.'

'*Exactly* as I like?' she enquired innocently. She watched his eyes widen and darken as she slowly pushed the sheets down, starting to uncover her naked body to his gaze once more. Then she reached out and pulled his belt undone with a single sharp tug. She let her gaze travel down his splendid body. He was fully aroused. For her.

She flipped the sheet away so that she was totally exposed. And so that he could not ignore the empty space beside her. 'What I should like, my lord, is a little…er…energetic male company. Of course, if you are not in the mood to provide it, I could always—'

He was beside her, and kissing her, before she could say another word. They had been passionate before, but this was different. This was passion between lovers who were no longer afraid, lovers who had at last recognised that, together, they made a single, perfect whole.

Jon was holding her in his arms as though she were as delicate as a snowflake and as likely to melt away. But she would not. She was strong now, and lusty, and she wanted to love him with her body as well as her heart. 'Love me,' she whispered, wrapping her legs around him and pulling him close. 'Love me. I am yours.'

Epilogue

Beth rolled over sleepily and reached across the pillow. 'Jon?' she murmured. She wanted to be in his arms again, rejoicing in his touch.

He was gone!

She was jerked fully awake. She sat up. No, she was not mistaken. Jon's side of the bed was empty. He had loved her. And then he had left her. But surely it made no sense now? Why would he not stay?

She scrabbled about for the tinder box and lit her bedside candle. What was she going to do? Tonight, she had been so sure he would stay that she had not even asked him. She must ask him now, this minute, or she would never have the courage to do it. Then she would be condemned to sleeping alone for the rest of her life.

She swung her feet out of the bed and dragged on her wrapper. She could not find her slippers. No matter, she would go barefoot. After all, she would be returning to bed very soon.

She lit a branch of candles, leaving the first one by her bed. Then she crept out into their shared sitting room. It was silent, and dark. The fire had gone out long ago. She set the candles down on the little table by Jon's door and put her ear against it. Still silence. She took a deep breath and eased the door half open.

He was lying on his back, asleep. She could hear his deep, even breathing. She pushed the door a little wider and reached for her candles.

'No! Stop! Release her or I will shoot you down. Oh, good God, no, no!'

Candles forgotten, Beth raced across to the bedside. Yes, he was still asleep, but now his breathing was shallow and rapid, and there was sweat on his brow. A dream. No, a nightmare! Something terrible. For a moment she stood frozen, wondering whether to wake him, or leave him.

She did neither. She let her wrapper slide to the floor and slid into the bed beside him. He was shaking. And muttering. Tentatively, she reached out to place her palm on his naked chest. After a moment, his shaking stopped. She slipped both arms around him and allowed her body to stretch down the full length of his. He groaned and tried to pull away, but then his whole body relaxed and he returned her embrace.

Beth smiled against his skin. She would wait.

'Beth?' It had taken at least ten minutes for his body to emerge from that nightmare and for him to realise that she had joined him in his bed.

She touched a kiss to the line of his jaw. In the dim light

from the sitting room, she could see his profile, but little more. 'You were having a terrible nightmare.' She understood only too well what they could do. She took a deep breath. It had to be now. 'Is that why you insist on sleeping alone? Because of nightmares?'

He groaned. He started to push her away, but then he pulled her back into an even closer embrace. 'I…yes. I had hoped you would not find out, love. It was—' He shuddered.

The dark might help, Beth decided. 'Tell me. Perhaps if you speak it aloud, here in the dark, the memory will stop tormenting you.'

After a long silence, he said, 'Very well. It was after Badajoz. I was in the town, with two young subalterns, trying to restore some order. It was impossible. The men were all roaring drunk, and— They had a woman, an innocent Spanish woman. They were going to rape her. I tried to stop them. I…I shot at the ringleader, but my pistol misfired and then the blackguards struck me down. My companions carried me back to camp. They were too young and too frightened to do anything else.'

Beth closed her eyes against the horror of it. 'And the woman?' she said in a tiny voice.

'I found her body. Later, after the looting had stopped. My only consolation was that the rapists were also dead, killed by their comrades' wild shooting. There was so much death…'

'It was after Badajoz that you sold out?' She had to know it all.

He nodded against her hair. 'They left their wounded comrades to bleed for two days while they drank the town dry. It was sickening. So when Mama wrote about George trying to ruin the estate all over again, I took it as an excuse to resign my commission. But I should have saved her. She died because I failed.'

Beth did not have to ask what he meant. She stroked his hair back from his damp brow and snuggled against him. 'You did all you could, my love. You risked your life for her.'

'Wellington should have stopped it. He knew the horror of it all, and he did nothing. For two whole days, he did nothing.'

It was no wonder Jon had sold out after such disillusion. But Beth would not say that, not ever. She would simply hold him while he slept, until the nightmares subsided.

'Come back to bed with me, love.' She took his hand and sat up, pulling him after her. 'You have nightmares here. In my bed, we have only love and passion. Come, sleep with me till morning. The memories will not dare attack you there.' She smiled at him, even though she was sure he could not see.

'I swear your goodness could heal anyone, and anything, my love.' He caught up his dressing gown and, together, they padded across the floor and back to their marriage bed. Soon they were peacefully asleep in each other's arms.

It was Christmas Eve at last. Jon felt more contented than ever before. His beloved wife was by his side and, thanks to her, he had spent his first undisturbed nights in months. He owed her so much. Yet, when he had offered her the moon, she had asked only for a chance to drive his horses!

He waited until the curricle had come to a stop and the groom had run to the horses' heads. She really drove extremely well. He reached across and squeezed her fingers gently. 'Perhaps you would like to tool the curricle round the lanes for ten minutes or so and then return for me? I have business with Miss Mountjoy, but it will not take long.'

'I am flattered that you should trust me with your precious horses,' Beth chuckled.

'More to the point,' he responded with a grin, 'I am trusting my horses with my precious wife.'

They both laughed, though Beth was blushing, too.

Jon climbed down. 'Go with her ladyship, Sam. She is going to drive around the lanes for a short while.' He watched until the curricle was out of sight before marching up the path and knocking on the cottage door.

'Lord Portbury!' Miss Mountjoy gasped as she opened the door.

'May I come in, ma'am?'

'I—' She stood back and dropped a polite curtsy. 'Very well. It is, after all, your house.'

Jon ignored that and walked into the neat parlour. 'Miss Mountjoy, I have come to enquire about your future plans.'

She drew herself up very straight. 'Our meeting at the Abbey was to be our last, you said. Or have I misremembered?'

'Forgive me, Miss Mountjoy, I should much prefer it if we did not repeat the substance of that last interview. Harsh words were spoken, on both sides. And on both sides they are better forgotten.'

She frowned, puzzled.

'Miss Mountjoy, much has happened since our last meeting. I have come to realise, and to regret, the cruel way

I treated you then. I do still think that you should leave King's Portbury—partly for my family's sake, but for your own sake also, since there must be many unhappy memories here for you. I cannot comprehend your feelings for Alicia, nor hers for you, but I do understand—now—that they were sincerely felt. I know that love is a gift, wherever it strikes. I should like to change the terms of our agreement.'

A slight shudder ran through her frame. She was afraid.

'For the better, Miss Mountjoy.' He drew out a sealed document and offered it to her. 'This is the lease on a cottage by the sea. It is on the south coast, a long way from King's Portbury, but it is a delightful house. If you wish, you may have it for the rest of your life for a peppercorn rent. I ask for nothing else. I am certain that you will respect Alicia's memory and keep her counsel, for I know the bond between you was very strong. I do not suppose that death can break it.'

'There are no other conditions?' she whispered, in disbelief.

'None.' He set the lease down on the table.

'Lord Portbury, this is more than I deserve after what I tried to do to you. In return, I…I should warn you to beware of your brother. He…it was he who encouraged me to poison your wife's reputation. He hoped that you and she would part. That there would be no heir. I am sorry.' She hung her head.

Jon took a deep breath. George had been the cause of all this? His brother? Jon knew he had every right to have George thrown into the gutter for such wickedness. But he knew, too, that he could not do such a thing. Not any more. He would threaten George with penury, and make sure he believed it, too, but that would be all. 'Thank you, Miss Mountjoy.' She looked up, surprised by his tone. He smiled at her. 'I wish you a long and contented life in your new home. Let everything else that has passed between us be forgotten.'

She did not speak but her face cleared. As she picked up the lease that guaranteed her future, Jon fancied that her eyes were shining. There was nothing more to be done now. He bowed.

She sank into a deep curtsy.

'I will show myself out. Goodbye, ma'am.' Jon closed the parlour door gently and made his way out into the fresh, crisp air of the winter morning. He felt as if a huge weight had been lifted from his shoulders by an unseen hand. Alicia was gone. And all the heartache that had been part of his first marriage was gone, too, washed away by Beth's love and the generosity she showed to everyone around her. Jon would never have a fraction of his wife's goodness, but he would try to learn from her example. Today's gift to Miss Mountjoy had been his first small step on that hard road. Dealing with George would be the second.

He walked through the cottage gate to see his curricle approaching at a fast trot. He held up his hand, waiting to judge how well Beth was handling the ribbons. She halted her pair very successfully, but not before they had gone a good thirty yards beyond him. He marched down the lane until he stood at the side of the curricle, arms akimbo, and shaking his head. 'Dear, dear. Is that the best you can do, Lady Portbury?' He climbed up beside her and held out his hands for the reins.

She ignored him, smiling wickedly. 'You were clearly

much in need of the exercise, sir. As to what I can do…'
She rearranged the reins in her gloved fingers and tightened
her grip on the whip. Then she grinned. 'Watch!'

Seconds later, the Countess of Portbury was springing her
horses with such vigour that her husband was thrown back
in his seat and robbed of the power of speech.

His laughter was echoing round the lane as the curricle
disappeared from sight.

* * * * *

REGENCY
Silk & Scandal

*A season of secrets, scandal and
seduction in high society!*

Volume 5 – 1st October 2010
The Viscount and the Virgin
by Annie Burrows

Volume 6 – 5th November 2010
Unlacing the Innocent Miss
by Margaret McPhee

Volume 7 – 3rd December 2010
The Officer and the Proper Lady
by Louise Allen

Volume 8 – 7th January 2011
Taken by the Wicked Rake
by Christine Merrill

8 VOLUMES IN ALL TO COLLECT!

www.millsandboon.co.uk   M&B

"The arrogance! To think that they can come here with their town bronze and sweep some heiress or other to the altar."

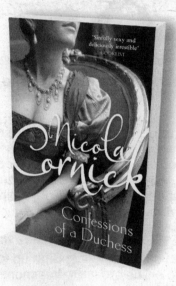

When a feudal law requires all unmarried ladies to wed or surrender half their wealth, the quiet village of Fortune's Folly becomes England's greatest Marriage Market.

Laura, the dowager duchess, is determined to resist the flattery of fortune hunters. Young, handsome and scandalously tempting Dexter Anstruther suspects Laura has a hidden motive for resisting his charms…and he intends to discover it.

www.mirabooks.co.uk